Praise for
The Queen's Pa

"*The Queen's Pawn* is a powerful portrait of two dynamic royal women and the men who controlled their lives—or is it the other way around? Treachery, betrayal, lust—and an unusual and compelling love story, beautifully told."

—Karen Harper, author of *The Queen's Governess*

"*The Queen's Pawn* by Christy English resurrects from misty legend Eleanor of Aquitaine, Henry II, Princess Alais, and Richard the Lionhearted. I knew the outlines of their stories, but now I have come to know them as fully, emotionally human, both flawed and magnificent. The French princess Alais comes as a child to England to be raised by Eleanor for marriage to Richard, the queen's favorite son. But the child becomes a beautiful woman and catches Henry's eye, starting an ever-escalating palace war of intrigue, betrayal, and passion. Almost 850 years have passed, but English brings the complex time of unrest and deceit to full, lyrical life for us. A captivating love story of Richard and Alais beyond the story I thought I knew of a young woman trapped between Eleanor and Henry in their lifelong struggle for mastery over the English Crown and each other. A jewel of a novel."   —Jeane Westin, author of *His Last Letter*

"What a promising debut! With deft strokes, Christy English transforms Alais from the innocent child her father sends to England into the cunning woman her surrogate mother, Eleanor, teaches her to be—while the crafty and sophisticated Eleanor is ensnared and nearly brought down by helpless love for her adopted daughter. The complex love-hate quadrangle between Eleanor, her husband, Henry, her son Richard, and the ever more wily Alais is a fascinating and original take on this juicy historical footnote."

—Ellyn Bache, award-winning novelist of
Safe Passage and *Daughters of the Sea*

continued . . .

ALSO BY CHRISTY ENGLISH

The Queen's Pawn

TO BE QUEEN

A NOVEL OF THE EARLY LIFE OF
ELEANOR OF AQUITAINE

CHRISTY ENGLISH

NAL

NEW AMERICAN LIBRARY

NEW AMERICAN LIBRARY

Published by New American Library, a division of Penguin Group (USA) Inc., 375 Hudson Street, New York, New York 10014, USA · Penguin Group (Canada), 90 Eglinton Avenue East, Suite 700, Toronto, Ontario M4P 2Y3, Canada (a division of Pearson Penguin Canada Inc.) · Penguin Books Ltd., 80 Strand, London WC2R 0RL, England · Penguin Ireland, 25 St. Stephen's Green, Dublin 2, Ireland (a division of Penguin Books Ltd.) · Penguin Group (Australia), 250 Camberwell Road, Camberwell, Victoria 3124, Australia (a division of Pearson Australia Group Pty. Ltd.) · Penguin Books India Pvt. Ltd., 11 Community Centre, Panchsheel Park, New Delhi - 110 017, India · Penguin Group (NZ), 67 Apollo Drive, Rosedale, North Shore 0632, New Zealand (a division of Pearson New Zealand Ltd.) · Penguin Books (South Africa) (Pty.) Ltd., 24 Sturdee Avenue, Rosebank, Johannesburg 2196, South Africa

Penguin Books Ltd., Registered Offices:
80 Strand, London WC2R 0RL, England

First published by New American Library,
a division of Penguin Group (USA) Inc.

First Printing, April 2011
1   3   5   7   9   10   8   6   4   2

LIBRARY OF CONGRESS CATALOGING-IN-PUBLICATION DATA:

English, Christy.
To be queen: a novel of the early life of Eleanor of Aquitaine/Christy English.
p. cm.
ISBN 978-0-451-23230-4
1. Eleanor, of Aquitaine, Queen, consort of Henry II, King of England,
1122?–1204—Fiction. I. Title.
PS3605.N49T6 2011
813'.6—dc22   2010052167

Set in Adobe Caslon Pro • Designed by Elke Sigal

Printed in the United States of America

For William X, Duke of Aquitaine
Count of Poitou

ACKNOWLEDGMENTS

As always when writing a novel, there are many people to thank. I must begin by thanking my parents, Karen and Carl English, for their unswerving support throughout my life. They gave me the gift of exploring my own mind as a child, and I reap the benefits of their generosity to this day.

I thank my brother, Barry English, for always making me laugh and for not letting me take myself too seriously. I thank Marianne Nubel for always believing in me, and for seeing the success of my novels alive in her own mind, before that success was ever an accomplished fact. Thanks to LaDonna Lindgren and Laura Creasy, both for their unwavering support and for reading this novel in early drafts. I offer thanks to Amy Pierce, Audrey Forrester, and Hope Johnston, who have always stood behind my work, urging me on, even in the darkest days, when it seemed my writing would never see the light of publication. And I must thank my godmother, Vena Miller, and my dear friend Susan Randall for their unflagging support.

Once again, I must thank the brilliant team at New American Library for their work: Michelle Alpern for her

ACKNOWLEDGMENTS

eagle eye in copyediting, Kaitlyn Kennedy for getting the word out about Eleanor, and Maureen O'Boyle, who designed the beautiful cover. As always, I thank Margaret O'Connor Chumley, Jhanteigh Kupihea, and Claire Zion. Without their continued devotion to Eleanor, rivaled only by my own, this book would never have been possible.

TO BE QUEEN

Prologue

❧

Abbey of Fontevrault

County of Poitou
April 1204

I WAS MY FATHER'S FAVORITE. I KNEW THIS FROM THE DAY I was born. I seemed to take this knowledge in with my mother's milk.

Men came to my father's court in the early days, patted my head, and fed me sweets. They took in the stone walls and tapestries of my father's palace as if they might see beyond them to my father's lands, stretching from the border of Burgundy to the sea. Those men leaned close to Papa and said, "One day there will be a son to rule all this." But my brother died, along with my mother, and there was never another heir. I was left, the only child with the strength to follow my father.

I find the thought of my own death a comfort now that I

1

am so old that my skin is pale and translucent. Now that the loves of my long life, the father who shaped me, the husband who fought me, the son who was loyal to me alone, have all gone down into the dust. My father died far from Aquitaine, but Henry and Richard both lie buried in this abbey. Soon I will lie between them, my body separating them for the last time.

I raise my arm and think to see the sunlight shining through the skin of my palm, so thin have I become. And my back pains me now, as it never did when I was young and rode a horse for days on end, seeking something always, a place I never reached, not with all my lovers, not even with Henry.

Death, my last lover, holds me closer than any man ever has. If the Church is right, I will soon burn for all eternity in a fiery pit, where demons cast coals on the flames and all who see me will mock me and laugh.

I have always loathed being laughed at.

I have little faith in the teachings of the Church. The priests and their followers seem to me a simple people, telling tales by the fireside to keep away the dark. I have never been afraid of the dark. My father taught me to look into it without blinking, so that I would be ready for whatever comes out of it.

If, as the Church says, I am to suffer the fires of hell, so be it. To avoid such a fate, I would have to repent of my life. That I will never do.

My priest never gives me penance, for he knows that to do so would be wasted breath. So after I have told him the tales of my life, we sit together in silence and listen to the wind as it moves through the fig trees above our heads.

The priest is the only man allowed here in the women's cloister at Fontevrault. I spent my life in the world of men, and loved it, with all its pain. But I have made this place where women can be free of men. All men but God. Even I cannot stand between these women and Him. In that last battle, they must fend for themselves.

As my life begins to fade from me as a dream fades at morning, I find that I have no regrets. My priest listens to me speak in lieu of penance or prayer, for my life is a story worth telling.

In honor of my father, in honor of all the love he gave me, all the statecraft he taught me, as well as the strength, I dedicate this tale to him. For without him, and his unswerving regard for me, the story of my life as you read it here would never have been possible.

PART I

To Be Duchess

Chapter 1

❧

Hunting Lodge at Talmont

County of Poitou
July 1132

THE GRASS WAS HIGH AND GREEN, STILL SOFT TO THE TOUCH, for the barley would not be harvested for months to come. I would dance at the harvest festival, and give out prizes to the peasants. Papa would hand them to me.

At ten years old, I was the lady in my mother's place; she and my brother had been dead two years already. Papa's brother, Raymond, lived far away in the Holy Land. He was king in Antioch and would never return to the Aquitaine. I was my father's heir.

I slipped away from my nurse, Alix, and my other women, though Papa had forbidden it. The beauty of the day called to me; the sun and the wind beckoned me from the keep. I could not stand to stay indoors.

It was dangerous for me to roam without a guard, without a woman to call for help if I was to need it. Though the duchy of Aquitaine and the county of Poitou stretched from Burgundy to the ocean, though my father's power was great, even he could not protect me when I went out alone. No woman or child was safe even on my father's lands, and as his heir, I was in more danger than most. A man might take me for ransom and hold my father by the throat; Papa would have paid any price to get me back.

But in spite of the danger, I was never one for obedience. Papa knew that, too.

That summer, the court of Aquitaine was at my father's hunting lodge of Talmont, near the coast, where my mother and brother had died. Every year we came back, always at the same time. Papa had no masses sung for their souls, for he did not believe in the afterlife the Church promised. He had caught the Church in too many lies to believe in their claims of eternal life, and he had taught me to see through their lies as well. But he mourned my mother and brother in his own silent way, and I mourned with him.

On the day they died, Papa had said to me, "I have no son."

"You do not need a son," I told him. "You have me."

The day I ran out alone, I was restless from being too long indoors. Though my father had promised to let me ride my own horse on our next hunt, I was too small to have a falcon of my own. But there was no hunt that day, so I ran outside by myself, slipping away from Alix and my ladies like a thief.

I moved into the barley fields, triumphant in my escape, heading pell-mell for the sea. But I was not the only one beckoned by the green fields and the sky. As I ran, I saw my father's favorite lady, Madeline, standing in the barley with Theobold, one of our troubadours. He was a tall man with wide shoulders, as if he spent his time at war and not in song. His dark eyes beckoned to my father's mistress, and as he took her tiny hand in his, I saw her breath catch.

Madeline was a beautiful woman, the younger daughter of one of my father's knights. Instead of remarrying upon her husband's death, at twenty-five Madeline had come to the court of Aquitaine, where she caught my father's eye. Papa had not offered her marriage, but he had offered her honor, as well as a place beside him on the dais in the great hall, and a place in his bed. She had even been kind to us, making my sister a doll with yarn for hair, dressed in the same silk that had been used to make her own gown. Petra loved that doll. She slept with it still.

So I thought at first that my eyes were dazzled by the morning light. Surely it was another woman who took Theobold's hand, and lay down with him among the barley grasses, laughing.

I crept closer, the sound of the wind covering my approach. I lay less than ten feet from them, and as I listened, I heard Madeline's high, sweet laughter, and her voice, speaking low, her words lost to the wind. I crawled on my knees and hands, heedless of my good green gown.

I crouched, so close that I might have cast a stone at them. But the high barley grass, which came almost to my shoulders when I stood, hid me well. They did not see me. I froze where I was, my father's strictures coming back to me. He reminded me that to sit in the seat of power is to be constantly betrayed, but I had never known such a thing for myself. That day, for the first time, I saw what betrayal was. I felt it in the pain above my heart.

Even then, I hoped that they had simply fallen. But when I came close enough to peer at them through the waving grasses, I saw that there was no sprained ankle, no twisted knee, nor scraped shin between them. They kissed, as I had seen Madeline kiss my father.

Madeline's long blond hair slipped from her braids, falling about her shoulders in a golden mass that lay against the green of the barley like sunlight. She took her lover into her arms with no thought for my father, or for any of us.

When my mother died, I learned that pain was not something I could run from, something that I might defeat by hiding. Now, as I watched the woman I loved betray my father, my sister, and myself, pain came, and I breathed it in like a fire that burned my lungs.

I sat in silence, the wind and the barley brushing against my face and over my hair. I heard Madeline moan. Instead of pushing Theobold away, Madeline clutched him closer. Papa would not have this woman under his roof, in his bed, once he knew what she had done.

Her moans reached a crescendo, as the fife and tabor do in music, and then she screamed. Theobold covered her mouth with his hand, and he groaned, shuddering over her. Then they both lay still, clutching each other and gasping.

My heart pounded, my breath came short, and my hands shook. Nausea rose in me, for I caught the scent of something between them, a musky scent that made me gag. I raised both hands over my mouth, until I was certain I would not be sick.

I moved slowly when the wind moved the barley, so that Madeline and her lover did not hear my passing. They thought, no doubt, that the wind simply sounded strong so close by the sea. I slipped away, bits of grass clinging to my skirt and to my hair. I kept my head below the barley, careful to stay low even when they no longer would have been able to see me.

When I had left the fields and entered the copse of maple and birch trees by the road, I ran toward the keep, the wind from the sea at my back. My lacerated heart pounded, and I gasped for breath, but I did not slow or stop. The hunting lodge at Talmont was no great seat, but we had stone walls around it instead of wood. My family had held that keep for ten generations. I felt as if Talmont were opening its stone arms to protect me as I flew through the castle gates. My father's men-at-arms knew me at once and let me pass.

Once I entered the haven of Talmont's walls, I stopped running. Alix was forever telling me that young ladies did not race the wind, nor did they pant like dogs. I tried to release my pain and anger with my outgoing breath, but I failed. My father hoped to teach me to control my emotions, both the good and the bad. I was not sure I would ever learn.

I turned my mind from what I had seen. My veil was lost; the swatch of linen had fallen away when I had run. My fillet was still in place, a gold circlet that bore the crest of Aquitaine carved into its shining brightness. The gold caught the warmth of the sun and held it against my temples. The fillet was too large for me, and hung too low, almost reaching my eyes, but I was stubborn and wore it anyway. Once, it had been my mother's.

I straightened my gown, pulling away the bits of grass that clung to it. The cloth was not stained as I had feared. Gold threads shot through the green of my favorite dress, catching the light of the sun. The gold matched the bronze fastenings of the leather belt at my waist. Emerald green brought out the green in my eyes, making them shine like jewels better than any other color could.

My breathing even, my dress smooth, I stepped into the darkness of my father's hall. Alix had been looking for me, but she had been too frightened to tell anyone I was missing. Her pale blue eyes were filled with tears. My headstrong ways always caused her pain and I was sorry for it, but I could not help it. I was as I was born to be. I was myself.

I went to Alix where she stood by the fire. Her thin blond hair was falling down from her linen coif. I kissed her, drawing her away from the smoking flames.

I let her hold me as I took in the sweet smell of warm bread and honey on her skin. Though she did not bake herself, she was always in the kitchen, fetching out bread and honey for me. They were her favorite foods, and she was sure that if I would only eat enough of them, I would grow plump and content, and settle down in the women's solar with my embroidery for the rest of my life.

"Where were you, my lady?"

I met Alix's eyes, as serious as a bishop in church on Sunday. "I was at prayer."

I saw her disbelief, but I did not waste the time it would have taken to come up with a better lie.

"I am going in to see Papa," I said.

I had run here to tell him my news, and as I reached the hall, I had seen that it was the appointed hour for our daily time together. The same time each day, my father met with me, unless he was on a hunt or riding to war.

At the mention of Papa, Alix smiled, and the sight of her smile warmed my heart. Only she had seen the weak side of me, the girl that had wept at my mother's and brother's deaths. The part of me that I had buried with them beneath the stone of Talmont's chapel floor.

I pressed her hand, then turned to climb the wooden stairs that led to my father's room.

My father, Duke William X of Aquitaine, Count of Poitou, was waiting for me, a scroll of vellum in his hand. Though Papa had clerks to do his writing, he was unique among noblemen in that he could read and write in Latin, as well as in our langue d'oc. My father's eyes were light blue, lighter than the blue of the sky on a sunny day. He was a tall man, and slender in his blue gown, which fell in soft folds past his knees, caught by a bronze-studded belt at his waist. His sandy hair fell over his forehead, but was not long enough to hide his eyes. Even at the age of thirty-two, he wore it short always, for he was often at war.

Papa rose when I entered the room, and offered his hand. I took it, and he drew me close; it was he who kissed me.

His clerk Baldwin had been standing with him, ready with the next scroll of vellum to be signed. Though a priest, the only kind of man that could read or write in Christendom, Baldwin served my father first, and the Church second. He had been raised in my father's household since he was a boy.

Baldwin bowed low in his black cassock, his blue eyes smiling. He was not yet thirty, but already his mouse brown hair had thinned, and a paunch had started above the low-slung belt of his rosary. When Baldwin saw me enter, after making the proper gestures of respect, he left us alone. He knew that there would be no more business done until my father called for him. Our time alone was sacred.

I faced my father with no one else between us.

"Daughter, how fare you this day?"

"Well, Papa."

I kissed him, the knowledge of all I must say heavy on my heart. "Papa, I have news. News that cannot wait."

"Indeed?"

He took his chair once more, and I sat beside him on a low stool brought close for the purpose. My father's dog, Gawain, came to sit at his knee, and whined. Papa petted the great wolfhound absently. I watched the creature, wary of it, but it came no closer. It was obedient to my father, as I was, when I could bring myself to be obedient to anyone.

I told him what I had seen in the barley field. I managed to keep my voice even; it shook only once. My father listened to my story, his face unreadable. I saw a flicker of pain behind his eyes, but that was all. His face was a study in stillness.

"Will you put her away?" I asked him.

His face opened a little, just enough to smile at me. "No, Alienor. I will not."

"But she has betrayed you," I said.

"Yes," Papa answered. "Now tell me why."

I forced myself to put aside my anger, and to think, as he had taught me. "She has betrayed you because she has betrayed the duchy. If you were ever to marry her, and if she were to bear the musician a son, she might pass him off as the next Duke of Aquitaine."

Pride lit his eyes, and his smile widened.

"Very good, daughter. You gained information and used it wisely, by bringing it to me. Let this be your first lesson today. Madeline betrayed me, but you have been my eyes and ears, and now she will never have my trust again. We will keep watch on her, and see to it that she does nothing worse to put our court in danger."

"But, Papa, does it not hurt you that she loves another?"

I saw his pain then, only a flash of it, before he masked it. I wished my words unspoken.

"Yes, daughter, it hurts me. This is the second lesson you must learn today: you must set aside personal emotion so that you can see the world as it is. Only when you see clearly will you know how to act."

He stood then, and crossed to the wine he kept on a sideboard. He poured himself a glass of burgundy, and watered it with his own hand. I watched, surprised, as he also poured a glass for me.

"Do you remember the story of Charlemagne?" he asked.

This, too, was part of my catechism. Charlemagne was my idol, but I did not understand what he had to do with the Lady Madeline and her betrayal of us.

"Charlemagne began our line, long ago, before the Church held sway in these lands," I said. "He united the lesser kings, and made them swear fealty to him. And when he died, he left the realm strong for his sons."

He smiled at me. "And his eldest son, Pepin. Do you remember him?"

"He was a great king. He held the lesser kings to his rule, after his father was dead."

Papa brought our wine back to the table beside his chair. He handed a goblet to me. It was glass from Murano; it had come far by sea and land. Its value was beyond anything I had ever held. He kept these goblets in his rooms, and brought them out only for his most distinguished guests. Today, he offered one to me.

I held the glass between my hands. Before, I had taken only white wine at table; now I sipped the deep, fragrant burgundy. The taste was harsh on my tongue, and burned my throat. I swallowed it down, and took a second sip.

"Pepin became king before his time, through treachery," he said.

I almost dropped my glass. I had never heard this before.

"This was a rumor only. Only one priest wrote it down, and he did not live long after the telling of it. But my father told me, and his father told him. Now I am telling you."

"Why, Papa?"

"Because I want you to know that betrayal lies every-where. Even among our kin. You must be careful, always."

"I would never betray you."

Tears burned my eyes and threatened to spill from the

prison of my lashes. Since my mother had died, I prided myself on never weeping. As my father watched, I fought for control, and won. Papa did not praise me, but nodded once before he leaned across to his table and rang his silver bell.

Baldwin stepped into the room from a hidden doorway, bringing yet more scrolls with him.

"Daughter, I send out a decree to one of my vassals. Today, you will sign it with me."

This, then, was my reward. Never before had he offered me such an honor. I knew that this would not be the last time.

I held out my hand to Baldwin, who handed me the scroll. I read it aloud, careful to keep my Latin perfect.

When I was done, my father signed the vellum. "And you, daughter, sign beneath my name."

Baldwin stood close, holding the writing table aloft for me, his pride in me shining as a sun at midday. I wrote my name with a flourish, Alienor of Aquitaine, then met my father's eyes.

"Your first step into the larger world, Alienor."

"I will walk far, Papa, with you beside me."

Baldwin rolled the vellum, then melted wax on it, sealing it with my father's ruby signet ring. The clerk left us, and Papa stretched out his arm, catching my hand in his.

"Now, Alienor, sing for me, before I hear more of your Latin."

I often sang for him when we were alone. I was still too young to raise my voice in company, but Papa loved to hear the cadence of it. He slid the ruby of his signet ring onto his finger as he listened.

I did not choose one of the lays of the court, for they all spoke of love. Instead, I sang a short song that I had written for my little sister, Petra, to cheer her when she was sick with fever. I sang of a magic mirror that showed each woman herself as she truly was. The power of a woman's inner strength, held clear in her own mind, could conquer the world.

When I finished, Papa did not ask for another song, but sat in silence with me, as the court went on beyond the door of his private chamber. For those stolen moments, we lingered in a world of our own, the most important thing between us my father's hand, warm in mine.

Chapter 2

❦

Hunting Lodge at Talmont

County of Poitou
July 1132

I WAS ALLOWED TO EAT AT THE HIGH TABLE FOR THAT NIGHT'S feast, rather than in my rooms with Petra. Alix stood behind my chair. When no one else was looking, she leaned down and kissed me.

The food was good and the company merry. I swung my legs beneath the table; they did not reach the ground. I watched my father where he sat with Madeline, his hand in hers.

Madeline laughed as she leaned close to Papa. I ate a bite of venison, fighting to keep my face free of emotion. I saw the look in Alix's eyes, and knew that I failed. I lowered my head so that no one else would see my weakness, so that I would not give my father away.

Madeline called a greeting, and waved to me. I rose when my father bade me, and came to the center of the dais. I curtsied to her, as if it were any other day.

"Well met, Alienor. How lovely you look tonight."

Her voice was honey sweet, as smooth as it ever was. I looked into her eyes and could see no sign of deceit, no sign of guile. Had I not witnessed her duplicity myself, I would never have believed it.

I felt my father's attention heavy on me, though he seemed to look down the table to one of his high-ranking barons.

I gave Madeline a sweet, childish smile. Though I was ten years old, too old for such tricks, I saw from the softening of her face that she was taken in. I kissed her cheek, as if bile did not rise in my throat, as if I still loved her and always would.

"Well met, Lady Madeline. May your meal be a pleasant one."

It was a dull comment, unworthy of my father's table. But my voice was soft. I sounded trusting and hopeful to my own ears.

My father touched my hand once, very lightly, and I knew I had done well. I curtsied to both of them as if I were a biddable, obedient girl. I sat down once more on my bench, and Alix patted my shoulder, well pleased with my sweetness and courtesy. She had drilled that courtesy into me endlessly, though often I chose to ignore it. I had deceived everyone, even her.

I felt the gulf of my loneliness open like a chasm at my feet. I must be strong to walk the path to power, to stand as duchess after my father. I must stand in front of Petra and protect her, all the days of my life. It would take power to do those things. But this was the price: never to be known, not even by those who thought they loved me.

I met Papa's eyes. His gaze seemed to anchor me, and the chasm at my feet closed up. My loneliness receded.

I was not alone. My father was with me.

After the fruit was brought out, Papa did not wait for the songs to be sung. His chief troubadour, Theobold, the man who had cuckolded him in his own fields, rose to play. My father waved him back. As I watched, fear crossed Theobold's face. I wanted to laugh out loud, but I held my tongue. My father noticed my self-control and winked.

No one else saw this pass between my father and me but Theobold and the Lady Madeline. Madeline turned pale, and almost choked on the wine she drank. My father raised her up and led her onto the dance floor.

Music swelled, and the company rose when my father did, men and women laughing, taking their places in the dance. Had it been any other night, I would have risen to dance myself, but that evening I was satisfied to eat my pears from Anjou and drink my watered wine. When Papa sat once more, the dancing went on without him. The Lady Madeline came to sit beside him.

My father kissed her, his hand roaming over her backside. He let his hand linger, and as I watched, her fear softened to desire. Papa swatted her once, sending her back out among the dancers. Madeline went reluctantly, her eyes on his, until one of his men-at-arms caught her hand and led her out among the courtiers.

Papa watched her go. If I had not been staring at him, I would not have seen his hand beckon me beneath the table.

Alix steadied me as I rose from my bench. I went to my father and knelt to show my obedience. He leaned low, and whispered in my ear. His smiling look never turned from Madeline on the dance floor.

"Go to my antechamber. Place yourself behind the arras by the hidden door."

A thrill of excitement ran up my spine and into my heart. My father was offering to let me spy for him, and in his own rooms. He had a network of spies that served him in the French court, among his own vassals, and in Rome, but today was the first time he had ever offered to place me among them. He would punish her in private, and I would get to watch.

I kissed his ruby signet ring. He shot me a look for that bit of foolishness, but I could not contain my joy. I smiled back at him, and curtsied, as if he had simply sent me to bed.

Alix trailed me as I made my way out of the great hall and up the wooden staircase to my bedroom. She followed, but had to hurry to keep up with me, for her long skirts trailed behind her, and I was quick.

When we reached my chamber, I did not wash my face as Alix told me. "I must go to my father in his antechamber," I said. "This is a secret. You must stand guard here, and let me go."

Alix had seen my father speak to me in whispers. She hated the thought of letting me go out into the world alone, but the time for her to protect and cocoon me was over. I must learn to make my way in the world of men.

I opened the secret door hidden behind one of the

tapestries in my bedroom. I stepped into that dark, narrow corridor with only the lamp in my hand to light my way. I moved down the passage quickly and silently; only my father and I knew where it led.

I came out in his antechamber, where he and I worked on my lessons every day. My father's manservant Matthew saw me enter, but he said nothing as I slipped behind the arras. I fastened the heavy stone door closed behind me and hid myself just as Papa and the Lady Madeline came in from the hall below.

Matthew stood to one side of the room and waited for the duke's instructions. His eyes did not tend toward me even for a moment, and I knew that my father had warned him of my coming. I saw that Papa trusted him more than I had known; even a man as strong as my father needed loyal servants to shore up his power.

I loved Alix, but could not trust her to obey me blindly. I swore to myself, standing behind my father's arras, peering out of a slit made low in the fabric of the tapestry, that someday I would find a woman to follow me, wherever I led.

"Thank you, Matthew. You may leave us."

The Lady Madeline clung to my father's arm. Instead of drawing my father into the bedchamber with her, she cast herself at his feet, weeping.

"William, you must forgive me."

I saw that she had never loved him, or me, or Petra. All her sweet words to me and to my sister were only so much air. Madeline had pretended to love Papa in the hope that, one day, she would be duchess after my mother.

"Madeline, stop this. Stop this at once."

My father raised her up, and she clung to him, the warm softness of his voice spurring her on. I looked at my father's face as he pressed his mistress against his heart. I saw pain in his eyes, but I saw hopelessness, too. In spite of his soft words and honeyed tone, he had not forgotten what she had done.

"William, I have wronged you, and I am sorry. So sorry . . ."

Still the woman wept, as if the heart she did not have were breaking. Had I not been under orders to my father, had I been even a few years older, I would have called for guards and had her thrown out into the night. As it was, I raised my thumb to my mouth and bit down, so that I would not speak.

Hot blood rose and caressed my tongue. The sharp pain of my teeth in my own flesh kept me quiet and still, reminding me where I was, and who. If I was to be the next Duchess of Aquitaine, I would have to learn to listen to worse lies than this. I wrapped my thumb in the linen of my discarded veil, stanching the flow of blood before it dripped onto my fur-trimmed sleeve.

My father soothed Madeline, smoothing her hair with the palms of his hands, stroking her back.

"I betrayed you, William, and with a servant!"

Papa drew her close, so that she could not see his face.

"It happened only once, Madeline. You will not do it again."

She wept on, babbling this time, relieved and amazed at her good fortune. She thought, as I had, that he would cast her away. But I knew that though he did not, he would never forgive her, or love her again. I learned in that moment that a man's love, once lost, is lost forever.

The next day I realized something else, too, something

Papa had not sought to teach me. The next day, I saw the sly glances exchanged by the men-at-arms in the bailey and the great hall, looks that I had never noticed before, and that my father did not notice at all.

Madeline had weakened us among my father's barons. Because of her treachery, because he would not cast her aside, Papa would lose face among his men, and his barons would lose respect for him. I remembered his lessons well: the respect of one's fighting men was all; it was the foundation of a duke's power.

I saw for the first time that my father was not perfect. He was not the perfect knight, nor the perfect duke. He did not see his own weakness, though he had taught me to master mine.

❀

The next morning Papa called for me to meet him in the bailey just a few hours after sunrise. I stood before him in the courtyard, the stones wet beneath our feet where the servants had washed away the muck from the day before. His large hand, gloved in rough leather, reached down and took hold of my chin, so that I might look him in the eye.

"Is this wound got in my service?" he asked me.

He raised my bandaged thumb. I stood still as he untied the dressing. The bite was deep, but it would heal. I watched him swallow hard at the sight of my punctured flesh as he rewrapped my wound.

"Perhaps in future you will carry a strap of leather to bite on to help you keep your temper."

"I did not cry out," I said. "I did not speak."

"No, Alienor, you did not." Papa stared down at me, and I could not read the expression behind his eyes.

"I would give you a treat, to reward your faithful service. My vassals have land from me, and gold. What would you ask of me?"

I had thought long and hard about this question, though I had never expected him to ask it. At the age of ten, I knew what I wanted, above all things in the world.

"I would be Queen of France," I said.

My father did not smile at me indulgently, or laugh, as any other man might have done. He did not treat me as a child or a fool. He stared down at me for a long moment, and the wheels of his mind began to turn in this new direction I had set them in.

"You will have it, Alienor. Leave it to me."

The king had a son of an age with me. And no girl in five hundred miles had a dowry to match mine. The Aquitaine and Poitou were lands that rivaled and surpassed even the kingdom of France for beauty and wealth. I knew all this, for it was my duty to know it. I would be duchess one day.

And now, Papa would make me queen.

My joy and hope spilled over each other like pebbles in a rushing stream. My son would be King of France, as well as Duke of Aquitaine. My marriage would begin a new golden age, creating a united France that could rival any other power in Christendom. With the royal armies of Paris and the cultural heritage of my father's house, my son could become a second Charlemagne.

My father raised me into the saddle. I had just learned to

ride the summer before, and my horse was a lady's mount, a filly with delicate bones and a light step. Someday, I would be tall enough to ride a stallion. Papa had promised me that once I could control a warhorse, he would give one to me.

"In lieu of the throne of France, today I will take you on a hunt."

My father gestured, and a groom stepped forward with a beautiful young falcon. Triumph rose in my breast, that Papa would trust me to hunt with such a bird. My falcon's feathers were brown and gold, her claws sharp. I wanted to reach out and touch that beauty, but I knew that such familiarity would earn me a bite worse than the one I had given myself. I held back, and waited.

"Very good, Alienor. Caution is a necessity, even for the very brave."

Papa mounted his own stallion and led our party out of the keep into the clean, bright air of the morning. We rode for hours over our lands, and over the field where I had seen Madeline lie down with our troubadour. My father laughed as we passed it. Whatever pain he was feeling, he would never let even me know of it again.

My falcon brought back a sparrow fresh in her claws the first time she flew for me. She landed on my arm, as smooth and as disciplined as I was, dropping her catch deftly into my open palm. I fed her a piece of that sparrow, its hot flesh disappearing into my falcon's beak.

My bird turned her head to one side and looked at me. I saw myself, reflected in her eyes. I, too, would become a bird of prey. One must, to be queen.

Chapter 3

❧

Palace of Poitiers

County of Poitou
Easter 1136

THE PEOPLE WERE CHEERING. MY FATHER AND I STOOD JUST inside the door of the palace, listening to them. The procession to the cathedral had already begun, as it did every Easter. Only this time, the people waited to see not just the statue of the Virgin in her gold and blue paint, nor the flower-decked cross and the cloth-of-gold tympanum that sheltered it. They had come to witness the ceremony that would make me my father's official heir.

My younger sister, Petra, ten years old, stood with us. She was no coward, but she hid behind my shoulder, as if the people were shouting for blood and not for joy. I was fourteen now, and a woman. The cries of the people did not frighten me.

I squeezed Petra's hand before stepping out into the sunshine. She returned my smile, but kept close to me.

We walked among the people, down the winding road that led to my father's cathedral. The creamy stone of the church shone in the morning light. The old Roman basilica reminded me of the time that had come before, when the Church had been in the service of the duke. We had followed the old Roman ways during the days of Charlemagne, when the king's law reigned supreme. Now the Church vied with my father, with all kings and lords, for power. But the basilica of my father's cathedral reminded me of the power of the dukes of Aquitaine under Charlemagne, when the Church had known its place.

Flowers were strewn in the path of the Virgin and before the cross, but a bounty of spring garlands was held back for me, for Petra, and for my father.

Papa spoke close to my ear, so that only I would hear him. "Let them love God," my father said. "But let them love you first."

As I moved, I saw a dark-haired man standing among the barons who walked with us. His deep brown eyes met mine, and heat rose in my cheeks. My breath came short as if I had run upstairs too quickly. I searched my memory for his name. He was the Baron Rancon, a vassal of my father's.

We reached the church, and I tore my eyes from his. When Papa and I stepped into the cathedral, it was as if a great hand had closed over us, blocking out the sun. I stood in that darkness, letting my eyes adjust to it. My father's barons filed in behind us.

Our throne sat midway into the church, with the altar and the bishop at our backs. Though in Paris the Church held sway over all things, religious and otherwise, my father kept to the old Roman ways. The business of the state was a separate thing from the business of the Church. It was a concession to hold this ceremony in a church at all.

I took our throne, and Papa stood at my right hand. He was dressed in cloth of gold as I was. His blue eyes gleamed bright, even in the darkness of the basilica. This day was a beginning, but it was also a triumph, the end of an arduous path to make me his heir. My father and I had walked that long road, together.

My sister, Petra, dressed in blue silk to match her eyes, stood behind us to remind the barons that if I died, there was another to follow me. Her gaze sought mine, her skin pale, her soft blond hair coming loose from its braids, making a halo about her face, as if she were an angel. I winked, and she lost her frightened look.

One by one, my father's barons knelt, swearing me fealty, as they had once sworn fealty to my father. The ceremony gave every man his lands again, this time from me. These men would stand with me in time of war. When they entered that cathedral, they thought to serve me only out of duty to my father, but I took each baron's hand before he stood, and caught his eyes with mine. Each man rose, ready to serve the woman I would become.

The lords dressed well that day, in leather leggings and tunics of woven silk that reached past their knees, bound about their waists with leather belts studded with bronze and silver.

But Baron Rancon stood out even in that handsome company, his gaze dark where so many of my vassals had eyes of blue and green, his hair chestnut brown where other men's gleamed fair in the darkness of the church. Baron Rancon's hand lingered over mine as he swore to serve me every day for the rest of his life. My breath came short, but my father had taught me well. I smiled at him, serene, as if he were any other man.

Baron Rancon stepped down from the dais and took his place among my lords. The mass went on after the ceremony was through, but I heard not a word of it. The words of the priests and their incense spilled over me without touching me, as my father stood beside me.

The people were waiting for us when we emerged from the darkness of the cathedral, and they had more flowers to spread in our path as we walked to my father's castle against the old Roman wall. I turned back only once, at a curve in the road, and met the Baron Rancon's eyes. Heat flamed from my throat to my cheeks; I knew I blushed with it. He smiled to see my color rise as I turned away from him.

My father's palace was a short walk from the church. Built from the same cream-colored stone, the palace was not cut off from light and air as so many keeps were. Safe on a hill, high in the center of the city, the palace had long windows, all sealed with expensive glass. The light came in from those windows to the north and the west, brightening our hall even in winter, when the light was at its lowest ebb. Now, in spring, sunlight shone into my father's hall, casting shadows where the columns raised the wooden ceiling high above our heads.

When I stepped into the great hall, I found the stone walls decked in flowers. My chief lady-in-waiting, Amaria, had been at work all week to make the hall perfect for this one feast. I had excused her from her duties in my rooms. She watched over my women and the tapestries sewn in my chamber, altar cloths that served to keep my ladies busy and out of mischief, at least for part of the day. Alix, my old nurse, loved to work on such embroidery, for she was a religious woman, devoted to God. She no longer ruled my rooms, but she stayed close by, for love of me.

Petra had risen to the position of chief woman in my rooms in Amaria's absence. Only ten years old, she was too young for such work, but my sister had done well, better than I had expected. I always thought of her as too young and sweet to be of any real use except in the marriage she would make. That week I saw that there was a mind behind her pretty smile, if I could only teach her to use it.

My father's hall was hung in sweet-smelling flowers, and fresh rushes scented with thyme and rosemary covered the floor. I took my place at the high table, with Papa on one side of me and Petra on the other. The highest barons sat with us, and the rest of the company kept to the lower tables, where the feast was just as grand.

Course after course was brought out. We had borrowed from all our estates for this one day, to show my father's largesse. Roasted peacocks with their feathers still attached gleamed in the light of the lamps; dishes of eel and comfrey were brought, one after another, feeding everyone, from the barons to the servants, until the remains of the dishes were carried out to the poor. Our duchy was rich, and that day we shared our riches with our people.

When the fruit was brought, my father rose to his feet beside me. His voice filled the hall without effort. He had trained himself to be heard a long way off without strain. Papa had taught me to do the same, down by the river's edge. He had stood with me by the old Roman wall of our castle keep, until I could hear my voice bounce back to me from a hundred feet away.

Though I would never need to cast my voice over a battle-field as my father had done, there were other fields on which I would fight all my life, and my father knew it. A woman in the world of men is always at war; a strong, melodious voice was only one weapon in my arsenal.

"My daughter sits before you this day, the flower of Aqui-taine. Serve her well, as you have sworn to do. Follow her, as you have followed me. She is worthy of you."

Papa turned back to me, and took my hand; his eyes were full of tears. The years we had worked together to make this day come to pass had been hard on him. He had no way of knowing whether his men would accept me, if his barons would indeed swear fealty to me, as he called on them to do. He had gambled on me, and won.

Papa gave me the kiss of peace, then sat beside me. His barons raised a cheer, their wine lifted high. I squeezed my father's hand, and stood to speak in the strong voice he had given me. "I will serve you in my marriage, and all the days of my life. I will put you and our lands first always, whatever comes. This is my oath to you, as you have given your oaths to me this day."

The barons cheered again. As I took my place beside my father, I caught the eye of the Baron Rancon. His dark hair gleamed in the firelight, and his brown eyes met mine. He was a young man, not yet married. His arms were thick from wielding a sword; they strained the silk of his tunic. His was a body made to wear chain mail, not silk. For half a moment, I almost wished myself free, that I might choose such a man for myself.

The negotiations for my marriage had already begun between our duchy and the King of France. Though it took years for such an alliance to be forged, one day I would marry the heir to the French throne. The politics between Aquitaine and the kingdom of France were delicate, made more so by the interference of the Church, which wanted a hand in everything. But I knew whether the Church supported us or not, my father would see my marriage made.

Papa's troubadour, Bertrand, bowed low to me. As Bertrand stood to sing, I found Baron Rancon still watching me. His eyes cradled mine, and warmth began to pool in the center of my belly. I sipped from that pool of languid pleasure, but did not drink deep. That pool could drown me, and I knew it.

I drew my mind from Baron Rancon, and focused my attention on the troubadour who sang in my honor. Bertrand's poetry told of my beauty and its power, of how it would rise from the Aquitaine to hold all men in its sway.

As the song ended, I sent my voice, melodious and light, into every corner of the great hall. "I thank you, Bertrand. You have outdone us all in honor."

I took a ring of silver and gold from my finger, cast in my father's crest. I raised it for the company to see, then pressed it into his palm. For once, Bertrand was struck dumb. For all his practiced poetry, he had no words to speak. He bowed low, drawing my ring onto the little finger of his right hand. He touched it reverently. I had never shown him such favor before.

"Who else might sing for me?" I asked. "Who among my barons would stand and honor me?"

My barons murmured among themselves, like wind through a field of barley.

"I will choose from among the men who sing for me a song of their own devising. The man I choose will be the first tonight to dance with me."

The men laughed, delighted at this challenge. All my people, men and women both, loved poetry and music, and they loved a contest more. Ever since my grandfather's time, men had written their own songs and sung them in company to win the favor of their ladies. They hoped only to draw a woman into their beds for an hour, or a week. That night, I would challenge that tradition. I would remake it into a tradition of my own.

One baron after another rose to sing for me, as if to woo me for his own. But I was to be their duchess. They could not so much as touch my hand, much less have me in the dark, and they knew this as well as I.

As I listened to their songs, my father caught my eye and smiled. He knew that by setting myself above them as a prize to be won, as a woman to love but not to touch, I hoped to bind every man in my court closer to me. Each man in that hall must love me at least a little, for barons who loved me would not rise up in arms against me. Or so I hoped.

Time would tell.

The last man to sing was the young Baron Rancon.

Rancon sang alone, strumming his own lute, with no musicians to play for him. He gave the company a song of how my beauty rose with the sun each morning, and did not fade when night came; of how I ruled the sun and the moon both, which were mere spheres in the sky, come to circle my throne.

My blood raced, though I schooled my features to cool politeness. His song done, I extended my hand, and let him take it.

My voice did not shake, and neither did my hand, though my heartbeat was loud in my own ears. "The Baron Rancon has carried the day. Let him be the victor, then, for he has conquered me."

The barons laughed and applauded Rancon, and my father applauded with them. Rancon did not smile, but held my gaze. His palm was warm on mine as he brought me down from the dais onto the dance floor.

Amaria whispered to the musicians at one end of the hall. They struck up a dancing tune, and the men at the lower tables took up their women and came onto the center of the floor as if they had waited all day for it.

Geoffrey of Rancon led me into the dance seamlessly, and I fell into step with him. We moved as if we had danced together before, as if our bodies knew each other already.

His eyes were the brown of chestnuts in autumn, and his gaze was warm with more than lust as he stared down at me.

He looked at me as if I were his lady in truth, as if he might offer me marriage and all the kisses and sweet words men offered women alone in the dark.

It was a heady feeling, that first sip of power. I had been raised to rule men all my life, but the heat that rose between us was a different matter altogether.

"I would see you again," he said.

I stepped away from him, and did not answer, having to count carefully to keep time in the motion of the dance. I hid my hesitation and did not falter. His heated gaze still followed me, until I drew close to him again.

"You will see me many times for the rest of your life," I said. "I will be your duchess."

My light tone hid the elation I felt. I had learned to lie as a child, so that now, when my blood was pounding in my throat, I did it easily. But for the first time in my life, the effort of a lie cost me something. I breathed deep, keeping my hand back from his, touching only his fingertips with my own.

"I would see you again tonight," he said, his gaze hot, his flesh warm on mine.

I drank in his scent, the hint of some unknown spice on his skin. My heart pounded so loudly that I thought Rancon might be able to hear it.

I raised my eyes to his, and took in the sight of him. He was a man of the world with many mistresses; he had sung their praises before he ever sang mine. But in that moment, as my green eyes cradled him, I saw the Baron Rancon falter.

"My lady, you are the most beautiful woman in the world."

I stood on the slippery slope of a man's desire. The choice

and the power of this moment were mine. I might slide into Rancon's bed, and seal the promise of the heat that rose between us.

I drew my hand from his as the music ended. "My lord," I said, "you flatter me."

I spoke as if I were a modest maid, but my eyes held the same heat as his own. I watched him pause, searching my face, before he turned to lead me back to the dais.

As we walked, I tripped, catching myself on his arm, as if I feared that I might fall. I bent to adjust the dyed leather slipper on my foot, and he leaned down to balance me.

"Meet me behind the curved staircase on the second level three hours before dawn," I said, my voice low so that only he would hear. When I stood again, still clinging to him, Rancon's breath was as short as mine.

He said not a word and did not meet my eyes again, but delivered me to my father.

I danced every dance, the fire of new-discovered lust mounting in my belly. As I whirled and touched hands with each young man in turn, one after the other, I felt Baron Rancon's eyes on me. I did not look at him. Instead I wove a spell over each man I danced with, so that they all began to love me, at least a little. What else is beauty for, if not to hold all men in your sway?

Chapter 4

❧

Palace of Poitiers

County of Poitou
Easter 1136

WELL AFTER MIDNIGHT, WHILE ALIX SLEPT SOUNDLY ON HER pallet, Amaria helped me dress to meet Rancon in the hallway of my father's keep. Her dark blond hair lay neatly across her forehead. Her clear blue gaze met mine without judgment. She said not a word, knowing that any warning she might give me would fall on barren ground.

Amaria had been with me for more than three years, and she knew me well. I would never injure my chances to be Queen of France by losing my maidenhead to the Baron Rancon. But I would have my will, or why else be queen at all?

At the appointed time, hours before dawn, I slipped out into the corridor, carrying no lamp. I knew my father's palace at Poitiers so well that had I been struck blind, I would still have found my way. So I moved along the corridor toward the curved staircase, my hand trailing along the damp stone, until I felt warm flesh beneath my fingertips, and the Baron Rancon's hand closed over mine.

He whispered low, "My lady, I have waited for you."

He drew me close, retreating with me beneath the curved staircase. There was a little space for both of us to stand upright. He turned his back to the corridor, pressing me against the stone. My heart leaped in my chest. I had thought him biddable, completely my own creature, but here, alone, without my father's court between us, he was a man, and I, a girl.

My heart thundered in my breast, and my breath came short as my lust rose, a great tide that almost swamped my reason. Rancon pulled me to him, his hands on my waist beneath my cloak, his breath hot on my cheek.

"I did not mean to keep you waiting," I said.

The sound of his laughter caressed me, like hands running up my spine and into my hair. I shivered, and Rancon drew me closer, the heat and weight of his body against mine.

I felt a tremor of fear, but my lust rose to conquer it. Rancon leaned down and took my lips with his.

I drew back from his mouth before I fell to him completely. I forced lightness into my voice, a tone that belied my desire. "How do you know who I am? I might be any number of women, come here to meet you . . . one of my ladies, perhaps."

Rancon laughed low, and again, I felt the heat of the sound on my skin. His hands moved up from my waist to caress my rib cage, as he pressed me back against the stone wall. "My lady, I would know you anywhere."

"Then let me be clear," I said. "I will not give you my maidenhead. That is for another."

He kissed me, but drew back almost at once, as if to seal a bargain between us. "I swear I will protect you, my lady. Even from yourself. You will beg me to take you, but I will not. I seek only to give us both a little pleasure."

He leaned close, and I felt his smile against my cheek as he bent down to nuzzle my throat. "After all, it was you who invited me."

I thought to reprimand him for his impertinence, but his hand moved to cup my breast, and his lips trailed over my throat. He opened his mouth on mine as his hands caressed me.

I understood now why women must guard themselves so carefully before marriage. It would have been so easy to slip, to give myself and my future away for a trifle.

But it did not feel like a trifle, with Rancon's tongue on mine, his rough, large hands caressing me. Just as I thought to push him away, his touch turned gentle, and his lips caressed my cheek, his breath warm in my ear.

"Lady, forgive me. I can go no further with you. I do not trust myself to stop."

Rancon laid his forehead against my own, and we clung to each other. He caught his breath before I caught mine.

"You will soon be bound in marriage to another. But know this, lady. Nothing is over between us."

His promise was a warm balm against my already heated skin. He covered my lips once more with his, pressing his body against me for one long, delicious moment. Then he pulled away and left me without his heat or touch.

The cold of my father's castle surrounded me, and crept along my flesh beneath my gown, for Rancon's hands had laid my cloak open. I was light-headed, and my blood still thundered in my ears. I knew that I had come too close to the abyss.

But how sweet it was, to touch a man like that. When I was married, I would touch my husband that way, and no one would stop me.

I made my way back to my rooms. When I scratched on the door, Amaria drew me inside and brought me close to the fire. I did not let her undress me right away, but sat by the brazier, my cloak wrapped around me. Rancon's scent lingered in its woolen folds.

I remembered his last words to me as I sat safe in my rooms. I heard the promise in them, and I shivered, as if his hands were once more on my body.

❀

The next morning, my father called me to him. I had slept little; I still felt the heat of Rancon's touch. Amaria dressed my hair with pearls and gold, covering her handiwork with a veil of silk. My bronze hair hung down my back in braids, in case my father wished to go on a hunt, as he had promised me we would.

I entered Papa's antechamber and found a tall, emaciated monk whose tonsure revealed a network of veins and bumps on the crown of his head. Never before had I noticed a monk's tonsure, but never before had one looked so hideous to me.

My father stood when I entered, but the monk remained seated, as if to show that he had no more respect for me than if I had been a common drab. I felt the first flame of my temper rise, but I tamped it down. I curtsied to my father, including the monk in the gesture of good manners that Alix had spent years of her life drumming into me. The monk had hoped to see me falter. I saw from his annoyance that I had succeeded in hiding my ire from him.

"Daughter, may I present Bernard of Clairvaux, come lately from Paris with greetings from our esteemed lord King Louis of France."

I had heard of this man before. My father had abased himself once to him in public, out of political necessity. I was surprised to find Bernard of Clairvaux in my father's rooms, but there were times when even enemies needed to be placated.

The monk still did not speak, furious that he had been presented to me, and not me to him. I saw his throat working, as if to swallow bile.

Bernard rose from his chair as if scalded. I think he had expected some show of subservience from me. When he did not get it, he lost his temper. I wondered then why my father had ever abased himself to this man, begging for forgiveness that he did not need.

"A daughter of Eve cannot be lord in these lands. Not today, and not tomorrow. William, you are a fool. Marry at once, before it is too late."

I raised one eyebrow, shocked that this enemy, a man who had the ear of the king, would reveal himself and his position so quickly.

We were negotiating my marriage to the king's son, the

Aquitaine as my dowry. The king would never encourage my father to remarry and sire a son, for that would cost his own son the duchy. It was clear to me, and no doubt to my father as well, that in this moment Bernard spoke not for the King of France but for the Church.

I felt the creep of fear along my skin. Could the Church block my marriage to the king's son? My father worked night and day to place me on the throne of France. And though two years had passed since formal negotiations had begun, the deal was not done yet.

Bernard's blue eyes were chilling. He looked at me not as if I was a woman but as if I were a contagion, a disease he must guard against. He drew his brown robes back as if to retreat from me, so that I saw his horned toes beneath the hem, gnarled where they poked up from his sandals.

My father sat down to his breakfast once more, and I sat beside him. When Papa gestured to a third chair, Bernard stood fuming over us.

Breakfast was laid out for us as it always was, but this morning there was enough bread, fruit, and honey for three. I accepted the small gold plate my father offered. When my father ate of the soft, good bread, I dipped my own in honey and took a bite.

These common gestures angered Bernard more than anything else we might have done. He saw himself dismissed, and my father had not even opened his mouth to speak.

"No woman can hold these lands, nor any lands in Christendom. No oath of fealty to a woman can be kept. Every man who swore to follow your daughter in the house of God on Sunday is forsworn, and need not burn for it. For they cannot be held to an oath that has no power!"

Bernard of Clairvaux finished spewing this last bit of bile, and drew himself up taller still, as if he was certain we would collapse before him and his holy fire.

As I ate my pear, my hand shook once. I was fortunate that the old man did not see it. My father reached for me, as if to offer fresh linen, but his eyes met mine and I saw his strength.

The monk's argument against me would appeal to many. The Church preached that women were weak vessels fit only to birth the next generation of men. From the point of view of the pope, the monk's position held validity.

The remnants of the old Roman, secular tradition had begun to fall to the Church's laws in the last generation. Always before, the law had come from the king, and from his vassals. Now the Church sought to make all laws come from the pope in Rome, and his minions among us. My father and I stood against this encroachment from the Vatican, but not all our barons did.

Bernard's voice softened for a moment, as if he was certain that, upon reflection, my father would agree with him, and cast me aside. "William, you must marry and sire a son. Only a son can hold these lands for you."

"Brother Bernard, please, sit and eat with us. I hear your words, and I consider them. I have considered them all my life."

The monk sat with us finally but did not touch the plate my father offered him. I finished my bread, and ate the last of my pear. I did not look at Bernard directly, but caught a glimpse of him through my lashes. This demure show did not fool him; clearly stories of my true self had preceded me. Or perhaps he simply knew me at once as an implacable enemy, just as I knew him.

"William, you will marry before the summer is out. You must listen to me, and to my lord the king. The duchy of Aquitaine is too valuable a property to leave undefended by your death."

I froze where I sat, a piece of fruit poised at my lips. I heard the threat, thinly veiled. My father heard it, too.

Papa's voice was soft. "The king is my lord, and I owe him my allegiance. Even now, he works with me to secure my daughter's marriage to his son."

The monk's threat still lingered in my ears like poison. "As to my death, the king and I have looked to that as well. I have made my daughter a ward of the crown. The king has taken my family as his own. You would do well to heed it." The honeyed tones were gone. His speech was like an unsheathed blade. Only now did he draw his malice out, and show it to our enemy.

Bernard's face darkened as if a summer storm had risen in him, blotting out the sun. He had no words to spit at us, no weapons from his keepers in Rome to cast back at us. He had known nothing of my father's dealings with the king; that much was plain from the look on his face. Though the king kept this monk close, there were things he did not tell him. The fact that I had been made the king's ward was clearly one of them. The shock of this news was Bernard of Clairvaux's undoing.

"The Church will see to it that you are brought to heel," Bernard said.

My father only smiled. "And no doubt the king will do the same with you. Best you look to him, Bernard. As Christ teaches us, you cannot serve two masters."

I thought the monk would run from the room, but a tall man can move quickly without running. This one did, as if the devil were at his heels.

We sat in silence, my father and I, the remains of our breakfast forgotten. I heard my father's words again; the king had taken me as his ward. The marriage was a fait accompli. I had only to wait a few months more, or perhaps a year, just long enough for the marriage contract to be drawn up and signed.

Joy rose in me, and with it relief that we had vanquished our enemy, that our years of hard work had not been undone. I laughed my deep, throaty laugh. My mirth filled my father's antechamber, and reverberated off the stone walls. Even the tapestries could not muffle the sound.

Papa drew me close, covering my mouth with his hand. "The walls have ears, daughter, even in our keep."

I needed to be reassured, though my heart told me we had won. "Is it true, Papa, or were you merely stalling?"

My father smiled. In this moment, even he could not maintain his iron control. We had triumphed over two enemies, the Church and Bernard of Clairvaux, and this victory was sweet.

"It will be true. The papers making you the king's ward in the event of my death have not been signed yet, but they will be. I expect them any day."

"But you made him think that it was an accomplished fact."

"Of course. Always lie to your enemies."

My laughter filled my throat again, and spilled from my lips. I could not catch it, or hold it back. My admiration for my father rose in me as my fear had done, but stronger. If I lived to be a hundred, I would never know another man like him.

"I love you, Papa."

"And I love you, Alienor."

❊

The next day my father and I rode out on our hunt. After another evening of eating, music, and dancing in our hall, most of our barons had gone. Bernard of Clairvaux left the keep after his interview with my father. The taste of that victory was still on my tongue. I knew my father savored it, too.

I rode a war stallion, a destrier far too large for me. Papa had finally given me permission to train on a man's mount. My Merlin was too broad and strong for any lady, but that was why I loved him.

My horse was as black as a moonless night, with a patch of white on his forelock and on his chest. This patch of white was like a knight's shield. Merlin loved it when I stroked him there, raising his head so that I would have clear access after I fed him his apple and cheese.

A groom rode beside me, bearing my falcon on his arm. I wanted to hunt with a hawk, but Papa said such birds were far too big for me. I told him that Merlin was too big for me as well, but that all men must bend to my will, even hawks, even stallions. Papa laughed and kissed me, but did not change his mind.

So I rode out at my father's side with the little brown falcon he had given me years before, on a stallion more beautiful than any but his own. That day we rode for hours, and my bird brought down five doves. Our kill would be dressed when we returned, to be eaten at the feast.

As we turned toward home, my father drew his mount close to mine. I kept a firm rein on Merlin, but he knew Excalibur, my father's horse, and did not shy from him. The two great beasts stood close, more like mules than stallions, breathing into each other's faces.

Papa pulled a small gold bell from his saddlebag. It jingled merrily, with a clear, clean sound that only the highest-quality gold can make. I took the bell in my hand and rang it once, listening to its music. Papa drew it from my hand, and tied it to my falcon's jesses.

"So this is a gift, Papa? Thank you. It is beautiful."

"Do not thank me, Alienor." My father leaned close, so that no one else would hear him. "Thank the King of France."

I touched the golden bell where it hung from my bird's leg. My falcon shifted on my gloved arm, and a sweet, high note rang out.

The answer to our years of negotiation dangled from my falcon's jesses. The papers making me a ward of the king in the event of my father's death must have arrived with this gift. The documents betrothing me to the heir of France would soon follow.

My father's smile lit his face. My groom came to take my falcon from me, her new bell ringing. Papa leaned across his pommel and kissed me.

Our barons would not be pleased with a French overlord. While the marriage contract was concluded, we would have a year or more to make them used to the idea. I would tame them to my hand, as my falcon and my stallion had been.

Chapter 5

❧

Palace of Ombrière

Bordeaux
Easter 1137

ALMOST A YEAR LATER, I STOOD WITH MY FATHER ON THE ramparts of our white palace at Ombrière, looking down at the river below. We had come to Bordeaux for Easter, but he would not be staying to celebrate with me.

Papa would leave on the morrow for a pilgrimage to Compostela, in Spain. He had rolled the dice, played for political power in Rome, backing a pope who had proved too weak to hold the Holy See. Our candidate for the papacy had lost. Now my father must abase himself before our enemies in the Church, and ride to Compostela on the pilgrim road, and be absolved of his political missteps at the shrine to Santiago.

I was troubled to see him go, for my betrothal to the son of the King of France had still not been signed. It took years to negotiate such marriage contracts, and this one would have to be as airtight as a cask of wine, strong enough to hold long past my father's death.

The marriage had been delayed, for there was a clause in the contract that the king did not like, a position from which my father was immovable: the lands of the Aquitaine and Poitou would not pass directly to my husband at our marriage, but to our son once he was of age. The king would gain the wealth of the Aquitaine. He would be able to draw on our gold, and call upon my vassals in time of war. But the Aquitaine and Poitou would become the property of the throne of France only after my son was crowned.

The King of France bided his time, saying that his heir was still too young to marry, all the while hoping to frighten us into making his son the sole ruler of Aquitaine. My father would not agree to this; only I or my son would rule these lands after him. Though in the end we were sure to win, as the Aquitaine was a prize too sweet to be let go of, the king was slow to admit defeat. I was only fifteen; I had time to wait. But my father would leave for Spain to face his enemies with my marriage contract still unsigned.

The whole situation rankled, filling my throat with bile. I swallowed, the sour taste lingering on the back of my tongue. If it was this bitter for me, how much worse must this defeat be for him? I knew how much it pained him to leave me and my sister undefended, while he went to make amends with the Church. But as always, my father hid his pain behind a mask of stone.

"I must go alone, and you must stay here," Papa said.

He did not speak just of his travels to Compostela. He feared a different journey, that death would meet him there, in the form of poison, or an assassin's knife. Our enemies in the Church had taken one slight too many from his hands, and we knew they might now work to be rid of him completely.

I clung to one hope: perhaps he was wrong. Perhaps his fears of assassination were unfounded.

Papa's hand was warm over mine; the wind in our faces was bitter. The sun did little to warm it. I could feel the hunger of the cold wind on my skin. I shivered, drawing my fur-lined cloak close around me.

"If I am lost, you will turn to the king in Paris," he said.

"I know, Papa. We spoke of this already."

"You may also turn to Geoffrey of Anjou. I fought with him in Normandy. I sought to help him win his duchy back."

"He failed," I said. I knew the story of Geoffrey of Anjou well. His wife, the Empress Maude, had been heir to the throne of England, but her barons had rebelled, not wanting to swear fealty to a woman. The usurper Stephen had tried to take her throne, but he had been too weak to hold her lands, either in England or in Normandy. So Geoffrey, Count of Anjou, fought for his wife, both in Normandy and in England, but he had never been able to defeat Stephen completely, and take his wife's lands back. Though my father honored the count as friend and ally, I would turn to my own barons in time of need long before I ever sought help from Geoffrey of Anjou.

"Geoffrey fights still," my father said. "The Angevins never give up, as you do not." Papa raised my chin, and looked into my eyes. "I tell you this, because you must hear it. If you are ever in dire need, turn to Geoffrey. He will help you, if he can."

I did not mention to my father that a man who could not hold his own duchy, a man who could not enforce his wife's claims to the throne of England, surely could do little to help me. The plan we had in place among our trusted barons and bishops would serve me far better than reaching out to the Angevins. It showed my father's fear for me that he spoke not of our carefully laid plans but his friend Geoffrey, far away in Normandy.

"I promise you, Papa. I will remember. The Angevins are our allies."

He kissed me and held me close. Papa thought to draw his enemies away from us by going to Compostela alone. He hoped to leave me and Petra safe behind the walls of Ombrière.

I knew well the depths we swam in, and the razor-sharp teeth in the mouths of our enemies, ready to consume us and the Aquitaine both.

"I taught you not to fear the dark," Papa said.

My father waited for me to finish. It was part of our catechism, part of the truth he had begun to teach me when I was eight years old, the year my brother died.

"In the dark, I must keep my eyes open, so that I might see whatever comes out of it."

How my father would have answered me I never knew, for my sister, Petra, came outside to meet us then, her women hurrying to catch her. Though she was a sweet, biddable girl, she was often restless; no one ever could keep her close and settled for longer than an hour. Petra had finished her lessons and her afternoon embroidery, and now she ran to us, her soft hair coming loose from the veil she wore.

"Alienor!"

She hugged me as if we had been separated for months and not hours. She kissed my cheek, and I took in the sweet scent of her skin. Her soft hair was blond, where mine was bronze. Though I had been named for our mother, it was Petra who favored her in looks and temperament. Her blue eyes took me in as if she knew all there was to know of me, as if she loved me anyway.

Petra was like a little bird in my arms; she did not linger long, but flew at once to our father. She was eleven years old; in a few years, she would be old enough for marriage, but to me she still seemed very young.

My father held her close. He met my eyes over the top of her head. I understood him as if he had spoken the words aloud. We would say nothing of our fears to her. We would keep her safe, as we always had, as I always would.

We went inside, Petra chattering between us. Our family feasted at my father's high table, I on one side of him, and Petra on the other. We did not linger in the hall that night, but sat up late with Petra in the room that had once been her nursery. I sent her women away, and relaxed beside her fire, my father's hand in mine, listening to Petra's plans for a new altar cloth, as if Papa's cathedral at Bordeaux needed yet another one.

Finally, even my sister's energy tapered off, and she lay down on her feather bed.

"Papa, you are going away tomorrow," Petra said. "But you must come back. Promise me."

My father never lied to us, not even to offer comfort. He did not turn away, but kept his eyes on hers. "I promise that I will be careful, and do all I can to come home to you," he said.

As I watched, Petra's eyes filled with tears. I squeezed her hand. Lies fell from my lips easily, even then. I would have done more than lie to comfort and protect her. "He will be back, and with us in a month's time," I said.

I thought at first that Papa would contradict me, but he said only, "God willing."

Petra heard our father's words, but it was my eyes she sought as she lay against her bolster. Her blue gaze pierced mine.

"God willing," I said.

She heard the prayer I uttered to her god, and she was satisfied. Her eyes closed then; my father and I stayed beside her, until her breathing deepened.

Papa leaned over and kissed her, murmuring into her hair something that I could not hear. Those words were lost, for she did not hear them either; she slept without stirring.

My father moved with me toward my own rooms. We walked alone, though we were rarely alone in our keep. His men slept on the floor of the great hall, waiting to escort him to Spain on the morrow.

"I will love you always, Alienor, until the day they put me in the ground. And if the Church is right, my soul will remember you, even beyond death."

There were tears in my eyes, but I laughed in spite of them. "I will see you then. We will recline in hell together."

Papa did not speak, nor did he laugh with me. He wiped my tears away, but they fell too fast, and were too many. He could not stop them, even with his linen kerchief. He left me the soft white linen with his crest embroidered on it. At the door to my room, Papa kissed me, his lips lingering on my forehead as if to bless me, though he and I believed in no gods, and had no saints to succor us.

I still felt his lips on my skin the next day, when I stood in the castle bailey and watched him ride away. Papa raised his gloved hand before urging his horse down the road that had no turning. I did not weep there in front of all our people, but watched him go dry-eyed. Petra wept for both of us.

❧

It was weeks before we heard the news. Petra and I sat in the garden of the keep among the flowers. The white stone of Ombrière rose around us but did not choke off the sunlight and air. Pear trees clung to the inner garden walls, their blossoms white against the vivid green of the leaves. Their bark was darkened by rain, as were the limbs of the fig trees that waved against the deep blue of the sky. Every few moments, some cool rainwater would shake loose from those leaves in the wind, and fall onto my sister's embroidery. Since she did not mutter under her breath against the sprinkles that fell from the leaves above our heads, I knew that she embroidered simply to stay calm, as we waited for word from our father.

Though I feared for Papa, I felt sheltered in his favorite

keep among the flowering trees my grandmother had planted. It had rained that morning, but the sun had come out at noon, and my sister and I had emerged from the castle keep with it.

Petra continued to work her needle while I read to her in Latin. She had little interest in words or books, but at eleven, she had begun to notice men, so that I had to keep a close watch on her. I made sure that she was observed at all times by every old crone I could find who was trustworthy. Still, I feared Petra might slip my nets and get herself with child before her marriage could be arranged. So far, my sister stayed obedient to me, though her eye wandered over every virile young man in sight.

I was sitting in our grandmother's flower garden, worrying over how to rein my sister in, when news came of my father's death.

The boy who brought word was pale with his task, gasping from the hard ride he had made. I learned later that he had traveled straight to Bordeaux from Spain, driving almost six horses into the ground. My father's squire was barely fifteen, a boy named Guillaume.

I held the letter in my hand, its old vellum as soft as a caress. I knew what it contained before I opened it, from the dark and frightened look on Guillaume's face. He had brought this letter straight to me. I recognized the seal of wax from my father's signet ring, still unbroken on the vellum in my hand.

As I peered into his face, I saw that this boy acknowledged me as duchess, as had every man who had ridden with him. My mind was one large bruise; I could not even feel pleasure in the fact that my father's people had come to me before the archbishop of Bordeaux, my father's friend, in whose keeping I was supposed to be. A gray fog stole over my eyes, and over the contours of my mind, as I broke the seal. I read the Latin of that letter, words of condolence that seemed sincere. The priest from Compostela who had written of my father's death had not had a hand in it.

My father had died within the Church precincts after drinking bad water, and sickening from it.

I could not feel the pain. Someone had killed him; I knew the term "bad water" was a euphemism for poison.

Fear rose in my throat, unexpected and unlooked for. Grief I had anticipated, as well as tears, but neither came. I would have welcomed them. Instead, the gray fog over my mind turned black, and terror rose from the ground as if to smother me and mine, threatening to block out the sun for the rest of my life. My life, which would be short if I did not think clearly, as Papa had taught me.

If I faltered, men would come. They would attack our keep. If my own barons could not reach us in time, the walls of my father's palace would fall, and my body would be forfeit.

Rape did not frighten me. All women faced such danger every day of their lives. A coronet was no protection from that. I feared worse, for with my body would go the Aquitaine. Some brigand might make himself duke if I could not complete the contract to wed the king's son.

I was driven from these thoughts by the sound of my sister crying. I had not spoken, but she had seen the look on my face, and had read the words of the priest's letter. It was the only time I ever regretted that Papa had taught her to read Latin.

I heard Petra's screams before I felt her clutching me, her small hands fastened on my gown. I came to myself, looking down at the blond braids that bound her hair. The letter that held my father's death lay discarded on the stone walkway where I had dropped it. I lowered myself to a bench close by, and brought Petra with me. As my sister wept, the last of my childhood bled out of me with her tears. I felt it go as I sat and stroked her hair.

The plan of action that my father had laid out for me began to form in my mind. I clung to it, as if it were a scrap of vellum with my father's last words written on it to guide me. My fear lay down, like a dog that would look to bite me later.

I met Amaria's eyes. She stood by, silent as she always was, ready to do my bidding. She was only one year older than I, but she was steady, a high rock in the world when the waters rose to drown me. I held fast to that rock, and took strength from her.

"Send for the archbishop," I said. "He must know at once."

She did not hesitate, but took up the letter I had dropped.

No doubt the archbishop had heard already of my father's death, for once such news reached the keep, it would spread through the city like wildfire in dry summer grain. But I must begin as I meant to go on. I must summon the archbishop to me. If he acknowledged me as duchess and as my father's heir, he would come when I called for him.

Amaria left at once. Guillaume had begun to weep when

Petra did, but he still knelt by me, though his knees trembled with exhaustion. He reached into the pouch at his belt, and brought forth my father's signet ring. Its ruby gleamed in the light of the dying sun. I raised it above my sister's head, and looked at it in the fading light. The last time I had seen it, that ring had been on my father's hand. It was too large to fit even my middle finger, so I slid it onto my thumb.

The archbishop came to me in my grandmother's garden instead of sending a clerk to fetch me back to him. With that one gesture, he confirmed me in my state. That more than anything told me I was duchess now: the sight of my father's proud churchman, bending one knee to take my hand in his. He kissed my father's ring, and met my eyes.

"I am sorry, my lady. I am sorry for your loss."

For this man to humble himself before me spoke more of his love for my father than anything else he might have done. I pressed his hand, unable to speak, for a rock had lodged in my throat. I had to swallow hard to discard it.

Petra still clung to me. Her sobs had quieted, but her tears ran down her cheeks, raining on the satin of her brocade gown. When I looked at my father's friend, my eyes were dry.

"He has been buried at the cathedral of Santiago de Compostela in Spain," Archbishop Geoffrey said.

Grief gave way to fury when I saw that our enemies had stolen even his body from me. I looked at Guillaume, who still knelt before me, and at the archbishop, who waited to see if I would falter. Guillaume looked frightened; I saw that he had feared my anger too much to give me this news himself.

It was Guillaume I spoke to first. In spite of his fear, he

had served me well, when he would have been well paid to hand the news of my father's death to another. "Go inside and sleep. I will send for you on the morrow. From this day forward you are esquire no longer, but a knight. I will outfit you with horse and armor from my father's treasury myself."

Guillaume bowed lower, even as he kept to his knees. I felt his lips on my hand, on my father's ring.

I turned to Amaria, who stood back just a little, enough to show respect to the archbishop, but still close enough to hear my orders.

"Take Guillaume inside, and give him a bed and food. Pay the men who rode with him in gold."

She did not question me, but raised one hand. Maria, another of my ladies, stepped forward from the shadows, tears on her cheeks. She curtsied to me, and after Amaria had whispered instruction in her ear, she went at once to do my bidding.

The archbishop was impressed by this small show, but I knew, as he did, that I would have to be able to conquer more than my household to save the Aquitaine.

I was a marriage prize now. I must lock myself tight within the stronghold of our palace at Bordeaux. I could not stir to hunt or even to take the air on our ramparts. I must hide, as a coward might, while I waited for my marriage arrangements to be completed.

"I would have seen my father buried at Talmont, next to my mother."

"You could not travel to see him laid to rest, my lady," the archbishop said.

As I watched, he gathered himself to speak against my traveling anywhere, for any reason, as if he needed to explain to me the deep danger I was in until I took my marriage vows. As if my father's death by poison had not taught me of my danger already.

I would have laughed on any other day, that a man would think me so blind and so stupid. But Papa was dead. I would never see his face again. I did not laugh, but clutched my sister to me. I would not fail. As I met the archbishop's gaze, I saw for the first time that he knew it.

"I must stay here, locked behind my father's walls, a rabbit beneath a stone, still and silent, in the hope that the hunter will not see me. And you . . ."

The archbishop who had been my father's friend took strength from the certainty behind my eyes. Whatever he had thought of me before, this man would serve me now, and for the rest of his life.

"You must send for the King of France."

Chapter 6

⁓⁓⁓

Palace of Ombrière

Bordeaux
July 1137

I STAYED SAFELY HIDDEN BEHIND THE WALLS OF MY FATHER'S castle at Bordeaux. The life of my duchy went on beyond those walls, and reports were brought to me daily. My father's spy network was still in place, and now had become mine. Its ranks were made up of many people, from the great to the small, all gathered into my father's service over the course of his lifetime. Each man was paid in gold for his information, but each also served my father out of loyalty, and out of love for him. The bishop of Limoges was a member of this corps of spies, as were a dozen other priests scattered throughout my father's lands. More than a dozen knights were enlisted in my father's service in the houses of both his friends and his enemies. This network of spies was a secret, even one member from another, but I knew them all. My father had made me memorize each man's name from the time I was a child.

That network served me well, now that I was trapped in Ombrière. No one was allowed into the city gates, nor into my keep, for fear that an enemy would sneak in and take my maidenhead and the duchy before my marriage contract with France could be signed. Marriage negotiations took the rest of the spring, for the king knew he had me by the throat, and hoped to make the most of it. But I knew his son was getting the wealth of Aquitaine and Poitou, if not complete dominion over the lands themselves. He would have to be content with that.

My representative, the bishop of Limoges, made the king see reason, for in the month of June, my betrothed left Paris with an escort of five hundred knights. At last, the young king, heir to the kingdom of France, was riding to Bordeaux to marry me. No doubt his father, Louis VI, would live another ten years or more, but the throne of France sought to safeguard its future by crowning its prince early, during the old king's lifetime. The man I would marry would not need to be crowned when his father died, for his coronation had been celebrated in the cathedral of Reims already.

Young King Louis sent word to me a week before he arrived, so my women and I were ranged in my father's castle keep to greet him. The sky was a clear blue overhead, with no hint of clouds. The warmth of the wind beckoned me to go on a hunt, but I knew my duty, to myself and to my father's memory. We had both worked for years to see this marriage done. I would stay inside the palace where I was safe, until my husband-to-be and his five hundred knights arrived.

His men could not stay in the keep, for there were too many of them. I arranged for tents to be set up in the fields surrounding the city, so that Louis' troops would not come inside the city walls. I had no doubt that the Parisians would take offense at this, for they were a touchy people, or so I had been told. No matter. We would begin as I meant to go on. I was duchess here.

Summer was rising, and the fruit was thick on the boughs, not yet turned ripe. I saw Papa's pear trees twining along the garden wall. I would not be here when that fruit was eaten.

I pushed that thought aside. I would be Queen of France. I would have pears sent up from Anjou to please my palate. When I was queen, the world would lie at my feet.

When Louis, my betrothed, rode into the keep, I turned to the gate, a smile on my lips. The soul of courtesy, Louis left most of his men outside. Only twenty warriors accompanied him through my father's castle gates, a number easily welcomed. My hospitality would not be overwhelmed, even when my barons came to see us married.

At first sight, Louis took my breath away. Only sixteen years old, my husband-to-be was tall and fair, with soft blond hair falling to curve against his cheek. He wore no outer finery, no crown or diadem, but his clothes were of the finest silk, even for riding. I saw then that he had looked forward to this meeting, as I had. He sought to honor me.

Louis came down off his horse and stepped toward me without hesitation. He knew me at once, as I knew him. Tales of my beauty had preceded me. But when he stopped dead in his tracks, I saw that in his eyes I was more beautiful than tales could tell.

"My lady duchess," Louis said, bowing low before stepping forward to take the hand I offered.

"My lord king," I said as I curtsied.

Louis kept my hand. His eyes were as blue as the sky above our heads. His lips looked soft and sensuous, curved in a smile that did not fade. I caught my breath and reminded myself who and where I was. I spoke in my public voice, but he seemed to understand that I wished we were alone.

"You are welcome to this place, my liege. Come inside and take refreshment. Let my ladies entertain you."

He flushed with pleasure and bowed so that his pink cheeks might be hidden. I saw then how young he was, much younger than I in his mind and heart, though I was a year his junior. Louis had been raised among monks, before his elder brother was killed falling from his horse, leaving Louis as the only heir. Young Louis was not used to politics. No doubt he needed a guiding hand.

I offered him my arm, and he took it. Perhaps my guiding hand would do.

❁

For hours my ladies sang and smiled for Louis. He sat beside me on my dais, and was gracious to all who welcomed him. The afternoon festivities turned into the evening meal, and all the while, Louis sat at my side, saying little, and looking beautiful.

I longed to get him alone. As I caught his eye, he blushed once more, almost as a maid might. It occurred to me that he was a virgin, as I was, and I felt a touch of foreboding. I dismissed it at once; was this not the marriage my father and I had labored for almost a decade to make?

We did not speak alone, for Louis did not stay for the dancing. The churchmen he had brought with him stood after the fruit came out, and bowed low to me, making ready to leave.

"We look forward to seeing you again tomorrow, my lady duchess," Louis said. I saw that his men had not even asked his permission to go. He had seen them rise, and trained to come when his churchmen called, he rose with them.

Louis pressed his lips to my fingertips, and the warmth of his breath sent a shiver down my spine. His blue eyes met mine, and for a moment, I lost myself in them.

Louis gave me a soft, sweet smile that made me long to reach out and touch his cheek. He lowered his voice so that only I could hear him. "Good night, Eleanor."

It was the first time he had used my given name. His Parisian accent mangled it almost beyond recognition, but his voice was soft, his breath hot on my skin. I thought that I might overlook such a flaw, even come to find it charming, in exchange for the crown he would soon place upon my head.

The Parisians were gone from my hall almost as soon as Louis turned from me. How they moved so quickly, with their stiff, contained walks and their furtive glances at my people, I was not sure. My ladies and knights sighed with relief to see them gone, but a few of the Parisian churchmen still lingered. I raised my glass to them, and sent round the fruit once more, this time from my own table.

Their leader, a monk named Francis, smiled and bowed from his seat below the dais. Though there were spies in my midst, I was well aware of them, as my father had taught me to be.

The remembered loss of my father was like a blade driven into my side. It came upon me as an assassin might, and took my breath. Papa was not here to sit in triumph with me. It was his careful diplomacy as much as the duchy itself that had brought this alliance about. I missed my father more in that moment than I had since I first learned of his death.

Petra heard me gasp, and pressed my hand under the table, careful not to look at me, since I had told her that we must both be cautious while the Parisians were about, careful never to reveal our true thoughts or feelings in public. Petra had shown more grace at subterfuge than I had hoped for. Perhaps we had sold her short by protecting her for so long. But it was done. I was duchess, and I would keep protecting her for as long as I drew breath.

My pain passed, though the memory of it lingered like a pall over the rest of the evening. I stayed in the hall until the lamps burned down.

My people were relieved to see me dance once more. They sang for me with pride, and I listened to their songs. We had heard little music since my father died. Tonight, my knights and ladies danced not just for the joy of my coming marriage but for joy in the simple freedom to move and sing once more.

I was not as lighthearted as they, but I laughed at their bawdy jokes as if I were. It was almost midnight when Amaria and my women climbed the stairs to my rooms. Petra had been asleep long since, safe in her bower, with double guards to keep the Parisians at bay, if any gentlemen were to try her door.

Amaria undid my braid until my bronze hair hung about my shoulders like a cloak. She began the long task of combing it out, as she did every night. She knew that such soothing motions helped me sleep.

"The young king is at prayer," she said, almost idly.

I blinked, and sat up straight. The cushion supporting my back fell to the wooden floor so that Amaria had to bend down to retrieve it. The rest of my ladies had been sent away already.

"What? Where is Louis?"

She blinked to see such emotion from me. She knew as well as I that our marriage was not for my pleasure, nor for his, but to secure the throne of France for my sons.

"Young Louis," I said, as if there could be more than one in my keep. "Where is he?"

"He is at prayer, my lady. He wanted to go to the chapel, but when he found there was none such within the palace, he went to the cathedral in the city."

Such idle gossip had come to her in the hall. My spies would have brought me such news directly, if they thought for one moment that I cared. I saw that I would have to take them in hand. It was not for them to decide what information they carried to me.

"In the cathedral," I said. "Is he there still?"

"He was when we left the hall, Your Grace."

From the formal title she gave me, not only could she see

the way my thoughts were tending, but she did not approve. I rose at once, and called for my cloak.

"I feel the need for prayer," I said.

She did not snort in derision, for to do so would have been beneath her dignity. Amaria stared hard at me for one long moment before she went to do my bidding. As she returned from my trunks, she wore her own cloak across her shoulders.

"I, too, feel the call of God," she said.

I did not speak but only smiled as I led her into the hidden corridor beyond the wall of my room. The door into the hallway was tucked behind a tapestry. Its hinges were well oiled, and the door opened easily after I unlocked it with the key I kept in my alms purse. I carried few coins for alms, but there were many hidden doors in my father's castle. I held the only key to each of them.

I felt Amaria's displeasure as she walked behind me, but I did not heed it. It was for her to follow me, whatever I set out to do. This night was no exception.

We slipped past my men and the few Parisian guards who dozed on the great staircase. We moved through another hidden door into the bailey, where one of my men, a great hulking warrior named Bardonne, fell in behind me without questioning my purpose. I took him in, memorizing his face before I walked on. I could use a man who asked no questions at my back. I would bring him with me to Paris.

We moved to walk from the bailey through the gates to Bordeaux itself. There was a small door, tucked in close by the portcullis. My gatekeeper knew me at once, and moved to open it for me. Before he could do so, a shadow rose out of the darkness, and stepped into my path so that I could not move, forward or back. The shadow spoke.

"My lady duchess, where do you go, so late in the night and unattended?"

I heard the Baron Rancon's voice, and knew him well, even in the dark. Bardonne had made no noise, but had drawn his short sword. He stood now between the baron and myself, the tip of his blade at my baron's throat. I raised one hand, and Bardonne stepped back. He did not lower his blade but kept watch on Rancon as if he were an enemy.

"I go to the cathedral for prayer, my lord. Will you escort me there?"

The night was dark, but the moon had risen, coming out from behind a heavy cloud. I saw Rancon then in the moonlight. I saw his anger and his jealousy and his desire for me, all bound into one great mass over his heart. These emotions chased one another across the handsome planes of his face. I felt my own heart seize within my breast. I wanted this man, but I was bound for another.

Rancon stepped away, clearing the path so that Bardonne, Amaria, and I might walk on unencumbered. "I will not go with you, my lady duchess. It seems your man has all in hand."

"I have all in hand. I thank you, my lord baron."

I stared into the chestnut brown of his eyes. I wished us alone in that moment, myself in his arms. The hunger of lust rose in me, caressing my tongue. I saw answering lust on the baron's face, along with the knowledge that we were not alone in the dark of my father's keep. I was duchess now, and Rancon could not touch me, on pain of death.

Rancon took one more step away from me, and I walked on, though every sinew in my body cried out to stay with him, and to leave Louis forgotten. But Louis could never be forgotten. Baron Rancon was beautiful, but I could not have him, that night or ever.

The great cathedral my grandfather had constructed stood a short walk from my father's keep. I entered quietly, hiding myself within the shadows of the church. No one else was there save for Louis and two of his men. Both of his guards slept, but my husband-to-be knelt before the altar, his head bowed, his hands clasped. I watched the play of the lamplight across the blond brightness of his hair.

I left Amaria guarded by Bardonne in the shadows behind me, and went to kneel beside him.

Louis did not sense my presence at once, so deep was he in his devotions. I was fascinated. Never before had I seen a man who prayed in truth and not for show. I felt humbled in his presence, though I believed in nothing that he prayed to. His silent reverence called to me. I wondered if someday he might be as devoted to me.

I moved and my silk gown rustled. Louis crossed himself, then turned to me, his blue eyes meeting mine in the dimness of that church.

"You came," he said.

"I am here," I answered.

"I waited," he said, "hoping you would come."

His generous lips stilled; his voice fell silent. I watched his mouth, waiting to see if he might speak again.

When he did not, I leaned close to him, and pressed my

lips to his. It was a chaste kiss, an offering of sorts, a question. I was not sure what the answer was. Neither, it seemed, was he.

Louis' lips were soft beneath mine. He did not respond, nor did he touch me. He stayed as still as stone, though I could hear his breath catch, and then quicken.

I drew back from him. Louis' eyes were still closed. He seemed to realize only then that I had pulled away. His blue eyes flew open, and his gaze rested on me.

"Forgive me, my lady."

I thought at first he apologized for not taking me in his arms. I wondered if perhaps he was shy, for his men were awake now, and Amaria and my own man stood watching.

"I have sinned," he said. "I have kissed you in the house of God."

I smiled, thinking that perhaps he was joking. "No, my lord king. It is I who kissed you."

He flushed, and his pale cheeks turned red. I watched the blood rise beneath his skin, and was reminded once more of a shy maid. I told myself that he had been raised in a church. He had not always known his destiny, as I had always known mine.

Louis did not speak. I rose to my feet and offered him my hand. I watched him hesitate. He seemed tempted, and I wondered if he did not want to lean on a woman to help him stand. Then he spoke.

"I must pray a little longer, my lady. I must ask forgiveness, and seek absolution from my confessor."

A man in black stepped out from behind the altar then, and I recoiled instinctively. It was Brother Francis, the lead priest in Louis' entourage, the man who had accepted the gift of fruit from my table with a smile earlier that night, as if tribute from a duchess were his due.

Louis' priest smiled at me, a calculating smile that seemed to speculate on what he might gain from catching me alone with the heir of France. I saw that I would have to send this one a bag of gold on the morrow, to buy his silence.

I bowed to Francis, knowing him for the first time as an enemy. I pushed the priest from my mind, as I had pushed the Baron Rancon from my mind half an hour before.

I focused on the young king at my side, on the man who would be my husband.

"Do sleep sometime tonight, my lord king. Tomorrow, we ride out on a hunt."

Louis turned pale at my words. I thought for a moment he was afraid to hunt with me, but he swallowed hard and nodded. "As you say, my lady. Until tomorrow."

I curtsied to him, and moved to go. I expected to feel my betrothed's eyes on me as I went, as I would have felt any other man's. But when I turned back at the door, Louis faced the cross above his head. He still knelt, his rosary between his hands, his lips moving in silent prayer. Brother Francis stood over him, as a black crow over a carrion feast, waiting to hear his confession.

Chapter 7

༄

Palace of Ombrière

Bordeaux
July 1137

MOST OF MY BARONS BEGAN TO ARRIVE THE NEXT DAY. THEY all came to the great hall to bend their knee to me and to my betrothed. We had to cut our hunt short in order to greet them. I was sorry, but I saw after only a few minutes in the saddle that though Louis was a competent horseman, he did not care for hunting.

When I showed him my hawk, newly tamed to my hand, he shrank from the great bird as from an apparition. His eyes were shadowed with sleeplessness, his pale face almost gray with fear. I handed the bird off to my groom at once, but it took many moments for Louis to regain his color.

That afternoon, we sat on my dais in my father's hall, the great hall that had become my own. Petra sat behind us to remind the barons that if I was to die, the duchy would go not to France but to her.

As each baron stepped forward, I asked him about his fields and crops, his peasants, and his wars. Each was surprised, some pleased and some not, that I knew him and all his doings so intimately. They each bent their knee to Louis, but only after first having spoken to me.

As the fourth baron approached the dais, I began to realize that Louis was still saying my name with his heavy Parisian accent. Though we all spoke French out of courtesy to him, he could not make his tongue and lips form the word *Alienor*. The flavor of the langue d'oc did not sit easily on his tongue for even that one word.

Louis did not notice, but my barons began to frown, and to take offense. My men were touchy, and needed careful handling, but Louis would be my husband. Here was one way I might establish his authority, while losing nothing but my name. I did not consider the price, for it was a personal matter only. As to the duchy, Louis' authority was my authority, once I went away.

"The Duchess Eleanor greets you," I said to Baron Rancon.

The memory of our meeting the night before lived still in the dark brown of his eyes. My own lust rose, as I sat there with Louis beside me.

Geoffrey of Rancon saw the desire on my face. He also understood when I insisted on the new pronunciation of my name. He was the first after Louis to speak my name as I would bear it for the rest of my life.

"My lady Eleanor, you grow ever more beautiful."

Rancon behaved as if he had just arrived, as if he had never seen me the night before, sneaking out of the castle keep.

I laughed at his words, and the sound carried to the far end of the hall, warming the cold stone. I had never before drawn out my laughter, and let it caress all who heard it. All the men in the room stopped their conversations, and turned to me.

"And your tongue is ever silver, my lord. It puts me in mind of the contest a year ago, when you won a dance from me with a song."

I pitched my voice to fill the great hall without strain. Though I kept my eyes on Rancon, I saw that all my other barons and their wives turned to listen. I had never commanded in my own hall before, without my father standing by. It was a heady moment, but in spite of the warmth of the Baron Rancon's hand on mine, I kept my wits.

"It was more than a year ago, Your Grace," Rancon said.

"Indeed. How well you remember." I smiled at him, and made him feel for a moment as if my smile were for him alone, though of course it was not. Louis shifted beside me on his borrowed cushions.

"My lords and ladies, I call for a song. Tonight, in this hall, my lords and knights will sing for me. Each man must compose a new song, using my given name: Eleanor."

My barons, who had been rapt to this point, began to shift on their feet, and cast glances at one another.

"Among our people, we have the most artistic and talented knights in this land. Indeed, I would stake a claim that my lords might set a poem to music that would rival any man's in Christendom."

Though my praise was flowery, and calculated to draw them in, I did not lie. The Court of Love had begun in my grandfather's time. Though many great castles now fed and housed countless troubadours, the best songwriters in Europe still came to our halls. And my barons stood to sing with them, bringing songs and tales they had written themselves. I had set my court a challenge, and as I watched, they drank it down.

I infused my voice with just a hint of laughter. "And if you take care with the scansion of my name, you might use your songs again, to woo your own ladies."

There was a long pause, during which I thought they had slipped my nets. But then they laughed, not because what I said had much wit, but because it was the simple truth. The only reason my men wrote poetry at all was to coax their ladies into their beds.

Baron Rancon and Louis were the only two men in the hall who did not laugh. Louis, no doubt, because he did not get the joke; Rancon because his eyes had still not left my face. I had used him to enforce the new pronunciation of my name, and he did not like it. But I knew he would not question me, there in front of all my men.

I lowered my voice, so that only he and Louis could hear me. "And will you sing again this night, my lord? Will you raise your voice in song for me?"

I knew I was pushing my luck, but I could not seem to stop myself. I still wanted this man. Even now, as I looked at his great wide hands, I remembered how they had felt on my body.

I reminded myself that my husband-to-be sat beside me, feeling lost and out of place, for Rancon and I had begun to speak in the langue d'oc, a language Louis did not understand.

Baron Rancon answered me, his eyes cradling mine. His voice was soft, all traces of anger bled out of it. I saw only his pain, that he must yield me to another.

"No, my lady duchess. There are too many rivals for your affection. This day, I will respectfully retire from the field."

Rancon bowed low, first to me, and then to Louis, who still sat frowning. Geoffrey left me then, and took a stool at the far end of the hall. He was not alone long, for women found him, and drank with him, simpering and offering themselves, for he was young and unmarried still. I forced myself not to look his way again, but from time to time, all that afternoon and that evening, I felt his eyes on me.

I turned back to Louis, for I had neglected him long enough. I spoke to him in flawless Parisian French of the contest I would hold that night. I reached out to take his hand. Louis blinked, surprised at my boldness.

"You see, my lord king. Now they will use my new name and it will become a byword. Never again will you be misunderstood when you speak of your wife."

Louis' face, cloudy with worry and doubt, cleared as the sky does when the sun rises in the morning. "You did this for me?"

I felt my heart twist inside me. This young king's childhood had shaped him so that he was forced to such diffidence now. I thought of my father; what a man Papa might have made of him.

I schooled my face to blankness, save for a soothing smile. "Of course, my lord king. All I do, I seek to serve you."

Louis' hand closed hard over my own, and he raised it to his lips. His eyes filled with tears, and for a moment, I thought he might shed them.

I saw then that Louis was weak. He was not a man to shelter me, as the Baron Rancon would have been, but someone else I would have to protect.

I stared down at Louis' bent golden head, pushing away all comparisons with the baron and what might have been. I told myself that it was better this way. A weak king would lean more heavily on me, and on our son.

This thought did little to comfort me as I sat in my great hall that night, listening to the songs sung in my honor. My barons used my new name as seamlessly as if I had never had any other. Louis listened and applauded, though I could see he did not like to hear my name lifted in song at all.

I judged the contest, and gave the winner a golden cup from my father's treasury. Louis eyed it almost avariciously, and I wondered if he coveted it for himself. I saw his priest, Brother Francis, eyeing it as well, and the look that passed between them. Louis wanted that goblet not for himself but for the Church.

I felt a touch of ice slide down my spine, but I shook it off. I could train Louis out of such proclivities. Soon he would be drawn to me alone. Once I had Louis in my bed, the Church would be relegated to its place, in the service of the throne of France.

❦

After two weeks of feasting and dancing, my wedding day came. The sun rose bright that morning, and there was not a cloud in the sky. As my women dressed me in emerald silk and cloth of gold, I stared out of the window and thought of my father.

For the last two weeks, I had been distracted from his death, both by Louis and by all my knights and barons gathering in one place. I had laughed and danced, schemed and heard the reports of my spies. For the weeks after our wedding, I had planned a progress through my lands so that all my people might see my husband, and, more important, his five hundred knights. I would show the people and my barons the might of the King of France, as well as the control I exerted over that might. I would leave for Paris soon after that progress, so I wanted to make a strong impression.

Politics seemed to fade with the dawn of my wedding day. My father and I had worked so hard to achieve this marriage. Today, that work would bear fruit, but my father would not see it.

Papa lay everywhere as I looked around his favorite palace. I had been mewed up in the keep at Bordeaux for so many months that it had grown tiresome to me. Now I was leaving, and I did not know when I might return. I must be about the business of birthing kings, and raising them to follow not just in their father's footsteps but in mine. But today, I thought not of my future but of my past. I thought of Papa, and of how I wished he stood beside me.

Petra seemed to know what I was thinking, as she often did, in spite of my care to keep my feelings hidden. She reached out, and took my hand. I kept her hand in mine, and smiled for her, though I knew the smile did not reach my eyes. She would have said something to me, but a knock came at my door.

Before my women could speak, I called, "Come." And the door opened.

The Baron Rancon strode into my rooms, as if he were my betrothed, as if he had the right.

My women drew back, startled, then moved to stand in front of me. They were all thinking that he had come to abduct me. I knew better; he was loyal. Rancon would not have come to me unless the need was dire. He was no romantic fool, set on begging me to reconsider my marriage. He was there for some other reason altogether.

When Geoffrey of Rancon looked at me, standing there in my green silk and cloth of gold, he stopped dead, whatever he had first meant to say forgotten. I savored the feel of his eyes on my skin, and let him look.

I stepped out from behind my women. "My lord Rancon, what brings you to my rooms on my wedding day?"

"Treason, my lady."

I raised one eyebrow. My ladies twittered like birds in a hedge. I let them murmur among themselves for a moment, before I raised one hand.

"What treachery, my lord?"

"There is a plot to kidnap you after the ceremony, on the way to your wedding feast."

Our vows spoken and the mass after were two steps in the process of my marriage to Louis, but neither was the most important. If I was taken by another man before Louis bedded me, the duchy could be claimed by the first man who had me. A few hasty words with a priest and a quick coupling were all that was needed for any brigand to make himself Duke of Aquitaine. Vows taken before God and masses sung in the darkness of a church would mean little if another man laid siege to my body, and, by taking hold of me, took hold of my duchy.

Though my barons might rise up against such a usurper, they could be subdued, and bribed with gold after, once my new brigand husband had his hands on my treasury. And in spite of Louis' five hundred knights, there were some men who would not mind risking war with France if they could gain my duchy first.

"Is this common knowledge?" I asked.

"No, my lady. Only I know it, and now you."

I nodded once, thoughtful, as if considering. It was no secret that men wanted to kidnap me, to take hold of my duchy. I had a strategy in place to thwart them if my enemies made it past my castle gates. I met Amaria's eyes, and she left us to spread the word among a few well-chosen men. My people would soon be at work, seeing that my will was done.

"Then we will give them a hunt," I said.

"What, my lady?"

I smiled at him, and in spite of his worldliness and his courtesy, I saw that he loved me still.

"If my enemies hope to catch me like a rabbit in a snare, we will give them a chase."

My women said nothing to this, and the baron stared at me, uncomprehending.

"My lord Rancon, your castle of Taillebourg lies hard by. Might I prevail on you to spend a night there when the wedding is done, myself and the king?"

Baron Rancon's face darkened, and he bowed to hide it. "My house is yours, Your Grace, whenever you have need of it."

I closed the distance between us, and extended my hand. "Thank you, Geoffrey."

The use of his given name was almost his undoing. I felt a pain next to my own heart, and I wished once more that he were the man I would bed that night.

I thought for a long moment that he would not accept the hand I offered. When he did take it, his palm was warm and dry. He kissed my fingertips, then backed away.

"Send word to your men," I said. "I will get word to the king."

Rancon did not speak again, but bowed to me. He turned and strode from the room, and my women sighed as he left. Had I been free to express myself, I would have sighed as well. As it was, I met Amaria's eyes. She would dispatch word to the king's guard. After the ceremony, we would ride for Taillebourg.

❊

My wedding was almost anticlimactic after so much excitement.

I met my husband on the cathedral porch, and we pledged ourselves to each other in front of his people and mine. The archbishop of Bordeaux heard our vows and blessed our marriage there under a blue sky a shade darker than my father's eyes.

At the end of the ceremony, Louis hesitated one long moment, but finally, he gave me the kiss of peace. My women relaxed then, for they had feared he would avoid kissing me out of shyness; he was famous among my people for diffidence already. It had never occurred to me that he might turn from me in front of all our people, and I felt a wash of relief as his dry lips touched mine once, very gently. Louis turned from me to stare after the archbishop as he preceded us into the darkness of the church.

I laid my hand on Louis' arm and waited, but he did not move. In the end, as we stepped into the church, it was I who led him.

I did not listen to the mass, but knelt on my embroidered cushion and thought about the night to come. I was sorry to leave directly for Taillebourg from the church and miss the wedding feast I had planned so carefully. But I could not risk being kidnapped at the feast itself, or on my way from the church to my own great hall. I would have to flee as soon as the wedding mass was sung. I knew that Amaria and Petra would see to it that my lords and their ladies ate well, drank deep, and slept it off after. After all, it was my wedding my barons had come to see, and they had seen it.

I was the young queen now. I would not have my own coronation, as no French queen ever did. But my barons and Louis' men-at-arms had seen me bound in marriage to their lord and king. My marriage vows were all it took to make me queen. All my father had worked for had come to pass. I wondered in that moment why I did not feel the triumph of it.

Louis listened to the mass, and prayed fervently when directed by my archbishop. I watched my young husband and realized that he would be in my bed and in my life for many years to come. The whole day seemed like a dream suddenly, and fear rose in my throat. I swallowed hard, but could not dislodge it.

Though my will was strong, this boy beside me now held the power of life and death over me and mine. Though in truth I would continue to rule in Aquitaine, though I would continue to rule my own life or see myself damned, by the laws of France and the Church, this boy was now my lord and master.

The archbishop placed the coronet of Aquitaine first on my head and then on my husband's. I looked at Louis in my father's diadem. He was Duke of Aquitaine now. I was a lone duchess no longer.

The mass ended, and the congregation rose. Louis stood first, for I had been distracted by my dark thoughts, and had lost the thread of the ceremony, dropping my mask of calm serenity for the briefest moment. Louis must have seen my fear.

A lesser man would have preened, or planned how to use my moment of weakness against me, but Louis was a true gentleman. He did none of those things. In the darkest moment I had known since I first heard of my father's death, Louis reached out and took my hand.

"My lady. My queen. Fear not. I am here. No harm will ever come to you, so long as I draw breath."

Louis' hand was warm, as warm as Rancon's had been. His blue eyes held mine. He took a new oath, standing there beside me. I leaned on him, and let him help me rise.

"My men-at-arms will protect you, Eleanor. Come with me now. Let us leave this place. Your women will follow with your baggage train."

I smiled that he thought I worried for my bags, for my gowns and slippers. He looked down at me, standing between me and all the court. He seemed to want to block their view of me, until I was in control of myself again.

Louis took me by the hand and led me out into the sunshine of the cathedral steps. My people waited to see us, and cheered themselves hoarse. Louis stopped and took one step back, that they might admire me.

Still holding his hand, I drew him up beside me. The people called my name, but when they saw me smile, when they saw me turn to him, they called his name as well.

I saw him as they did, this bright young boy, full of promise, his golden hair gleaming in the sun, his strength a bulwark for us to hide behind in time of war. Standing with me on those stone steps, my husband's face bloomed with the kind of open smile I had never given anyone, the smile of someone who was truly young.

Louis flushed, this time from unexpected joy. He met my eyes, his hand still in mine. I saw him then as I believe he truly was, a man meant for love, had he only been strong enough to claim it.

PART II

To Be Queen

Chapter 8

✤

Castle of Taillebourg

County of Poitou
July 1137

AS WE STOOD ON THE STEPS OF MY FATHER'S CATHEDRAL after our wedding mass, Louis' men-at-arms led two horses forward, festooned with ribbons and flowers. We would ride hard for Taillebourg to evade the unknown men who hoped to kidnap me. My destrier, Merlin, was nowhere to be seen. The horse Louis' people had prepared for me was a delicate mare with a clean step and bright eyes. She looked at me as if she knew me, and I offered her my hand.

As she breathed in the scent of my skin, I wondered what they were thinking, to saddle such a delicate mare when we soon would be riding for our lives. Perhaps one of Louis' men was in on the plot to abduct me before we could consummate our union. I scanned the crowd for anyone suspicious, but soon dismissed the thought. This beautiful horse had been a wedding gift from Louis.

Louis did not move to his own mount, but stayed beside me. His hands went around my waist, raising me into the saddle. I was impressed by Louis' strength; his slender build was deceptive. But since he had placed me on my horse side-mounted, I hoped I would keep my seat once we were past the city walls, and running full out. I was an experienced horsewoman, but only a fool would ride sidesaddle when pursued by enemies. I slung my knee over the wooden haft rising from the front of my saddle, making sure that my skirts lay smooth afterward. I would hold my place. I had come too far in pursuit of this marriage to fall off my horse, into my enemies' waiting hands.

I positioned myself so that I might hold to my horse, even at a gallop, still waving to my people. They did not know that our plans had changed. I did not know who among them might have aided my unknown enemy. And if it came to an open battle, between Louis' men-at-arms and the enemy who hoped to kidnap me, I would rather Louis' men fight for me. I would save my own barons to fight another day, when I might need them more.

My lords stood ready, waiting for us to lead them back to my father's palace. No doubt everyone thought we had mounted steeds to better show ourselves as we made our progress to the castle.

I met Amaria's eyes over the crowd. She nodded to me once, then disappeared. Baron Rancon was nowhere to be seen. I waited for Louis to mount his own horse and then I moved off.

At the turning in the road, I waved one hand and headed for the city gates. The people along that road cleared out of my path at once, casting flowers down for my horse to tread on. I led Louis out through the nearest gate, then touched my heel to my horse's side. She responded as if we had known each other all our lives. She leaped under my hands, joining Louis' troops that waited for us just outside Bordeaux's city walls.

I was pleased that Louis' men-at-arms were ready for us. They fell in before and behind, flanking us so that we could no longer be seen from the city. I heard an annoyed murmuring from my people, but I had left Petra behind to soothe their fears. She and I had said our good-byes in the keep. I would send for her once I reached Poitiers.

We were out of the hands of any attackers planning to take me in the city, but I knew that there would be more warriors lying in wait beyond the walls of Bordeaux. I felt my vulnerability in spite of Louis' knights flanking us, but then I saw Baron Rancon waiting for me by a turn in the road.

Surrounded by Louis' men, I rode to meet him. My horse got a little ahead of the young king, and foolishly, I let her. It was then that I heard the shouts from a nearby hill, and saw men bearing no standard riding for us as if the devil were on their heels. Our enemies hid not only within Bordeaux, not just within my keep, but waited for us here as well. For the first time I wondered if this attempt at escape was folly. But I would be damned before I let my enemies hem me up inside my palace again. I had been locked inside my keep for too many months already. Louis' coming had set me free. I would never cower behind stone walls again, but ride out to meet my enemies head-on. I was queen; I would do as I saw fit.

I did not look back for Louis but left the road at once, my new mount responding under me. I felt the first tremor of fear as I heard the sounds of battle behind me. I hoped we were far enough from the city that none of my people would come and fight with us. Louis' men would hold off the would-be abductors, or what else was this marriage for?

Fifty of Louis' men kept pace with me, and when I turned once to look back, I found Louis close on my heels. I smiled at him, and watched as his fear warred with his newborn love for me. I called to him, "Come, my lord, this is a race. A race we must win."

Louis did not respond, for he had lost his breath. He was not the horseman I was, but he kept up with me as the Baron Rancon led us deeper into the forest. I knew that the baron would take us to his keep at Taillebourg, staying off the roads where other men might lie in wait.

I wondered if I would ever know which lord hoped to kidnap me before my wedding night. No doubt he was a man of daring if not courage, for no man of courage would attack a helpless woman.

Of course, I was not helpless. I was Duchess of Aquitaine, and I was surrounded by the fighting men of the King of France.

We made Taillebourg by sunset; my horse was tired, though she never flagged. I did not wait to be handed down but slid from her back myself, standing close against her side.

"I will never ride any horse but you," I told her, whispering in her ear. She rolled her eye at me, and whinnied as if she understood me.

Louis came down off his own mount, and I threw myself into his arms. He caught me, though I shocked him. I pressed myself against him, my lips on his.

"My lord king, we won. We left them in the dust."

The exhilaration of the day left me breathless. Fear had given way to the joy of the hunt. Adventure was sweet, much sweeter than I had thought it would be. After being locked away in my father's keep for months on end, I found that I had a taste for it. Even as I pressed myself against him, I could see that Louis did not.

Louis had lost his breath. At first, I thought it was from our frenzied ride, but as his eyes met mine, I knew that it was from my nearness. I felt his desire pressed hard against me. I smiled up at him, only to see him blush like a maid.

I kissed him again, lingering over his lips, heedless of all who stood nearby. Louis did not spare them a glance, but kept his eyes on me.

"Life with me will never be dull, my lord king."

"I believe you, Eleanor."

He kissed me then without my prompting. Though his lips were clumsy and his touch feeble compared with the Baron Rancon's, I felt the swell of victory in my breast. I would bed him this night and take him away from the Church he loved so dearly. I knew this as certainly as I knew that I would draw my next breath. I was young, and had never known defeat.

As I drew back, his blue gaze seemed to gleam with the same hope and the same joy. Louis grew bolder. He kissed me once more, his palms lingering on my waist, before he took my hand and led me into the keep.

❀

Baron Rancon met us in his great hall, where food and music waited. From politeness, we ate with him, though I wanted to be upstairs, alone with Louis.

Geoffrey saw this in my face, for he cut our meal short, waving one hand before the servers could bring the last course. "I will have my women serve your fruit in your rooms, my lady."

"Thank you, my lord. And might they send warm water for my bath? It has been a tiring day."

Baron Rancon saw that I lied. I was not weary from the ride or from the fact someone had tried to take me by force. My cheeks still glowed with the challenge I had faced and overcome. Geoffrey's eyes darkened with desire as he looked at me, though my husband sat at my side, half-asleep with his goblet of wine.

"It will be my pleasure, my lady, to serve you in this, as in all things."

The king's men stood and herded Louis toward the stairs. He looked back to find me, and I smiled at him, and raised one hand. Satisfied, he smiled back, and let them lead him on. He was a trusting soul; I would see to it that I deserved his trust. I owed him that, for the crown he had given me.

Geoffrey was at my side then, drawing out my chair. I offered him one hand, careful to keep a seemly distance between us. I saw that he would have taken my maidenhead then and there, had we not been surrounded on all sides by Louis' men. I felt the weight of their gaze on me like hands. As soon as Geoffrey kissed my fingertips, I drew back.

"Thank you for offering us sanctuary, my lord. The king and I will never forget it."

Geoffrey did not reply, but bowed low. I left him there, and climbed the steps to the upper floor alone with the eyes of Louis' men on me.

❀

Geoffrey's women had come with fruit and wine. The rooms set aside for me looked to be the best rooms in the keep. I wondered idly if Rancon had given us his bed to spend our wedding night in. I shivered as I looked at the great carved bedstead with its dark woolen hangings. I thought of Geoffrey's hands, so large they might span my waist. I thought of how he could lift me easily onto that bed, and my skirt afterward.

I let the women leave me in my shift. They combed my hair smooth, for it had snarled while I was riding pell-mell from Bordeaux. I missed Petra, and Amaria's calming touch, but I reminded myself that Amaria would be there on the morrow, with my gowns in tow. Petra would meet us in two days' time in Poitiers, to see us crowned as Count and Countess of Poitou.

Louis came to me dressed in his shirt and cloak. The cloak was the one he had worn at our wedding, and the shirt was stained. I suppressed a flicker of disappointment that he would come to me so dirty, thoughtless of the fact that this was our wedding night. I felt slighted, until I saw his face. He gazed on me with eyes of worship tinged with fear.

It was I who moved toward him. Louis swallowed hard, and his eyes shifted from my breasts to my face. I realized then that he could see the outline of my body through the thin linen. I moved slower, that he might look his fill.

I stopped just short of brushing against his body with my own. I stood not an inch from him, raising my lips to his without actually touching him. His breath caught, as my own did. He might be shy and Church raised, but surely nature would take its course, if only we let it.

Louis did not touch me, nor did he kiss me. I felt the first icy tinge of fear. He was a man. This should be his doing. I had ordered the rest of that day's proceedings. Surely now he would take a man's part and do what must be done.

Though I could see his manhood rising beneath his long linen shirt, he did not move to touch me. I lifted his cloak from his shoulders, and draped it across a nearby chair. He gasped when I touched him, but still he did not move. I pushed aside my misgivings, and followed my own inclinations. I took his hand in mine.

"Come, my lord," I said, suddenly inspired. "Come into the bath with me."

Alarm crossed his face, and at first I thought he feared to see me naked. I raised my arms and drew my shift off in one smooth motion. I saw that my nakedness was not what he feared, but the strength of his own desire. Louis' eyes filled with a longing so intense, it made Baron Rancon's lust look like the rutting of a boar in a thicket. Louis worshipped me from the first, and never so much as when he first saw my naked body in the firelight, with nothing and no one between us.

I stepped into the hip bath, and held out my hand. As I watched, he warred with himself. I held steady, my eyes on his.

There was no priest with us now. Louis left his Church leanings to one side, for he lifted his own linen gown and tossed it after mine. His body was slender and finely made. He was no man for the outdoors, so his skin was pale all over, but his muscles were toned and smooth. I watched them play beneath his skin as he crossed the room to me.

"My lady." Louis could not speak again. But he was man enough to take my hand.

I drew him into the bath with me, and the warm water caught him as I wished it to. He moaned, and I thought for a moment that he had never felt the pleasure of warm water on his flesh before.

I took the cake of soap between my hands. It was not my own soap, scented with lilac, but some harsh lye stuff that Rancon's people had left us. I laid it by at once, and smoothed my hands over Louis' skin. Let the water do what it would.

Louis stood stock-still while I washed him. I thought for certain that he would take me up in his arms then. His manhood swayed of its own accord, though I did not touch it. But my husband only stood and stared at me. I felt another touch of fear, but I set it aside. His shyness was just one more challenge, one I would face down and win.

I moved back a little, and began to wash myself, while Louis stared at me. I faltered, but swallowed hard. I was a maid, but he was a virgin, too. I had nothing to fear or be ashamed of.

Louis seemed to see my weakness, for he reached for me

then, and took my hand. He stepped from the hip bath, and held my hand while I climbed out behind him. He raised a folded linen sheath that had been warming by the fire. He dried me with his own hands, his touch gentle and light, almost like a bird's wing. I thought I would swallow my tongue, my lust rose so quickly.

I thought to do the same for him, but he dried himself, then drew me with him toward the bed. He knew his duty, as I did, and he watched as I climbed onto the bed before him. He drew the curtains closed behind us, but I could still see the outline of his body in the firelight, as I knew he could see mine.

I lay back, and let him take the man's part. Finally, he sought to lead, and I would follow. I waited, my eyes half-closed with lust.

He began to pray.

He prayed in Latin, that our marriage be fruitful, that our bed be blessed with children. He asked for forgiveness for the sin of loving me, and promised God that he would do penance for it on the morrow.

I lay before him, my ardor blown away like so much dust. Humiliation rose to swamp me, and I closed my eyes against it. It was humiliation I felt as Louis leaned awkwardly over me, and pressed his manhood against my thighs.

I had a horrible thought that he might not be able to penetrate me, for I was a virgin true, and my passage was tight. It seemed he had a prayer for that, too, which he murmured over me, almost as if I were a sacrifice. He pushed into me then, and I gasped with the pain. Without a caress or loving touch, my maidenhead was taken in one swift, blinding stroke.

Tears rose in my eyes and I blinked them away. For Aquitaine, I would do anything. For my son to sit on the throne of France, I would have suffered worse.

I lay beneath him as he used me like a whore. As worse than a whore: as a vessel for his seed, and nothing more.

After a while, I felt a little quickening in my womb, in spite of his cold touch. A tiny bit of heat seemed to build in me, once the pain was gone. But I had known already that I was a woman for men.

I thought of the Baron Rancon, turning my face from Louis. I remembered Geoffrey's big hands, their grip hard on my waist as he pressed me up against the wall in my father's keep.

This thought stoked the heat in my nether parts, but then Louis groaned, and stopped moving altogether. The touch of his seed swamped the lamp of my own lust, and put it out.

Louis lay on top of me as one dead. But in the next moment, he drew away and left me.

The curtain stood open behind him, and I felt a draft of cool air on my skin. I shivered, though it was late July. I drew the cover up over my naked body. I would not leave the bed, for fear of seeing him. I did not fear him, but that I might strike him, if my gaze was to fall on him too soon.

As I listened, he drew his dirty shift on once more. I heard the rustling of his clothes. Then he began to pray.

I would have forgiven him even this, for I wanted to love him. But as I listened, he wept, begging his god for forgiveness, for absolution for his descent into carnal lust.

I listened to this for what seemed like an hour. I do not

know how long I lay there, and listened to the boy I had married as he wept. The scent of sex clung to me, and to our bed. I drew the bedclothes back once, and saw that there was enough blood on the sheets to show well in the morning.

I turned on my side. Tears formed in the corners of my eyes, and leaked down into my hair. I struck them away.

If I had been a better woman, a softhearted woman like my sister, I would have pitied him. As it was, as I listened to his tears, and to the weakness that no prayers would free him from, I began to hate.

❈

I slept after many hours, and woke to find Amaria leaning over me. "My lady," she said.

I did not let her finish her thought, but threw myself at her, clinging to her as I would have clung to my own mother had she been there. Amaria was only a year older than I, but she knew how to play the mother's part. She held me close, and stroked my hair.

She dressed me and we rode out into the morning sunshine, our horses set on the road to Poitiers. The sheets had been displayed and applauded over. The Parisians congratulated Louis on his prowess, as if he were a conquering hero.

If Geoffrey of Rancon was there, I did not see him. I kept my eyes unfocused, except when I looked up at the sky, a shade of blue darker than my father's eyes.

My heart was bleeding, but no one but Amaria knew it. This was the path I had chosen.

When Louis reached for my hand, and kissed my fingertips encased in my leather glove, I managed to smile at him.

❦

It was easier after that first night. Sometimes I even began to
feel a quickening in my womb, though the heat never rose to
its completion. It was as if there were a distant country hidden deep within my body that I saw only glimpses of.

But I had my husband. My people were safe from war, as
was my sister, as was I.

We were greeted throughout my lands with cheers and
late-blooming flowers. We paced through my lands for a
week, and all along our way to Poitiers, the people called to
me. My people loved me, as they had loved my father and
grandfather before me. They loved me for my beauty and my
strength, and for the largesse they received from my hands.
Always, I had sat at my father's side and listened to their
petitions. We judged them fairly, giving justice to those who
asked for it. No great lord could buy my favor, for I was rich
already, and so the townspeople and peasants of my lands
might come to me, and be heard, if they ever had need. In
times of famine, we saw to it that all the grain held in my
own walls was given out to the people, so that their children
would not starve. This was how my father had ruled, and in
the few months since I had been duchess, I went on as he had
begun.

Once we reached my capital at Poitiers, Louis and I
were crowned with the coronets of Poitou, and feasted in

my father's great hall. The burghers of my capital looked at Louis with loathing, for Parisian overlords were not welcome. I smoothed the way for Louis and for his men as much as I could, but my people were loyal only to me.

We were in Poitiers when the news came to us, after only a week of marriage. A fast messenger brought it from Paris, his horse half-dead from his frantic ride. The elder king was dead of dysentery after a weeklong illness. Louis was the young king no longer.

I heard this news as from a far distance. All around me, my people made a show of sorrow, though no doubt they rejoiced to see their duchess brought so high, so quickly. I ordered masses sung for the king's soul at once, knowing that Louis would like it.

I sat surrounded by my own people as the Parisians began their maneuvers. Some left at once for Paris, though what they hoped to gain from a corpse I did not comprehend. Other, younger lords stayed by Louis' side, and fawned over him as if he were Christ come back to earth. Some of them even fawned over me.

My man Bardonne met my eyes across the hall at Poitiers. He had come in my retinue, though he was of low birth and was considered slow in the head. After he had guarded me unasked as I went to seek Louis that night in the chapel at Bordeaux, I had spoken with Bardonne, and found his mind quite sound. I had welcomed him into the ranks of my spies, people I had begun to gather into my service, as my father once had done. All would speak easily in front of Bardonne, thinking him too stupid to understand what they were about.

The day we heard of Louis the Elder's death, I nodded to Bardonne across my father's hall. He needed little prompting to do what must be done. He would make his way among the French who stayed in my court, not the lords, but their men-at-arms, who no doubt would know all their lords' doings. Bardonne would listen well, never speaking a word, so that they all might think him mute as well as stupid. And later, he would come to me alone, and report all he had seen and heard.

As for the French lords who stayed by Louis, I watched each of them to learn their ways. I sent word to my spy in the Church, the bishop of Limoges; no doubt he would report back to me what I already knew. We were in a new world. It was one thing for my father to be murdered when he was away on pilgrimage. For the King of France to fall dead in his own hall was quite another.

Though no one said it, I saw from their faces that others thought as I did. "Dysentery" was an ailment that came after drinking bad water. "Bad water," like the water that had killed my father, meant poison.

My hatred for Louis burned away in the fire of that new world. He wept openly, and I saw that he had loved his father, as he now claimed to love me.

Each morning, he went to his priests and begged absolution for what went on in our marriage bed. I wondered what he would say if I told him that those same churchmen, or men just like them, had killed my father, and very likely had killed his.

With the old king dead, the Church would reach a height

of power in Paris that it had never before seen. My husband was weak, and had been Church-raised. Now that the elder king was dead, my young husband would no doubt fall into line with whatever the Church might want. He would do as he was told, for he was easily led, and the priests knew it.

I saw Louis and myself as those priests would see us: two weak-minded children, one of us Church-raised and biddable, and the other a woman. Louis now held both the Aquitaine and the throne of France; with his father dead, the Church was sure that it held them, too.

I sat in my father's hall and listened to the uneasy talk among the people, while Louis wept beside me. Darkness had risen to engulf us. Evil had raised its hand to press against the clean daylight world I had been raised in. I knew that politics was built on blood, but that day drove that truth home better even than my own father's death. Papa's enemies in the Church had been open in their hatred for him, but no one could have suspected that the elder king was in danger until he lay dead.

The Church thought that they had won, but I would prove otherwise. When lifting their knives in the dark to murder, they had not reckoned on me. Louis was weak, but I was not. I would take the reins into my own hands. Through Louis, I would rule France, and my son would rule after me.

Chapter 9

✦

Palace of the City

Paris
August 1137

WE RODE INTO PARIS ON A DAY OF RAIN AND FOG. THE DAMP rose from the ground, just as it fell from the sky in a steady drizzle. I rode my new white mare, which I had christened Melusina after the fabled sorceress, much to Louis' and Amaria's annoyance.

Today was a day for witches and water, I thought as I looked at the gray walls of Paris. My father had spoken of Paris as if it were a new Rome, full of learning and culture, where men came from all over the world to study Greek and Latin, so that the old Greek and Roman ways might not perish from the earth. But the enlightened Paris of my dreams and my father's stories had little to do with the dirty city I found, crouched low under rain clouds.

The streets that led up to the city gates were narrow and crowded by wooden shanties and lean-tos built against the stone walls of the buildings. Soot coated the wood as well as the stone; buildings rose four or five stories above the street, choking what little light made it through the clouds overhead. At the sight of the dirt of Paris, Melusina tossed her head. If not for my elaborate headdress, I might have done the same.

But I wore a heavy veil, as Louis had asked me to, covered by both diadems of Aquitaine and Poitou, as well as the crown of France. It seemed the Parisians wanted me to wear all my finery at once, for he had also called on me to deck myself in jewels. I wore somber blue in honor of Louis' father. Though all this finery was covered by a canopy, my gown still got ruined. Our covering was made of silk, which was charming in the sunlight of Poitiers, but in the rain of Paris, it did us little good.

During the three weeks of our journey to Paris, Louis and I had fallen into an easier way with each other. He had not come to my bed since his father died, so we did not have that constant irritant between us. Louis left the making of an heir for another day and instead spent his days and nights praying for the soul of his father.

The Parisians met us at the gates of the city, looking dispirited and cold in the rain. No doubt some official had meant to welcome us with fanfare, but the blooms of late summer had lost all their petals, and the garlands looped over the gate had begun to fall.

I nodded and waved to my new people, who stood and

stared back at me as if seeing an apparition. Not one of them had taken a bath in a year, if ever, and here and there a peasant squinted at me. I was tempted to reach up and make certain that my diadems were straight, but I kept my hand on Melusina's reins. A murmur crossed over the crowd, like the wind over a field of barley. My beauty did not seem to impress them, or my many diadems. When Louis rode up behind me, the Parisians gave a small, halfhearted cheer. I could see that they had been paid for it.

Then we were through the gates, and over the bridge. The Seine's dark brown waters stank, though the day was cool. Louis' priest Francis put it about that the constant rains meant that all the world wept for the passing of their king. I had never known Louis the Fat. I would have to take their word for his goodness and largesse.

It was a short ride to the palace, which was good, for by that time I was wet through to the skin. Amaria came to me, and the lords and ladies of Paris greeted us in the courtyard.

The French nobility were well dressed in silks and satins, bright spots of color against the drab gray of the palace bailey. Rain dripped down even there, but each nobleman had a servant to cover him with a well-oiled canopy which seemed to keep the rain off. Now that we were here, no doubt Louis' chamberlain would do a better job of keeping the royal persons dry as well.

The Parisian lords and ladies seemed accustomed to the damp, so much so that they ignored it completely. I took my cue from them and smiled as if the sun were shining, as if I were not cold and dressed from head to toe in wet silk.

Louis' Parisian nobles knelt to us there in the bailey. I saw that they were a practical people even when first greeting their new king. They had taken care to have oiled cloths placed beneath their feet, that they might not kneel in mud.

Louis raised his hand over them, as if he were a priest and not a king at all. They did not seem surprised or look askance at this. They simply rose to their feet when he bade them, each smiling on him as if he were Christ come down to earth.

My own people helped me down from my horse. Bardonne stood to one side, his hand near his sword, as if ready to do battle in my name. I made a small, subtle gesture, and he stepped back, lowering his hand. Only one or two of the Parisian lords were quick enough to see the exchange between us.

The Count of Valois stepped forward and bowed low, first to Louis, and then to me. He was a tall man with fair blond hair and cold gray eyes. I saw his loathing for me, though he masked it quickly with a smile something like a crocodile's. No doubt he could shed false tears, too, when called upon to do so. Though this was the first time I had seen him, I had heard of the Count of Valois and his faction already.

The bishop of Limoges had warned me before I left Bordeaux that there were many in Paris who did not approve of my marriage to Louis. The details of the marriage contract were known everywhere, and many Parisian lords were insulted that my lands fell not to Louis' control, but remained in my hands until the crowning of our son. No woman was allowed to hold such power in Paris.

As I looked around me, the ladies of the royal court seemed like flowers that bloomed behind damp stone walls. I wondered how many of those pretty faces hid fine minds. A few of them might be tired of serving their lords and masters. Perhaps one or two among them might be willing to throw in their lot with me.

I would look into the matter before nightfall. My spy system was growing from the network my father had built, but I wanted more people of my own, who owed loyalty to no one but me.

Louis led me solemnly into the castle by the hand. The great hall held large sprays of flowers, but the rushes underfoot smelled of the meal that had been served the night before. I would give instructions that new rushes be laid out before the feast that night, and I would see to it that such things would not be neglected again.

Louis did not stop to break his fast, though food and drink were laid out, and a smoking fire warmed the chair of state. He led me deeper into the keep, where torches were lit, casting light and smoke onto the gray walls. Soot rose against the stone like thick black tar. Amaria, who met my eyes as Louis led me into his private rooms, took note of the soot as well as the dirty rushes. She nodded to me, and I put the matter of the keep from my thoughts. She would give orders to care for it all; the hall would be put right long before the evening meal.

Inside Louis' antechamber, only one gentleman stood by, one lady, and a priest. The rest of his lords and ladies had been left in the great hall behind us. My husband, shy as he was, was clearly relieved to be away from the prying eyes of the court.

The gentleman and the lady who waited on him in his antechamber bowed low. Louis greeted them, looking weary and heartsick; his face was drawn still with grief for his father. The gentleman, Louis' chamberlain, rose when my husband spoke, but the woman held her curtsy.

The priest, dressed in simple robes, did not bow at all, but came to Louis without prompting, and took him in his arms. I drew back, taking Amaria with me, looking around at once for the king's guard. My first thought was *assassin*, and I cursed in silence, that my marriage was to end so early, with me and mine so far from Poitiers. But the priest drew no dagger. Louis went into his arms without hesitation, as if such a display were seemly, as if a simple priest had the right to embrace the King of France.

"My lord," the priest said. "Your Majesty. Welcome home."

My husband wiped his eyes on the sleeve of his gown as if he were a boy of eight and not a man of sixteen. Louis turned to me then, and held out one hand. After a moment's hesitation, I went to him, for I was his obedient wife.

"My lord abbot, let me present my wife, Eleanor of Aquitaine and Poitou."

I stood dumbfounded in the silence that followed. The woman and Louis' chamberlain both stared as if their eyes might fly from their heads. I was not the only one horrified that a mere abbot was not presented to me, but I, to him. The priest seemed to understand, but he took Louis' faux pas in stride, and worked at once to set it right. He knelt to me, there in those dirty rushes. Straw clung to his cassock where his knees touched the ground, but he seemed not to notice or to care. His bright blue eyes met mine, and he smiled.

"My lady queen. The tales of your beauty are far reaching, and well deserved. Welcome to Paris. May your days among us be bountiful, and full of joy."

This speech was almost worthy of one of my own lords. I extended my hand and let the abbot kiss my ring. I still wore my father's signet. I had the ring cut down to size before I went away. I would never give it over to my husband, but only, someday, to my son. My father's signet ring was mine, as Aquitaine was.

Louis still wept, and the abbot still knelt. I would do well to end this scene as quickly as I might.

"I thank you, Father," I said, careful not to give him any title save for the one any priest might bear. "Your kind greeting warms my heart, and the hearts of all the people of Aquitaine. I look forward to many years as France's queen."

"Indeed, my lady. God willing."

I looked at him sharply, but saw no sign of mockery or threat in his clear blue eyes. It seemed he was a true priest, if I could trust my instincts about something so far beyond my ken. Still, I would set my spies on him, and see what I might find, as soon as I knew his name.

He rose from his obeisance, and the woman stepped forward as if called to lead me to my rooms.

"Until tonight, my lord," I said to Louis.

I thought at first he did not hear me, so focused was he on the abbot. But at the last moment, just before I turned to go, Louis caught my hand. "Yes, Eleanor. Tonight in the great hall. I will send your women to you, that they might help you settle in."

"Thank you, my lord king."

I brushed his cheek with my lips, not to be outdone by the kneeling and grasping abbot. Louis had not come to my bed in more than three weeks, but there was a hint of warmth between us that shocked me. It seemed that it shocked him more. He did not blush as he used to do, but met my eyes steadily. Perhaps his father's death had made him cherish me more.

"You are welcome, Eleanor. I will always have a care for you. I hope you know it."

I kissed him again, this time on his lips. Louis' chamberlain shifted on his feet, and the abbot rose, displeased. But I gave no care for what stewards and prelates thought of me. I followed Louis' woman deeper into the palace with Amaria beside me.

"My dear," I said to the Parisian lady before we had walked far down the smoky, damp corridor. "What is your name?"

She was not much older than I, less than seventeen summers old if I made a guess. Her blue gaze was clear and sweet, like clean water from a well. There was no depth to her, but I saw that she was a good girl, and kind. I wondered if she was married yet, or if I would make her marriage for her. Perhaps she might join the ranks of my spies, for married yet or not, she looked biddable, a woman who might become obedient to me.

"I am the Lady Priscilla, Your Majesty." She was shy, but she spoke clearly. I smiled at her, and she seemed more at ease.

"Well, Lady Priscilla, welcome to my service. May I ask, who was that churchman who greeted us so kindly?"

She seemed shocked that I had to ask. I wondered what else I might have missed, and what it would cost me.

"He is the Abbot Suger, madam." She spoke his name as one might speak the name of God, with reverence, and with a casual assumption that all under heaven must know of him already. I did not show my ignorance, but continued to smile.

"Of course. Lead on."

Lady Priscilla, who led us deeper into the darkness of the palace, was well dressed, but her hair was completely hidden under her veil. I saw that Parisian women covered their hair like Saracens. This did not please me, but neither did it concern me. It was a fashion that I would change.

Priscilla showed off the audience chamber, where Louis often saw the lords of the kingdom. The high stone walls echoed with our footfalls, and the stench of the rushes filled my nostrils, making my eyes water. I did not lose my smile, though Amaria reached for her scented handkerchief and covered her nose.

If the rushes in that room had been changed in the last month, you could not tell it now. The men-at-arms ate there, when the king was not seated in state at one end of the hall. The smell of rotted food and bones rose from underfoot. The trestle tables had been taken up, and a great fire burned in a pit in the center of the room. That fire was the only light.

Though it seemed well tended, its red haze cast our shadows along the stone walls. I stood and stared for one long moment, but forced myself to move on. Priscilla did not see me falter, but Amaria did.

The lords of the kingdom had not been in this room since the old king had stopped taking audiences, and clearly the palace servants had neglected the place since the king's death. Or perhaps, the standards of cleanliness in Paris were low enough to allow such filth. Even among our men-at-arms, such dirt would not have been tolerated indoors in Aquitaine or in Poitou.

I managed to walk through the hall without speaking and without reaching for a pomander. We climbed some narrow, curving stairs to the second floor, our footfalls echoing against the stone. I shivered; though it was August, it was as cold and damp indoors as it was in December back home.

The woman opened the doors to the queen's rooms with a flourish, then stood back, that I might enter first.

If the audience chamber was a stable, the queen's rooms were a chicken coop. Fetid straw lay on the stone floor, and the walls bore no tapestries to make them brighter.

There were three rooms given over to my keeping, one for my sitting room, one for my bedroom, and a tiny one for my trunks and clothespress. The whitewashed walls in the antechamber had once been bright, but had now turned gray from time and from smoky fires lit in the room's braziers. There was little furniture, but I had brought my own. I wondered where the dowager queen's chairs and bedstead had gone. Indeed, I wondered where the dowager queen herself had disappeared to. I had been in Paris an hour and had not yet seen Louis' mother, Adelaide, anywhere.

As I stood, taking in my surroundings in a stunned silence, Priscilla watched me proudly, waiting for my praise.

"How charming," I lied. "Priscilla, might you do an errand for me?"

"Of course, Your Majesty." She curtsied low, and I saw in her eyes that whoever she had been before I came, she would soon be loyal only to me.

"Send word to all the heads of staff in the palace, all who do not work to prepare the evening meal. Bring them here, that I might speak to them."

She curtsied and left at once, eager to please the new queen.

I stared at the clumps of dirty rushes on the floor, and at the narrow windows above our heads. Their panes of glass set in lead casements had not been washed in weeks. Though I was grateful for the luxury of glass windows, the overall state of the queen's rooms depressed me. Once more, I wondered where Louis' mother was. Surely these rooms had been clean while she was living in them.

"This will pass, my lady," Amaria said. She stood beside me and did not falter. "I will see to it."

❀

I paid the staff of the palace in gold from Aquitaine, coins with my father's name carved into them. I held back some for myself, that I might keep the distorted image of his face. But more gold would arrive from Poitou with my sister, so most of the contents of my purse I paid out to my husband's people, that they might make my rooms habitable, clean the audience chamber, and change the rushes in the great hall to keep us from sickening from some dread disease while we ate.

It took dozens of the palace staff all afternoon to make my rooms less horrible. They cleaned and scrubbed as Amaria watched them. My own women began to arrive and after their first moments of horror, they, too, set to work, directing the palace servants.

My antechamber, the one that had first brought to mind a chicken coop, was indeed small, but once it was cleaned, I began to see how a Queen of France might welcome guests there. As I stepped deeper into my rooms, I saw that my bedchamber was spacious and had high windows. Once clean, and once the rain stopped, if it ever did, those windows would bring in sunlight. The third room, the dressing room, was lined in cedar for my gowns to be hung in, a luxury I had never seen before. I would have my men take its measurements, and re-create such a closet for me at home in Poitiers and in Bordeaux.

Petra arrived and stood in the door of my antechamber as if she hoped she had come into the wrong room. I went to her, blocking her face from all who stood near. She looked so horrified that, at first, I thought she might faint. I spoke low in the langue d'oc. "It is only a little dirt, Petra. It will soon be gone."

Eleven years old, she swallowed her tears. She missed our home as badly as I did, and she was still a child, with no crown to succor her. I took her in my arms as if to greet her, offering her comfort instead. Her own rooms and those of my women were close by. I was having those cleaned as well, so that none of us would have to sleep in filth that night.

My clothes arrived at last, along with my furniture and my own tapestries. I did not have those hung yet, but waited until the walls could be whitewashed on the morrow.

My bed arrived and was put together in the center of the largest room. I did not want it near the walls until I knew that everything was clean enough that vermin would not mount my bed. I hoped I might coax Louis to spend the night with me. Whether he touched me or not, I did not want him sleeping in his own rooms until I had a look at them. I could not leave my husband in the dirt, to be bitten by fleas and to sleep on straw. He was King of France, whether he knew it or not.

When I saw Louis that night in his banquet hall, I saw that he was not well pleased with my arrangements. He spoke low to me as we entered the hall, and I wondered if I had truly offended him by cleaning out some rushes.

"Eleanor, you have set the palace in an uproar. Queens of France live quietly, and do not bribe the royal servants with gold. It is unseemly."

"Louis, it is unseemly for your home to be left in a state of disarray. I am shocked at it. Where is Queen Adelaide, your lady mother, who I thought to be running the household while you were away?"

At the mention of his mother, Louis' face grew dark. He would not speak of her.

"That gold might have been better spent serving Our Lord and His Church," Louis said.

I could not answer him, for we had come into the fire-light, and were surrounded on all sides by his vassals, who welcomed us.

The lords and ladies who had greeted us earlier in the bailey stood now when Louis and I entered the great hall. They bowed to us and called his name. A blush mounted his cheeks, but he nodded graciously, inclining his head to them.

We sat together, and with great ceremony washed our hands in the silver basin his chamberlain held out for us. We dried our hands on the soft linen cloths Amaria handed to us next. Only as the first course of meat was brought into the hall did Louis meet my eyes.

"My lady mother is indisposed. She rests abovestairs. She is not well."

His face was closed, his mouth pinched, his pale face red with fury. Clearly his mother was out of favor. I would have to find out why.

I saw that I would get no sense from Louis on the subject that night, so in honor of peace, I pressed his hand and leaned over to kiss him. He turned to me, his blue eyes on mine.

"Let me make you cheerful tonight, my lord king. It is not every night that a man is welcomed back into his own hall."

My closeness brought a blush to his cheek, this time a blush not of fury but of desire. For one long moment he stared down at me, and I thought he might carry me from that place and have me in my rooms at once, or up against a wall in some quiet, soot-stained corridor. But he did not.

Louis kissed me, and offered a bite of squab from his own plate. I ate it from his hand, my lips caressing his fingertips, but his color did not rise again. He turned from me to listen to the Count of Valois, who sat at the high table with us. As the count described some matter of state that had lately been settled in the city of Orléans, he watched me down the table, to see if I might try to draw the king's attention back once more. I did not, but instead listened to the men's talk of politics as if I did not have a thought in my head. The Count of Valois frowned to see me so silent, and so seemingly biddable. He had heard tales of me already.

After the feast, I raised my hand and my troubadour Bertrand stood to sing. The Parisian lords and ladies looked askance at this, some of the women going so far as to laugh softly behind their hands. I saw at once that a troubadour's song after supper was not the tradition in the French court, but Louis politely gave his attention to my man, so one by one, his lords and ladies did as well.

Bertrand sang a song of my beauty, of how all the world would come to Paris to kneel at my feet and worship me, as the Greeks had once worshipped Aphrodite. Louis turned puce when he heard that, and the courtiers around us began to mutter. Bertrand, always quick to take the mood of his audience, brought his song to a close two verses early. My own people applauded him, but the Parisians sat in stony silence. Louis nodded once to my troubadour, and I smiled at him. Bertrand took his seat quickly, wiping the sweat of fear from his brow. I saw for the first time, as he did, how different this court was from my father's. They could not stand to hear a woman praised, not even their queen.

Louis said nothing, nor did he look at me. His confessor,

Brother Francis, rose from his place below the dais. "We love and honor our queen, but we must first love and honor the Queen of Heaven. Let me now lead the company in an Ave Maria, that we might remember the Virgin and Her Grace."

No one knelt, but all around the hall my husband's courtiers took up rosaries from their belts. I had none with me, but I closed my eyes and murmured the prayer along with the rest. My own people, seeing me do this, fell into prayer as well. For a moment, I thought the whole place might have run mad, but then I remembered: this was Paris. There were more churches in this city devoted to the Mother of Christ than in any other, save Rome itself.

Once my father had spoken to me about French courtiers and their love of the Virgin Mary, but I had never before witnessed it. I knew that Queen Adelaide had held power in her husband's court, for my father had told me so, using her as an example of how I would rule at Louis' side. But as I raised my eyes from false prayer, I saw that whatever power Queen Adelaide had once held had died with her husband. I would have to look to Louis, and shore up my power with him, for these courtiers would grant me nothing.

The Count of Valois nodded to Brother Francis, who bowed low in return, as if Valois were royalty. My husband's confessor supported the count and his faction, and wanted to be certain that I knew it. Francis stood with those who did not favor my marriage to Louis, those courtiers who did not wish me well.

I held my smile in place and lowered my eyes as if in piety. I would take control of this moment, and wrest the focus of the court away from the Church. I would return the devotion of the court to where it belonged, to my husband, the king. I turned my gaze first to Francis, then to Valois, before touching Louis' hand.

"My lord king, Brother Francis does well to remind us of the Holy Mother, and of God's Grace. We thank him for his prayers, both for your rule and for the kingdom of France."

The Count of Valois' face darkened at the return to the secular subject of the kingdom of France, as did Brother Francis', but my people knew what I was about. My barons who had traveled with us to see me safe in Paris rose together and saluted the king. When they did, the Parisians could do nothing but join them. Thoughts of the Virgin Mary and Her Church pushed aside, the court raised their glasses and called on Louis. I did not rise with them but sat beside my husband, nodding my head as he did, accepting the tribute with him.

When his people had finished cheering him, Louis rose to his feet, bringing me with him. "My good people, Queen Eleanor has yet to learn our ways. Let us welcome her into our bosom, into the very heart of our halls, that she may become one of us."

This bizarre and cryptic statement chilled me, for surely marriage to Louis had made me one of them already. But as I looked around that hall at the faces raised to us, I saw that not just Brother Francis and the Count of Valois hated me. Some wished me ill simply because I was a duchess in my own right, with power a woman would never be allowed to hold in Paris. I was a foreigner, and a wealthy one, a foreigner who had the ear of their king.

Louis did not make love to me, but neither did he spend the night praying. He lay in my great bed, as trusting as a child. I lay beside him long after his breathing deepened into sleep, his hand still in mine. How I would watch over him and keep his eye always turned on me among power-hungry courtiers like Brother Francis and the Count of Valois was beyond my comprehension.

❀

The next afternoon, after the whitewash had begun to dry, I sat in my rooms while my women set up their tapestry frame in the center of the antechamber. They were to make a new altar cloth for Louis' favorite church, the old cathedral at the center of Paris. I had not seen the church yet, but I knew that I was sure to. Let my women show piety for me, since I had none.

The room got the afternoon sun. In spite of the narrow windows, some light streamed through the heavy glass. The newly whitewashed walls gleamed, their paint not yet dry. The constant rains that had dogged our steps to Paris had lifted, and I longed to be outdoors. I would first get my household in hand, and then the government. The palace gardens would have to wait.

One of Louis' many priests came to me then, bowing low just inside my door. I stood to greet him as a courtesy, a courtesy I saw he had not looked for.

"Your Majesty," he said. "I have come to show your chamberlain the list of the properties settled on you since your marriage."

I raised one eyebrow. I knew my marriage contract by

heart. Louis the Fat had signed and sealed it, as I had. I got no lands in the bargain, and I brought no dowry other than the coronets of Aquitaine and Poitou. I was not sure what this clerk was referring to, but I would find out.

"My chamberlain is abroad in the palace, seeing to the needs of my household," I said. "I will hear your report."

"My lady queen, the report is written in Latin."

I did not raise my voice to him as I would have done at home, had anyone there had the temerity to question my learning. Of course, everyone on my father's lands knew that I read and spoke Latin, as well as a little Greek. A very little. I had never taken to it as my father had.

The Greeks were too long dead, too far from the world I lived in, to fire my mind. I was glad that the scholars of Paris kept the language of the ancients alive, but for myself, I would stick to languages that might actually serve my purpose in the here and now.

"You may hand it here," I said.

He swallowed hard and stepped forward. He had enough sense that, in spite of my youth, he feared me. He had seen Louis and me in the hall the night before. He knew well that I had the ear of the king.

I perused the vellum quickly. It was only one page, drawn in a clear hand. The dower lands that had belonged to Queen Adelaide were hereby given to me. This meant that Adelaide, now dowager queen, had nothing but a pittance from her son to live on.

This was a message, telling me that if I was not careful, I, too, might be relegated to nothing and no one. The document in my hand showed me the power the Queen of France held once her king was dead, or once she had the misfortune to fall from favor.

Though Louis had signed the order, his even, monkish hand clear at the bottom of the page, I knew that the order had not come from him. No matter how angry he was at his mother, he never would have thought to disinherit her himself. Louis was too softhearted; someone else had encouraged him to do it.

The Lady Priscilla agreed to take me to Queen Adelaide's rooms. I would have visited Louis' mother in any case, whether she was out of favor with Louis or not, but with the loss of her dower lands, I knew I must seek her out in earnest.

Priscilla took me deep into the bowels of the palace. Queen Adelaide's rooms were far from the court, down a long stone corridor. There was no light in this corridor, and no windows. The torches in their sconces were damp, and were not lit. I saw at once why Priscilla carried a lamp with us, though it was early afternoon, and the sun was still high.

Priscilla knocked on a plain door set deep into the stone wall. We did not wait long before the door swung open, held by an old woman. It was not Adelaide; this woman was the gatekeeper. I was glad to see that not everyone had abandoned Queen Adelaide when her son left her in the dust. Her face was wrinkled and worn, but the look she bore was one of pride. I was not used to finding power in the eyes of a woman, save for my own in the mirror. But as I gazed at this old crone, I saw she was one who had stood fast and had seen much. The experiences of her life had left deep rivets on her forehead, and in two lines around her mouth.

She stared at me without speaking. I touched Priscilla's arm, and she fell back to stand behind me.

"I am Eleanor of Aquitaine," I said.

I saw by the look on her face that she recognized me at once as her mistress' usurper. For all she knew, I had killed Louis the Fat myself. My youth would not dissuade her from such thoughts. Some people looked at me and saw only a girl of fifteen. This woman did not make that mistake.

"I know who you are." The crone's voice was dry, and rasped. She stared at me from above her beaklike nose, her gaze impassive.

"I have come to see Queen Adelaide," I said. "If she will receive me."

"You ask permission to enter," she said. "You do not demand it?"

"I would demand nothing of a queen."

The old woman did not take her eyes from mine. After a long moment, she stepped back, and let me pass.

Adelaide sat behind her protector, a slender blonde dressed in dark blue silk. Her gown was lovely, and cut in the latest fashion, for her husband had been dead only a few weeks. Only a month before, she had ruled alongside him. But now her rooms were poky and small, as dark and dim as the corridor outside. The stone was damp with mildew. As I watched, the queen dowager sneezed delicately into a handkerchief.

"This is an outrage," I said. "I will not endure it."

Adelaide wiped her nose as delicately as she had sneezed. Her gaze was as blue as her son's, and as clear. I saw that she was no fool, though I had assumed she might be, since Louis was.

"I endure it, Queen Eleanor. If I can, so can you."

"Who has placed you here? I will have his head on a pike."

Adelaide surprised me then. She laughed. Her laugh was musical and sweet, like the soft chime of a bell. I swallowed my anger. If she could laugh at her plight, I could set my anger down.

"Have you no income besides your dower lands?" I asked her.

"How rude you youngsters are," she said. She herself was not old, only a few years past thirty. Her face smoothed, and her laughter fled, but her eyes still held a soft light when she looked at me. "Come here," she said. "Come here and let me look at you."

I drew close to her chair. She sat between two braziers to ward off the chill of the damp. I curtsied to her, and she took my hand.

"You will keep him safe," she said. "I can see in your face that you are a strong woman, as I am not."

"I will settle money on you," I said. "I have estates in Poitou that will serve you. You may go there, and be lady in my place. My people will look after you. I will not leave you here to rot."

Adelaide laughed again, and drew me down onto the chair beside her. I felt that I took a liberty to sit in her presence. She had a way about her, after so many years as queen. It had not faded yet. Nor would it, I saw, until her days passed from this earth.

"There is no need," she said. "In one week's time, I travel to meet my betrothed. With my son's reluctant permission, I have arranged to marry Lord Matthew of Montmorency. He will care for me. You need not trouble yourself over my fate. I am well provided for."

I was shocked by the marriage she was about to make. This woman had once been a power to be reckoned with in the kingdom; next to Bernard of Clairvaux, Adelaide had always held old King Louis' ear. Now she was to marry some minor lord, her dower lands taken from her. Louis might as well have openly banished her from court. There was something she was not telling me. A lone woman would not have been allowed to arrange her own marriage in Paris, not even a queen.

"Who has done this to you? Who chose your husband for you?" I asked.

Adelaide did not drop her gaze, or dodge the question. I saw then that she wanted her revenge. She was not like Louis, save for the soft blue of her eyes and the golden light of her hair, which even now, in the midst of that dread dark, shone like the sun at midday.

"Suger," she said.

One word only, but I felt it rise before my eyes like an apparition. The churchman who had met us in the antechamber, the abbot who had taken the King of France in his arms without pause or leave. He, then, was my enemy.

I stood to go, thinking that I would walk to Louis that hour, that very moment, and throw his treatment of his mother in his face. Adelaide held tight to my hand. I looked down at her, surprised by her strength. Her blue gaze held mine. I, who rarely listened to anyone, attended on her.

"Fear him, Eleanor. He is a good man, a man of God. But fear him. He was born a peasant, but now that my husband is dead, Bernard of Clairvaux has fallen from power, and no longer has the ear of the king. Suger is the new man behind the throne. He raised Louis from a child, and my son loves him above all others. Heed me. Fear him."

No doubt Suger wanted Adelaide out of the way, that she might have no more power over the king. He had arranged her marriage to a minor nobleman, knowing that such a marriage would estrange her from her only living son. Suger had taken her lands from her and had given them to me, perhaps to buy my loyalty, perhaps simply to show me that he could.

I stared down at Louis' mother, at her soft golden hair.

"I cannot leave you here, alone in the dark. You must sleep in Louis' rooms until you leave for Montmorency. Louis does not need them."

Before the dowager queen could answer, her old woman nodded to me from where she stood guard by the door. I had won her over, just as Adelaide had won me.

"Thank you, Eleanor," Queen Adelaide said. "And where will you go?"

She smiled at me, and I was certain she knew the answer before I spoke.

"I, Your Majesty? I go to seek the king."

Chapter 10

❦

Cathedral of Saint-Étienne

Paris
August 1137

OF COURSE, I DID NOT RUN OUT AT ONCE, HUNTING DOWN Louis and shrieking like a fishwife. I saw to it that Adelaide was safely ensconced in Louis' rooms, with a fire burning in the brazier beside her. She declined my invitation to sit with my ladies, many of whom had once been her own.

I looked in on my women, and made sure they were out of mischief, while Amaria went to find the king.

"He is at Saint-Étienne, my lady. At the cathedral school."

"Is he indeed?"

I knew Louis had been raised in the care of monks as a child. I should not have been surprised to learn he was hiding among them now.

I could see him in my mind's eye, reading scripture and

praying, leaving his kingdom to lie like some discarded thing for whoever might claim it. It was clear that if I did nothing, Suger would control France, as he controlled St.-Denis, the rich abbey outside Paris that was the seat of his power.

I sent word to Abbot Suger, asking him to my rooms. I was not one to hide in the dark from my enemies. I would face this one head-on.

I did not have long to wait to hear his answer. It seemed that the abbot was too busy to visit the Queen of France. His messenger thanked me prettily, but said that he was about the work of the Church, serving God, and could not leave the cathedral grounds.

Things at the court of France were worse than I thought if a prelate of the Church could so openly defy me. I called for a handful of my most trusted ladies, and a few from the court of France. Led by Bardonne, burly men-at-arms joined us to hold off the peasants, in case someone wished to accost us in the streets. Then I set out for Saint-Étienne on foot, for it was close by. When I did not ask for my litter, the Parisian ladies were shocked, but they were all young, and somewhat flighty. They were happy to walk out into the sunshine, to be admired by all we passed.

The streets of Paris were narrow and dirty, but the people were happy to greet me. Even without my crowns they knew at once who I was, and they called and waved to me as they had not the day we entered Paris in the rain. No doubt they had heard of my generosity to Louis' palace staff. I had my men-at-arms scatter silver coins, and then the people cheered me.

The low buildings of Paris huddled together, the streets

that ran between them more like narrow alleys. As my women and I moved toward the cathedral at the center of the island, the smells of street cooking mingled with the smell of goats. I saw one woman milking a goat beneath the leather of an awning. She drew the milk from her goat's teats and offered it to me as a gift. I smiled at her, and my man Bardonne gave her a piece of silver with my father's face on it. I thanked her prettily, but did not touch the filthy crock she offered, moving slowly but steadily toward the cathedral.

The church was a gray stone building done in the style of an old Roman basilica, as my father's cathedral was in Poitiers. But unlike the cathedral in Poitou, Saint-Étienne seemed to squat, low to the ground, as if dreading the inevitable time when more rain would fall. Its gray bricks were soot covered from the fires of the houses nearby, and in the cathedral porch men sold relics and pieces of the True Cross, while others begged for alms.

Bardonne cleared a path for me, and my ladies followed, tittering behind their hands. This day was the closest they had come to the peasants of the city in years, if ever. I nodded to the Parisians who stood and stared at me as I passed, but I did not waver. I knew where I was going.

The interior of the church was as dark as a tomb. Some windows of dirt-streaked glass rose above our heads, but below torches were lit, lining the walls and the chapels tucked into the nooks and crannies of the cathedral. As I watched, a whore in garish paint drew her mark into the shadows of a sepulchre, and I thought of how similar this place was to my husband's court. I saw members of the court here and there, masked to hide their faces, swathed in plain wool cloaks to hide their finery. All could travel to church, men and women both, with the excuse of prayer. There, in the shadows of the cathedral, men drew their lady loves into the darkness, and called it romance. I preferred our romance in Aquitaine. At least there the women got a song first.

Beyond the altar lay a cathedral school like the one in which my husband had been raised, taught to read Latin and to think like a priest. My ladies waited for me in the darkness of the church, left to pray or light candles or make mischief as they willed, surrounded by my men-at-arms. Only Bardonne followed me into the inner sanctum.

Though women were not allowed inside, I ignored this stricture. The monks who guarded the door knew better than to stop me. They, too, seemed to know who I was, and respected my position, even if Suger did not. They bowed low to me, and for a moment I thought they might cross themselves in their fervor, as if I were the Virgin come down to earth. Pleased by this reverence from churchmen I had expected to despise me, I was smiling when I stepped into Abbot Suger's domain, looking for my errant husband.

The inner sanctum was bare, save for a few very fine pieces of sculpture, all carvings of the Virgin and Her Son. A rock crystal vase on a marble stand caught my eye. It looked like the vase my grandfather had brought back from Crusade, the one I had given Louis as a wedding present.

My eye was drawn from the crystal vase to Brother Francis, dressed from cowl to sandal in black. His robes were as dark as midnight, his eyes pinched and close together. His hair was shaved for his tonsure on the crown of his head. The rest of his fair blond hair straggled across his scalp, almost colorless. His skin was pale, as if he never saw the sun. Though he smiled, I saw the loathing behind his eyes. I wondered if it was me he hated, or all women.

Brother Francis was my husband's confessor, the priest who had come with Louis to Bordeaux to see him wed to me. He was one of the Count of Valois' faction at court, one of the men who did not favor my marriage to Louis. No doubt they favored claiming the Aquitaine, but they were furious that my lands were controlled ultimately not by Louis but by me.

I was surprised to find him in the abbot's rooms. Suger did not strike me as a man who would use the services of a double-tongued monk like Francis. But then, I supposed all men who strove for greatness had to dirty their hands by dealing with many people, no matter how unsavory.

Abbot Suger came in. His black cassock was as dark as Francis', and dirt lined the fabric over the knees. He had been out in the garden, seeing to the herbs that grew there. He was peasant born, whatever heights he had been raised to since.

As he stepped across the stone floor of his private chamber, extending his hand to me, I realized something that I had never before understood. Suger believed in God and Christ, in all His glory. But he believed in the Church first. It was the Church he sought to succor by disarming Adelaide, by blocking my power. By taking away any power the Dowager Queen of France might hold over the king, Suger sought to increase his own. In this man's mind, his power and the power of God were one and the same.

I felt a chill as Abbot Suger took my hand in his.

"Good day, Your Majesty. Welcome to this place."

"Am I indeed welcome?" I kept my tone light, though my intent was clear in my eyes. "I sent word asking you to join me in the palace. I was given to understand that you were too busy to visit the Queen of France."

Color rose in his pale face and he bowed to me. "Your Majesty, forgive me. This message only lately came to me. My people were remiss. I hope you will accept my deepest apologies."

Abbot Suger called for fruit and wine, for bread and cheese. He seated me himself in the best chair in the room, offering me a cushion for my back.

I accepted all this as my due, watching him all the while for signs of mockery. I saw none. Brother Francis watched the abbot welcome me, his pale face darkening with ire.

The food brought was fresh, the figs succulent, the bread soft. I ate a little to show my appreciation for the abbot's largesse.

I saw Louis then, standing silent by the door to the cloister garden. His green silk gown was marked with streaks of black soil. He, too, had been pruning the herbs.

I stood at once, and curtsied. I knew what was due a king of France, even if my husband did not.

"My lord king," I said. "I am glad to see you here. There is a matter of business between us, touching on your mother, that I hope you can put right."

Louis came away from the doorway where he had been loitering like a recalcitrant schoolboy. He stood next to his mentor, and a little behind him, as if he feared to speak to me.

"What business have we, Eleanor, concerning my lady mother?"

"The business of her dower lands, my lord king. Her lands were offered to me by mistake. But they are set aside for the dowager queen, so that she may live off their income after the king's death."

"I know what dower lands are, Eleanor." Louis spoke sullenly, the first time he had ever done so to me.

I was surprised, taken so aback that I did not at once reply.

The Abbot Suger spoke for both of us. "My lady queen, there has been a misunderstanding once again. The Queen Adelaide goes to Montmorency to marry in two weeks' time. She has no need of the dower lands, so His Majesty, out of his largesse, has gifted them to you."

I saw at once that Louis believed this tale. His face was set in stubborn lines, the closest I had ever seen him to anger. He deeply resented his mother's coming marriage.

I simply said, "I would give them back to her, my lord king, if you will permit me."

Louis' face softened at my tone. He had never yet heard me ask for anything without at once granting my request. But Suger stood between us, and Louis looked to his mentor. The churchman did not hesitate to speak for the king.

"My lady queen, this is not possible. The papers have been signed, the thing is done. But your kindness to your mother-in-law does you credit. You have a soft heart. Anyone can see that."

I understood then that this man would stand in my way if I let him. I must pry Louis from his grasp, as one sometimes had to pry the kill from the talons of a badly trained hawk.

I would give Adelaide income from my own property. The battle for her dower lands was lost, but it had taught me much. I knew now beyond any doubt who my rival was for power behind the throne of France.

"Thank you, my lord abbot. My lord king. I worried for Queen Adelaide, but you have set my mind at rest."

I stood, fluttering my hands a little in my long sleeves, looking to Louis as if I needed his strength to lean on. He moved to my side at once, like a hound come to heel. His sullenness had fled, replaced by a look of worshipful devotion. It seemed he would swing back and forth between these extremes, devotion to me and devotion to the Church. I would have to see to it that he let his Church leanings go, and placed all his confidence, all his love, in me.

"Your concern does you credit, Your Majesty," Suger said as he bowed low to us.

"Thank you, my lord abbot. I will not forget your kindness."

Suger smiled, for he did not understand me. Louis beamed, elated that Suger and I suddenly seemed to get on so well. It was Francis, the pale monk with the midnight robes, who stared at me with venom, who understood exactly what I had said. I would forget nothing Suger had done. I would watch him closely, and make certain that he would not thwart me again.

As we passed from those rooms, I looked close at the rock crystal vase. I stopped by its marble stand, my hand on the king's arm. The vase was indeed the wedding present I had given Louis, a prized possession that had been in my family for generations. My grandfather had brought it back from the Levant, as he had my mirror of gold-trimmed bronze.

A bit of gold had been added to the base of the rock crystal, as well as a bit of additional gold to the top. Suger had carved an inscription onto the golden base stating that I had given the vase to Louis, who gave it to Suger, who in turn gave it to the saints.

Louis saw the tears in the green of my gaze. He knew already that I was a woman who never wept. He turned pale.

"Eleanor," he said.

I pressed his arm, and led him out. My ladies waited for us in the church, beyond the door of the abbot's private rooms. My men-at-arms and Louis' men surrounded us, and my women followed us home chattering, the afternoon in the cathedral a great adventure for them.

All I could see in my mind's eye was my wedding gift to Louis, so carefully chosen, so lovingly polished, passed not to our son but to the Church I despised. The saints would never see it, whatever Suger said. The Church would have it now. I could not get it back.

I was quiet all through dinner. Though he was still furious at his mother's coming marriage to Montmorency, when Louis found Adelaide in his rooms, he simply kissed her cheek. I saw that he was ashamed of giving away my wedding gift to him, and that with this gesture to his mother, who was now under my protection, he hoped to keep the peace. Louis said not a word, but stepped into my room with me.

My ladies left me alone with him, my soft shift covering

my body in the firelight, my bronze hair brushed out, trailing down my back.

Louis was not a stupid man, though he often behaved like a fool. He had not meant to hurt me by giving away my grandfather's vase; all he valued, all he loved, he gave to the Church without thought. They had trained him to it.

He came to me and took my hand in his. His blue eyes were clear in the light of our one brazier. Louis kissed my hand, and held it between his own. He did not defend himself for giving away the heirloom of my family, as so many other men would have done.

"I am sorry, Eleanor."

I did not say I forgave him, because I could not. Instead, I offered him something he might do for me. Though it would not be enough, it could be a beginning.

"Louis, when spring comes, promise me that you will take me home to Aquitaine."

Relief dawned in his eyes. Here was a boon he could grant me, to make up for the pain he had caused. He leaped at it, as I knew he would. His sweet eagerness to please me softened my heart.

"I will take you home come spring, Eleanor. I promise you."

I let him kiss me, and let him run his warm hands over my body, above the outline of my shift. His breath quickened as it always did, and for the first time since our wedding night, my breath quickened, too. He took me on my bed, there in the center of my newly whitewashed rooms.

Louis climaxed quickly, so quickly that I had barely begun to feel the heat in my own loins before he spent himself inside me. But it did not matter. I had long since stopped expecting pleasure from him.

Instead, I took pleasure in his warm arms around me, from the scent of his minty breath on my cheek. Louis held me close all that night. He did not pray even once. I forced myself to be satisfied with that.

Chapter 11

❧

Poitiers

County of Poitou
April 1138

I SPENT A LONG AND THANKLESS WINTER IN PARIS. THE COR-
ridors of that palace, cold in August, were dark and bone-
chilling in December. And in spite of all my efforts, I could
not bring the Parisian lords to sing or write music in honor
of me, or of anything else. The Court of Love would not
take hold in my husband's hall, no matter how I rewarded or
encouraged it. My powers of seduction, which worked so well
in Poitiers and Bordeaux, held no sway in Paris. They wanted
to sing only to the Holy Mother, and then only in church. My
first night in Paris, when Louis and his courtiers had been
scandalized by my troubadour singing praises of me, had
been only a taste of what was to come.

Parisians had no objection to dalliance, however. The

men of my husband's court sported with any woman who came to hand, as the men in Aquitaine had done. But they would never extol a woman, not in public nor in private.

Abbot Suger came to dinner in the great hall one night and listened to my troubadours. He smiled at the lays they sang for me, all of which had been shortened and toned down in their praise, in the hope that I might persuade the Parisians to embrace the Court of Love. But even in their modified forms, Suger did not like my songs; he, like all the Parisian courtiers, seemed to think that voices should be raised only in praise of the Queen of Heaven. After that night, Suger sent a sweet-voiced choir of boys from St.-Denis to give us music while we dined.

I listened to that choir and applauded them, leading my people in polite acknowledgment of the abbot's gift. I paid the children in silver and sent them out again before my own man rose to sing. I was sure if they understood one word in ten of the langue d'oc, Bertrand would set that choir of virgins blushing.

Abbot Suger was not there the night his choir sang for us, but I sent him a basket of dried flowers from my garden the next morning. Louis was pleased by this gesture, and came once more to my bed, so neither the choir nor the flowers were wasted.

When spring came, rising from the damp ground like a blessing, I found I was with child. I had missed my bleeding for two months running, and on the third month when it did not come, I summoned the court physician.

"Your Majesty, it is a great day for you," he said after examining me without touching me. He had asked me questions, one after another, and I knew that I would need to send for midwives to learn any woman's truth. If this man knew about matters of birthing, he would never tell me.

"A great day for France," I said.

He bowed low to me. "And for His Majesty the King," he said.

Amaria paid the learned physician in gold, but I knew he would not keep his mouth shut. The court would know of my pregnancy, and tell the king. Before the door had even closed behind the doctor, I sent word to Louis that I must see him alone, at once.

Louis must have known something of my condition already, for he did not keep me waiting. He had been with his ministers, planning our journey to Aquitaine. Louis and I had made arrangements already for our households to work together. My women ran my rooms, cared for my gowns and silks, saw to it that the wine I favored was always in stock in the palace. Louis' chamberlain ordered his rooms separately, and had ever since we came to Paris. This arrangement of separate households suited us, and we had never changed it. Now Amaria and Louis' chamberlain consulted each other so that our return to Poitiers would be seamless.

Louis left his ministers, the men who had counseled his father before him. He came to me alone, without even his men-at-arms. He scratched at my door, and when Amaria opened it, Louis bore a bunch of flowers. He had picked them from my garden on the way, and his hands were full of daisies and asters, primroses and columbine. He did not hand them off to Amaria, but held them out to me.

"For you, Eleanor."

As if he would bring flowers to any other.

Tears rose in my eyes, the easy tears of early pregnancy. Louis saw them, and stepped close to me, blocking me from the sight of my women. He did not wait for my ladies to file out behind him, but kissed me in full view of all my people. I knew then that he loved me truly. He had left his shyness behind and followed his heart.

I felt a piercing warmth stir close in my chest. I leaned against him, breathing in the scent of his perfume, the musky scent he had his perfumers press for him and no other.

"I love you, Louis." I had never said those words to him before.

Tears rose in his eyes, tears to match mine. My women were gone, Amaria closing the door behind her. Louis held me close, as if I were made of spun glass. He kissed me lightly, gently, letting his tears fall. He was the only man I ever knew who was not frightened by his own tears.

"A son," he said. "A son for France."

I did not answer, but nestled close to him, as if he were my protector in truth. We stood together, the first flowers of spring between us, our child in my belly, hope rising in both our breasts.

❧

We left for Aquitaine the next month, though the Count of Valois and Louis' churchmen were against my traveling at all. Valois and his faction counseled the king to leave me behind in their tender care. I saw in their smiles only sharp teeth and in their gestures of obedience only narrow fingers that looked like claws. I did not want to give birth to my son among them. I would have been gone from that place, even if we were not headed home.

The spring came with May, and the sun lit our way every day we traveled. The roads were dry and Melusina stepped lightly, as if she, too, knew that I carried the next King of France.

Louis rode at my side, and I thought once more that we might indeed be happy. I was sure that all I had ever wished for with my father at my back would come to fruition. My son would be a new Charlemagne and would rule a united kingdom at peace.

I was still very young.

We rode into the lands near Poitiers and my people did not stand to greet me. The ones who saw us coming as they worked in their fields stopped work, but only long enough to bow before turning once more to their crops. I felt the first chill then, though the sun was warm above us, burnishing my bronze hair. In place of crown and coronet, my mother's fillet rested on my brow. It fit me now, engraved above my temples with the crest of Aquitaine.

My people knew me, though I rode with a party of Parisians. They bowed to me, but none would meet my eyes. I remembered a spring two years before when my father and I had stepped from our fortress in Poitiers, greeted by the calls of the people. They had cheered us for joy that day. As we rode through the countryside now, no one so much as raised his hat to me. I did not know why my people might have turned from me. I swallowed my confusion, and rode on. Louis and his men did not notice, for their people cheered for them only if paid to do it.

We slept that night in tents five miles outside the city of Poitiers. We would ride the rest of the way in the morning, an easy distance on horses as fine as ours.

Melusina tossed her head as I came down from her back. Louis stood by, ready to catch me if I fell, though of course I did not. To be cherished by my husband, even a weak husband, warmed my heart. Louis did not come to my bed now, for fear of harming the child, but he would sit by me, his hand in mine, until I slept.

At first, this made me uneasy; I feigned sleep so that he might leave me in peace. But over the last week, I had grown to find comfort in the warmth of his touch.

Louis and I dined alone that night, a luxury we never would have had in Paris. Amaria attended us, and Louis' page Alfonse, but that was all. The rest of my women had a tent of their own, well guarded by knights who would turn their backs if one of my women wished to entertain a suitor elsewhere. This leniency did not extend to the young girls in my care; I would make marriages for them. But for the widows and the women older than twenty summers, I let them take their ease as they pleased. If one of them had the misfortune to fall with child, I would arrange her marriage then.

So Louis and I sat alone, the fire in the braziers burning beside us. Louis held my hand, and I drank the last of my wine. It was well watered; in my pregnant state, I could not stomach heavy burgundies. Only the lightest wines and the purest water would satisfy me. Louis indulged me in this as he did in all minor things. It was statecraft and policy that he turned to Suger for, unless I kept a close watch on him. During the months of my marriage, there had been a constant battle between myself and Suger to keep the king's ear. But I held it now; his son was in my belly.

That night, statecraft was far from my thoughts. We sat in comfortable silence, as if we had been married nine peaceful years and not nine grueling months. Louis toyed with the ring of Aquitaine that I wore next to my wedding band on my right hand. My father's ruby glinted in the half-light. I wondered that Louis had never asked for the signet of Aquitaine. I would have had to muster some excuse then, for I would never give it up. But he never asked.

The chief of Louis' guard, Jean, came to us as we sat alone in my tent, and knelt to my husband. I sat up straight, my warm, comfortable haze clearing like a fog at morning.

Alfonse stood by the flap of the tent, looking as if he wanted to run through it, and away from us. Jean stayed kneeling before us. I stared at him, the scent of his sweat-stained tunic filling my throat with bile. Louis took his hand from mine.

"What news?"

"There is word from Poitiers, my lord king. The people there have risen. The burghers have cast out Lord Philip, and set a council of their own in his place."

I did not breathe or move. My people had not waited a year before turning me out of my own capital. For my husband's man was my man; his representative was my own.

The citizens of my lands hated the Parisians, but that was the first day I understood how much. I also realized that the remnant of my father's web of spies was worthless. I had paid them as my father had always done, and even increased their fees. I had assumed that each man would be loyal to me, as he had once been to my father. I saw now that I was wrong. At the very least, the bishop of Limoges should have sent the news of this uprising to me. Instead, I had to hear it from Louis' man, not half a day's ride from the city. My father's men were not loyal, in spite of the gold I paid. My own spy network, a few men and priests gathered into my service since my marriage, would not be enough to keep information flowing into my hands. I would have to rebuild my father's network, one man at a time. Such a task might take years, and my people had risen up against me in Poitiers already.

Fear rose to swamp me, the taste of it bitter in my mouth. I felt the flutter of my heart beneath my rib cage, like a bird that wished to fly free. All I had worked for, all my father had died for, might go up like so much smoke and ash. I looked to Louis.

He was as calm as any bishop.

"My lord king," I said, "I am sorry that I have not gotten word of this before."

"And how would you, Eleanor?" Louis took my hand, and pressed it between both of his. "This is men's business. Politics is not a woman's province."

I stared at my husband, searching his eyes for some trace of mockery. I saw none. He truly believed what he said. After nine long months, he still did not know me. At that moment

I felt encased in a cocoon of velvet, as if all the world were muffled and distant, as if I were already in my grave.

Louis sent for his army, and we rode up in three days' time to the very gates of Poitiers with his knights at our backs. The sight of Louis' army quickly had my people singing a different tune. Hating the thought of a Parisian overlord, they had risen up and formed their own government, assuming my husband too weak to defend his rights. But when they heard that his army was coming from Paris, they realized that not only did Louis command countless knights, but he would use those knights against the city. Like the Babylonians when Alexander the Great threatened their walls, the city of Poitiers came out to greet us, flowers in their arms and songs of praise on their lips.

The velvet shroud that wrapped me almost burst when I saw that. These were still my people, fickle and fractious though they were. They called my name in that spring sunshine. I felt my father's presence beside me so clearly, I knew that if I were but to turn my head, Papa would be sitting on Excalibur beside me.

So I went into my father's palace with an army of Parisian knights and foot soldiers at my back. I saw my own lands held by an enemy, and my heart bled all over again. Then I remembered: these soldiers were my husband's. These soldiers were also mine.

This thought heartened me, and the next day, Amaria stopped giving me the curds and whey with my breakfast; before, she had offered them to me in an effort to build up my strength. Amaria knew me better than anyone alive, and watched me as I came back to life. My statecraft returned to me then, and I told Louis to take hostages, one child from every rebelling family. Like the Pharaohs of Egypt, I instructed Louis to take the eldest son; if there was no son, to take a daughter.

Louis blanched at this, but I explained to him slowly and carefully that we would not kill these children. If we did not take hostages, if we did nothing at all, my people would rise behind us, and the rebellion would spread from the capital at Poitiers to all my lands. Even the knights and foot soldiers of France could not hold that much land by force of arms. The threat of arms as well as hostages in hand would suffice.

Louis stared at me, but gave the instructions to take hostages as I looked on. I felt a cramping in my belly like an ill omen, but I ignored it. Though my father had warned me of the possibility, I had never truly believed that my people would ever turn from me. Now I did. I must put their hearts and minds to rights and remind them, not only of their love for me, but of their obedience. I must convince them that I was still duchess, and that I ruled with a firm hand. I might be married to a French king, but I was my father's daughter.

Still, I was uneasy, and could not sleep. I was five months into my pregnancy and my belly had begun to swell; all could see that I was with child. After almost a month in Poitiers, I left my rooms only once a day, when I went out among my people, my husband's guards attending me, my women left behind. Louis did not like it, but I knew that I had to remind my people of a different time, of a time when they called my name with joy, a time when my father stood beside me.

The swelling of my belly seemed to comfort them. They saw this child not as my husband's son but as mine. One woman came to me, and pressed her hand against my stomach.

"A son for Aquitaine," she said.

"Please God," another answered.

And I, who believed in nothing but myself, said, "Amen."

Louis came to me that same day, when I was taking my ease among my women in the solar of my father's keep. He sent them out without so much as a by-your-leave, and I felt another cramp in my belly, as I had already three times that day.

"Eleanor, I have word from Paris."

"Has the populace risen up against us there, too?" I asked.

Louis looked shocked at my feeble joke, as if I had called down a curse upon our heads. He crossed himself. "God forbid, my lady."

"God does forbid it, Louis. Sit down."

He sat down beside me and took my hand in his. I felt a flutter of pain close to my heart, matched by another cramp in my belly. I bit down on the pain, and ignored it.

"What news comes to us from Paris, my lord king?"

"Suger has written. He has taken me to task on the order of the prisoners."

My mind, still wrapped in velvet, could not at first understand what he said. That Suger would reprimand the King of France was beyond my comprehension. But as I looked at Louis' face, I saw the guilt there warring with the sense of righteousness he always displayed after he had made up his mind to be a fool.

"I have let the prisoners go," he said.

"The hostages?" I asked. "But they are the only insurance we have that my people will not rise again behind us when we go."

"Eleanor, I cannot take children from their families, mothers from their sons, fathers from their daughters. Suger said that this was evil, that God would curse us if I did this thing. I have been at prayer and have been shriven. You must go and do the same."

My people would not think him a fool if he went back on his given word. They would think him weak, and me, his plaything.

My fury rose to consume me. Suger ruled here, not me, a man too feeble to keep hostages, even when it was necessary. The lands that had belonged to my family since before the time of Charlemagne were now held by a mere abbot and my husband, who was his pawn.

The cramp in my belly doubled me over, the pain so sharp I could not speak, nor breathe. I heard Louis shout for Amaria, who took one look at me and called for the midwife.

My women had to carry me to my bed, for I could not walk. The pain rode me as I would ride a stallion. Wave after wave of it washed through me, taking my reason. I felt something inside my belly give way, as if a ship inside me had slipped its moors unbidden, and I knew. My child had flown. My son for Aquitaine was dead. Suger had killed him.

My father's bed was covered in my blood. The fur coverlet was drawn off to be washed, and my women washed me. All that time, Louis would not leave, though I cursed him and told him to stay far from me. His abbot had killed our child because Louis was too weak to hold fast, to do what was necessary.

I do not think I said these things aloud, but I was so out of my head that I might have said such things and more. Louis was as white as snow, as gray as death, but still, he would not leave me. Indeed, he would not let go of my hand. He stayed beside me, as close and as loyal as a dog to his master.

I wanted to curse him then in earnest, but reason had come back to me, and I held my tongue. Where was his loyalty to me when Suger beckoned to him? Why would Louis betray me to those who would rise against us when one lone abbot told him to? I had no answers; I knew that I would never have them.

The midwife came to us when it was done. She wiped my brow, and touched my cheek as she would have touched her own daughter's. By way of comfort, she whispered low to me, as if to salve my pain.

"It was a girl, lady. You did not lose a son."

Her words were like a knife in my ear. My tears had long since dried on my cheeks, but at those words, my pain rose again, another cramp in my belly, though my child was already gone. I did not speak, but waved the woman away. Louis wept beside me. He had heard her, too.

"Eleanor, forgive me." Louis laid his head on the bed beside me, his tears wetting the fine lawn of my sheets. "Forgive me, Eleanor."

That day, I learned that marriage is not just playacting and manipulation. It is not just making moves on the dance floor, fitting your steps to those of your partner, leading him while he thinks that he is leading you. That day, I learned that marriage is built on lies. It must be so if one is wed to a king.

"I forgive you, Louis," I said. "I forgive you."

He lay down beside me then, not touching me but to hold my hand. He slept finally, hours later. I did not. I stared into the darkness, into the shadows that rose from the fire and climbed the curtains of my bed. I thought of my daughter's face, the face I would never see. While Louis slept, when I was alone with his hand on mine, only then did I weep.

Chapter 12

❧

Poitiers

County of Poitou
August 1138

TWO DAYS AFTER MY MISCARRIAGE, I FORCED MYSELF OUT OF bed. Louis spoke of returning to Paris, but I knew that I could not go without securing Poitiers behind us. My people would see our backs, and start to think once more of setting up their own government of burghers in place of Louis' Parisian stewards. I needed an alternative. As soon as I could sit upright in a chair with pillows behind my back, I asked to see my uncle Raoul de Faye.

Raoul de Faye was my mother's brother, a man I had seen little during my childhood, but one my father had always relied on to watch his back, as he relied on a handful of faithful vassals, who were always eager to serve the duchy. Now, in my hour of need, I would call on Raoul de Faye to serve the duchy again.

My uncle came to me as soon as I sent word. Weeks before, he had heard of the insurrection in my capital, and had traveled to Poitiers while I was still pouring out my first child's lifeblood in my father's bedchamber. Three days after I lost the baby, my uncle entered my bedroom, and bowed over my hand. The stench of blood and death had been cleaned from that place, but it still lingered in my mind like a curse. Raoul de Faye, a slender man with dark brown hair and deep blue eyes, seemed to bring sunlight and fresh air into the room with him. He also brought my sister, Petra.

Weeks before, Louis had called for Petra to come south from Paris, that she might wait with me for the birth of our child. She had just arrived that morning, now that there was no child to wait for. My uncle brought her in to see me.

Petra, now twelve years old, was slight and delicate, as our mother had been. Her soft blond hair was falling from its braids, coming loose in a halo around her face. I saw from her traveling cloak and from the dirt on her gloves that she had not even stopped to wash, but had come to me straight from the road. I took her in my arms, thinking to hold her close, but as she stood next to my high-backed wooden chair, it was she who held me.

"I am sorry, Alienor," she said. "I am sorry about the baby."

I could not speak. My voice was silenced by the heavy sorrow that lodged in my throat. I simply held on to Petra, and fought for control of myself. In this, my uncle helped me, his dry voice sounding in the room like the toll of a bell, calling me from self-pity to my duty as Duchess of Aquitaine.

"Alienor, Petra. We have no time for tears."

I pulled back from my sister, and pressed her hand, drawing her to sit down beside me in Amaria's cushioned chair. Raoul de Faye was right. My sorrow would have to wait until Poitiers was safe. Since Louis would not take steps to secure it, my family and I would.

My uncle stood before me, waiting for me to turn my eyes to him. He was slight, as all my mother's family was, more a politician than a warrior. But as Papa had taught me, a good politician can always find other men to fight his battles for him. A thinking man chose which battle to fight. We were going to have to fight another battle now, for the hearts and minds of the people of Poitiers.

"Alienor, you cannot leave the city behind you with no assurances of the burghers' continued loyalty. But your husband and his bishops will not hold hostages to keep the peace. Do I understand the situation clearly?"

"You do, Uncle."

"It seems to me that you need someone from the family to hold the city in your place."

I raised one brow. "You, Uncle?"

He smiled, and amusement warmed the chill of his blue eyes. "Indeed. I will hold the lands of Aquitaine for you, while you are about our family's business in Paris. But the people would not accept me any more than they accept Louis. We must have a bridge between the people's emotions and the world as it is."

Almost as one, my uncle and I turned to Petra.

She did not understand us. She had not been raised to

politics and war, as I had been. I took her hand, my voice soft as I spoke to her. She was a young girl at twelve years old, but today, I would ask her to become a woman.

"Petra, we will need you to stay here, to keep the peace among the people."

"But I cannot rule," she said. "I do not know how."

I saw the panic rise in the clear blue of her eyes. I gripped her hand. "No," I said. "You will not have to. Uncle Raoul will advise you."

"He will stay with me? He will deal with Louis' men?"

"Yes," I said. "But you will have to keep state in the great hall, in my place. You will have to listen to petitions, and mete out justice, in my name."

Petra was pale, but I saw her strength. I saw for the first time that she, too, was our father's daughter.

"And Uncle Raoul will help me?"

My mother's brother met my eyes over my sister's head.

"He will," I said.

We wasted no time but took Petra at once out among the people of Poitiers, with my uncle and myself walking beside her. Our people had heard of her arrival from Paris, and they welcomed Petra with song and dancing along the roads, with flowers and a feast. In those first weeks, while I watched, the people of Poitiers made much of her, and pretended to listen to her edicts, all the while taking note and obeying my uncle, who stood behind her in my place.

Though my uncle began to administer my realm in Aquitaine and Poitou, it was Petra's presence that would keep the

peace. Her sunny smile lit all the countryside around our capital. Over the next two weeks, people came for miles just to
greet her, and to welcome her home.

She was young for such work, younger than I had been
when our father died. But the people loved her. They saw her
strength, which she herself had just begun to learn of. They
saw her kindness, every time she was called on to deal out justice in the great hall of my father's palace. In Petra, the people
of Poitiers saw a reflection of both my father and myself. Her
blue eyes shone like his, and her finespun hair hung like gold
down her back, lit by the sun, shining bright like a blessing
from God. My people believed in God as I did not, and they
saw Him first in us.

Petra had my laugh, and a ready smile. It was enough.
Poitiers embraced her as one of their own, as indeed she was,
all the while dealing with my uncle in matters of state, trade,
and war. My people were in good hands, and so was Petra. The
burghers of Poitiers would not rebel again. As we listened to
the city cheer Petra from the front steps of my father's cathedral
after Sunday mass, I saw this knowledge reflected in my uncle's
eyes. His support, like all things, would have to be paid for.

I expected him to ask for more land or for an income
from my husband, but he did not. I should have known before
we met, alone in my father's old bedchamber, what Raoul de
Faye would ask of me.

"Toulouse," he said.

One word only, but in a moment, I knew exactly what
he wanted and exactly how difficult a task granting his wish
would be.

"Toulouse," I answered.

It was dark already. The feast in the great hall had ended an hour before, and Louis had gone to the cathedral to pray with his confessor, Francis. I had seen Petra put safely to bed with her women. She was tired from the weeks of dealing with my people. And she had many years ahead, until I had a son to secure the Aquitaine and Poitou both. My shoes were hard to fill; as young as she was, Petra knew that, but she was determined to try, and to make a success of it.

Of course, without my uncle to support her and to rule from behind the ducal throne, she would not succeed. Petra did not understand this, but my uncle de Faye and I did. Toulouse would be his price.

"Toulouse is in the hands of our enemies," I said. "They have held that city since my grandfather's time."

"Yes. But now your mother's family wants it back."

Toulouse, a city so beautiful that even my own troubadours had sung of it. That city had belonged to my mother's family for generations, and had fallen into the hands of the Saint-Gilles family only in my grandmother's lifetime. And now, after two generations, my uncle wanted me to take the city back.

I laughed and sat down in my high-backed chair. Amaria had left us alone, so I had to arrange my own cushions. My back still pained me from my miscarriage the month before. I used this bit of business to look away from my uncle, and to buy myself time to think.

"You would have me call on Louis," I said. "You would have the throne of France take Toulouse for us."

Raoul smiled. He did not have to answer.

"What if Louis will not agree?" I asked.

My uncle's smile did not falter. "I think he will agree to anything if his loving wife asks it."

Raoul de Faye paused for a moment to allow his comment to sink into my brain. "You knew nothing of the rebellion in Poitiers before it happened," he said.

"No," I said. "I did not."

"You will build a new web of people loyal to you, then? People who owe their allegiance to you alone? The spies you inherited from your father are worse than useless."

I was not surprised that my uncle knew of my father's spy network, but I was displeased that he knew of its inefficiency. I found myself forced to swallow sudden anger that even this man, after all he had done for me, would speak ill of my father.

"The old network is useless," I answered. "I will build a new one."

"Good," Raoul said. "I will help you."

He rang my father's bell, the bell that had once called for Baldwin, my father's steward. I saw that I would have to remind my uncle that I was duchess here.

A young, slender man stepped into my bedchamber. He had been waiting for the sound of that bell, and as he entered the room, he met my uncle's eyes. But he bowed not to Raoul, but came at once to me. He knelt, just two feet from me, close enough to be seen in the firelight, but not so close as to be taking a liberty.

He lowered his head in obeisance, then met my eyes.

"My lady duchess, I am Stefan of Gascony. I am here to serve you."

His eyes were hazel with flecks of green hidden in their depths. His dark blond hair was almost brown. Only here and there in the firelight did hints of honey gold gleam.

Raoul de Faye smiled. "Your father's family is not the only one that wishes you well. You are not alone in the world, Alienor. I know what burdens you bear. I will help you bear them."

"For Toulouse," I said.

He smiled, pleased that I understood him. "Yes. For Toulouse."

I lifted my hand then and Stefan of Gascony took it gently into his palm. He pressed his lips, not to my diamond wedding ring, but to my father's ruby signet.

"I will serve you all the days of my life, until you no longer have need of me."

Stefan spoke with fervor, but he did not seem a zealot. I looked into the brown depths of his gaze, searching him out. If there was a lie behind his eyes, I did not find it.

"You will serve me and no other?"

"You and no other."

I took my hand from his. "So be it. I accept your fealty."

Stefan rose and backed out of the room, closing the door behind him.

"He is a good man," my uncle said. "He will serve you well, and keep watch over your enemies."

"And my allies?"

My uncle's lips quirked, but he did not smile.

"You will have Toulouse, Uncle. But first I must ask Louis to besiege it."

"Of course." The curve of Raoul's lips drew an answering smile from me. "What else has a young king to do but to besiege a city at peace?"

My uncle did not kneel, but when he took my hand in his, he, too, kissed my father's signet ring. He would serve me, and I would serve him. That is what allies did, whether family or not. He would not betray me; he cared for me, as much as his cold heart would allow him to, as much as he cared for having Toulouse back again. To keep this bargain with my uncle, Louis and I would take that city. It had been too long in the hands of others already.

❁

Petra and our uncle de Faye stayed behind in Poitiers to rule Aquitaine and Poitou in my stead. Louis thought they were his stewards, but we and all my people knew better. Though it cost me something to leave my sister behind, alone but for my uncle and her women, I knew that I must do it. A woman must tear out her heart to be queen.

It took me until the summer of 1141 to turn Louis' mind to Toulouse and to make it stay there. I had to bide my time, much to my uncle de Faye's displeasure, for it was important that Louis think the conquest of Toulouse his own idea. With my encouragement, he came to see himself as a knight errant, righting a wrong for his lady love.

Finally, four years into our marriage, I sat with my husband in his tent outside Toulouse's city gates. We were perhaps a week away from winning the siege and taking the city back for my family. Louis was elated with the taste of victory. I was nineteen years old, and it was the first time I had ridden to war. I felt the elation of certain victory, too.

"Eleanor, I will crown you Countess of Toulouse in their very cathedral."

The firelight from the braziers around us cast a warm and mellow light on Louis' handsome face. His soft hair hung down, caressing his cheeks in a fall of gold. At times like these, all memory of his rejections melted away, and I longed for him to touch me again.

Louis had avoided sleeping with me after my miscarriage, the memory of my blood filling his mind with death and loss. He came to have a morbid fear that I would die, especially that I might die in childbed. No matter what I said to dissuade him from this notion, he would not let go of it. And even when my miscarriage was years behind us, Louis avoided my bed as if he might catch the plague there, preferring instead to moon at me over goblets of wine in the great hall, then praying for forgiveness of his sin during the hours when he should have been getting a son on me. I drew him into my bed from time to time, but never often enough to quicken my womb once more. I hoped that a victory at Toulouse would fan his ardor, and confirm in his mind that he was blessed by God. Once we conquered the city, I hoped that Louis would claim my body every night until he had given me a son.

I reached for him, running my hand up the silk of his sleeve. The heat in his blue eyes caught fire and he held my gaze. He leaned close, and for one blessed moment, I thought he would kiss me, then lead me to the bed that lay behind the damask curtain. The walls of his tent were made of the finest waterproofed leather; there was no wind that night, so the walls did not move. I could pretend that his men-at-arms did not guard us, standing less than ten feet away, separated from us only by thin leather. I could pretend that we were alone.

Louis kissed me, and I drew him close without seeming to lead him. He raised me to my feet, for we had been sitting together in the firelight, drinking the last of the wine. His hands were soft in my hair.

But just as Louis' mouth warmed over mine, his chamberlain came in. As I met Gerald's embarrassed eyes as he knelt to us, I wondered for one brief moment if he might not be in the pay of the Count of Valois. The count would love to see me barren; the count would love to see the throne of France without an heir forever, that he might pluck that prize for himself. The fact that Louis seldom touched me was a great joke in the Parisian court, as if this lack of a son were somehow my fault.

Louis pulled away from me at once. His voice sounded pained as he spoke, and I took heart. Perhaps he would simply send Gerald away, and draw me back to the bed in spite of the interruption. He had never done so before, but there was always a first time.

"My lord king, there is news from Bourges. They have chosen a new archbishop."

Louis' fair skin darkened with anger. "I know this,

Gerald. I sent my chancellor to fill that post. Why do you wake me in the night to tell me what I already know?"

"No, my lord king. A messenger came straight from Bourges. The brothers in the Church have chosen a different archbishop."

"Not my chancellor?"

"No, my lord king. A monk of their own house."

Louis said nothing, but waved one hand in dismissal. Gerald stood at once and stumbled from our sight. My husband's anger was a rare thing, but when it rose, it was like a storm that might shake the very foundations of the earth. I always waited for it, and sometimes hoped for it. The sight of his fury gave me hope now.

Never before had the Church openly defied him. We had worked steadily over the past four years to shore up the power of the throne of France. Louis' ministers were still mostly churchmen, but he took most of his advice from me. With Suger safe in St.-Denis, running the great cathedral there, even the Count of Valois and his faction had stayed quiet, save for spreading rumors of my barrenness. But now the brothers of Bourges had openly defied Louis, denying him the appointment of their archbishop, an appointment that had been in the hands of the throne of France for centuries. Louis felt the sting of their contempt. Their defiance, instead of making him meek, as they no doubt had hoped, made him strong.

"How dare they? How dare they defy their king?"

I did not step close to him, but waited and listened. In

those first few moments of fury, he had forgotten that I was even in the room.

"It is for me to choose the archbishop of Bourges. For myself, and no other. I must return to Paris. I must take counsel with my lords."

"But, husband, what of Toulouse? The city will fall in a few days' time. Let us stay here, and finish what we started. Then let us return to Paris, and settle with the Church."

Louis' face was puce with anger. I was not sure he even heard me until he spoke.

"No, Eleanor. Toulouse has sued for peace. I will allow it."

"They sued for peace because they know that they are losing!" I could not keep my own anger from my voice, and Louis heard it. He turned the force of his blue eyes on me. For the first time in our marriage I saw that there truly was strength in him, if only he would learn to use it.

"I will show mercy. I will let them go."

I thought of my uncle de Faye, of how he had waited so patiently for this city to fall into his hands. I felt it all slipping away, as sand with a tide that is rolling out.

"Louis, please, do not abandon our work here. Let us take the city. If they sued for peace, they will soon open the gates to you. It is only a matter of time."

"I abandon nothing!" Louis' fury was turned on me for the first time since I had known him, and I felt a chill along my spine.

"We will return to Paris. I will take counsel with my ministers. I will speak to Suger. I will have that bishopric."

I saw that his mind had let Toulouse go altogether. He

cared nothing for the foot soldiers already lost, or for the fact that by turning from the task only half-done, he would look weak before all our vassals and our men-at-arms.

I thought of my uncle, and how I might appease him with no city to gift him with. I pushed the thought from my mind at once. I needed to pay attention in the midst of Louis' ire; I needed to stay in the here and now. The game was shifting, and I must shift with it.

For the moment, Toulouse was lost to me, but this new battle with the Church was not. If I hoped to be a player in that battle, I must regain my husband's ear. I moved now to Louis' side.

"If you go to Paris, I go with you. I will stand at your side, and fight with you." My next words stuck in my throat, but I spoke the lie without flinching. "I am your obedient wife."

Louis drew me close, and pressed me against him. He pulled me behind the damask curtain, and forgot his Church nonsense of sin and death, and embraced me as a man.

He was quick and clumsy, but he made love to me for the first time in many months. And for once, he did not pray afterward.

As Louis lay asleep beside me, his ardor and his anger spent, I laid my plans. I would send word to my uncle and, for the time being, put Toulouse from my thoughts. For I knew that, no matter whose counsel Louis took in Paris, the Church would not concede.

Ultimately, the archbishopric of Bourges was a small matter. It was the power of the throne of France that concerned us, for it was the power of the throne that the Church had attacked. If the Church began to usurp the power to name bishops in a king's realm, what other powers might they take next?

I lay beside my husband, my breathing quiet as I watched his face. The cast of Louis' features was implacable, even in sleep. I saw that if the Church did not give way, there might be open war.

Chapter 13

Palace of the City

Paris
September 1141

OF COURSE, LOUIS DID NOT TAKE UP ARMS AGAINST THE
Church. He was far too pious for that. Instead, he turned his
mind and the minds of his ministers to defending the power
of the throne of France. Though I had lost Toulouse for the
moment, I was heartened to see Louis defend his realm from
the political machinations of the Church. The loss of the
bishopric of Bourges was something Louis did not forgive or
forget.

One morning, when we had been back in Paris for two
months, my ladies sat working on yet another tapestry for the
altar of Suger's cathedral at St.-Denis. Amaria entered my
rooms with only the slightest curtsy, and came straight to me.
She whispered in my ear, and at once, I sent all my women away.

As soon as they had gone, Petra rushed in, her hair falling from its braids, her riding cloak still clasped around her shoulders.

She was fifteen and as beautiful as a summer morning that has not yet felt the heat of noon. She stood in the doorway of my rooms, her hair falling down around her shoulders in soft golden strands, her blue eyes wild, until they settled on me.

"Eleanor, you must help me," she said.

I had last seen her at the feast of Christ's Mass in Poitiers nine months before. We had eaten and drunk together, and I had cast my eye over my uncle's work in my lands, and had found it sound. Petra, too, had seemed happy, as content as she had been when I first left her under my uncle's care.

I took her hands in mine as Amaria left, drawing the door shut behind my women. I placed Petra in my own chair, and poured her watered wine. She drank it, her hand shaking.

My sister turned her great blue eyes on me. "Eleanor, I am married."

Of all the words I had expected from Petra's lips, I had not thought to hear these. I sat in Amaria's chair, for my knees had given way. The cushion behind me fell to the stone floor, and there was no one there to set it right.

"He is with me, just outside your chamber door. They would not let him in, as he is a man. But he loves me, and I love him. I am two months gone with his child. We married in haste, as soon as we knew, and then we came to you."

My sister spoke all this in a rush, throwing down all my hopes for her marriage to come, all hope of a good alliance with a man of my own choosing. I had indulged her, and left

her with only my uncle for too long. She had chosen for herself already.

Petra cast herself at my feet, her wine discarded.

"Forgive me, Alienor. You must forgive me."

The sound of my true name on her lips touched me as
nothing else might have done. Petra did not calculate to strike
at my heart, nor did she lie. I knew from the look on her face
that she loved this man, whoever he was, whatever he had
done. She had married him in secret, and came now to tell me.

I took her in my arms, and we knelt together for a moment
on that cold Parisian floor. I drew her back onto her chair and
began to smooth her braids, taking them down, reworking
them with my own hands. She calmed under my touch, as a
frightened foal quiets when she sidles up next to her mother.

"I thought you would be angry. Say something, Alienor."

"I love you, Petra, no matter what you have done. Let me
meet your husband. Then I will take you both in to see the
king."

When her husband stepped into my rooms, I realized
that things were worse than I had thought. I knew the man
on sight. Not only had the opportunity to make a good alliance been lost with my sister's marriage, but enemies had been
made. She had chosen Raoul of Vermandois, a man thirty-
five years her senior, a man already married to the Count of
Champagne's sister. No doubt he wished to cast aside his first
wife in order to align himself with the throne of France.

My sister, in all her sweetness, did not see this. Petra
knew only that she wanted him, and that if she asked, I
would arrange to set him free from another so that she could

have her heart's desire. She had no mind for politics, nor for the lengths power-hungry men were driven to. She thought he loved her truly, just as she loved him.

I could only think what my husband would say when presented with this folly. Louis would call for my sister to be sent to a nunnery, and for Raoul to be sent back to his wife. For all the trouble this relationship would cause us, both with the Church and with our vassals and allies, I was tempted to let Louis prevail in this, and to let his scruples rule my sister's fate. She had made her bed; now let her lie in it.

But as I watched, Petra clung to Raoul of Vermandois' arm as if he were the bulwark of the world. Her frightened eyes did not leave his face from the moment he stepped into the room. She looked not to me for sanctuary but to him. The love she felt for him was written on the curves of her lovely face, as well as her longing for him. I saw then, and for the first time, all that our father's death had cost her.

Lost and alone, left behind by me, with only my uncle to guide her, she had found this hulk of a man. This one-eyed warrior, with wide shoulders and hard hands, promised her not just pleasure but a safe haven from the world. The kind of haven she and I once had when our father was still alive.

I would give her the safe haven of her choosing. I would arrange the annulment of Raoul's first marriage, though his wife was still living, though she had borne him children already. I would see those children disinherited by the order of Louis' bishops, for Petra's sake. And in return, Raoul of Vermandois would protect my sister, forsaking all others, or I would see him dead.

"You have dishonored my sister," I said. "You have thrown her to the dogs, and now you come to beg my leave for having done it. Who do you think you are?"

Raoul of Vermandois knelt at once, and my sister knelt with him, tears rising in her eyes as she clung to his hand. He smoothed back her hair, and kissed her. It was a pretty gesture, and I saw from the tenderness in his touch that it was not an empty one. With my sister comforted, her would-be husband turned to me.

"I mean her no dishonor. I seek to make her my wife."

"You have a wife already." My voice was harsh, my face unreadable.

"She has given me no sons. She is the sister of the Count of Champagne, your enemy."

I was silent for a moment, letting him sweat. The Count of Champagne was a disloyal vassal who had refused to send us troops in any military operation we had accomplished since Louis took the throne. This insolence had gone unpunished. Raoul was offering his marriage to my sister, and its insult to the Count of Champagne, as a bond between us.

If Louis ordered his bishops to annul the marriage of the sister of the Count of Champagne, he would show all his vassals the price of defying the crown. We had enough bishops loyal and obedient to us to follow through with this scheme. Some of our more unruly vassals might even take note of it.

Raoul saw that I was weakening. He had seen the closeness between my sister and me. He knew that I would not cast Petra into a nunnery. He knew that I would care for her always, no matter what it cost me.

"I will defend Petra with my life," he said.

I did not speak but stared at him. He did not flinch or turn away under my gaze.

"Very well," I said. "I will back you with Louis. And when the Count of Champagne comes calling, asking for his sister's husband, I will back you then, too."

Vermandois came closer and knelt again, this time not as a suppliant but as one swearing me fealty. I offered him my hand, the one that bore my wedding ring, and my father's signet.

My sister's husband ignored Louis' ring as if it were not there. He pressed his lips instead to the ruby of Aquitaine, the ruby that was never off my hand since my father died.

"I will follow you, my lady queen, unto the ends of the earth. I swear it."

"Rise," I said. "I will not lead you so far. Just into the neighbor room. The king takes counsel from his ministers. He will see us there."

Chapter 14

❧

Palace of the City

Paris
September 1141

"ELEANOR, YOU CANNOT BE SERIOUS."

Louis faced me from his place beside his prie-dieu. Newly risen from his prayers, he stood close by the bed of state, where I was certain our son would one day be conceived. I had gone in alone to see him, leaving my sister and her would-be suitor alone with Amaria.

I fought down my irritation as I looked at Louis. The sight of his piety, of his judgmental dismissal of my sister and her woes, made my heart burn with fire. But I kept my tone even, and a welcoming smile on my face. I needed Louis to support me with Petra almost as much as I needed him back in my bed.

Anger still burned beneath my breastbone at his abandonment of Toulouse. Though he had left the city that

belonged to my family to languish in the hands of my enemies, Louis had made no headway in his conflict with the
Church. Louis' will was still thwarted; the archbishop chosen by the Church still sat in state at Bourges. My husband's
assertion of his right to appoint bishops across the land fell
on deaf ears in Rome. As always, Louis seemed caught in the
middle of things, between what he wanted and his inability
to work his will against the Church.

I pressed all thoughts of Louis' weakness, all thoughts of
Toulouse, from my mind, focusing all my energy on Petra's
marriage to come.

"Louis, it is very little to ask. My sister wishes to marry
this man; she considers herself married to him already in the
sight of God. She needs only your blessing."

"And an annulment for her lover from my bishops."

The comment was so astute, so unlike Louis, that I could
not at once find my voice.

Louis' thin lips pursed in distaste. "And you say your sister is pregnant, out of wedlock, with his child?"

"She hopes to bear Raoul a son."

"That is for God to say."

Louis stepped away from me, and fiddled with a piece of
parchment on the mahogany table by his bed. "You ask that I
support your sister as a favor to you?"

"Husband, I would ask this as a boon, yes. I know that
in your generosity you will grant me this small thing. But it
occurs to me, by granting this blessing to me and to my sister,
you will also be striking at the Count of Champagne."

Louis heard that name, and the parchment he held fell

once more to the table, discarded. The name of his enemy made his eyes gleam. "Champagne's sister is married to Vermandois?" Louis asked.

I stepped toward him, so that he might catch the scent of my lilac perfume. "She was. Now my sister will marry him. As soon as your bishops call for the annulment."

Satisfaction lit Louis' eyes. "So you say, Eleanor. We will support your sister. It is time the Count of Champagne learned not to defy the King of France."

"You are wise, my lord king. You lead us all into the light."

Being Louis, he did not catch the irony in my voice. He took my hand in his, and instead of kissing me, he pressed his lips to my fingertips. I hoped that something more might come of our accord, but he did not draw me back onto his bed. He gave me his support for Petra, but that was all I got from Louis that day.

❈

I soon saw that Petra's marriage would not be as easy to procure as I once had hoped.

Though the French bishops granted Raoul of Vermandois an annulment at Louis' request, as soon as the rest of Christendom heard of it, the annulment was condemned by churchmen all over Europe. The pope himself stated the annulment was void, that Raoul's marriage to the sister of the Count of Champagne still was valid.

The month before, Petra had left Paris with Raoul. She and her errant husband had gone to his seat at Vermandois, while his first wife languished in her brother's protection in

Champagne. Petra would be delivered of their child in mid-winter. I hoped that by the time her baby was born, I would have purchased the annulment of her husband's first marriage.

I took the matter into my own hands and called Stefan of Gascony to me. Stefan had been my eyes and ears, both with the Church and with Louis' lords, since my uncle de Faye had brought him into my service.

Of course, I could not meet a man alone in my rooms, even with Amaria to attend me. So I made sure that our meeting looked like chance, as I stood in the simples garden, watching Amaria cut down the last of the lavender. The scent of those flowers was sweet, and soothed me, even in the midst of Paris, even in the middle of my husband's court. Though it was late October, the rains had ceased, and for that one day we had sunlight. I stood, my face to the sun, and drank in the warmth of it. I knew from all my years in Paris that it would not last, as nothing on earth does.

"My lady queen."

Stefan did not draw attention to himself by kneeling, but he bowed low to me, and met my eyes.

"You are welcome, Stefan of Gascony." I waved one hand, and the Lady Priscilla caught my eye. She saw the way my gaze was tending, and she curtsied, leading my other women back into the keep, so that I was left alone with Amaria and Stefan.

Amaria did not turn and acknowledge him, but simply stepped deeper into the plants, and cut another sprig of the purple flower.

I did not waste time, for I knew we had little. I must soon go inside. In a few hours, the evening meal would come, and

I would have to sit at my husband's right hand and pretend that this meeting with Stefan had never taken place.

"You serve me, Stefan, do you not?"

"It is my honor to serve you, my lady queen."

I met the maple brown of his eyes. "You no longer serve my uncle de Faye, though he sends you gold?"

This time, Stefan did kneel. "Your Majesty, I accept his gold, but I serve you."

"Indeed," I said. "I have an opportunity for you to prove it."

"Command me, lady. I am yours."

I hid my smile. He was an earnest young man, or at least could pretend to be one. Who truly knew how deep his loyalties lay? The task I was about to give him would prove his worth to me, better than anything else ever would.

"I need a man in Rome."

"I will leave tomorrow."

With a gesture, I gave him leave to rise.

"You will walk among the bishops of Rome. You will listen. You will keep watch in the halls of my enemies. And when the time comes, you will hand out the bribes that will secure my sister's marriage."

I saw from the look on his face that even he had heard of Petra and her troubles. "My lady queen, I will do all you ask, and more."

He bowed again, and I gave him my hand, which he kissed with fervent devotion. I saw that he fancied himself in love with me, and for the first time in months, I felt young again. I could still command men with my smiles. My time in Paris had almost made me forget.

Stefan backed out of my presence, leaving me alone in the simples garden with Amaria. Her calm blue eyes met mine over the waving lavender as she stooped down to retrieve the last cutting needed for my rooms.

"He will do as you ask," she said. "He will fulfill your wishes, or die trying."

I simply smiled, and led her back into the shadows of my husband's keep.

Chapter 15

❧

Abbey of St.-Denis

Île-de-France
April 1144

IN THE SPRING OF 1144, I WAS ALMOST TWENTY-TWO YEARS old. For a queen who had never borne a living son, I might as well have been fifty. Louis' courtiers looked at me and whispered behind their hands, not even troubling themselves to hide their contempt. The court knew that Louis did not stir himself to come to my bed, and as each month passed, the smirks of the Count of Valois were more and more like acid on my skin. All the courtiers in Paris were united in the idea that the fact that Louis behaved like a monk and not like a king was somehow my fault.

Just as Louis would not come to my bed, he also would not make peace with the Church. He still struggled to make his old chancellor archbishop of Bourges. The pope had denied the annulment of Raoul de Vermandois' first marriage, but still Louis clung to his tenuous authority in that matter, saying that indeed his bishops could annul a marriage where and when they wished.

In spite of the fact that her marriage was not yet blessed by the pope, despite that one faction in the Church believed her married while the pope himself did not, Petra was happy, safe from the court and the Church both, tucked away on Raoul of Vermandois' lands, while my uncle de Faye continued to rule in Aquitaine.

Petra and Raoul had two children already, sweet, towheaded daughters who were lively replicas of my sister. Those children reminded me that I still had no son, no heir of Charlemagne to follow in my footsteps, or in my father's. And in spite of all I did, Louis would not touch me. Louis still made confession to Brother Francis, and every month would visit his mentor, Abbot Suger, at St.-Denis. But these visits did not bring him to me; he would not come to my bed, and give me an heir. Once Louis had set his mind to a course of action, he was implacable.

Earlier that year, the pope, the old enemy of my father, finally died. Abbot Suger was a holy man, but he had not risen to the heights of power by being a fool. He saw the pope's death as the opportunity it was: a chance to make peace between the Church and the throne of France.

So at Suger's request, we all came together, the Church and my husband's ministers, many of whom were churchmen themselves. As I traveled with my husband on the few hours' journey to St.-Denis, I could only hope that Louis would stick to his current resolve, that he would hold fast to the power of the throne, and force the Church to concede, both on the matter of my sister's annulment and on the archbishopric of Bourges.

I would have raised my voice in the discussion, or at the very least, I would have sat next to Louis and quietly made my voice heard through him. But I was locked out of the debates. Because I was a woman, the Church was certain that I could have nothing to say.

I sat with my women outside the halls of power, my heart hot with fury beneath my gown, a bland smile on my face. I allowed the monks of St.-Denis to fawn on me, bringing me tisanes and braziers to warm me in the cold reaches of that cathedral complex. I waited for my husband to emerge, for Louis to tell me what was taking place beyond the doors of Suger's private rooms.

As I waited, Bernard of Clairvaux stepped out from the halls of power. My father's old enemy smiled on me, and I returned his look with equal insincerity. I knew he was baffled by my easy welcome, and my quiet grace.

"My lady duchess." Bernard of Clairvaux bowed low to me, his tongue lingering on the title I was most proud of. "My lady queen. Might I speak with you, alone?"

The smile on my face did not waver. I stood, and extended my hand. "Indeed, my lord abbot. It would be my honor."

Though he loathed women with a depth and breadth that would have staggered a lesser man, Bernard reached for me, there in front of my husband's courtiers, and took my hand. He touched the fingertips of my right hand, where my wedding ring and the signet ring of Aquitaine gleamed, even in that dim light. He led me into yet another antechamber, and I saw that this church was a rabbit's warren, full of holes and hidden places, where two might sit alone to plot, or to do whatever churchmen did to while away the hours when they were not at prayer.

Bernard offered me a chair, almost as if he were a gentleman. I had left my women in the hall behind me, in spite of Amaria's dark looks and my women's shocked gazes. As if I would slip away with the likes of Bernard of Clairvaux for a dalliance. As if such a man could bring himself to touch even the hem of my gown. The ridiculous thought made me smile, and Bernard blinked. He hesitated, before taking the chair next to mine.

This unlooked-for familiarity shocked me. That Bernard would lower himself to sit in my presence was strange enough that I did not resent his sitting without my leave. Any other man in the country, save Louis, would have had to ask permission to sit in my presence. But I let the matter go.

"We have come from opposing camps to this place of truce, my lady queen."

"My lord abbot, you speak as if we are at war." This man wanted something from me, and wanted it very badly, to take such trouble to speak with me.

Irritation crossed the icy blue of his eyes, and my smile faded. I had scored a point, but I could not drive it home. There were things I needed, too, things he might be able to give me, things that Suger withheld.

"Your sister has been very brazen, my lady queen."

"Indeed. The women of my duchy are known for it."

He swallowed his first reply. I saw how deeply he loathed me. I leaned against the high, hard back of my chair. It seemed Suger did not believe in cushions. I waited then, for Bernard to make the next move.

The monk could not speak of women without bile, so he changed his tactic. "Queen Eleanor, France has desperate need of a son."

I lowered my eyes to examine my rings. My father's ruby gleamed on the third finger of my right hand. The diamond of my wedding band shot fire at me, as if in reproach. I had chased Louis for years, and I still had not gotten a son off him. What more did Bernard think I could do, save tie the King of France to his bed and not let him up until I was pregnant once more?

This idea was oddly appealing. A feigned illness, a worried queen who would not leave her husband's side. This thought brought another genuine smile to my face. Bernard shuddered to see it, but he soldiered on.

"The king, long may God bless his reign, perhaps has not been as diligent in the service of the crown as he has been in the service of his prayers."

I laughed then. The warm sound reverberated back to us from the cold stone walls of that little room. The gloom seemed to lift a little, and I began to see that perhaps Bernard of Clairvaux was not all bad. He wanted what I wanted: my son to sit on the throne of France.

"Indeed, my lord abbot. And what would you suggest? How do we bring the king to service me?"

Bernard's color rose as if I had exposed myself to him. I bit my tongue, and chastised myself for going too far. I did not have to like him, but I had to keep a civil tongue in my head. Allies were never friendly. Allies simply wanted the same things, and would walk a few steps on the road together for necessity's sake, no matter what had once happened between them, no matter what might happen between them in the future.

I leaned forward, and met my new ally's eyes.

"My lord abbot, France needs a son. How do you propose we turn Louis' thoughts from God to me?"

"Suger and I are of one mind in this. It has been decided: he will lay the groundwork, and then I will speak with the king on your behalf. For the good of France, our lord must return to his duty in the marriage bed."

My eyebrows rose. It was not the first time that day Bernard had shocked me. "You and the Abbot Suger are allies, then?"

Bernard did not answer but bowed his head. I saw how deeply it cut him to join with Abbot Suger. Almost as much as it cut him to attempt to ally himself with me. No doubt Suger could not bring himself to speak to me on the subject of Louis' coming to lie with me. Suger had called on Bernard to approach me in his place.

"And what will you and Suger ask from me, my lord abbot, in exchange for this generous talk with Louis?"

"Persuade Louis to keep peace with the Church. Today Suger will bring him to an understanding, but his power over the king lasts only so long as Suger is in the room with His Majesty. But you . . ."

"I, on the other hand, am always there."

"Yes."

That one word cost him more than anything else he said that day.

"And my sister's marriage?" I asked. "What of that?"

"His Holiness the Pope will not grant the annulment of Raoul of Vermandois."

"Not today," I said.

"Not ever," he answered.

I bowed my head. Bernard of Clairvaux relaxed in his chair, taking my lowered eyes for defeat, as I knew he would. Little did he know my man Stefan was still in Rome. Ever since the annulment from Louis' bishops had been overturned, Stefan had sought an annulment from the Roman bishops. It would take years and gold, but in the end, I was certain I would win.

However, Bernard need know nothing of that.

"I will pray with your husband, Queen Eleanor. I will guide him back to God, and to his duty to France."

I spoke then for the ears that listened to our every word. I knew that I must be clear, and show my own obedience, or at least some semblance of it.

"I am a weak woman, my lord abbot. I thank you for your kind intervention, and I ask that you bless me."

His blue eyes met mine, lit with fire. At first he thought that I mocked him. When he saw that I did not, Bernard rose, one hand above me. He made the sign of the cross over my head, and intoned something in Latin to the effect that I would bear the next King of France, with the blessing of God and the saints.

I crossed myself, and managed to look contrite as he led me back out among my husband's people. They saw us emerge, and took heart. I seemed to have been brought to heel by the great churchman, as my husband had been brought to heel by Suger.

Louis himself had emerged from his council meetings while I was gone. I stepped into the hall once more with Bernard of Clairvaux at my side. Louis smiled to see that I had allowed a great man of the Church to guide me. My husband took my hand to lead me to the meal Suger's people had set out for us.

Whatever else he may have been, Bernard of Clairvaux was a man of his word. After he spoke with the king, Louis came back to my bed. And a month after that, I was pregnant again. At long last, I would bear a son for France.

Chapter 16

꧁ꙮ꧂

Palace of the City

Paris
May 1145

MY DAUGHTER'S CRIES WERE SHARP IN MY EARS. AMARIA moved to take her away, but I raised one hand, and she left the child in her crib. I gestured once more, and the wet nurse handed my daughter to me.

I looked down into Marie's face, and I could not feel defeat. This living daughter brought my father back to me in all his glory, with the soft blond down of her feathery hair and the piercing blue of her eyes. For now, until I bore a son, she was the heir to Aquitaine. One day, she might be duchess after me. But I knew I could not indulge myself in that fantasy, nor in any other.

Though my breasts leaked with the desire to feed my

child, I could not. I needed to be ready to bear another child as soon as possible, as soon as I could entice Louis back into my bed. No woman of greatness could afford the time to feed her own daughter, nor even a son.

As I handed Marie off to her nurse, Amaria came to me with cloths. We bound up my breasts, and the pain was like dull knives. But I had borne worse pain, and would again.

Louis came to my room when I was gowned in silk and my hair had been brushed out. Marie had drunk her fill of the nurse's milk, and now she slept once more in my arms.

I knew I could not indulge myself in this. I would have to give her up, give her over to the care of others. I could not rule my lands, rule Louis, and be a mother, too. But for now, I held my daughter close, and raised her in my arms, so that her father might look upon her.

"Is she not beautiful?" I asked him.

Louis stared down at our daughter, the child it had taken eight years of marriage and the blessing of Bernard of Clairvaux to conceive. Louis looked at Marie as if searching for something else, as if my daughter might somehow reveal herself to be another creature altogether: a creature of the fey perhaps, or some kind of changeling. As if his son, his rightful heir, had been spirited away.

"She is a girl."

I did not shield my child from his eyes and curse him. Instead, I met his gaze, and smiled.

"Louis," I said. "She is a child of God."

He could not hold on to his disappointment, not when I looked at him. He pressed his lips to mine, then to my baby's forehead. I let my breath out once, softly, and my daughter sighed with me.

"She is a beauty, like her mother," Louis said.

"Our son will be as beautiful."

Louis kissed me again, then remembered himself, and that I had not yet been churched. I would not be ready for his bed for another six weeks. Though I wished I might spend those six weeks with my daughter, I knew that I could not.

❀

Talk of a Crusade began in the kingdom almost immediately as the Holy Land and all its riches caught the eye of the new pope. Support for this Crusade took little time to catch on among the bishops and the kings of Europe like wildfire in a dry field. The new pope was hungry for the wealth that a Crusade might bring, and our vassals were hungry for war, and for glory in the name of God.

After Marie was born, Louis returned to prayer, and shunned my bed once more, for in his own mind, he feared himself too sinful to produce an heir for France. He thought that God had turned His Face from the throne. I sighed, and said nothing, for I knew that when God came to the foreground, the only way to win with Louis was to retreat.

Once more it was Bernard of Clairvaux who set things right, though he had not meant to. He hated me more since the birth of my daughter. Our short-lived alliance had ended almost as soon as it had begun. He felt it a personal affront that his work with my husband, as well as all his prayers, had produced only a princess.

But Bernard's thoughts were not on me, nor on my supposed failure to produce a son. Like everyone else, he was caught up in the fever for the Holy Land. He called to dukes and princes everywhere, as the pope did, to rain fiery wrath down on the Turkish infidels who had taken Edessa, a city close to the Christian kingdom of Jerusalem. Bernard called on the princes of Christendom to ride to the Levant, and to set all of the Holy Land free.

Louis refused to listen to this talk of a Crusade at first, but I heard it. My uncle Raymond was king in Antioch. I had never seen him, and the hope of meeting my father's brother made me long to begin the journey.

I also thought of Louis' obsession with guilt, and of the absolution that could be received in the city of Jerusalem. Murderers and evildoers of all kinds made their way to the Holy Land, fought against the infidel, and were shriven, forgiven of all their sins. Louis thought himself steeped in sin. There was no more decisive way to free him from this belief than to travel to Jerusalem, as the pope and Bernard of Clairvaux called for us to do. If Louis could be freed from his ideas of sin, he might return to my bed, and give me a son.

I sat with Louis alone after dinner in the great hall. Though he would not come to my bed, often he would sit with me of an evening once my ladies had gone, when he was not at prayer. That night he had left off praying to be with me. It was yet another beginning.

"Louis," I said. "What think you of this talk of war?"

"War, Eleanor?" he asked me. "What war do you speak of?"

"The war for God," I answered. "The war to free the Holy Land."

Louis said nothing for a long time. He turned his eyes from the fire to gaze on me. "I think to fight for God is a blessed thing. I think the great warriors who free the Holy Land from the infidel will be blessed, their names called on for generations to come."

Bernard of Clairvaux had been at him in private, then.

"And their souls, Louis? Do you think they will be forgiven of all sin? Will they be allowed through the gates of paradise?"

The light of God came into my husband's face. I had rarely seen that light turned on me. Instead of warming me, the sight of that zeal chilled the marrow of my bones. But I had gone too far to turn back. I must free him of his obsession with sin, even if I had to walk barefoot to Jerusalem to do it.

"You speak of God as if you have seen His Face," Louis said.

"I would never presume to look upon the Face of God, Louis. I seek His Grace, as all men do."

He did not doubt my lies. Louis rose from his chair, and came to kneel beside mine.

"Eleanor," Louis said. "I would follow God to the Levant, and beyond. I would follow the Cross to Jerusalem."

I pressed on, keeping my voice even. "Perhaps we might seek absolution from God in Jerusalem, that He might grant us a son."

Louis raised my hands to his lips and kissed them, not as

a lover would, but as if they were holy relics, as if my finger-tips held his salvation.

"Let us go on Crusade, Eleanor. Let us seek the grace of God."

He kissed me then, full on the lips. He lingered over my mouth, as if to taste my very soul. My heart leaped, and I ignored the fact that my blood was frozen, like a river in winter. This man was my husband. I had bound my life to his. I would raise our son to rule France as a great kingdom, stretching from Paris to Poitiers and beyond, as it had once been united under Charlemagne.

If I had believed in a god, that is what I would have prayed for.

PART III

To Be Free

Chapter 17

✦

City of Metz

Empire of Germany
June 1147

THOUGH BERNARD OF CLAIRVAUX HAD BEEN KIND ENOUGH to plant the idea of a Crusade in my husband's head, he could not let us leave for the Levant without speaking out against me. He did not go so far as to make a sermon proclaiming my evil, as he had called on all of Europe to fight against the infidel from his pulpit. Instead, he used his fiery eloquence to speak ill of me among certain churchmen and clerics, all of whom hated me already. He spoke long enough, and well enough, that his words were carried to Louis.

My people also carried them to me.

For the first time, Bernard of Clairvaux asked aloud whether God had turned His Face from us. Were we too closely related to please God, being distant cousins? Should we not seek an annulment from the pope in Rome, that Louis might be free to begin again?

In all the years of our marriage, not one man, no priest, bishop, or pope, had ever thought to question the validity of my marriage to Louis of France. Now that Bernard of Clairvaux did, I saw all his old hatred for me rising once more, and all his old hatred of my father. He would bring me down if he could, for since he had joined the pope in calling for a Crusade, Bernard had the ear not only of my husband but of all Europe.

But with Louis, Bernard had miscalculated. At court, in the months before we left on Crusade, Louis began the practice of leading me into dinner on his arm, and seating me himself at the high table. He did not fawn on me like a green boy, for we were both in our mid-twenties. The time for youthful foolishness had passed, even for Louis. But he poured wine for me himself, displaying to all who might be watching that I was his lady, his queen, and that no other woman would ever be.

The rest of Europe ignored Bernard of Clairvaux's words about my marriage, as the throne of France and the Emperor Conrad of Germany prepared for the march on the Holy Land.

As we assembled our knights and barons, gathering them for war, Bernard of Clairvaux's words stayed in the forefront of my mind. I had questions of my own. What if even a Crusade in the Holy Land would not turn Louis from his ideas of sin and death? What if Louis never gave me a son?

Charlemagne come alive once more in my own flesh and

blood was a dream I had cherished since childhood. But as I sat among my husband's courtiers, and drew furs around me to ward off the chill of that hall, I wondered if the men and women of Louis' court would follow even a Charlemagne. Parisians were shortsighted, hating all things new. Perhaps my son would not be able to bring them to heel, even after a lifetime of training from me. Perhaps they were simply an intractable people for whom the south and all its glories would always remain just one more country province to be sneered at.

For the first time in my life, I considered: if Louis annulled our marriage with the blessing of the pope, I would be free.

At first, this thought burned as a firebrand in my side. I lost my breath, sitting among my husband's people, so that Louis noticed and took my hand in his. I wondered as I looked at him: if he never gave me a son, could I leave him?

I remembered the warmth of my own homeland, and the joy life would hold for me if I never left there again. I might marry one of my own barons, and raise our son to follow as duke after me. To be a Duke of Aquitaine in the unbroken line of Charlemagne was no small thing.

But I could not relinquish my father's dream. My ambition was bred into my bone; I could not give it up. I would lead Louis to Jerusalem; I would call on him to release his fear of sin, and come once more to my bed.

The day before we left on Crusade, I went to the nursery and cradled Marie in my arms. She was less than two years old, but very solemn. Her dark blue eyes looked up into mine.

The light of my father's eyes was gone; I saw nothing but Louis reflected in her face.

I kissed her. "Marie, my love, I must go away."

She blinked but did not answer. This news was not surprising. I was often gone from her. Her nurses cared for her, and were true mothers to her, as I could never be.

"Your papa and I are going to a holy place, the city of Jerusalem, very far away. We will be gone a long time. Longer than a year, and maybe longer. Do you understand what I am saying?"

I saw from the shadows in her eyes that she did not. She knew only that I had always left her alone, though I saw her whenever I could, and came to her rooms daily whenever we slept in the same keep. I drew Marie close, and pressed her against the softness of my breasts. This child would never know me. But I would love her, every day for the rest of my life, whether we were together or apart.

"I hear you love music," I said. "Will you sing for me?"

Marie raised her head from its resting place above my heart, and she gave me a smile, nodded, and then began to sing.

It was a simple song about a spring flower that sat on her windowsill. She stood alone in the center of the room to sing it for me, as if she had a great hall filled with knights to be her audience, instead of only me. I listened as carefully as I had ever listened to any of my troubadours, and when she finished, I applauded her as if she were Bertrand himself.

"I will see you when your papa and I come home again."

Marie did not answer me, but came to me without her

nurse's prompting. This time, I did not have to draw her close. She climbed onto my lap, and laid her head against my breast herself. I remembered a truth then, as I held my daughter. One must cut out one's heart to be queen.

The next day Louis and I rode out from St.-Denis. It was a sunlit day in June, and Melusina pranced beneath me, her harness ringing like the sound of a bell. The bells of Paris and of Abbot Suger's grand new cathedral sounded us on our way as we rode out, Louis' men leading the vanguard.

Louis and I rode together in the center of our troops, with my barons from the Aquitaine and Poitou following behind us. Geoffrey of Rancon, my old suitor, rode before us as Louis' standard-bearer. The rains of spring ceased as we took to the road, white clouds drifting above our heads, the flowers of spring rising along the roadside at our horses' feet. We rode to the city of Metz in one long celebration. The Emperor Conrad of Germany was to meet us there, and continue with us on through his vast territories to Byzantium itself.

I brought all my ladies with me, both Parisians and Poitevins, and as we left the confines of France behind us, I felt them all begin to relax, even Priscilla, who was Parisian born and bred.

We had been on the road four days when Priscilla came to me, a sly smile on her face.

"Your Majesty, may I have a word?"

I smiled at her formality. Like all my ladies she had more than a word with me each day as we traveled safe between my husband's men-at-arms and my barons.

"You may, Lady Priscilla."

Instead of speaking, she waved to a servingwoman, beckoning her to step closer. The woman unrolled a silken sack, from which a pair of fine-combed woolen leggings emerged. The leggings had been dyed an emerald green, and were too small for any man to wear; my smile began to widen.

Priscilla waved to another servingwoman, who brought forth a gown in elegant emerald silk. Priscilla drew the skirt out for my inspection, and I saw that it was slit up both sides. Once I put it on, the skirt of the gown would reveal the leggings beneath.

I laughed out loud in sheer delight.

"We are women, riding to war," she said.

I laughed harder. "Amazons indeed, Priscilla."

"Yes, my lady queen."

I discovered that this scheme of dressing as modern-day Amazons, though concocted by Priscilla, was shared by all but the most staid of my ladies. They had their seamstresses sewing for months before we left, and now, the night before we entered the German city of Metz, they presented the gowns and leggings to me.

They had also fashioned leather vests for us to wear over the bodices of these gowns. Each bit of leather was soft and supple to the touch, beautifully embroidered in colors to match the gown it would be worn with. From a distance, the leather vests would give the semblance of breastplates.

Amaria had known of Priscilla's preparations but had said nothing to me, thinking that my women would never have the courage to reveal such a thing to the Queen of France. But when Priscilla presented Amaria with her own blue silk gown with its split skirt, woolen leggings, and fine embroidered vest, Amaria accepted them.

The next day, we rode into the city of Metz, and peasants lined the roadside to be blessed by the crusading priests in our entourage and to see a King and Queen of France riding through German lands to meet their emperor. As we rode close to the city gates, my ladies and I cast off the traveling cloaks we had been wearing to keep the dust of the road off our clothes, revealing our Amazon garb for the first time. The people saw our leather vests, and the divided skirts and leggings that we wore. At first, I thought they might revile us, but after a long moment of near silence, the people began to laugh and cheer.

I waved to them, and they began to cast flowers in our path. The Emperor Conrad rode out to meet us as we approached his city, and he drew his horse close to mine, giving me a rakish smile.

"Your beauty is as dazzling as the sun at midday," he said, after first offering his compliments to Louis as his brother king and crusader. Conrad's dark blond hair was cut short, for war was his constant pastime. His smooth tanned features and the strength of his hand as he grasped mine reminded me what a real man was like. I had been so long among courtiers that I had almost forgotten.

"And will you fight at our side, as the Amazons of old?" Conrad asked, his blue eyes sparkling with mirth.

I had opened my mouth to respond to his casual jest when Louis reached over and took my gloved hand from Conrad's. "No, my brother king. She will not."

Louis' face was drawn and pale, almost gray with horror at the contours of my legs revealed beneath the leggings and the split skirt of my gown. He was furious that my women and I had made such a display of ourselves. He threw his own cloak over me, and Conrad saw that it would be best to let the matter rest.

"Come into my keep, brother," he said in his flawless French. "Let us offer you a feast, for you have had a long journey, and we have farther still to go."

Louis nodded to the German emperor, but did not answer. We followed Conrad, our mounts trailing behind him, Louis' hand clutching mine. It was awkward to ride with our two horses side by side, but Louis would not let go of me.

Once we were in our adjoining rooms inside Conrad's keep, Louis would not leave me alone and in peace until I had stripped off the gown and leggings, and replaced them with a modest gown of cloth of gold. He left me then to go to his evening prayers, and I wondered what else this journey might hold, and if I would have the patience to bear my husband's constant company until we reached Jerusalem.

❀

Conrad feasted us with a great banquet of roasted boar and vast wooden kegs of local beer. I sipped at it only, for I found the concoction foul, but my barons and Louis' men drank deep, their laughter reverberating off the stone walls of Conrad's great hall. Only Brother Francis sat alone in the midst of the Germans with a frown on his face.

I retired with my ladies as soon as it was polite to do so,

for Louis still glowered at me. The Emperor Conrad's attentions were too solicitous, and I left knowing that though Louis was jealous, he would not come to my bed that night. But then, he never did.

I had brought a full retinue of ladies on Crusade with me, and most of them slept in the room that led into mine. Amaria saw them bedded down, though we both knew that they would not stay there. They, too, were happy to be away from the Parisian court, where prying eyes held them always under scrutiny. Here, they could meet their lovers unencumbered. While on the journey to Jerusalem, they could enjoy themselves. I envied them that.

Amaria saw my restlessness, and without a word, she handed me a long, heavy traveling cloak of wool. The cloak might have been worn by any woman, and was plain, with no embroidered border; no one who saw it would ever suspect that it hid the queen.

Amaria and I kept to the shadows and walked in silence through the torchlit keep. She made it her business to know all the outer doors and secret passages of any castle we slept in, for she trusted no one, and always wanted to see to it that I had a method of escape in case of fire or war. Her caution had never been necessary, but now we made use of her intelligence, climbing to the ramparts without calling a man-at-arms to accompany us. Bardonne alone followed us, moving with great silence and stealth for so large a man. He spoke not a word, but simply kept to the shadows as we did.

On the ramparts of Conrad's castle, I could see the village below made of stone huts, all outlined by the half-moon that rose above our heads. The town's cathedral rose on the next hill, and moonlight softened the rounded edges of the Romanesque basilica. The sight reminded me of my father's cathedral in Poitiers, and for one long, piercing moment, the view of that foreign church made me long for home.

"Your thoughts are far from here."

I knew that voice well, though it had been years since we had spoken alone.

"My mind was at home, in Poitiers," I said.

Bardonne stepped between us as Geoffrey of Rancon emerged from the shadows of the castle wall. Conrad's men-at-arms, posted on the ramparts to watch the grounds below, saw us talking, and assumed no doubt that I was his lady love, and that this meeting had been prearranged. They gave us a wide berth, for which I was grateful; they did not recognize me.

I raised one hand. "It is all right, Bardonne. He may pass."

My man stepped back, but kept his hand on his short sword. He wore one not for formal battle; he had been born little more than a peasant and did not fight as an archer or on horseback. But hand to hand, in close combat, Bardonne had no equal. To guard my life was his only duty, besides spying among my husband's men-at-arms, and he took his duty seriously.

Amaria frowned deeply, but when Bardonne stepped back, she did the same. Both she and my man-at-arms would hear every word we spoke, but we kept our voices low, to give ourselves the illusion of privacy.

"The people of Aquitaine and Poitou miss you," Geoffrey said.

I smiled at him, for that was nonsense. I had been to

see my uncle de Faye for Christ's Mass the year before, and had celebrated in my own hall among my own people. It was Rancon who missed me. Though he had served me faithfully, he had done it from afar. I had rarely seen him in the years of my marriage to Louis. The time he spent near us on our wedding day, and our wedding night, was all he could bear.

I saw the longing in Rancon's eyes and found that it mirrored my own. For the first time in my life, I wondered what might have been had I not married the King of France.

I dismissed such thoughts as folly. But I had been miserable with Louis for so long, and Geoffrey of Rancon stood close, his head bent low over mine. I took in the spicy sweet scent of his skin, and remembered how his hands had felt on my body so many years ago. I took one step back. Rancon was a man of honor and did not follow me, though his eyes were hot with desire.

"You would have made a fine Amazon, my lady."

My smile was wry. "My husband did not think so."

"Then he is a fool."

I pressed my hand to his arm to silence him and looked over my shoulder, in case any of the Emperor Conrad's men might be listening. They stood more than ten feet away, staring out into the night over the castle walls.

I met Rancon's eyes. "Do not take foolish chances."

"I would do more, for your sake."

He bent low, and took my hand in his, pressing his lips to my fingertips. For one heady moment, I thought he might turn my hand over and press his lips to my palm, but he did not. He let my hand fall and took a step back from me.

"My lady, I have not forgotten the vow I made you in your father's keep."

He did not speak of his oath of fealty, but of the promise he had made me while we stood alone in the dark, in the shadow of my father's curved staircase. I had been fourteen when he swore that there would come a night when he would not let me go. Years had passed since then; I had borne a child and married a man I did not love since those words were spoken. But still, I remembered.

"My lady, I always keep my word."

Rancon faded into the shadows. I inhaled deeply of the night air, for my breath had turned shallow at his nearness. I pressed one hand against the cold stone of the castle rampart. Amaria took that hand then, and drew it into her own.

"We must go in, my lady. You must sleep. The road ahead is long."

Her steady blue eyes met mine without judgment or rancor. I let Amaria lead me back into the keep. Bardonne followed us in silence. Amaria put me to bed with no more words between us, but as I lay down, she pressed a kiss to my forehead, almost as my mother might have done, had she been there. She took a liberty, but I did not rebuke her. For years she had been my friend as well as my lady-in-waiting. Amaria knew me and loved me for myself, as few others ever would.

I lay back on my bolster, but I did not sleep. The light from the braziers crept up the hangings of the bed, and raised shadows on the tapestries that lined the walls. I watched the shadows dance. At dawn, we would take to the road again, this time with Conrad and his Germans beside us. Baron

Rancon would carry my husband's standard. I would treat him as a stranger, as I had done for years already, as in the sight of my husband, I always must.

❧

The good weather did not last as we traveled deeper into Germany. The rains began outside Metz and stalked our path as we rode on horseback from one principality to the next. We were five months on the road from St.-Denis to Constantinople, and as we moved, the company of our troops grew until our ranks swelled to more than twenty-five thousand fighting men, their ladies, and their servants.

Most of the baggage was sent ahead by river at the city of Regensburg, so that our army, as large as it had become, might move faster. Conrad continued to host us at each castle he controlled, but most of the horde of crusaders remained in their own tents. I was relieved when we left Germany, and my women and I had our own tent raised along the roadside. As charming a host as Conrad was, I was happy to be queen in my own hall, even if my hall was made of waterproofed leather trimmed in silk.

Late in the month of September, we were well away from Conrad's territories and had entered the outskirts of the empire of Byzantium. The banner of Aquitaine flew above the tent I slept in, as it flew with the fleur-de-lys of France over the large tent that passed for Louis' great hall. Though many Parisians had traveled with us, Louis' hall became my own, for I had my own barons and ladies from Poitou and Aquitaine traveling with me.

On the first night we camped outside the city of Sofia in Bulgaria, I spoke with my troubadours before the feast. We had experienced no hardship or warfare along the path of our Crusade thus far, so there was much to celebrate. Like all Poitevins, I was always willing to celebrate being alive, so I called my troubadours to me, and instructed them to sing that night old songs my father and grandfather had written, as well as one of my own.

As the fruit was being served, one troubadour after another stood to sing. Louis glowered at this break in Parisian formality, but we were not in Paris now. This was a new country. We might carry the Court of Love into the East, and with it all the music that I had known in my childhood.

My barons cheered after every song, for they knew each of them well, as I did. Even some of the Parisians who traveled with us listened with attention, as they never would have done if Abbot Suger or Bernard of Clairvaux had been there, watching them.

Brother Francis frowned as if he would bring down thunder and lightning on all our heads. Brother Matthew and Father Gilbert, two more priests that Louis had brought to pray for him in Jerusalem, listened to the music of my homeland in stunned silence, as if they had never heard songs of love before. They sat together at a lower table, blinking like bovines that had just been struck between the eyes.

The German emperor Conrad applauded my troubadours as loudly as my own people did, and offered them sacks of silver discreetly in payment for their talent. I had paid them all beforehand, but I smiled as Bertrand and his lute player took the German's money, scraping before Conrad as if he were their lord.

The night ended early, for we had a few days' march still to the city of Adrianople, the last city that would rise in our path before we would come to Constantinople. All the barons and their ladies, save for a few of the Parisians and Louis' favorite confessor, Brother Francis, left my husband's tents with smiles on their faces. For the first time since I had been made Queen of France, my husband's people had embraced the Court of Love, as I had always longed for them to do. That first taste of cultural victory left me hungry for more.

I had thought to try to tempt Louis to my bed, but as I looked upon his sour, pinched expression, I simply kissed his cheek and bade him a good night. I would sleep with the sound of my grandfather's music still in my ears. I would savor the joy that came with biding among my own barons and among the Germans, who seemed to love music as much as we did.

From that evening outside the town of Sofia, my troubadours sang, and our lords and ladies listened. The songs of my family were carried deep into the East, right up to the gates of Adrianople, and to Constantinople itself. It seemed to me that my grandfather lived again whenever his music was played.

As we rode closer and closer to the gates of the capital of Byzantium, the land rose gently beneath Melusina's hooves, as if the country offered a greeting to me and mine. The windswept plains outside Constantinople had not changed in a thousand years. I almost expected to see the wild men of

Herodotus riding down upon us as we came closer and closer to the great city's gates. Our fighting men surrounded us and became ever more vigilant. At any moment, the Turks might attack us, even in Byzantium itself, and strike to cut us down. Those Turks, with whom we were at war, were the heirs of the ancient tribesmen who had terrorized that land centuries before.

The danger in the air around us, the spiced heat that rose from the ground even in the autumn, filled my heart with joy. The hills were green and brown with the ash and myrtle trees that grew along the Lycus River leading into Constantinople.

I rode Melusina among my own barons, as each vied with the others for precedence beside me. Louis rode far behind me, and I savored the first taste of freedom I had known since my father's death. The first sip of that nectar was sweet.

Each step on the road to Byzantium left me wanting more.

Chapter 18

City of Constantinople

Empire of Byzantium
October 1147

THE CITY OF CONSTANTINOPLE ROSE ON THE HORIZON LIKE A great curved beast. Even from a distance of five miles, the buildings and domes, the towers, and the great walls could be seen as we approached on horseback. Melusina seemed to step more lively, and the Parisians fell silent. Even in Germany, we had not seen a city as great as this. The walls and ramparts towered above us as we approached, blocking out the sun. The city's huge wooden gates bound in worked iron opened before us, and we stepped into another world.

The scent of spices was the first thing that struck me as Melusina carried me into the city, with Louis beside me. The smell of cinnamon and nutmeg rode on the air, and the scent of pepper and salt. The Byzantine emperor Manuel's people cast flowers at our horses' feet, blooms of such strange and vivid colors, orange, purple, and mauve.

Constantinople spanned the great water of the strait of Bosporus as a corridor might bridge the gap between a woman's solar and her bedroom. The city was as dirty as Paris, but I forgot the dirt at once as I craned my neck to look upon the heights of those buildings. Constantinople's towers and domes gleamed gold and white against the landscape, a jewel of gold and pearl set against a backdrop of ochre.

My ladies fell silent behind me as Louis and I entered the city. None of us had ever seen a place so large, or so grand. Rome itself could not possibly rival it. Constantinople was a city apart.

The towers shone like jewels in the late-morning sun. The great dome of Hagia Sophia beckoned to me, cupped like a woman's hand over a flame. Its elegant, graceful lines spoke of a distant past, when the Empress Theodora had ruled at the side of her Justinian.

The buildings of Constantinople were all made of stone. Different-colored marbles caught the light as we rode past, framing the wide cobbled street. Refuse flowed in neat rivers into drains along the edge of the road. In Paris, dirty water flowed into channels carved in the center of the streets, so that people and horses alike were forced to walk through the filth. I breathed deep, and though the scent of camel dung mixed with the scent of flowers and cinnamon, I did not catch the stink of human refuse as I had throughout Europe.

At the sight of the marbled buildings and the murmuring fountains, the Parisians drew close together, muttering and anxious. Brother Francis brought his mule as close as he could to Louis' mount, as if the presence of his king might protect him from the exotic landscape, an elegance so different from anything Paris had to offer. Even as Louis' people shrank from all they saw, I felt my spirit open like a flower under the sun after a winter of snow and ice.

Though I loved the Aquitaine all my life, with its deep green forests and its rolling hills, I loved the East as much from the first moment the towers of Constantinople rose around me. Here at last was evidence of the achievement mankind was capable of, the beauty of the mind of man that my father had always spoken of when he taught me of the Romans and the Greeks. Here was a city that housed the remnants of the ancient world. I took in the sight of that beauty, and it fed my soul.

I looked to Louis, whose horse walked close beside mine, and I saw that he knew nothing of what I felt. His eyes were cast forward. He looked neither right nor left, but followed his own standard deeper into the most beautiful city on earth. No thoughts of ancient Rome or Athens entered his mind; I could see that from the look on his face. I turned away from Louis then, and cast my own eyes back to the wonders around me. We did not plan to stay more than two weeks in this place, so I would drink in all the beauty that I could.

Constantinople's buildings were close together, built one on top of the other, as the buildings were in Paris. But this city was much larger than Paris could ever be, hemmed in as it was on its small island in the middle of the Seine. As we moved deeper into Constantinople on horseback, my husband's troops of twenty-five thousand men and all my ladies with our baggage train were dwarfed by the countless people and the endless streets that fanned out around us in a great arc off the wide road we traveled on.

We came to the Lycus River at the center of the city. The river was surrounded on all sides by buildings six stories tall. My ladies and I were brought down from our horses by imperial slaves. These slaves, dressed in thin silk robes over linen trousers, lifted us down from our mounts.

I blinked, shocked to be handled by a servant without permission, but the man in his fine jeweled silk touched me without meeting my eyes. His hands were indifferent on my waist, as if I were a vase that his lord had asked him to set on a table. My ladies tittered together, for these slaves were clearly chosen for their beauty as well as for their strength.

Later that evening, I was told that these were not men at all but eunuchs, gelded half men who had been trained to guard the empress with their lives. My own men-at-arms were separated from me and my ladies by these towering hulks, but there was no time to question this arrangement, for we were handed at once into flowered litters made of fragrant cedar wood stained dark brown. These litters were carved with flying beasts, dragons with sapphires and rubies inlaid for their gleaming eyes.

We followed the path of the river to the Bosporus, the strait that separated one section of the vast city from the other. This water divided Europe from Asia, and the imperial palace from the rest of Constantinople itself. Once we reached the edge of the Bosporus, we were handed by more slaves into wooden barges with canopies of silk to block the sun. These canopies were covered with fragrant, jewel-toned flowers of vermilion, lapis, and saffron. The peasants of Constantinople lined the quayside and waved to us and cheered as we set off across the water to the imperial palace. My women were silent until we were on solid ground again, clutching one another's hands, for none of them could swim.

Nor could I, but I was thrilled by the new world that had sprung up around me; it never entered my mind to be afraid.

My ladies and I had been separated from Louis and his Parisians as well as my own lords from Poitou and Aquitaine. But as our barges reached the palace on the other side of the strait, I saw that the men had crossed the Bosporus in barges of their own. My ladies climbed onto dry land one by one. When I rose to step out of the barge, the Baron Rancon was there beside me, offering his hand. He helped me onto the marble quay within the inner walls of the palace.

"My lady queen."

"Thank you, my lord."

I addressed him formally, keeping my tone light. All around us my ladies stood staring. Never before had he singled me out for attention in public.

My husband came to stand beside us then, and Baron Rancon dropped my hand. Louis stood close but did not touch me, his eyes trained on the high stone walls around us. The water gate closed behind us, a heavy wooden barrier edged and enforced with bands of iron.

For the first time since entering Constantinople, I felt a chill as those great gates were sealed shut. Our fighting men and most of our baggage were left outside. I later discovered that our people were given lodgings in the city and that our baggage was brought into the palace by a separate gate. But in that moment, behind those gates of iron and wood, I wondered if we would as easily find our way back out again.

I pushed this thought from my mind almost as soon as I had it. Louis met my eyes, and smiled. "I have been told that the gentlemen are housed separately. I am off to greet the Emperor Manuel, but I will see you at this night's feast." Louis kissed my cheek as a brother might, before the Emperor Manuel's attendants led him and our men away. Only Baron Rancon lingered, his eyes on me. My safety was his personal trust. He did not like to leave it to another.

I had heard on the road to Byzantium that in the palace at Constantinople men and women lived separate lives, save for their daily meetings in the great hall, and for love play. There would be little of the latter with Louis, and while I would rather have gone to see the Emperor Manuel for myself, I soon relaxed in the presence of my own ladies. The Empress Eirene did not come to greet me, but sent her head woman, Esmeralda, to see to my comfort. My ladies and I were led through a different entrance from the one the men had taken into the depths of the palace.

The interior walls rose around us, but light still shone through the latticework that covered the windows. The outer walls were strong for defense, but were set far back from the living quarters of the palace. Sunlight came into the rooms through windows that stretched from floor to ceiling. The painted white latticework kept out the direct heat of the sun, so that even in that climate, the rooms were never too warm.

My ladies and I were taken into the women's quarters. In the East, women not only led separate lives from men but were cut off completely in their own section of the palace. I did not care for this arrangement. But this city was only one stop on our road to Jerusalem. We would leave in two weeks' time, and take the long journey to Antioch to meet my uncle Raymond. Until then, I would enjoy the beauties that surrounded me, and overlook the flaws of Byzantium.

The rooms that the Empress Eirene had set aside for my use were the most elaborate I had ever seen. It was a day for firsts, for I had never before seen entire rooms laid out in marble: floors, walls, and ceilings. The beams of the high ceilings were inlaid cypress wood carved in swirls, images that brought to mind the waves of the ocean. Marble columns rose throughout the sunlit rooms, each in different shades of rose and cream, each column gilded at the top in Corinthian splendor. Low divans lay against the walls, and were scattered throughout the room, that one might sit in comfort the moment one thought to rest. These were carved from rich mahogany and covered with cushions of silk and damask in shades of rose, mauve, cream, and gold.

The effect these rooms had on the body and the spirit was immediately soothing. I felt the tension leave my shoulders for the first time since coming down off my horse in the hands of that palace eunuch. As Amaria and I led Priscilla and the rest of my ladies into these rooms, palace women scurried like mice to get out of our way, their faces veiled like Saracens. One of the Parisians crossed herself when she saw them. Amaria met my eyes. She would send word to Bardonne to find a quick and secret way out of this palace. I would not rest easy under the roof of a man who kept his women always veiled.

I still did not see the empress, but her veiled women were everywhere, offering me sweetmeats, hazelnuts braised in honey, and candied dates and figs. I took one of each for politeness' sake, and sent the rest among my women. After I had eaten and taken a glass of watered wine from Cyprus, the empress' ladies brought me into the baths.

The four deep pools lay in the shape of flower petals, large teardrops curving off from the center of the room. These bathing pools were sunk into the marble floor, as a pond or a lake might be at home. But this was no forest pool of brackish water. The empress' baths were man-made lakes lined with pink and cream marble. Beneath the floor of each, furnaces were stoked day and night, so that the water in those pools would stay heated, that the women of the palace might bathe any time they desired.

Great marble columns rose among the curves of these bathing pools, gilded as the columns in the outer rooms were.

The empress' women offered me a bath, and I accepted. The ladies of the palace all bathed in long linen shifts so sheer that they might as well have worn nothing. I would send Amaria to the bazaar to buy such material for my own shifts. No doubt the cloth would be too thin for warmth in

Paris, but in the Aquitaine, I might wear that beautiful cloth beneath my gowns in summer.

Once more I thought of what my life might be like if I were to leave Louis, and live among my own people in the Aquitaine. I might take one of my own barons to my bed, and wear such a shift for him. Baron Rancon came to mind, and I almost lost my breath. The memory of his hands on my body came back to me as if he had touched me only yesterday, and not many years ago, when I was still a green girl. I had forgotten him, and his touch; I had made myself forget. But the scent of the East, with its spices and its heat, made me remember the heat he had drawn from me that night in my father's keep. My body had never forgotten him. As if I were a young girl again, my skin flushed pink with the knowledge that I would see him at that night's feast.

I pushed the thought of the Baron Rancon aside, but the memory of his touch lingered on my skin. As the heat of the water surrounded me, it was as if I could feel his hands once more.

That warm, scented water was the first truly sensual experience of my life. I had thought I might find such pleasure with my husband, given enough time. But Louis was for the Church; marriage to me had not changed that. Only in that city on the threshold of the East, far from anything I had ever known, could I admit that, if only to myself.

Three of the empress' women stepped into the bath with me. The water in the deep sunken tub came up to my shoulders, and I was a tall woman. The empress' bathing women were tall as well, and they were so smooth in their motions, so practiced in their work, that I wondered if they had been bred for it, as I had heard Saracens bred their slaves for beauty and cut out their tongues for silence.

These women had kept their tongues, but as I did not speak to them, they said nothing to me. As I lay back in the water, practically floating in the peaceful warmth, two women scrubbed my arms and back, while the third washed my hair.

I relaxed beneath their competent hands; bathing while completely submerged in heated water was only one of the many benefits of living so close to Saracen rule. The drawbacks, constant warfare and imminent death, could surely be overlooked in favor of such luxuries as deep bathing pools and linen as fine and strong as silk.

There were other drawbacks, I was to discover that night as I took my ease among the empress' ladies, seated at her right hand in the place of honor. I saw how the women were separated from the men at table, set far from the seats of power. Having been raised at my father's side since the age of eight, I found it vexing to be so far from Louis, Manuel, and Conrad. I could see Louis speaking with both emperors, nodding as the heir of Constantine smiled on him, as Conrad spoke of politics and war. Of course, I could hear nothing of their talk from across the hall.

The Baron Rancon sat close by Louis, given precedence not by right of birth but by the fact that he ordered my troops and carried Louis' standard. The Lady Priscilla, who always kept her ears open for me, had made an interesting report.

Empress Eirene had heard that Baron Rancon had helped me from the flowered barge when we first arrived at the palace. Though the empress said nothing outright, his care for me had convinced her and others at the Byzantine court that Rancon was my lover. Eirene was smiling and charming to everyone of rank, but she favored Rancon, sending candied fruit from our table to him, with a message that it came from me.

In spite of the distance between us, I felt the baron's dark chestnut eyes on me. He nodded, acknowledging the gift, and the unprecedented nature of it. Louis noticed that the baron was watching me, and frowned. Rancon, while not a courtier, was careful to gauge the moods of the king. He turned at once to the man at his side, leaving the empress' candied dates untouched beside him.

I felt the heavy gaze of the imperial ladies as they watched for some fault, some evidence of my feelings for the baron that would sow seeds of dissent between Louis and my men from Aquitaine, damning both me and our Crusade. Eirene's chief lady-in-waiting, Esmeralda, smiled with malice, and the empress turned her bland, friendly gaze on me. I was not fooled. They would like nothing more than to cause trouble between me and Louis. For all their shows of welcome, the Emperor Manuel and his empress did not appreciate an army of twenty-five thousand men riding through their territory.

As I sat among the Byzantines, eating their food and drinking their wine, I wondered if the tension between our courts went even deeper than that. The Church in Rome and the Church in Constantinople were at each other's throats, vying for power, as all churchmen did everywhere. But as I took a sip of sweet wine from Cyprus, another thought occurred to me. Though we had come to the East to win Edessa back from the Saracens, perhaps the Emperor Manuel wanted that city for himself.

Whatever the emperor's true intentions, I knew what was at stake for my own people. I did not want an open rift between myself and the Parisians over Rancon. I was careful to ignore the baron for the rest of the evening. But still, I felt the currents of deceit just under the surface of the Byzantine pleasantness, the desire to see our Crusade against the Saracens fail, and miserably. It would amuse the Emperor Manuel to see us turn tail and run back to France in defeat, leaving the city of Edessa for him.

When I rose to leave, I was surrounded once more by the empress' ladies, as all my women were. We were herded carefully back to our rooms, as if we might go astray and make mischief, which indeed my people might have done, had they been given time and opportunity.

I received a message from Baron Rancon as soon as I reached my rooms. He sent it by way of his latest mistress, the Lady Rosalind. Like many women of rank from Poitou, she had come on this Crusade to expiate her sins, and to have an adventure. Men were not the only ones who hungered for change. By sending Rosalind as his messenger, Rancon no doubt sought to remind me that just as I had a life beyond him, he had a rich life as well. For all the heated looks he sent in my direction, Rancon had not spent the last ten years pining for me.

And of course, Rancon knew that he could trust her as a messenger. Rosalind curtsied low as she offered his letter to me. The seal was unbroken, though I doubt she could read the Latin even if it had not been written in code.

The missive was brief. It was no love letter, and spoke nothing of our mutual lust. It said only: "We face heavy losses on the road to Antioch."

I burned the vellum at once, under the watchful eyes of the empress' women. My own ladies sat huddled by a bronze brazier, though it was warm in Constantinople. The luxury of the palace had ceased to comfort them. Though they had no true knowledge of the Byzantine subterfuge that surrounded us, they could still sense the depths we swam in, as a lamb might sense the butcher's intent before the blade is drawn.

I asked that word be sent to Louis, asking him to come to me.

The empress' woman, Esmeralda, smiled at me, her sharp front teeth reminding me of little spikes, her lips rouged so deeply it looked as if she had supped on blood. I thought perhaps my message would not be sent, but Louis entered my rooms in less than an hour, his own men trailing behind him. He had been allowed into the women's quarters, as all husbands were. I came to see that the separation between the men and women in Byzantium was not so much for the women's protection, as was claimed, but so that the men might control their women better.

I took Louis' hand, and drew him with me into the bedchamber I had been given. The bed itself was as big as a small room back home, with deep cushions in mauve and cream silk, trimmed with gold tassels and edged with ermine. I drew Louis down onto the bed with me as if to kiss him. I leaned close, so that my lips rested at the level of his ear. But before I could speak, Louis' voice rang out, echoing against the marble pillars and walls of the room.

"Eleanor, I have taken a holy vow. I cannot do my duty by you until I have been shriven in Jerusalem."

I took his hand in mine and caressed it, as if he had whispered an endearment. "I know, Louis. Keep your voice down. I did not bring you here to ravish you."

His pale face had turned bright red from riding all day in the sun, and now that color darkened. I kissed his cheek, but he was stiff with anger. I had made a bad beginning. The oppression of the court of Constantinople had begun to wear on me. I would have to do better, and guard my tongue.

"Forgive me, my lord king. It is urgent, or I would not have sent for you. They watch us, even now. We must be cautious."

Louis drew back from me, and made as if to rise. "Who watches us, Eleanor?"

His voice was low, but could still be heard if anyone was hidden behind the latticework leading into the women's garden, or if, as in my father's castles, the walls truly had ears.

"The Emperor Manuel and his men."

"The Emperor of Byzantium is a Christian king. He has made us welcome, and offered us a great feast. Surely you do not think that he wishes us ill?"

I did not point out to Louis that the emperor had an agenda of his own. It would never have occurred to my husband that perhaps Manuel felt that one Christian king in this land was enough.

"I have word that men of ours will be killed on the march to Antioch. And this word comes from a source I would heed."

"Who are you consulting, Eleanor? Has the empress sent you someone to read your palm? You know I do not care for such doings. They are of the devil, even in amusement. I forbid you to do such things again."

I breathed deeply. Perhaps exposure to the sun had scrambled Louis' wits. He was never this slow to understand me in Paris, where I always had his ear. I tried again.

"Louis, our army will be attacked on the road to Antioch. My source is no soothsayer but a man of action. He tells me that we are in danger."

"We are at war, Eleanor. We are always in danger."

I lowered my voice so that he had to lean close once more to hear me. I caressed his cheek, as if to invite him closer. Perhaps I was mad with suspicion, but it seemed to me that I could feel alien eyes watching me even as we sat there in my private rooms. There was a sense of menace in that palace, for all its gold, marble, and silk hangings. I would not sleep well until we were away from that place.

"Louis, Manuel is going to betray us. He has no wish to see us prosper here. We must go, and not tell him the path we take. We must march to the sea, and from there take ship for Antioch. My uncle Raymond will support us, and keep us safe until we know more. If we march through these lands, we will be as sheep to the slaughter."

"Eleanor, we do not need to be made safe from a Christian king. I will not discuss this further."

Louis stood, keeping my hand in his. He kissed my fingertips, and I saw that he was aroused, though he had sworn not to touch me. I would get no more sense from him that night, if ever.

"I promise, Eleanor, no harm will come to you. I have given you my sworn word of honor that I will protect you, and I meant it."

I sighed, and he kissed my cheek, before backing to the door. He watched me as if I were some woodland bear that might charge him. Instead of swiping at him with great claws, he feared I might drag him to my bed.

I would get no further with him on the subject, and I knew it. I would have to make my plans for the safety of my people on my own. The Baron Rancon would help me.

Louis bowed to me at the door, and left the way he had come. I let him go.

"Good night, Louis," I said, but he was gone already. My ladies came to me, leaving the empress' women in the outer rooms. They undressed me, and Amaria lay down beside me. I saw that she had a dagger in her fist as she slid her hand beneath her pillow. I did not laugh, as I would have done at home.

Chapter 19

❦

The Road to Antioch

WE STAYED IN CONSTANTINOPLE FOR TEN MORE NIGHTS, AND I slept little. Though the feather bed I lay on was one of the most comfortable of my life, I could feel the eyes of the empress' women on me even as I slept. No doubt Eirene kept watch over us always, even in the dark reaches of the night, and reported all to her husband.

The Emperor Manuel sent us off with as much fanfare as he had received us. I was well pleased to be gone from that place. I was not convinced of his goodwill, though Louis kissed him like a brother as we departed.

I met the Baron Rancon's eyes as I mounted Melusina outside the city gates. We had communicated by messenger already that morning. We would not take the route that Louis had told the emperor of, nor would we make camp where the emperor recommended. I did not trust that Christian king, as Louis called him. Caution would cost me nothing, where carelessness might cost me much.

But we would make our way overland to Antioch, instead of taking ship and traveling by sea. There were shrines Louis wished to visit between Constantinople and Antioch, and many of his lords hungered for war as my own people did not.

Though we met some Turks on the road, the German emperor Conrad rode in our vanguard and took the heaviest losses. Baron Rancon managed to keep my own men safe, while still bearing Louis' standard with honor. Beyond this one attack from the Turks before we reached Ephesus, our armies traveled unmolested. I waited, but as the autumn passed into winter, I stopped looking for an ambush around every corner. We were still hundreds of miles from Antioch, traveling slowly overland. But I began to hope that perhaps my fears of Manuel's treachery would prove unfounded.

The country leading from Constantinople to Ephesus was the color of ochre and dun, save for the green of the cypress trees that greeted us by every riverside. The warm blue sky rose above us each morning after sunrise like a dome of clouded glass. Though winter came upon us as we were on that road, it was as warm as Aquitaine in summer, and the sun as bright. It was my first full winter away from the confines of the palace in Paris, with its rain, and its damp walls and chill stone corridors that no braziers and no tapestries could warm. I drank in the rich browns and greens of that Eastern foreign land, and counted myself fortunate.

One day in January, after we had celebrated the feast of Christ's Mass in the city of Ephesus, I rode out ahead of Louis' army with my barons and my women. Louis and Conrad lingered in that country, visiting some shrine or other to Saint Paul. Their armies lingered with them, and sent word that they would meet us the next day. That night they would camp apart from us.

Those from Aquitaine and Poitou could not care less if all the Parisians in the world disappeared into the sea, so the separation for one night did not trouble them. I did not like having our backs exposed to Constantinople and to the Turks in the north, but Rancon assured me that in the place he had chosen, we would be safe.

Though he was Louis' standard-bearer, Rancon rode on to set up camp with me, and with my men. He chose the site where we would sleep, not on the exposed mountainside as Louis had instructed, but in a sheltered valley. Rancon had brought us this far with no trouble, losing few men. I decided to trust him once more.

My tent was set up on a bluff above the river, hidden in a copse of trees. Mountains rose on either side of us, but we were safe within our valley, with a wide view of all before and behind us.

Cypress and willows sheltered us from the sun, which, by the time we made camp, had begun to set already. There was a stream running close by, and the washerwomen brought up fresh water for my bath. I bathed in the silver basin that had been a gift from the Empress Eirene; it was far finer than anything I had at home. As I bathed quickly in tepid water, I sorely missed the deep bathing pools of Constantinople.

As the sun sank into the west, I sat alone but for Amaria, who stood by me. My other ladies were happy for a night without Parisians, and feasted with my knights and barons beside a roaring bonfire. Even had I wanted to join them, I would not have done so. Let them drink deep, and rest themselves, away from the prying eyes of the Byzantines and the Parisians both. There was little time for my people to enjoy themselves alone, and there were many leagues to go before we reached Antioch, and then Jerusalem after it.

I sat drinking wine from Cyprus, yet another gift from the empress, when the back flap of my tent lifted, and the Baron Rancon walked in.

Amaria's knife was in her hand. She did not lower it when she saw who had entered.

I stood, and pressed my hand to her arm. She lowered her dagger then, but she did not sheathe it.

"Baron Rancon," I said. "You are welcome here. You might have come in the front door."

I touched Amaria once more. She saw that I would brook no refusals. She sheathed her dagger and moved to leave me. She took up her place before my tent, and did not leave it all that night. No doubt my people saw that Geoffrey was missing, saw Amaria at my door, and knew why she stood there.

For the first time in years, the Baron Rancon and I stood alone, and looked at each other.

"Could you not have waited until dark?" I asked him.

"I have waited almost ten years. That is long enough."

He did not fall on me and ravish me. He stood still, and

waited for my leave. Even there, in that foreign land under a foreign sun, I was still his duchess. He had sworn to protect and serve me. He would not come to me, even then, unless I permitted it.

I raised one hand and he took a step forward. He did not leap on me but took my raised hand in his. I was fresh from my bath, and dressed in a light gown and shift, one I had ordered made upon coming into that country, for the heat there was more than it had ever been at home. I wore dark blue that day, like the sky at morning, with pearls around the hem, and at my throat. The blue silk beckoned him, and I knew he wanted to strip it off me. He leaned down, and pressed his lips to my palm.

He, too, had bathed, though it was not the custom among my men to do so, especially while on Crusade. I took in the scent of the thyme on his clothes, and the scent of soap on his still-wet hair. His beard was trimmed and smooth, and he was dressed in light, fine-combed wool, his boots polished to a sheen. Louis wore silk and satin for court occasions and in the great hall, but he had never taken the trouble to wear such finery for me when we were alone in my room. My husband had never come wooing; but then, he had never had to.

I moved away from Geoffrey, drawing my hand from his. I poured Cypriot wine from a silver urn into the silver goblet that matched it. Cool sweat beaded along the outside of that urn; it ran down the side, and caressed my hand as I poured. I shivered, with Geoffrey watching me.

I raised the cup between us, and took the first sip. His

eyes never left me all the while, and he did not draw breath. I stepped across the deep, rich carpet on the floor of my tent, and raised the goblet to his lips myself.

His hand was on mine then, caressing my fingers. He touched my ruby ring, the one my father once had worn. He touched the diamond Louis had given me when I married him, but neither my rank nor my married state stopped him. Geoffrey swallowed one long draught of wine, then took the goblet from me. He set down the cup beside its urn. He reached for me, and I knew my time to choose was over.

Geoffrey kissed me softly, gently, as if I were made of spun glass and might break between his hands. Louis loved me, and was often tender, but he had not the skill to cherish me, even after more than ten years of marriage. Geoffrey had both the skill and the fire of a real man combined.

When I did not shy from him, he drew me close, and pressed himself against me. The heat of his body melded at once with mine, and I lost my breath. His lips were on mine again, sipping from me, as if I were a fountain that would never run dry, as if he had lived all his life in the desert, and just now had the taste of water on his lips.

I let him lead. Always Louis had to be coaxed and cajoled into the act of love, drawn along by hints and whores' tricks. I needed none of those with Geoffrey.

He lifted me in his arms as if I weighed nothing, though I was a tall woman, full of strength. He laid me down upon my pallet of furs and satin, drawing first my gown from me, then my shift. His hands feasted on me as his eyes did, for a lamp was lit beside the bed, and cast its glow over us.

In spite of the gloves he wore when on horseback or at war, Geoffrey's hands were coarse and callused, as Louis' were not. It seemed I could not drive my husband from my mind, comparing him with Geoffrey: the darkness of Geoffrey's arms with Louis' fairness, the dark heat in Geoffrey's brown eyes with Louis' soft blue. Then Geoffrey reached between my thighs to caress my nether lips, and all comparisons ended.

A heat began to build in me, a tightening so intense that I began to fight it. But I could fight nothing with Geoffrey's hands on me. His own gown and hose cast off, he leaned close; his skin heated mine as a forge heats a sword. He pressed the hard length of his body against mine, the warm curling hairs of his thighs against my soft skin. Still, he did not enter me, though I shifted beneath him, trying to coax him closer. Had I not been a queen, I would have begged him, but still his hand rode me as he looked into my eyes.

I felt it then, the great wave of power as it rose in me. Louis had fanned that flame before, clumsily, but it had never caught. This time, it was a conflagration, and I was swept up in it.

The waves of power washed over me, pleasure after pleasure, so that I could not catch my breath. Geoffrey entered me. I would have screamed had his hand not been fastened over my mouth. He rode me then, his own gasps echoing in my ears. I had not thought that I could feel anything more, but his body was in mine and on mine, riding me as I rode my mare. I crested once more beneath him as he spoke my name.

I felt the warmth of his seed spill inside me, and for once it was not just a sordid but necessary end to a man's pleasure.

For once, I felt my own pleasure, and I knew how much I had been cheated of in all my years of marriage. There were depths within me that I would not have plumbed, had Geoffrey never touched me.

Had I been a weaker woman, I would have cursed Louis. As it was, I did not waste my breath. Instead, I drew Geoffrey close, that he might come to me again.

❈

Geoffrey loved me many times that night, and each time I rose to the pinnacle of bliss, and toppled over it. When he left me an hour before dawn, I lay spent on the satin of my bed as if slain. But I still lived.

"Alienor, I will not forget this night, now or ever."

"Nor I, Geoffrey. But you must not call me that."

"I will not, ever again. But that is who you are to me. Alienor of the soft bronze hair."

He kissed me then, and I tasted his regret. His lust had flown, as mine had done. My husband would return soon, and we would not be able to touch each other again.

"If you ever have need of me, I will come to you."

I pressed my hand against his cheek. The unkempt edges of his beard had grown back in the night. It rasped against my fingertips.

"That has always been true. And I thank you for it," I said.

"There need be no thanks between us."

He kissed me, his lips lingering on mine as if he wished time would stand still, as if time did not exist. But even then, he knew his duty, just as I knew mine. He left me without another word. There was too much between us ever to be spoken of, and we both knew it.

Amaria came in when he had gone, and helped me wash and dress. When my women entered my tent, fresh from their own liaisons, I was already breaking my fast. Not one of them looked askance at me, or asked any leading questions. If I had not been so deliciously sore, I might have thought the night before nothing but a dream.

I was soon to discover that while I was pleasuring myself safe among the cypress trees, the world was going on around me, for good and ill. Word came to us early that morning: Louis' army had been attacked in the night. The Turks had overrun them, and only two thousand Parisian fighting men had survived.

Louis was well, they were quick to tell me, thinking that I grew pale in my fear for him. Bile rose in my throat, and I pushed my food aside. It was a dark day. I had been proved right. The Turks had attacked.

Perhaps the Emperor Manuel still secretly resented our presence in his territory. I wondered if Manuel had heard of our route, and had learned that our forces had been separated overnight. I did not doubt for a moment that the Emperor of Byzantium was capable of selling information about his fellow Christians to the Saracens. Manuel might have told the Turks where Louis and his army could be found, busy at prayer and ripe for the scythe.

I sent at once for Rancon.

He bowed to me, no acknowledgment on his face of anything that had passed between us. I questioned him in front of my men. My women had been sent from the tent, save for Amaria, who was always by me.

Though all my barons no doubt knew that Rancon and I had spent the night in love play, I saw no evidence of that knowledge on their faces. I saw nothing but respect for me, and respect for the man who led them. Rancon had kept them safe. Had we heeded Louis, had we camped on the mountain, we would all be lying dead now, food for crows, and every one of us knew it.

"And you sent word to the king yesterday, in the afternoon, to tell him that we would be here?" I asked.

"No, my lady queen. I sent no word. I thought it too far, and that my messenger might be killed. It would have been a waste of a man, and his horse."

Rancon did not say it, though we were all thinking it. Louis had wasted more than one man's life by not heeding me, and taking ship to Antioch before this. I knew, however, that Louis and his Parisians would not see it that way.

"And the Emperor Conrad and his Germans, what of them?"

"The emperor still lives, my lady. Many of his men were killed at prayer, and others stood to fight with the king's knights. A few hundred are left alive. The Germans are making their way for the coast even as we speak."

I did not want to hear any more. I extended my hand, and Geoffrey bowed over it. He did not kiss my ring, but neither did he let my hand go.

"You have done well. Send word to me when Louis arrives. He knows by now where we are?"

Geoffrey's eyes met mine. "Yes, my lady duchess. My men have met him on the road. The king's knights are in retreat."

My barons bowed to me, before backing from my presence. They knew, as I did, that we would all pay for our night of safety in the valley. Baron Rancon was my war leader, but he was also my husband's standard-bearer. It was his duty to obey my husband in all things, but Rancon had remembered his oath to me first. He had chosen the safety of our people over Louis' foolish orders. My husband would not soon forget that he had been ignored, and that my people had been saved from an ambush in which so many Parisians fell.

We waited until past noon, and Louis' army still did not come to meet us. Only as the sun set did the French begin to straggle into our camp. One by one, man by man, they came among us. They drank deep from the water of the clear-running creek nearby, almost falling down where they stood. They cared for their horses, then lay down to sleep on blankets in the open air. None of the survivors set up tents, so my people did it for them. I began to see that what I thought had been a rout had been a massacre.

Louis did not come to me, but sent his man to fetch me to him. I knew then that we were in for deep trouble, the kind I had never before seen with Louis. I dressed in dark blue silk, with a rosary of diamonds and jet bound around my waist. My hair was braided down my back and covered with a linen veil. I thought I looked like a nun, which would suit my purpose. No doubt Louis had no use for a whore so soon after such a humiliating defeat.

As I came to the door of Louis' tent, one of his confessors,

Brother Matthew, beckoned to me at the door, giving me leave to enter. I thought for a moment that the churchman might stay with me and my husband, to hear all that we might say, but when he saw the look on Louis' face, Matthew left at once.

My husband had aged ten years in one day. His face was gray, as if he had seen too much death. He was a good man, with a soft heart. The last day's work had been his undoing. I could see it in the rings of dark blue around his eyes. The whites of his eyes were reddened with sleeplessness, and with tears.

Louis did not speak, but simply stared at me. He did not rise from his cushioned chair. I knelt in the center of his tent, where his people had not yet even placed the rug his brother king the Emperor Manuel had given him. I knelt on the canvas, with nothing to cushion my knees but the hard ground and my thin silk skirts. I lowered my head, as if I were a suppliant. If I had thought that might be enough, I was mistaken.

"I am sorry, Louis," I said. "I am sorry for the loss of your men."

He did not speak for a long time. When I raised my head, he was staring at me still, but his eyes were vacant, like a lost child's. I thought of our daughter, Marie, left behind in Paris. I wondered how she was faring, alone but for her nurse and attendants. I wondered if, when she thought of us, she felt as lost as Louis looked.

I pressed the idea of my child from my mind. I had a marriage to salvage, and little time to do it in. If I left this wound even overnight, it would fester. Louis would curse me, and set me aside.

I would not let it come to that. "You left us," he said. "We looked for you on the mountainside, and you were not there."

"No, Louis. I was not." I did not look away from him. Baron Rancon and I were justified in our decision to stay in the valley. We had defied Louis' orders, and we had stayed alive as a consequence. But always, with a king, one must take the blame onto oneself. "Forgive me."

He reached out to me, and I rose to my feet. I kissed his hand, and pressed my cheek to the back of it. I knelt once more before him, his hand still cradled in mine. I thought of the night I had spent in the Baron Rancon's arms. Louis' people would soon learn of it.

I had been foolish to take the risk. Louis was furious that Baron Rancon had defied his orders. If he learned of our night together while the French troops were being slaughtered, he would put me aside. I would have to send the Baron Rancon home by ship, and the rest of my vassals with him. I could no longer be the Duchess of Aquitaine and the Countess of Poitou on this journey, commanding my own troops through my lover. As in Paris, I would have to subjugate myself to Louis and his people in order to heal the breach that the decimation of his army had made between us. We still had more than two thousand living knights from Louis' train. Those knights would have to be sufficient to protect us as we continued our journey to Jerusalem.

Louis sat for a long time with my lips on his hand, my cheek pressed against his palm. His hand was cold in mine. I thought to chafe it a little, to warm it, as I would have warmed my own, but I did not dare. I would not take the risk of being overly familiar. Fool or not, real man or not, Louis was king.

"I forgive you, Eleanor."

I raised my head, and met his eyes. Louis' hand was still clutched in mine.

I would never love this man. The realization bruised my heart, as if someone had struck me. I wanted to love Louis; I wanted to hunger for him. I wanted his touch to transport me as the Baron Rancon's had. But kneeling before him, far from the world we had built together, I knew that I would never love him or desire him. There would be no son born to us, no Charlemagne come back to earth. As a child, I had learned to bear pain in silence. Now I set aside my pain, and kissed my husband's fingertips.

"I love you, Louis," I said, and for the last time. It was not true, but it would have been if I could have willed it so.

He raised me up, and stood beside me, drawing me close. He did not clutch me as the baron had. His hands were not firm on my waist. Louis leaned against me, as if gathering his strength.

"Go to your tent, Eleanor. Rest and make ready. Tomorrow we ride for the coast, for the city of Attalia."

Attalia held no distinction, except that it was a coastal town the Turks did not hold. Our journey overland had come to disaster. So we would take ship for Antioch after all, and travel by sea to my uncle's kingdom, where we might find a modicum of safety, and a moment of peace in this quest for war.

I saw on my husband's face that he had had enough of

fighting. He would go to Jerusalem. He would kneel at the shrines and beg for a son. But from that moment, alone with me, he laid his crusader's sword down.

Louis stood a little taller than I was. I easily met his eyes as he came into my arms, and clutched me close, as if he would squeeze the breath from my body. I longed to feel sheltered by his embrace, but the best I could hope for was that he felt sheltered for a moment in mine.

He kissed me, and sent me away. Brother Francis was tending to what was left of Louis' men. But Brother Matthew still stood at the flap of Louis' tent. Father Gilbert, an old Norman priest who had served both Suger and my husband for many years, stood with him. They both looked at me reproachfully, and I knew that they had heard of my liaison with the Baron Rancon.

I bowed my head to Louis' churchmen as I passed. Matthew and Gilbert were wise enough to bow to me, for Louis was there, and watching them. I still had the ear of the king.

That night, I stayed in my tent, giving out word that I was in prayer for the souls of the men who had died. No one came to me, not even my women. Amaria and I sat alone, eating fresh rabbit that someone had caught and put into a stew. It was rude fare, but savory. I sent the best part of it to Louis.

He did not leave me unattended. An hour after I had sent him the stew from my own pot, a gift came for me, much more elaborate. Wrapped in gauze and linen, in a box of mahogany and mother-of-pearl, lay a chess set so fine, it took my breath. The board was ebony and mother-of-pearl, lined with lapis. The pieces were cast in gold and silver, and stood as tall as the length of my palm. I took up one and hoisted it. It was heavy as only good gold and silver can be. I laid the piece back down, and sat at once to write a flowery message of thanks.

Louis sent no reply, but it was enough. He had sent the gift. Though he loathed chess and had no patience for it, though his newfound friend the emperor had gifted him with the set himself, still, Louis sent it to me. All was not lost between us. We would go on to be blessed in Jerusalem. Louis would still pray for a son.

I sat in that tent at the edge of the world, the soft, warm winds of the East on my cheek. The thought of a son to unite the kingdoms was far from me, like a mirage in the desert of my life, a phantom only, a shadow with no substance. As I sat alone in my tent, with only Amaria to attend me, I wondered. Perhaps it was time to build a new dream for myself.

Chapter 20

❧

City of Antioch

Kingdom of Antioch
March 1148

WE TOOK SICILIAN SHIPS FROM THE HILL TOWN OF ATTALIA, and spent two days on the sea sailing from Byzantium to the kingdom of Antioch. The rowers worked with the wind, and we made good time across the deep blue of the Middle Sea. I spent a great deal of my own gold to purchase that safe passage, for we still needed ships enough for all two thousand of my husband's men. Conrad and his German army took their own ships to the port of Acre in the kingdom of Jerusalem. The German emperor bade us farewell at Attalia, agreeing to meet us once more in Jerusalem.

Baron Rancon and most of my men from Poitou and Aquitaine left with the outgoing tide, as we did. The sight of my barons and men-at-arms, all alive and well, served only to remind Louis of his own losses at the hands of the Turks. As a concession to him, I agreed to send my own people back. Most had had enough of travel, and longed only to see their homes again. My barons had taken on many bolts of silk, cloth of gold, and spices. They loaded these wares onto other Sicilian ships, and sailed for home.

As we crossed the Middle Sea, my women, sickened by the motion of the waves, stayed in the cabin below and prayed for a safe delivery. Whether they wished to be delivered from death or into death's comforting hands, I was not sure.

Amaria and I did not sicken. We stayed on deck both days, and faced the wind. The sun was high and warm. We sat under a canopy, and watched the sailors work. It seemed that they showed a bit of flair for our sakes, but no doubt they were always adept at climbing the rigging.

I thought of Bernard of Clairvaux's words, that Louis and I were too closely related to be truly married in the eyes of God. I thought of how I might slip the leash of my marriage.

I wanted my life for my own, free from Louis and his court. More and more, I thought of what freedom might mean. I might live my life on my own lands, surrounded by my people, protected by my barons. Though the loss of the crown of France would be great, my hunger for freedom from Louis and from the French court grew as each day went by. The idea of freedom burned in my brain, a firebrand that would not go out.

I rode the waves of the Mediterranean to my uncle's stronghold, watching the dark blue water touch the blue of the sky. The world seemed too big a place to stay always in

Paris without a son and heir, at that court's mercy for the rest of my life. I was born for better things.

Of course, I did not speak of this, not even to Amaria. To speak these thoughts was to give another too much power. So I waited, and watched the water, and thought of home. I longed to be duchess in my own hall, with no man to rule beside me. To be Duchess of Aquitaine in my own right was a heady thought. It had never been done. Always, every duchess in the history of my lands had a husband to rule beside her. For the first time in the history of my people, I might be different. I could scent my freedom on the air, in the salt that rose with the waves.

I went to stand at the rail as we came to the coast of the kingdom of Antioch, the taste of freedom on my tongue. It was a tempting wine. I must guard against it. My stolen night with Geoffrey of Rancon had taught me that. I would have to plan, and carefully. Too much freedom, taken too soon, could be my undoing.

When we reached the port, there was no flower-decked fanfare as in Constantinople. But there was a barge waiting to take us upriver to the city of Antioch itself. I did not know my uncle, the king. Raymond, my father's brother, was only nine years my senior, but if I had ever met him as a child, I had forgotten it, as I had forgotten most of my childhood. I felt as if I had been born a duchess, a duchess preparing always to be a queen.

My father had told me that Raymond had been restless even as a boy. After he was fostered out among the nobility of Normandy, he never came back to Aquitaine. He served

King Henry of England before that old man died, leaving the kingdom to be fought over by Queen Maude and the usurper, Stephen of Blois. Raymond had left Europe then for the Levant, not wanting to die in someone else's war, intending to make his way in the world himself.

And so he had. When Raymond married the heiress of Antioch, he had become king there. He stayed away from the Aquitaine and Poitou, even when he might have come home and taken up his place as my father's heir. Now that I had breathed in the spices of the East and drunk deep of the colors of the Levant for myself, I could see why he never came home. Even the Aquitaine paled in comparison with this vivid place. It was a land that called on men to dash themselves against it, as a man might dash himself against the rocks on hearing the sirens' song. Like a woman of power, that ground called on all strong men to conquer it.

I had no taste for battle, but even I heard the song of that place. It called to the restlessness in me, fanning it, making it grow. I became something different there, something more than I had been. The Levant sang to me a siren's song of what it might mean to be whole, and to be free.

We came up from the barges on the river to the gates of Antioch. The gates of the city did not open until we were close at hand, when the fighting men of Antioch could see our faces as well as our standards from the ramparts. The men who greeted us were dressed for war, but their armor gleamed with inlaid gold and silver. Even the least of their knights were dressed in such finery, and counted it as nothing. The Parisians looked on those precious metals, then turned to one another, their eyes gleaming.

I was surprised to see Easterners among the men who waited upon us. I should have learned by then that in that place I could not tell Christian from Saracen, Frank from Greek. Even the fairest German was tanned a deep brown in that climate. After years under that relentless sun, even Louis would have gained some color other than bright red, had he not kept a canopy over his horse, and over me.

Louis and I stood together, his new standard-bearer a step behind us. At first I could not tell which man among those there to greet us was the king. We stepped through the gate, and it closed behind us, most of our army left to camp on the hills below.

It was then that I saw him. He looked like any other man, neither tall nor short, neither handsome nor fair. Until I saw his eyes. That blue struck me down. I stood frozen, caught in a strange alchemy. The web of that alchemy rose from the ground to swamp my reason, and drew me to him. I tried to fight it, to command the emotions that rose to steal my breath.

Then he spoke, and I knew it was beyond my control.

"Greetings, Your Majesties. I am Raymond, Prince of Antioch. You and yours are welcome to this place."

I do not believe in fate. But I felt what others call fate as Raymond stared down at me. His eyes were not heavy on my face. He did not leer or stare, as some men in my life had done. But there was something behind the deep blue of his eyes that told me he felt it. The alchemy between us had claimed him, too.

He reached out, and took my hand.

I felt the heat of his palm on mine, warm and sheltering,

as if I had stood on a plain of ice all my life and had just come in from the cold. Then the moment shifted, and he stepped back, and away from me. I could breathe again, and the sense of being stalked by fate receded.

Louis noticed nothing amiss, but took my hand in his to lead me up the high road, into the palace at the top of the hill.

The palace gleamed white. Once inside the cool of its thick stone walls, I saw that while the outer reaches of the castle were Norman in design, for strength and for defense, the interior was Eastern. The walls were lined with marbles of every hue, and the ceilings were of whitewashed plaster held in place above our heads with strong beams of cedar. Indoor fountains sounded in every public room, and when we reached the ramparts, in the far distance I could see the blue of the sea.

All the servants in that house had the look of Saracens, but here the women did not go veiled as they had in Constantinople. They met my eyes before bowing low to me, and I saw that Raymond and his men treated these people not as conquered chattel but as human beings. As I passed into my rooms, one small boy ran to us with clean water in a silver bowl. He bowed, and offered the bowl first to me, then to Louis, that we might wash our hands. I saw that this was a ceremonial cleansing only, one to signify that we had passed into the private rooms of the house, and that we were welcome there.

I sent the boy on his way, and Amaria handed him a piece of silver for his pains. Louis seemed dazed by all he had seen, pale beneath the red of his sunburn. He kissed my hand and left me at the door to my room, and Raymond left with him.

I stood in dumbfounded silence as my women moved about me, setting up my things in the borrowed rooms. They were not as fine as the rooms the empress had lent me, but where there had been gilt and marble in Constantinople, here there were great windows that opened onto a view of the hills outside the city walls.

A garden lay beyond a latticed door, with fruit trees bearing dates and figs, and soft flowers giving their perfume. It was in that garden that I first saw a Persian rose. I sat among those flowers for a full hour as my women made my rooms ready.

They took me into the bathing chamber that led off my sleeping quarters, and the tub there was large, if not as deep or as wide as the one in Constantinople. The water was scented with rose attar, so that the scent of the garden followed me into the bath, and perfumed my hair. I lingered in the water overlong, and found I could not bring myself to leave my rooms, even when the time for dinner came. I sent word to Louis that I was unwell, that the sun had blinded me, making my head ache. Louis sent back a basket of figs, and a flagon of sweet wine. He was kind to me always, though the divide between us was wide since the massacre.

I ate nothing and drank not even a sip of the wine. A torpor had come over me, but I was too restless to sleep. Amaria sent my women away, and they went to sup with Louis and the king's men, off to flirt and seduce as they might. I stayed abovestairs, and kept my doors locked.

Amaria knew me well, almost as well as I knew myself, but she had never seen this mood come upon me. Neither had I.

I sat outside in the walled garden and listened to the wind from the distant sea. I could smell the salt on the air even as the sunlight faded, and the moon rose, casting milky light and shadow over the roses. Amaria knew I needed to be left in peace, though she did not know why. She let me sit without her in the garden, my thoughts my only company.

I was alone when he came to me.

He stepped out of the shadows like a phantom, or an assassin, though I knew from the first that he was neither. He said nothing, but sat down beside me, careful to keep a distance between us on the marble bench.

He did not speak, and neither did I. After the first moment, my heart began to calm its frantic pace, and the silence rose from the ground around us, unbroken but for the sound of the wind.

"If I believed in God, I would say He has a sense of humor. Would you not agree, Alienor?"

He spoke my name from the first with the lilt of our homeland, in our own tongue. I savored the sound of it.

The moon was rising over the fig and almond trees. The scent of roses still clung to the warm air, and to my skin. I heard him draw a deep breath, and knew he was taking in the scent of the rose oil in my hair.

I did not meet his eyes. For the first time in my life, I felt shy with a man beside me.

"I would agree, Uncle. God would have a sense of humor. But He does not exist."

We sat in silence for a long moment before he spoke. "Never call me that again."

"No," I said. "I will not."

He reached out then, and took my hand. It was a simple gesture, and a natural one, fed not by lust or by fire but by the need to be known. By the need to acknowledge that we had both been alone for many years, until we laid eyes on each other. We could not speak of it, then or ever, so we did not. I saw that, like me, he was a man raised to necessity. He, too, saw the world as it was. He, too, had been forced to remake his world many times over, as I had when I married Louis, as I would again, when I forced Louis to set me free.

I knew with utter certainty that I could not stay married to Louis any longer.

"I thought to speak of politics with you before I saw your face," he said. "I thought to sway you to support me against the kingdom of Edessa, where the Saracens have taken the city from my friend."

"I will do all that," I said. "I will support you with Louis, and with anyone else."

"I know."

"So we need not discuss it further."

"Not tonight."

He still held my hand. "Did you like the figs I sent you, and the wine?"

"I thought Louis sent them," I said.

"No," Raymond answered. "They are my wife's favorites."

"Ah."

"Yes," he said. "We are both bound to another. But you already know that."

"I will soon be free," I said.

I spoke for the first time in my life without fear of who might hear me. It was as if, with him beside me, nothing could ever touch me, nor harm me, nor make me less than whole. I was Alienor of Aquitaine.

Raymond kissed my hand, and his lips were like a brand on my skin. But their heat did not burn me. I did not pull away.

"I will never be free," he said.

"I know that, too."

I turned and met his eyes for the first time that night. He saw me smile. In the moonlight, he was as fair as I was.

"We both accept the world as it is," he said.

"Yes," I said. "I would not want to live in any other."

His smile answered mine. The sight of it warmed my heart, even as it broke it.

"Nor would I."

He stood, and I stood with him. He kissed me once, carefully, his lips closed over mine. I did not kiss him back, but stood still; if I moved to meet him, neither of us could stop what happened next. So I would stop it, by never beginning.

We were both short of breath as he stepped away. He did not want to let go of my hand. I watched him struggle; I saw once more that, like me, he was a man of discipline. Otherwise, he would never have been king.

"Until tomorrow, then," he said.

"Until tomorrow."

He melted once more into shadow. I never knew what door he used to come to me, for I never saw it.

I went to bed that night, but I did not sleep, nor did I

feel the need of it. Amaria lay heavy, snoring beside me, but I could not hear her. I could hear only the wind as I breathed in the scent of roses that still clung to my hair.

❧

The next morning, I sent a coded message to Stefan in Rome. I had made up my mind, and I would have my will. I would ask not just for the annulment to sanctify Petra's marriage. I would ask for the annulment of my marriage to the King of France.

Of course, all this must be secret. I must be careful as I made the moves on the chessboard of my life, the moves that would one day set me free. My bribes to the Holy Father in Rome and to his bishops would have to be kept buried in the dark. Louis and his Parisians could not hear of it until I was ready for them to know it. For a woman to set herself free from a king had never been done. Many kings had set their wives aside, and many would again, but never before had a queen set herself free from her husband because she desired it. I would be the first.

Raymond came to me early with a retinue in tow. He brought both Louis' men and my women, and sent word beforehand that he would call on me in my garden. So we sat on the same bench, but this time in sunlight, with our count-less chaperones ranged around us. My husband was not one of them.

Raymond heard my question before I spoke it. "His Maj-esty King Louis has gone to visit a shrine outside the city. He sends his warmest regards, and asks that I look after your welfare while he is away."

"And how long will he be gone?"

"Until sunset. He must be back by then. I have told him so. I can only hope that he will heed me."

"Sunset? Is that the witching hour?"

Raymond smiled, and I saw a hint of his true self behind his eyes. But it was the courtier who answered me.

"No, my lady queen. That is the hour when the Saracens are on the move. Sunset, and just after dawn."

"But surely we are safe from them here," I answered. I did not smile, and I kept the irony from my voice. "This is a Christian kingdom."

I saw the amusement in Raymond's eyes, though his face was grave. "It is, lady. We fight hard to keep it so. But the roads are dangerous. I would not leave the keep past sunset."

"And what of before? Might we not ride out on a hunt?"

I had been in the saddle for so long that staying indoors made me feel trapped. This was true even in the beautiful garden Raymond had given me. I still had not met his wife.

"I would not take a woman hunting here. The larder is full. It will suffice. It is too dangerous to ride out. I would not be able to vouch for your safety."

I saw at once that he meant it. I let the matter drop.

"So perhaps we will stay indoors and play a game of chess, if your schedule permits," I said.

Raymond, Prince of Antioch, had many places to be, and many things to do other than hold court with me. I saw that he would do none of those things until Louis and I had set out on the road once more. He would stay with me, and I with him, for whatever time was left to us.

It would not be much, but we would savor what we could.

So we sat all that day, whiling away the hours as Louis prayed. We played game upon game of chess on the lapis and ebony set my husband had given me.

It was not long before our chaperones began to wander off, first to look at the rest of the garden, then to find amusement elsewhere. While chess interested us, and a few of Raymond's men, for my husbands' courtiers it held no power.

Amaria asked leave for my women to go, and I granted it, as long as they stayed in the keep. If they left it, they must take an armed escort with them. The city bazaar called to them, for they had gold to spend. Here in the East, there was much to spend it on.

I asked Amaria to fetch me a bolt of deep blue silk, and a silver belt, if one was to be had. She curtsied, something she never did when we were alone, and went to do my bidding.

So Raymond and I sat among the flowering trees, and played yet one more game of chess on the set from Byzantium.

"I have sent a man to Rome," he said. "He left last night, after we spoke."

"Indeed." I raised one brow. "And why would you do this? Did you feel a sudden surge of piety? You might have sent a man to Jerusalem instead, and saved yourself a great deal of expense."

Raymond smiled at me, and I was reminded that we were alone. "I did not send the man with prayers, but with gold. And I did not send him for myself. I sent him for you."

The wind in the trees whispered to me, but I could not

understand its language. I raised my head from the board in front of us and met his eyes. He was staring at my face as if he would drink it in.

"You take a liberty," I said.

"I do what must be done. My man will speak with the bishops there about dissolving your marriage, and setting you free."

I am not sure why, but his high-handedness did not anger me, as it would have from any other man. It made me want him more. The connection between us had blossomed in the night, and now simply sitting alone with him filled me with desire. That day, Raymond had not once so much as touched my hand.

"I have a man in Rome already," I said.

The light of the late-afternoon sun caught his hair, making it gleam russet and gold. The blue of his eyes reached out and cradled me, as if I were defenseless and needed his protection, all the while acknowledging to both of us that I was not and never would be. Raymond accepted what I was, and who, as no other man ever had, save my father before him.

"Now you have two."

I let the matter drop. I had sent word to Stefan just that morning. I would have my annulment if it took all the gold I possessed, and the rest of my life.

I raised my queen. "Checkmate."

Raymond laughed, the warm sound filling that walled garden. It was as if even the roses turned, that they might hear him better. I did not lean closer, though I wanted to. What my laughter did to men, Raymond's laughter did to me.

"We must go out among the others, Alienor. There is food in the hall, and music. Come and be my guest."

"And your wife's?"

His smile did not falter, but neither did he take my hand. "Yes. Come and meet Constance. I think she will like you."

The hall in Antioch was beautiful and open, larger than the great hall at Louis' palace in Paris. Its vaulted ceiling of white plaster arched above our heads, held in place by carved cedar beams. Its windows rose as high as that ceiling, and opened out onto the gardens beyond. Pomegranate bushes and date trees whispered together in the wind beyond the hall, and the scent of flowers drifted in on the warm evening breeze from the sea. The floors were done in mosaics of many shades, lapis and vermilion and saffron, outlining fantastical dragons and horses with wings. I walked over them slowly, watching every step, their colors like jewels beneath my feet. Those bits of colored glass were works of art, too beautiful to be on a floor.

When I finally raised my eyes, I caught Raymond smiling at me. The East made me feel like a country girl as no place ever had. I found I enjoyed it, seeing each new thing and taking it in. I wondered how I might make such things, like baths and tiled floors, come to pass in Aquitaine.

I was seated on Raymond's right side at the high table, which was made of mahogany inlaid with mother-of-pearl. Louis, who had just returned to the palace from his day of prayer and fasting, sat on Raymond's left. My husband nodded gravely to me from beyond my uncle's shoulder. The Parisians were talking low among themselves of how Raymond and I had been closeted alone for most of that day. Let them talk. One day, I would be free of them all.

I drank the sweet wine from Cyprus I had come to love and listened as Raymond's queen spoke at my right hand. She was a sweet thing, and quiet, except when she was praising her husband. I could see that she loved him, from the way her dark brown eyes shone when she spoke of him. When she could, Constance would glance at him past my shoulder, in small sips, as if he were a favorite dish that might be taken away if someone saw her looking.

Raymond's men, many from Poitou, had come to join him in the Levant and make their fortunes. They savored the taste of the langue d'oc on their tongues as I did. Louis frowned to hear it spoken, but for once, I did not heed and cajole him. I let him be.

The music was of Poitou as well. I felt as if I sat in my father's great hall once more as I closed my eyes and listened to it. But there was Eastern music as well, some blend of Christian, Saracen, Greek, and Frank that I had never heard before. Had I not known better, I would have said that I had fallen under an enchantment.

My women laughed and flirted with the dark-skinned men in Raymond's court, some darkened by sun, others by birth. The men seemed to find joy among the Eastern women as well, for in Raymond's court, the sexes mingled as they always had at home. He was no potentate with a harem here. He was simply a fair-haired, golden god who sat on his dais and let all who pleased come and worship him.

His troubadour sang to me, of my beauty and wit. I could

tell plainly that it was a standard song in that court, with my name slipped into the verse, as would have been done in Aquitaine. The men and women of the hall applauded as if the song were newly minted and had never been heard before. I smiled graciously, and sent the singer a sack of gold. Louis glowered to see me pay the man so openly and so well, but by now he should be used to my ways.

The Parisians frowned like thunder, unhappy since our arrival in Antioch. Now that I would be free, I found that their glowers had no power over me. Let them sulk. Let them return to Paris, to their rainy streets and their dark, smoky halls. I would wait for my divorce here in Antioch, among my own people.

I made that decision suddenly, sitting beside Raymond at his board. As soon as I had the thought, his hand caught mine beneath the table and gave it one swift squeeze.

He was talking and laughing again in the next moment, his hand once more aboveboard, his eyes on the company. I took his lesson, and smiled on his wife, offering her choice bits of fruit from the plate near my hand as if I were mistress there, though I sat in her castle, with her husband beside me.

Chapter 21

❧

City of Antioch

Kingdom of Antioch
March 1148

ALMOST TEN DAYS LATER, LOUIS CAME TO VISIT ME IN MY rooms. My ladies were braiding my hair in an elaborate Eastern style for the feast that night, and I was wearing a new gown of dark blue silk for which I had sent Amaria to the market. My new silver belt gleamed in the light of the lamps. Now that Raymond was near, I took pleasure in my beauty once more, as if it had been returned to me, newly polished. I could see Raymond took joy in it whenever he was with me.

It seemed that I was not the only one to notice Raymond's joy. Louis' people had seen it, too.

Louis came into my rooms alone but for his confessor, Francis. His other churchmen, the kindly Matthew and the quiet Gilbert, had been left outside.

I had spent the week in idle joy, visiting with Raymond and his men from Poitou, drinking in the East even as I spoke with the men on how to make war against the Saracens in Edessa. I had broached this subject with Louis twice already, asking him to lend some of his knights to support Raymond. Both times I asked, I had been rebuffed. My power with Louis had fallen low since the massacre, and I had little influence left to sway him.

I told Raymond in private that I would call on my men in the Aquitaine to come and serve with him if they desired, once my marriage was annulled. Raymond said that by then it would be too late. The French must move with him against Edessa, and move now, or the Turks, Nur ad-Din's men, would overrun the country of Antioch as they had Edessa in the north.

I sympathized, though there was little I could do. I planned to ask Louis yet one more time, though I was certain of the answer already. If I had been in doubt of what that answer would be, one look at Louis' face as he stepped into my borrowed chambers would have reminded me. I was on thin ice with him already. I must step carefully, that I might not slip beneath the floes, and drown.

I had been lax in my politics since coming to Antioch, but I had not known how lax until the sight of Louis' eyes brought it home to me.

I reached at once for the nearest rosary, a beautiful piece Raymond had given me of gold, diamonds, amethysts, and pearls. He had had it remade from a set of Saracen prayer beads, and had thought to give it me when he believed I was a pious woman, come on Crusade to save my soul. Once he met

me, and saw his own soul in my eyes, he gave it to me anyway, that it might be a bond between us. I took it up now, and
crossed myself, looking suddenly grave, sending my women
away.

"My lord king, have you come to me for evening prayers?"
I asked. "Let us kneel together and be shriven, since you bring
your confessor."

Brother Francis nodded to me, his paunch great beneath
his penitent's robes. He was one for outward show in religion,
as I was. Enemies though we were, we understood each other.

"Have you done something to be shriven for, Eleanor?"

Louis did not move his eyes from my face. He had heard
the wild rumors of my connection with Raymond. I saw that
he thought us lovers already.

I kept my face smooth, the blank mask my father had
trained into me. I knew who I was, and what I wanted. But
to get it, I would have to pay better attention to the world
around me. I was not free of Louis yet.

"No, my lord king. Only the daily sins that all flesh is
heir to."

"Like fornication?" Francis asked.

It was a clumsy move, and a foolish one. It turned Louis'
attention from me, and from my sins, imagined and otherwise. To speak so to a crowned queen was not permitted,
even so far from Paris. Francis saw his mistake at once, but by
then it was too late.

Louis did not speak, but stared him down.

I forced my voice into a soft tone, for I was my lord's obedient wife. "God forbid, Brother Francis."

Francis would have said something else, but Louis raised one hand to dismiss him. "Amen," the king said.

Brother Francis had the sense to back out of the room then, and close the door behind him. But I did not relax my guard. I had not won with Louis, if I could ever truly win a battle with him again.

"Have you played me false, Eleanor? With another man, or in any other way?"

I went to Louis and for the second time in my life, for the second time in half a year, I knelt to him. "No, my lord king. I swear before God, I am your faithful wife."

Louis gave me his hand, and helped me rise. He hated to see me abase myself, and I knew then that he had not truly believed the rumors that surrounded me. He pulled me close, his hand at my waist, the other in my elaborately styled hair.

"Thank God," he said, as if at prayer. "I knew it. I knew it was not true."

I drew back, for I could not bear his touch. Raymond was too near. I could not press myself against Louis, and think of the man I could not have.

"My lord, I must confess. My heart is troubled."

Louis' face darkened. "Why, Eleanor?"

I took his hand and brought him to sit beside me on my bed. He was roused, and I knew it, but I feigned ignorance, for I knew he would not touch me.

He had taken a solemn vow not to take me in the marriage bed until he had been blessed at the Holy Sepulchre in Jerusalem. I saw now that he had turned from the war he had hoped to win. His army was in shambles, the war lost before it had even started. Louis prayed now only for a son. A year before, I would have prayed with him, and meant it, had I a god to pray to. Now I wanted only to be free.

"We have no son, my lord. I fear it is my sin that makes this so."

"No, Eleanor."

The man who had come with his priest to force a confession of adultery from my lips now rose and stood over me like an angel avenging my benighted honor.

"Eleanor, you are a godly woman. I would not have thought to come to the Holy Land but for you. You are my wedded wife, and blessed before God. We will go to Jerusalem, and God will free me from my sin. And once He has done that, we will have a son."

I was careful to frame my speech in language that Louis would understand. I called on God, for Louis always heeded Him. "My lord king, I fear that God has turned His Face from me. I fear that He has cast me aside, and that now you must cast me aside also."

Louis turned away from me. He paced across the deep handwoven carpet almost to the door. I thought for one moment that he might leave the room altogether. When he stayed, I hoped that he had heard my words. And so he had, but he rejected all I said.

He was praying silently to his god, there in my borrowed rooms, words to a god who did not hear him, or at best would not heed him. I was done with Louis and all his praying. But I could not leave him yet. I must plant this seed, and water it to make it grow. Tonight was only the beginning.

"You must leave me behind in Antioch, my lord. Go to Jerusalem, be shriven, and cast your sins on God. Then go to Rome and ask for our annulment. You must be free, my lord king. France must have a son." I spoke fervently, as fervently as I had spoken a year ago for him to keep me.

I saw then that Louis wept. I went to him, and took his hand in mine. I kissed him, not as a wife, but as a mother who would soothe all his hurts, and heal him, if only she could.

"Forgive me, Eleanor. I am unmanned."

I lied once more. "You could never be."

I still held the rosary Raymond had given me, a prop to shore up my false piety; I pressed it into Louis' palm. Let him have the joy of it.

"Louis, take this rosary, given me by my uncle who loves you. Pray for our marriage in Jerusalem. Pray for us, that we might know the will of God. Only you can do it, Louis. You and no other."

My husband kissed me, and held me close. I think he knew it, too; the road we walked together had ended. That was why he wept. Our marriage was over.

But it did not take him long to deny that knowledge, even to himself.

"Eleanor, come down with me to dinner. We will eat your uncle's food and drink his wine. But on the morrow, we will leave this place. We will go forth to Jerusalem together, so that we might know the will of God, and be shriven of our sins. There is no sin so great that God cannot cure us of it."

I knew that to answer with my true thoughts would

be my undoing. Instead, I pressed my lips to his cheek, the words I spoke then yet one more lie between us.

"Let it be so," I said. "Let it be with us as God has wrought."

"Amen," Louis answered.

He took me down to dinner that night, and I drank in the sights and sounds of Antioch for the last time. For I knew that, in this, Louis was determined. We would take to the road once more, in his endless quest to find a god that ran ever before him, elusive, fleet, a dove of peace that could never be caught.

❊

I woke in the dead of night to men banging on the door of my room. Amaria had locked it, as a matter of course. She was on her feet in an instant, her dagger in her hand, her long braid trailing down her back. I rose to my feet more slowly. By the time I had wrapped a shawl of silk around my shoulders, Amaria had opened the door, for it was Louis who called for me.

"Eleanor, we leave for Jerusalem."

"Louis, you can't be serious. It is the middle of the night."

"It is three hours before dawn. Your women must pack your things and follow behind us if they cannot be ready in time. We ride out in half an hour."

"Louis, I will not leave my uncle and his Poitevins without a word. You go on, and I will follow with my women in a few days' time."

"No!"

Louis shouted that one word, his voice filling my rooms,

spilling out into the marbled corridor. No doubt Raymond's people heard it all, but they stayed away.

Never before had Louis screamed at me like any furious husband. Never before had I felt the helplessness of being a wife, tied completely to the dangerous whims of a man. I took a breath to speak, but Louis shouted once more.

"You will come with me now, Eleanor. You will not delay even one minute more. You will leave at my side, this very hour, or by God, I will call up my men who stand outside this keep and they will tear it down, brick by brick, and burn it all, until there is nothing left but ash."

I saw in the blaze of his blue eyes that he would do it. His jealous passion gave him a forcefulness he never had shown me in our marriage before, neither in bed nor anywhere else. My husband had taken on the look of a zealot. I wondered in that moment if he had worn that look always. Only now, in the midst of one of the worst pains of my life, could I finally see it.

I did not see or speak to Raymond before we fled. Louis' army was three leagues away from Antioch by sunrise. Though I turned back toward the city from the litter where Louis had imprisoned me, I could not see it. By the time the light had risen, we were too far gone already. All I saw were white distant hills, and the blue sky, arching above them.

Chapter 22

❧

City of Acre

Kingdom of Jerusalem
April 1149

THE NEXT YEAR WAS INTERMINABLE. LOUIS TRAVELED FROM Jerusalem, to Damascus, to Acre, and back again. After our flight from Antioch, Louis had abandoned his usual passivity. Dragging me from my uncle's keep in the dead of night had charged him with a fire I had never seen in him before. He was suddenly determined to make good on his promises to the pope for a great Christian victory. To have more to show from this campaign than a series of defeats. He fought one battle outside Damascus, and declared it a victory for God, though to my jaundiced eye, it looked more like a truce.

And though Louis visited shrine upon shrine in the months both before and after this one battle, I was not privy to what he prayed for. Once I would have sworn that Louis was petitioning God to cleanse him of sin and to give him a son. But now, looking on him as he knelt, I often wondered if he prayed for victory, both in war and over me.

Louis won nothing as far as I could tell, but he seemed to enjoy himself. He and the Parisians were full of fire after leaving Antioch, and seemed once more to be assured of their God, and of their place in His world. Namely, at the head of it.

As for me, I knelt when expected and feigned a piety I did not feel, all the while waiting for Raymond to come to me, knowing that he could not. This was the other side of the sickness I had once thought an enchantment, a yearning for a joy that could never be. I waited for Raymond with bated breath, like a young girl for her lover, or like a nun for the touch of Christ. But he did not come.

I still had a rational, sensible portion of my mind left to me, a piece of me untouched by this enchantment. That piece waited, almost bored, until I might be freed from the hand of fate. It was odd indeed, to be divided against oneself. I wondered if this was how Louis felt, whenever he looked on me.

The Parisians all thought me a whore by this time, the castoff of my uncle, a woman who had to be dragged out of her lover's house in the dark of night. No matter what my people said to discount this, no matter how many oaths Amaria swore to the contrary, in this Louis' courtiers were intractable. After a while, I left off denying anything. Let the Parisians think what they would. I would be their queen no longer.

My man in Rome was still working. Stefan had secured my sister's annulment; Raoul of Vermandois was married in the eyes of God to Petra, now and for all eternity. I laughed in triumph when I got that news, savoring the victory that had been so hard-won. I sent word to Petra at once, wishing only that I could deliver the news to her myself.

This victory was double-edged, for it encouraged me to continue to seek my own annulment. I had secured Raoul's freedom; I strove now to secure my own. So Stefan turned from the matter of my sister's marriage to mine. He had to be discreet, for Louis was a crowned king, and I, his queen. In the past, annulments came not because the woman asked for it but because the man did. Stefan had to use his charm, but he also had to be cautious.

For now, he sat in Rome, pouring wine down the throats of bishops and cardinals, making friends wherever he went, but without too much bombast. He made certain that all the money he handed out looked discreet as well, as if that gold were donations to build new monasteries, or contributions to pet projects that each cardinal held dear. Stefan knew the inner workings of the Church, and how to use them. I bided my time, and left him to it.

Finally, Louis and his French tired of the Levant. I wondered for a few despairing moments if he would be caught in the web of the Holy Land as Raymond was. But unlike him, Louis had no kingdom to stay for. We turned at last to the port city of Acre, that we might take ship for Sicily.

I was to travel on a separate ship from Louis. He had been blessed in Jerusalem, but had still not come to my bed. I continued to pretend to pray, and to don the facade of a pious woman. I never brought up the idea of our annulment again.

I did not think Louis would come to my bed on board ship, but I needed to be sure. After my time with Raymond, and the interminable months since I had seen him, I had taken my fill of Louis. I could not spend a month or more at sea with him beside me.

Louis indulged me in this as he did in all things that did not matter. So we sat in the palace at Acre, locked away in our separate rooms, Louis at prayer, me with my women. In the end, I sent all my women away.

I would not go to the great hall that last night in the Levant, but my women wanted to go to the feast. Each of them could feel the ties that bound them rising to circle them once more. What a woman might do under my protection in the East, far from home, was one thing. What a woman could do at court under the watchful eye of her husband or her father was quite another. I let my women leave me, to make merry while they might.

I sat alone with Amaria beside me in the garden attached to my borrowed rooms. Here, I had a view of the sea. The waves crashed below the palace walls, and I could hear the call of the gulls.

There were roses in that garden, too, Persian roses that climbed their arbors in brilliant colors of red, yellow, and white. I sat beneath them and took in their scent. The perfume of those flowers and the sound of the sea cocooned me. Amaria left me, so that I might sit alone.

He came out of nowhere, as he always did. I thought at first he was an apparition, that my mind had truly broken with the world. Then I saw his cloak thrown over his gold and russet hair, and Amaria standing behind him. She had let him in.

I did not ask how he had slipped past my husband's people. So many men fought under so many different banners in that place. Acre was one of the ports used by all Christian armies, and all men went through there at one time or another, many under false names, many of whom did not want to be known. As long as they paid in gold, no one asked questions. It was one of the things coin bought easily in that place: discretion.

Still, I knew that to come here was folly. He had risked his life and his kingdom to be alone with me.

Amaria left us. I knew that she would guard the door. No one watched me that night, for no one thought that I could get up to mischief one step from the quayside.

Raymond did not speak but came to me, his cloak falling onto the crushed seashells of the path behind him. He took me up in his arms without a word. There had never been a need for words between us. I pressed myself against him, thinking that he might feel for a brief moment like Louis, or that his muscled arms would remind me of the Baron Rancon. But they did not. When Raymond touched me, there was only him.

We had scarcely touched before. That one kiss in the garden on our first night was all that had passed between us. Occasionally, he had touched my hand, or our fingers brushed in the midst of a chess game, but that was all. That night, our restraint fell away. We had only those few hours to fill our lives to come. We took them, and gladly.

His lips were sweet, sweeter than I had thought they would be, soft, like the rose petals I bathed in. He tasted of mead, and warm honey. I pressed myself against him and he drew back long enough to laugh a little. There had never been laughter in Louis' bed. I had not known that I missed it.

I laughed, too, and tasted him again, but I did not lead for long. He savored me, as if I were the finest wine, and I drank him in, as if I could never get enough.

His body was firm and lean beneath my hands, but well muscled, from his time on the tiltyard and at war. He held the country of Antioch by the strength of his sword arm, while Louis held his lands through the strength of his barons, and through his marriage to me. I had never thought that such a difference mattered. But I had never before had a man touch me like Raymond of Antioch.

So the Parisians were right. Raymond and I would be lovers at last. It was something else to make me laugh, before he carried me into the bedroom beyond the garden we stood in.

Amaria had been there before us. Candles were lit on every surface, giving out soft pools of light, softer than any oil lamps or braziers filled with charcoal. Those candles made me think of the wedding night I never had, one a woman always longs for, even a woman born to a life of power. Even me.

Raymond drew my blue gown off me, and then the soft linen of my scented shift. I melted beneath his touch, and burned with the hottest, brightest flame of my life.

He took his own clothes off, and stood before me, tall

and proud, his scars drawn white against the tanned muscles of his arms. All his scars were on the front of his body. He led every charge he rode in.

Before Raymond lay down beside me, he caught my hand in his. We were not swept away by our madness. We did not rule it, but neither did it rule us.

The heat rose between us, like a flame that would never go out. But still, he waited. Though his deep blue eyes burned with it, he did not touch me.

"Say my name," he said, as if asking one last time for permission. I did not hesitate.

"Raymond of Poitou. Raymond of Antioch. Come here to me."

He rose on one knee and I drew him down beside me on that bed of silk. He kissed me again, and it was as if I were being kissed for the first time. The years of cold and loss in Louis' court, the courtiers who despised me, the child I had buried, the daughter I barely knew. All lay far distant the night he was with me. There was only he and I, alone together.

"I will love you, and no other, until my days pass from this earth," he said as he lay on the bed beside me.

I answered him, though before that day I never would have sworn such an oath. It was the madness that took me. That night, there was only Raymond, his skin soft on my lips as I kissed his chest, his heart beating over mine as he listened for my voice.

"And I will love you," I said, "until my life is done."

Our passion spent, he lay beside me until the hour before dawn when the deep indigo of the sky began to turn to gray. Neither of us had slept. We talked, trying to make up for all the years we had been apart, for all the years that would soon divide us.

I think he had some vain hope that I would leave Acre with him. That like some princess in a German fable, I would desert my husband and my lands, and fly with him to an unknown fate. He did not ask it of me, so I did not have to refuse.

He is with me still. That is what fated love means in the end. The hand of fate lies heavy on us, to show us the ones who will never leave us, the ones we will carry for the rest of our lives. And beyond, if the priests are right.

Though I do not believe in words like *forever*, I did when I looked into the blue of his eyes. I was grateful for that one night, carved out of the rest of my life. Those hours were worth the pain I paid for them, both before and after.

For nothing in this world comes free.

PART IV

To Be Known

Chapter 23

❦

City of Palermo

Kingdom of Sicily
September 1149

LOUIS KISSED ME AT THE QUAYSIDE IN THE PORT OF ACRE, and sailed before me. I watched his ship until it was out of sight; then I stepped onto my own. The tide was turning, and we needed to be gone.

I stood on the deck of that ship, rented at a high price from King Roger of Sicily, as my ladies sat below in their cabin. I was alone but for Amaria, who stood at my side. Raymond was like a dream gone at morning, but I felt his eyes on me as I stood upon the deck of King Roger's ship.

I watched until the city of Acre dwindled into nothing. I never saw Raymond, but I knew he was there. I felt his presence, as Louis so often claimed to feel the presence of God. Perhaps, in the end, I was as misguided as Louis was.

Night rose, and the sea rose with it. I went below for a few hours, but slept little. My ladies woke when I did, a few hours before dawn, but they soon went down into the belly of the ship again. The Middle Sea was a place that turned away the faint of heart. A great wind rose, and blew us off course. I welcomed it, for I did not want to step on land again, and see Louis standing there, waiting for me.

When we were two weeks at sea, I saw that we were lost in earnest. My women fell silent, their voices quieted by fear. I saw the most pious among them at prayer, and the worldly ones fingered their rosaries, their eyes turned always to the horizon, looking for land. I welcomed the deep waves and the swelling troughs that rose around us. I wanted freedom from the world as I had known it. If I could not stay in the Levant, I wanted to enter a new world altogether.

Our ship landed not in a new world but in Sicily more than a week later. We had been blown well off course, and came ashore not at Calabria, as Louis had, but at the port of Palermo. But even once we reached the Norman kingdom of Sicily, it was not a simple matter to come to land, for when we reached the waters close by Palermo, the Emperor of Byzantium's ships came upon us out of nowhere.

I laughed out loud when I saw Manuel's standard flying, thinking at first that the Byzantines meant only to greet us as we swept in from the sea. I laughed harder when I saw that they meant to take my ship. I was justified in my mistrust of Emperor Manuel yet again.

The Sicilians on board our ship were brave. They would have died to a man before letting the emperor's navy take me. But just as the imperial sinking catapults were turned on us, King Roger of Sicily's ships sailed up from the city, and fought off Manuel's navy.

I watched all this as a spectator only. I could not feel myself involved in the proceedings, though my very life was at stake. For all I knew, Louis' churchmen had paid the emperor well and in gold to see to it that I never made it back to my husband's side. It would have been like the Church, with their womanish ways, to pay others to commit their murders for them.

I was a woman. I should know.

If Brother Francis and his ilk paid for my death, they lost their money that day, for King Roger's ships took me under their protective wing as a mother hen shields her chicks from the hawk. The emperor's men must not have wanted me all that badly, for after a few parting volleys that went wide, they sailed away, heading for the open sea.

I came off ship at Palermo, knowing that King Roger would not be there to greet me. Of course, he was inland, running his court, as I myself should be. He held his land by the skin of his teeth. Sicily was a Norman conquest, but was full of bandits and rebels, with the Saracens across the Middle Sea in Africa, waiting always for the opportunity to raid the coast. Unlike myself, he could not leave his court to go on Crusade, or to seek his pleasure elsewhere. As my feet touched dry land once more, the hot plains of Sicily made me long for the verdant greens of the Aquitaine and Poitou. I had been gone too long already.

I fell ill from a sweating sickness, though I had never before been sick in my life. The sweltering plains of Sicily brought this sickness to my ladies as well, but it was worse with me. I was laid low with it for a week before we could move inland. I spent those days in a sort of twilight, in which my fever made me forget the past. I thought that Raymond was still with me, just a step away in the next room. I did not call for him, but I wanted to. That alone showed how weak I was.

My faithful Amaria guarded me, her dagger in its sheath on her wrist. She would not let any of King Roger's women attend me. Seeing all my food and water tasted, she fed me from her own hand.

After a week, I was in my own mind once more, and strong enough to travel, albeit slowly and by litter, inland to Roger's capital of Potenza. It took three weeks to make a journey that normally could be accomplished in two days. At the end of it, I was on my feet once more, if only barely.

At King Roger's keep at Potenza, I rose from my litter, Amaria gripping my hand. Louis and his confessor, Brother Francis, stood in the courtyard of Roger's palace, waiting for me. Amaria was angry that Louis had not come to me on the coast, to save me a journey in the midst of my illness. She loved me, almost to distraction. She did not understand that the King of France never put himself in danger of infection to travel to the side of another, not even his queen.

I stepped toward Louis under my own power. When I released her hand, I could feel Amaria's irritated displeasure as clearly as I felt the hot sun in the sky. She said nothing, but let me go.

"Eleanor. When your ship did not land at Calabria, I feared you were dead," Louis said.

Tears rose in my husband's watery blue eyes. I reached for him, and took his hand, as I would have taken a child's. I stood close to him, and let him hold me up. Only as I leaned against him did he see how weak I was.

"You have been ill," he said. "I am sorry."

I forced a smile. "I am mending now, Louis. But I had better get out of this sun."

"Yes."

And in the next moment, the King of France swept me up into his arms. I had lost a good deal of weight with the sea voyage and my long illness, but Louis' strength, so rarely seen, struck me dumb. He carried me into Roger's keep, and all our people, his and mine, moved quickly out of his way. He strode without speaking to a room deep in the interior of the castle. There was a little sunlight coming in from an open window, but the room was cooled by its thick stone walls.

Louis laid me gently on a feather bed, a bed far too soft for such a savage court. I missed the Levant already. I had grown used to the ever-running fountains and the rose gardens, the fresh fruit and the cold water. I would have to accustom myself to Europe once more.

We were alone, for Louis had closed the door of the bedroom behind him. I thought for a moment that he might have me on that bed, for his face was flushed with his exertion and his love for me. Whether he turned from me because of his sin or mine, or because of my long illness, he did not lie down beside me. Instead, Louis knelt at my bedside, lifting one of my hands to the softness of his lips.

"I love you, Eleanor. I prayed for you every day, while you were away."

I could not give Louis the answer he longed for, so I stayed silent. Even now, my men waited outside the door to report on the progress Stefan had made in Rome, to tell me whether or not the pope would set me free.

"You are a good man, Louis," I said. "Too good a man to be married to me."

"I am a sinner, Eleanor. You are my idol, and if I do not stay in constant prayer and fasting, I will burn for the sin of idolatry, when I am taken from the earth."

I considered the idea that Louis had set me up as an idol, and worshipped me without touching me for most of the years of our marriage. If that was true, it must have been worse torment for him than our marriage had been for me, because he was a pious man who could not even take the steps necessary to fulfill his own prayers for a son.

I caressed my husband's hair. We were not even thirty yet. Once I had left him, God might yet grant Louis a son. I believed in nothing, and in no god, but I hoped for Louis' sake that it would be so. For myself, I longed only to be gone from the Parisian court, and from him.

I gathered my strength and smiled. I had a long road to walk before I could go home again.

"Thank you for your prayers, Louis. If God listens to anyone, He listens to you."

Louis did not chastise me for my blasphemy. No doubt he marked it down as a shadow of my fevered brain. He kissed me, and left me then, so that my women could attend me. They brought cool cloths with which to bathe me, and wine sweetened with fruit. I recognized the Cypriot wine that I had first drunk in Emperor Manuel's palace, the wine I had come to love during my time with Raymond.

I drank that wine, and ate some honeyed dates, though I had no appetite. I had to gather my strength. More than Louis waited for me outside that door. His Parisians waited, too, and his churchmen. I must face them that night at King Roger's board. No matter how sick I was, or how tired, I must go on. They could not be allowed to see my weakness.

❈

Amaria drew a box from among my things, a box I had never before seen. Within it lay cosmetics, vermilion and lapis lazuli, powdered rose petals and kohl. I had never used such things, but I looked at my face, as gray as death, in the bronze mirror Amaria held up for me. Tonight would be the first time. Dressed in cloth of gold, with a bronze and silver belt at my waist, I stood while Amaria fastened my thin gold veil with the diadem of the Aquitaine. No doubt Louis' people would think less of me for it, and whisper evil tidings behind my back for not wearing the crown of France.

But I had long become accustomed to Parisians speaking evil of me, behind my back and to my face. I needed only to maintain my balance long enough to eat Roger's food without choking on it. It had been weeks since I sat among Louis' courtiers. After my journey and long illness, I knew I was not ready. I also knew that I had to be.

Louis himself led me into Roger's hall. The great stone walls were of Norman design, without even the grace of the vaulting I had so often seen in Paris. Here this castle was meant to be seen as it was: a fortress against the enemy. It was also a fortress against air and light.

I stood in the doorway of that great hall, looking at the gray stone walls that seemed to enclose me like a fist, and I almost faltered. I thought to turn back, to run to my room like a child, or a fool. Louis held my hand, and looked into my eyes. He stepped between me and all those who observed us, so that they might not see my face.

"Eleanor, are you all right? Do you need to lie down again?"

The soft sweetness in his voice was almost my undoing. Why had this man not come to my bed? Why, after so many years, had we never had a son? Why had he never become the man he was born to be?

Even these thoughts were weakness, which I pushed away. I caught my breath, and smiled. "No, Louis. I will stand, with you beside me."

This one phrase caught his ear, and his face opened as a flower in sunlight. He led me proudly then among his people, and seated me at the high table, between himself and the King of Sicily.

The Parisians frowned at this. I saw Brother Francis, Louis' confessor, whisper low to the churchman beside him.

I ignored all these people, and offered my host my hand. Roger took it gracefully. Gracious in speech as well, he made me welcome, though I did not hear his words. I drank from the wine at table. The alcohol did not fortify me, but made me dizzy, so I set the cup aside. I kept the false smile on my face, until it felt almost real.

The meat came in then, course after course of it. I took as little as was seemly, and Louis covered over my lack of appetite, praising the cook highly, though as far as I could tell, the clod did not deserve it. Thoughts of Raymond's table filled my mind, the succulent fruits, the light pastries, the honeyed almonds and dates. The year I had spent in the Levant apart from Raymond had faded as mist when sunlight hits it. All I could see, as I gazed at that stone hall in Sicily, were the wide avenues of Antioch, and the gracious fluted columns of Raymond's palace.

As if I had conjured him with my thoughts, someone spoke his name.

Brother Francis was seated at the high table, far above his station, for these things were overlooked in this foreign court as they never would have been in Paris. In Aquitaine, I would not have wanted Francis even in my hall. But among the Normans of Sicily, a lowborn peasant sat with kings simply because he was a well-placed priest. My wits sharpened just enough for me to think that once we returned to France, I must see to taking this churchman down. For everywhere I turned, he was there, mocking me.

Francis was mocking me now, though his smile was deferent, though he spoke Raymond's name with a sham of respect. I heard the contempt behind his words. No doubt everyone else did as well. Everyone save Louis.

"And the Turks rise once more in Edessa," Francis said. "The Emperor Manuel of Byzantium will have to go in and subdue them."

"No doubt the kingdom of Antioch will welcome the assistance," I said by way of dismissal.

The priest's eyes gleamed in the lamplight. He savored his next words as he spoke them.

"No doubt they will," Francis said. "Now that their prince is dead."

I was not sure, but I thought that I heard laughter somewhere in the hall. A woman's laugh, quick, high-pitched, and easily silenced. I listened hard after it faded, but it seemed I could hear nothing else. My mind had stopped, and my ears had fallen deaf, though Francis talked on, his mouth moving in mock sympathy, sympathy flavored with dark delight.

My mind was slow to take in the knowledge, and my heart lagged far behind.

Raymond was dead.

Francis went over the old tale there in my hearing, for old it was by now. With no one to fight with him, in June Raymond had gone to Edessa to negotiate with the Saracens there. On the road, he had been attacked; his men had fled or had died with him. Raymond fell, his head taken to be sold to the caliph in Edessa for gold. Francis told this story with such joy that no doubt he would have bid for Raymond's bloody corpse, had it been placed on sale at market.

"Well," the false priest concluded, "better men have died

at the hands of the Saracens. No doubt the Emperor Manuel will put that land to rights, once he is king in Antioch."

Roger made a gracious comment, and I could see he meant to silence my husband's priest. Louis turned to Francis and met his eyes unblinking. For the second time that day, I saw my husband's strength, and wondered what kind of man he might have made if my father had the training of him.

"You forget yourself, Brother Francis. You speak of my wife's uncle, and my own dear kinsman. Raymond of Antioch's passing is a great loss to all of Christendom. His sacrifice is not to be mocked, or gainsaid. He is in heaven now, at the foot of Our Lord, as all martyrs are, as we all one day hope to be." Louis laid his hand over mine as he spoke, but his eyes never left Francis.

The priest stood and bowed, and moved as if to kneel, but Louis raised one hand. "You may go. You are dismissed."

A black cloud of fury passed over Francis' face before his mask of righteous piety came to cover it. I would have laughed had my heart not been bleeding in my chest. Louis kept his hand over mine as Francis made his way from that foreign hall.

King Roger called for music then, and for some wine to go with the dancing, but my husband and I did not move from the dais. I sat for hours longer, my hand in Louis', looking on Roger's hall unseeing. All that came before my eyes was the sight of Raymond's golden hair, glinting in the sunlight, and the imagined sight of his bloody neck, sliced through by a Saracen's blade. I could see nothing but that red gold hair and the fair skin beneath it, colored in bright blood. But I did not weep. No good thing on this earth is meant to last.

Chapter 24

❧

Papal Villa

City of Rome
October 1149

WE TRAVELED NORTH TO THE PAPAL VILLA OUTSIDE ROME, where the pope waited to meet us. I lay still in my litter, the curtains drawn. My interest in wild, untamed country had faded.

I rode no horse, for Melusina, the beautiful white mare Louis had given me on our wedding day, had died while we were in Jerusalem. That she had walked so far with me on her back was a kind of miracle, Louis declared, though as far as I know, he never had his priests bottle and sell her blood as a relic. That is one kind of mercy, I suppose.

It was one of the darkest times of my life. Raymond was dead, left to the crows behind me. I lay alone in that great litter, as the bearers carried me ever closer to Rome.

Stefan waited for me there. In that city, I would make my next move in the game to set myself free. I must be awake and aware, fully alert, and ready for battle when I first set eyes on the Papal See. Pope Eugenius was just a man, a man who could be bought, as all men can. But as I lay adrift in that litter, I found I did not care if I never reached Rome, or ever saw Aquitaine again. It was the lowest point of my life, save for the day my father died.

If my father could see me laid so low, he would have stroked my hair, his wisdom and his calm conveyed to me in his gentle touch. Then he would have stood and said, "Alienor, I raised you to be stronger than this. Stand up. Live your life. Do what must be done."

I said these words to myself, over and over, expecting them at any moment to take hold of my mind, if not my heart. With each new hill town along the coast of Italy, I thought my mind would sharpen, that my heart would revive. They did not.

Amaria fed me teas and watered wine with bread soaked in it, as she would for someone dying. I was not dying, but I was not living either. As I rode ever closer to Rome and to my fate, I found that I did not have the energy to contemplate the future or the freedom I hoped for, much less to plan or fight for it. I was undone, and all of Louis' people traveling with us knew it.

It was Louis who came to me in the midst of my despair, as he had after my miscarriage. But this time I did not blame him for my losses or my pain. This time, my despair had nothing to do with him, so the sight of him did not gall me.

He sat beside my bed in the last abbey we stopped at on our way to Rome. The next morning would see us brought to the pope at his villa. We would be feasted and we would each be granted a papal audience, a time to confess our sins, air our grievances, and kiss the papal ring.

I could not think of it, of the reports I would hear from Stefan, briefing me on the lay of the land before me. I could not think of the battle to come. I, a lone woman, armed with nothing but my wit and the might of the Aquitaine, would come to the Vicar of Christ to barter for my life. This pope had already taken payment upon payment from my hands. But, as all good politicians, he had committed himself to nothing.

"Eleanor," Louis said. "It grieves me to see you so ill, and so out of heart. I have prayed for you constantly, but you do not seem to get any better."

I met his eyes, this man I had comforted and cajoled, manipulated and lied to, for almost thirteen years. He was a good man, and kind to me. His time in the Levant had not changed him, except inexplicably to make him love me more. His weakness still lay open for all to see, his unknown strengths hidden where I had never been able to reach them. Now that I had given up so completely on him and on our marriage both, I looked on Louis not as a husband or an enemy, but simply as a friend.

"You are good to pray for me," I said. "His Holiness will no doubt do the same, and I will be miraculously cured."

If Louis heard my jibe, he did not acknowledge it. He held my hand tighter, and kissed it, bringing it to his lips as he would a holy relic. I saw then that Louis would always love me, just as I loved Raymond, until his days passed from this earth. Just as I had not chosen Raymond, Louis had not chosen me. We were the same in this. Fate had not been kind to either of us.

I opened my arms to him, and Louis came up onto the bed. He clutched me close, but he did not draw me under him. Somewhere in his mind, unacknowledged and unlooked for since our time in Antioch, lay the truth that our marriage was over. Its death throes, long and painful, were upon us. They would one day subside, leaving us both with nothing.

Though I was full of sorrow, it was Louis who wept for both of us. His tears washed away some of my own pain, enough so that I could go on. Raymond was still lost. I would never look upon his face again. But Louis loved me enough to weep for me, as I could not weep for my own losses, that day or ever.

I found, as I held my husband in my arms, that it was enough. My heart began to heal. I began that night to do as my father would have instructed, had he been there. I began to rise from my living grave, to live my life, to go on. As we all must do, or perish utterly.

❁

His Holiness Pope Eugenius III was an urbane man of letters who greeted us inside his own gates with the aplomb of an emperor and the warmth of a priest. I knelt to him there in his courtyard, and kissed his ring. When I rose to meet his eyes, I found him smiling down on me, for he was a tall man, and full of fire. His brown eyes gleamed as he took in my form beneath the cloth of gold I wore. No man had looked at me so since Raymond, and I laughed out loud.

We were not alone, and all of Louis' Parisians frowned to hear my mirth. But Louis, rising from his own genuflection, turned to me with a smile.

"Praise God, Your Holiness. I thought to never hear her laugh again," he said.

"Indeed." Eugenius smiled. "And now you have."

I said nothing, but cast my eyes down in a false show of modesty, following His Holiness into his inner sanctum. Louis, ever the gentlemen, had allowed me to take my private audience first.

The pope and I walked in silence through empty gardens filled with jasmine and columbine, on paths lined with white marble that gleamed in the warm Italian sun. I raised my face to the light, loath to go inside to his rooms, as I knew we must.

Eugenius surprised me when he said, "Let us sit out here, between these fountains."

I sent a sharp glance toward him, and he smiled to acknowledge it. "We will be more alone here," he said. "These fountains will muffle the sound of our voices."

"So it will remain between us, all that we speak of," I said.

"Well," Eugenius answered, "between us and God."

His brown eyes gleamed with mirth, and I could not tell if he was baiting me with my faithlessness or acknowledging his own. He was the first man I had met, save those of my family, who looked to be my equal. I reserved judgment, and sat down on a marble bench when he bade me.

"Louis is a good man," Eugenius said.

"One of the best men I have ever known," I answered.

"And yet you wish to be free of him."

"Yes."

I thought for a moment to go into my long prepared speech of my own sin, of my fears that I was keeping the throne of France from a son and heir. But I saw that just as Stefan had reported to me, this pope had his own men hidden in my household. He knew that Louis would not touch me, on pain of death, and that this reason, more than anything, was why France had no son.

"You wish to be free to marry again," he said.

"No." I spoke without thinking. I took a breath, and chastised myself for foolishness. I was still on shaky ground. I had risen from my living grave, but I had not got my full strength back yet. I forced my eyes to his, and commanded my wits to be sharper. My life depended on this man, and what he chose to do with me.

"I may marry again, if that is God's will."

"But there is no one you have in mind at present," Eugenius said. "No man who calls to you, and bids you break your oath to your husband."

I met his eyes. For once, they were not smiling. "No," I answered. "There is no other man. Just as there is no son for France. Nor will be, I think, until Louis is free of me."

"So you plead for Louis' freedom?"

"And my own."

"But Louis has no wish to be free. He wishes to remain married to you, and to accept God's will in the matter of his son."

"Louis is young. It is all well and good to wait on God when one is eight and twenty. But when he is forty, and the wolves begin to circle, he will want a strong son to stand beside him, to hold them off. Whatever Louis is, whatever he hopes to be, he is king. A good king provides a son and heir for his people."

"I thought that was for you, his queen, to do."

"I have failed. I ask that Louis be given another queen, who will not."

"Such concern for people who hate you. I am sure the Parisians are touched by your hopes for their future."

I laid down my lies. I saw that Eugenius was not deceived by them. I could see nothing of his true thoughts, or his motivations. For all I knew, Louis' churchmen had been here before me, and had paid him for his judgment, just as I had.

If that was so, the truth would not harm me. And I had spent much gold lining the pockets of this man. Perhaps that gold, and the truth, would count for something with him. I had nothing else to bargain with, save my beauty. And in spite of what Louis' people said of me, I was no whore.

"I hate them as much as they hate me. But I would not curse them so, to leave them without an heir. I simply want to be gone. I wish to retire to my lands, and live out my life in peace."

"You would go to a nunnery, then, and leave your lands to France?"

I stood, my eyes blazing. All my father had taught me of hiding my true feelings while bargaining was gone like so much smoke.

"Never," I said. "Never, so long as I draw breath."

We stood facing each other like two enemies across a shield. I heard a bird singing somewhere in a hedge close by, and the wind in the tall fig trees, whispering above our heads. I stared Eugenius down. It was he who looked away first.

"Very well, then. You want to be free to return to Aquitaine as duchess in your own right."

"My right of birth," I said, "as my marriage contract states."

"Of course, of course." Eugenius spoke to soothe me, but I did not sit again. When he saw my strength, unsheathed before him, he let his own attempt at pretense go.

"Very well, Lady Alienor. I will consider your position. But please remember that I must consider your husband's position as well, and that of all of Christendom."

"You have much under your hand," I said.

Eugenius met my eyes, and for a moment, I thought I had made an enemy. But then the gleam of appreciation came into his gaze, and I saw that he admired not just my form and beauty but my mind.

"And if you are set free of this marriage, would you take counsel before bringing your next husband to your bed?"

"You mean to say, will I allow the Holy See to choose him?"

Eugenius did not speak but smiled, and bowed his head.

I smiled in answer, for I was closer to a victory than I had hoped. I knelt before him, my light veil showing the bronze of my red gold hair. I bent my head as if in prayer, knowing what a beautiful picture I made. What man can resist a kneeling woman?

"Let it be with me as God has wrought," I said.

For a long moment, there was nothing between us but birdsong and silence. Then, deep from Eugenius' chest rose a laugh that warmed my insides, curling my woman's parts with fire. The strength behind that laugh called to me. I was not dead yet.

That knowledge buoyed me as nothing else had in months. Still I kept my eyes down, my head bent, and let him take me in.

Eugenius offered his hand, his laughter done. He raised me to my feet. He met my eyes, and I saw his laughter still gleaming there. My blasphemy in quoting the Virgin Mary at the Annunciation had not offended him. I could not see what lay behind the doorway to his mind, but I knew he was no true child of the Church, as I was not.

"Perhaps God will send a Shepherd to lead you in your time of need," Eugenius said.

I smiled at him, my hand in his. "But, Your Holiness, He has sent me you."

❀

I waited in yet another garden while Louis met with Eugenius alone. Brother Francis, who clearly had thought to go in with the king, was left outside in the cloister garden with me.

I sat, fingering my rosary as if in prayer. Francis glowered, his hatred for me barely concealed beneath his anger at not being taken into the papal presence with Louis. I remembered well the night in Sicily when Brother Francis told me of my lover's death in front of all the company, and how he had gloated over my pain. I smiled at Louis' confessor, pleased with his discomfort at being left outside with me.

After my meeting with Eugenius, I was certain that the pope's time alone with Louis would not be long. But as afternoon began to fade toward evening, torches were brought out to the garden. Eugenius' steward came to find me and, on bended knee, offered to take me inside for some refreshment. Louis still had not emerged.

I broke my fast with a little bread and cheese, my eye turned all the while toward the inner door. Francis did not eat, nor did Amaria. They both kept watch, like two dogs eyeing each other over a coveted bone. In this case, I was that meaty morsel. I laughed out loud at that thought, and Eugenius' steward came back.

"His Holiness asks that you take mass with him in his chapel."

With a long look to Amaria to acknowledge this delaying tactic, I followed Eugenius' man deep into the bowels of his palace. The chapel was small, clearly one meant for His Holiness' private use. When I arrived, Francis was left outside the door, so that when I emerged into the candlelight within, I stood with only Amaria, Louis, and Eugenius himself.

"And will you celebrate mass?" I asked the pope. "You honor us."

Louis came to my side and took my hand, guiding me

toward the altar. Even then, I did not smell a rat, though one lay dead and rotting at my feet.

I met Eugenius' eyes, but he was the jocund conspirator no longer. Behind me, Francis stepped into the room from the shadows of the corridor. I saw that the lowly brother had dressed from head to foot in a robe of cloth of gold that almost matched my own in quality. The pope himself wore ermine with his papal robes, and on his head rested his papal crown.

"We come together to unite once more in the bond of matrimony these sons of the Church, Louis, King of France, and Eleanor, Duchess of Aquitaine. I raise my hand and bless you both, in the name of the Father, and the Son, and the Holy Spirit. May your marriage be fruitful. May, as God commanded, you multiply, and fill the earth."

Even two years ago, I would have been grateful for a full nursery, never mind a full earth. But that night, I heard the death knell of my hopes in Eugenius' voice. Louis had swayed him. For whatever reason, Eugenius had decided to support our marriage, and to leave me and my freedom in the dust.

I felt the floor slide out from under me, but Amaria was there to catch my arm, and hold me up. I drew strength from the dark blue of her eyes. She smiled at me, her dour countenance wreathed with light, and I remembered myself. I had lost the battle, but I would win the war.

Eugenius led us himself to his own bedchamber adjacent to his private chapel. His room was dressed in cloth of gold, as I was. Gilded tapestries depicting the life of Christ covered his walls, gleaming in the lamplight. A bright gold tympanum stood over the curved softness of his bed. The bedclothes were turned back, and I wondered for a moment if he had thought to have me there himself, before falling to Louis' fervor. No matter. I would live as I had been born to. I would take this day as it came.

There was no irony in Eugenius' voice as he stood next to his own bed, blessing the sheets with holy water, laying his hands over mine and Louis', joined in benediction.

His Holiness did not look at me, but left the room. Amaria followed him, though I knew she wanted to stay, at least long enough to help me take down my hair.

It was Brother Francis who left last. After a few murmured words to Louis, my enemy strode from the room as if he owned it, stopping only at the door to look back and smile on me in triumph. Like all who journeyed with us, Francis knew that I had asked the pope for an annulment. No doubt he thought that since I had been denied what I wanted, I would now become a biddable, obedient wife. It was clear from the look on his face that Francis was certain that I would give up all hope of freedom, and that the Aquitaine would stay safe in Parisian hands. Clearly, my enemy did not know me.

Finally, my husband and I stood alone in all our finery, the pope's words ringing in our ears.

"I will bed you, Eleanor. His Holiness has taken away the sin of it. He will pray for us, that we might have a son."

I turned from Louis and drew the crown of France from my head. I laid it on a table that stood between two braziers. I began to undress in the firelight.

Louis did not move, but watched me as I drew off first my veil, then my cloak, then my belt and overdress, until I reached the fine soft linen of my shift.

I began to take down my hair from its elaborate braids. The strands of pearls and diamonds laced through them I set on the table next to my discarded crown. Louis still did not move to undress himself, but watched me, as a snake watches its charmer.

My bronze hair fell past my shoulders almost to my waist. It would have covered me, but I had no need to hide. As always, I would do what must be done. One night would not mean pregnancy. I told myself this as I stepped forward, and took Louis' hand in mine.

"Husband," I said. "Shall I help you with your sword?"

He did not react to this double entendre as I had intended, nor did he laugh at the irony of it, for he heard none. Instead, he took his hand from mine and drew his sword belt off, and then his gown, followed by his shirt, until he stood in nothing but his garters and his shoes. I knelt before him then, and untied those. Louis caught his breath, to see me kneeling at his feet. I had never yet met a man not moved by the sight of a woman brought so low.

I meant to speed the progress of this night's affairs, so that Louis might turn to his prayers and I might get a little sleep. So once Louis stepped out of his shoes, I rose and drew my shift from my body in one smooth motion. I might be seven and twenty, but I had borne only one child. I was still beautiful, my breasts high and full, my belly a slight curve at my waist, beckoning a man's eyes lower.

Louis drank me in, as if I were water in a desert. Very gently, he touched my face. I was strong, but I knew I could not abide tenderness from him. Not this night. Not ever again.

So I took his hand from my cheek and drew him down with me onto the pope's borrowed bed. The tympanum above our heads swayed with Louis' motion. I took to looking at it as Louis moved inside me. We had been long apart, and Louis had had no other woman, so it was over quickly.

When he had done, he lay down, his arm slung across my waist, like a band of iron. Louis did not fall to praying as I thought he might, but went at once to sleep. So I was left alone with my thoughts, my husband beside me, the false tympanum of papal power above our heads. I watched as the firelight climbed that gilded silk long into the night. Though all was quiet now, I did not sleep. I simply lay still, as if waiting for Raymond to come for me.

I knew he would not. Even had he lived, Raymond could not have helped me. I must help myself.

I had been strong enough to make myself queen. Whatever this pope's leanings, I knew also that I was strong enough to set myself free.

❖

We stayed near Rome at the pontiff's villa for a few days more before setting off overland for Paris. My stomach roiled and heaved as we set out by litter. I could not face another sea voyage. It was autumn, not the best time to travel over the mountains of Italy, but I wanted to be gone from that place. Louis indulged me in this. He also stayed away from my bed.

It seemed, however, that the damage had been done. The pope's blessing had some effect, and our night under the papal tympanum. By the time we reached Paris, I knew I was once again with child.

Alix, my second living daughter, was born on a warm day in June in the year 1150. She was small, her blue eyes closed in tiny slits against the light. I kissed her forehead, and handed her at once to her nurse. I named her for my own beloved nurse, the woman who had stood as mother to me in place of my own. My Alix had died that winter, just after my return from Rome. Since little Alix was a girl, Louis did not care who I named her for.

Marie was brought in to me. She looked down upon her little sister, then kissed my cheek. I gazed into her sweet face, hoping to see some semblance of myself, or of my father, but there was nothing. She was Louis all the way down to the heart of her, even to her soft golden hair.

Chapter 25

❧

Cathedral Cloister of St.-Denis

Île-de-France
January 1151

LOUIS TOOK THREE MASSES A DAY, PRAYING FOR THE KING-dom, and stayed away from my bed. I left him to stew in the pot of his own folly, until the feast of Christ's Mass ended. In the early days of January in the year 1151, when the Yule log had burned out, I went to Louis' rooms once more to broach the subject of an annulment. But before I could speak, he wrapped me in furs and brought me down to the castle bailey without saying a word. His face was pale as he handed me into a litter. He stayed silent as we rode to the cathedral of St.-Denis. Louis was taking me to see Abbot Suger.

We had not seen much of Suger at court since we returned to Paris. He stayed at his new cathedral, and every month or so, Louis would visit him there, and take counsel from him. Suger had been ill all that autumn, but I had not understood how ill he truly was. As soon as we were brought into his presence, I saw that Abbot Suger was dying. His flesh was gray, and paper thin, like old vellum that had been used too often. His breath caught in his lungs, and rattled in his throat. Louis crossed himself when he heard it, and I did the same.

My husband knelt beside the bed of Suger, the man who, for all intents and purposes, had been his father. Suger had raised Louis in the confines of the cathedral cloister. He had taught him to be a good man, and to know God. He had never taught him to be king.

Louis wept though Suger's soul had not yet flown. Between my husband's hands was the rosary that I had given him, its diamonds, pearls, and amethysts pouring from his fingers down to meet the image of Christ.

Suger reached for Louis, and caressed his cheek. I wished that I might help my husband, though I knew I could not. He would have to bear his pain; no one could carry it for him. My father had died far from me. At least Louis got to see Suger at the last.

There was no help for Louis, and there would never be. He would simply have to rise from his father's deathbed and go on, by his own choice, as we all did. His crown and throne and scepter would not protect him. He would have to choose life, once his father's life had fled.

Suger clutched Louis' hand in his. "You must not let the Aquitaine go."

His voice rattled as he coughed, and I thought for a moment I had not heard him correctly. When that old man's words entered my ears, and were drawn into the contours of my brain, a fury rose in me so strong that had I let it loose, it would have been my undoing.

Louis did not answer Suger, and the old abbot could not draw breath to speak again. I would have to bide my time, and discover whether Louis had heard his spiritual father's dying wish, and if so, whether he took it to heart. Louis was sentimental. But even he knew that there must be a son for France.

He would not get one from me.

I knelt by Louis, my anger tamped down. I said a prayer aloud to the Holy Mother for Her blessing on Her servant Suger. Louis wept harder at the sound of my voice, and clutched my hand. The emerald rings he had given me during my pregnancy, when he still thought Alix would be born a prince, dug hard into my flesh.

I took in that pain as the tribute it was. With Suger gone, Louis might once more learn to lean on me. When he did so, I would lead him, inexorably, to ask Eugenius for our divorce.

I saw the path laid out clearly on the chessboard before me, and my heart rose. I hid my hope behind a veil of sorrow, and held my husband's hand while his soul's father took his last breath.

Suger's death rattle echoed off the stone walls of that tiny room. He slept in a bare cell, as all his monks did. Suger surrounded himself with no gold plate, with no silver crosses.

All the wealth of his cathedral he left on display outside, for the people to see.

Louis was beside himself with grief. His mind was undone by the loss of Suger, so that he could not remember the words to any prayer. So before we took our litter back to the city, I knelt in the sanctuary in his place, and lit a candle for Suger's soul.

Masses were already being sung in the great cathedral Suger had built, but we did not stay to hear them. I wanted Louis home with me, under my care, and under my eye. My husband leaned on me, as if his legs could not hold him up. Brother Francis saw this, and said nothing, but let me pass by unmolested, with Louis on my arm.

Our litter bearers saw the condition of the king, and made it back to the city by nightfall. I did not let Louis out of my sight, but brought him to my own rooms, where I placed him in my bed.

Amaria made him a cup of tea with a draught of poppy juice in it. I watched her carefully as she dosed him, for I did not want him too heavily drugged. I could have no rumors circulating in the court that, after the death of Suger, I tried to poison the king.

Louis lay sleeping, with his hand in mine. I sat by him all night. Once, his chamberlain and page came in. They saw him resting peacefully and left him in my care. Louis' household had never believed the lies told about me. They served my husband well, and saw how much he loved me. They had never hated me as his courtiers did.

I bathed Louis' face with warm water, but he wept for

Suger even in his sleep. He looked like an overgrown child who had lost his way. I did not sleep myself that night, but kept the lamps lit, in case Louis was to wake and need me.

Dawn came, and he slept on, though not as heavily. I washed my face and hands and changed my gown, leaving him finally to step into my sitting room. When I stepped into my antechamber, expecting to see the Lady Priscilla and the rest of my women waiting for me, I found only Brother Francis, in his deep robes of midnight black.

"Good day, Sister Eleanor," he said.

I almost laughed at his audacity. "I am many things, Brother Francis, but a nun is not one of them."

"Of course," he said, bowing low to me. "My lady queen."

I heard the insolence in his voice, but it had always been there. I could not cure him of it now, these many years later. If I had respected him at all, perhaps it would have stung me. I could not even hate the man that morning. I was too tired.

So I dismissed Francis from my mind, pouring myself a glass of Rhenish wine, certain that the churchman had come to my rooms only to see Louis. I sipped the watered wine, a gift from the German emperor, and waited for Brother Francis to ask my leave to see the king. He asked me nothing, but stepped closer to me.

"My lady queen, I come to offer you an alliance."

My lips quirked, but I was in control of myself and did not smile. I raised one brow.

"Indeed, Brother Francis. An alliance against whom?"

"Against the pope, my lady queen."

I did not answer, but went to sit in my best cushioned

chair. Amaria took up her place by the door leading into my bedchamber, and Francis did not so much as glance her way. I saw contempt in his eyes, not just for her, but for all women. I wondered that I had never noticed it before. I had always thought his contempt part of his hatred for me.

"His Holiness has all in his hands," I said, my meaning ambiguous, as I meant it to be.

"The Holy See means to set you aside, my lady queen. I heard the rumors when I was last in Rome. You will be forced into a nunnery, that my lord king might marry again."

I saw now which way this interview was tending. I called on all my powers of deception, and raised one hand to my hair.

"Brother Francis, God preserve me. Say it is not so."

He blinked, and for a moment, I thought my lies were too overblown, that he had not been taken in. I did not look to Amaria for fear I would laugh aloud. It was not a laughing matter. This man was my rival for power in the kingdom, now that Suger was dead. As Louis' confessor, Brother Francis had my husband's ear. No doubt the false priest hoped to frighten me into becoming his creature with this talk of setting me aside. He clearly believed that to escape the convent I would do anything, even join forces with him. I knew in that moment that I would do all in my power to see Francis eclipsed in the king's graces, and forever.

It is odd indeed when what we seek opens the door into another world altogether.

"I have even heard it said, among the king's barons, that

poison might find its way into your cup some evening meal. This would leave the kingdom with a vacant throne, and the Aquitaine both."

The word *poison* caught my ear, and drove away all thought of laughter. My people had brought no word of this treachery, but I was sure that Louis' people could see it done. Or perhaps Francis meant to warn me of some plot in the Church, some plot that might remove me, as my father had been removed. Cold crept into my chest, and lodged above my heart. I almost lost my breath.

"It would not be the first time poison found its way to curse a member of your family," Francis said.

My hand shook. I dropped my goblet, and the wine splashed onto my golden gown. The glass I had held shattered on the stone floor at my feet.

Amaria did not move to help me. She stayed still, and silent, in the hope that Francis had forgotten she was there. But I knew that I would need more witness to Francis' speech than one waiting woman.

I did not look to her, but I raised one hand to my temple as if in despair. As I did, my fingers fluttered once toward the door to my bedroom, where Louis lay, still sleeping.

Amaria moved at once, as silent as a ghost. The door between my rooms was well oiled, and draped with a thick tapestry to keep out the drafts in winter. My woman disappeared behind that tapestry, so that I was left alone with the man who had killed my father.

"Poison?" I asked.

It took no time for Francis to continue to speak, for he was overconfident, as all fools are. My woman had left and he did not heed it. He counted her as nothing, just as he counted me. Francis came close to me then, but he did not lower his voice. I saw that he was proud of all that he had done, and I had not yet learned the whole of it.

"Your father coughed blood at the last. Did anyone ever tell you that?"

My hand shook as I touched my hair. This time, I did not have to dissemble. My father's death was a wound that burned like acid. I would never be free of it. But I would hear this man's confession clearly, and from his own lips. Then I would act, as I had waited almost fourteen years to do.

I saw the tapestry at my bedroom door flutter once, as if in a draft from a window. I knew by that sign that Amaria stood behind it. I could only hope that Louis stood with her. Though it was not in my husband to dissemble or to hide, especially from a man of the Church, I fervently wished that, this once, Louis might stay hidden.

I raised my voice enough that it might be heard, even where Louis stood. I did not have to feign horror. I was steeped in it already.

"And the old king?" I asked. "Did he cough blood as well when he was poisoned?"

It was a clumsy move, but I had no way of knowing how long Louis might keep himself concealed. I hoped that my husband had enough sense to wait, and to listen to Francis' answer.

"Louis the king fell to poison, but his end was worse than your father's, or so my colleague said. He was three days dying of dysentery. Your father took only two."

Bile rose in my throat, but I swallowed it. "And your colleague . . . where is he now?"

"He was taken to the Lord's grace five years ago. I have lit a candle for his soul."

"No doubt he needs it."

Francis heard the acid in my voice, and took one step back.

I rose from my chair, and faced my enemy. "You murdered my father, and the king's father, for the good of France?"

"For the good of the Church," Francis said. "I wanted to make way for you and your husband to rule alone, unencumbered."

"With King Louis the Elder dead, my father would have advised us," I said.

"Yes. We knew we could not let William of Aquitaine live. He had made an enemy of us already."

I saw it all then, and it took my breath. This man had been in league with the old pope, the one we had worked against before I was ever duchess. That pope had hated my father for backing his rival, and had called for my father's penance, saying that he must go either to Rome or to Santiago. Francis had followed my father to Spain and killed him there. Months later, after my wedding, our enemy pope had sent another minion of the Church to Louis the Fat. The elder king had died by poison, just as my father had.

The Church had thought to control the wealth of the Aquitaine as well as the throne of France through my young, easily led husband, and through me. Only my strength of will had kept them from it.

I could hear nothing behind the tapestry, but I knew that Louis was there.

"Why do you come to me, and tell me all this now?"

"As I have said, I have heard rumors among the courtiers that some seek your death. I would give you my protection."

I did not laugh in his face. What protection could this bumbling fool offer me? A man so stupid that he would keep his silence for fourteen years, then reveal himself as my father's murderer? Did this baseborn cur think that I would ally myself with him? There would be time for vengeance, but I must hold my tongue and stay my hand. When I spoke, my voice was cool and calm, as if I spoke with my steward about the household accounts in Poitiers.

"And in exchange for your protection, I will help you control Louis?"

"Yes," Francis said. "Your father is dead, and the old king, and Abbot Suger. Now my brethren in the Church and I can control France altogether."

Louis stepped out from behind the tapestry, and Francis' face turned gray. Francis had thought my husband asleep in his own bed, or he would never have come to me. The false priest shook with fear at the sight of my husband's face.

"Get out," Louis said, his voice hoarse with weeping. "Get out of my sight."

"My lord king," Francis stammered.

"I am not your lord or your king. You are a treacherous dog, not fit to live upon the earth."

Francis ran from us, and left the door to the hallway standing open behind him. Amaria moved before I could beckon her. She would order my men-at-arms to catch the monk and hold him. My battle-hardened men, fresh from the Crusade, cared little if the prisoner they held was a man of God.

Amaria left us alone, closing the outer door behind her. Louis fell to his knees, and I knelt beside him. I took him in my arms, expecting tears, but he did not weep. Perhaps the horror of the last day had overwhelmed him. I was a strong woman, and it had overwhelmed me.

The cold of the stone floor seeped into my skin through the silk of my gown. Louis leaned his cheek against mine. I supported his weight, but he also supported me.

"Eleanor, I am so sorry."

"There is no fault in you, Louis."

"There is," he said. "There is. A true king would have known it. A true man of God would have seen what Francis was. Dear God, dear God, how may I be shriven for it?"

I kissed him, pressing my lips hard against his. He did not respond, but drew back from me, and lay down on the floor as if he wished to fall through the cracks between the stones and disappear.

"We have sinned, Eleanor. We are cursed. No marriage can be built on blood. My father and yours, dead through the greed of evil men. We can build nothing on that. This is why God never gave us sons."

I said nothing, for there was nothing left to say. I stroked his hair while he lay on the floor beside me. Amaria found us there when she came back.

She nodded once. Francis had been caught. I would look to him later. For now, I sat beside my husband, and offered comfort he could not take.

❖

That night, Bardonne drowned Brother Francis in the Seine. His body turned up three miles downstream, outside the city walls. There was talk of suicide, so that he could not be buried in consecrated ground. Louis, gray and pale all through those days, heard this news and said nothing. He did not know that I had taken Francis' death into my own hands. It was one more lie between us.

Louis agreed with me finally to petition the pope for an annulment. The murders of our fathers cast a pall over his mind, though he never spoke of it again. He looked harder at the men about him after that time. His own heart hardened a little, though never enough to be king.

I sat beside Louis on his throne as he dealt out death and judgment. I watched as his blue eyes took in the world as if seeing it for the first time. He would never be that sweet, golden boy again. I was surprised to feel the loss of that, even as Louis prepared to let me go.

My father had no restless spirit, no ghost to lie quiet, now that his murder was avenged. I was glad that Francis was dead. I begrudged him every peaceful night of sleep, every morsel of food, every bit of pleasure that he had taken from the day of my father's death until his own. But revenge did not soothe me as I had always thought it would.

The dead were still dead. I had no thought of heaven to comfort me, as Louis did. My father moldered in his grave at Santiago. He would not rise at some trumpet call. I would never see his face again. His murder was avenged, but it was cold comfort, too little consolation that came too late.

Chapter 26

Palace of the City

Paris
August 1151

IN THE SPRING OF 1151, PETRA CAME TO ME AS THE FIRST flowers began to rise from the thawed ground in Paris. I sent for her so that I might tell of her of our father's murder, and of the revenge I had exacted for it. Petra was a woman now; I could not hold back such news from her. I had also heard of trouble in her household, that her husband had taken a lover. I did not want her left alone on his lands, undefended. Let her roving husband remember that he was still married to the sister of the Duchess of Aquitaine.

I had planted a Persian rose garden when I first returned from the Levant, in the months before Alix was born. Now Alix was almost one year old, and the roses thrived, even in the damp wasteland that was my husband's keep. There was enough sun for them between those walls, though there was never enough sun for me.

I stood among those roses when Petra arrived at my gates. Amaria did not hesitate, but brought my sister to me.

When I saw her, I took her in my arms. Tears rose in my eyes. Her presence was a greater gift than I had expected. I had missed her, in the years I had been away. My love for her came flooding back, like a tide that would never go out.

Amaria took my women indoors to work at a new tapestry, so that my sister and I could be alone. The Parisian women of my household embroidered that cloth in honor of Abbot Suger. It would one day cover the altar at his cathedral at St.-Denis. If I had my way, by the time it was completed, I would no longer be in Paris.

It was the first warm day in June. Amaria had set out wine on a small table among the roses, as well as two chairs with cushions. Even now, Amaria was no doubt guarding the passage that led to the garden, so that my sister and I could be alone. I had news for Petra that no one else could hear.

Petra's soft blond hair fell from her braids, framing her face like a halo. My sister wept openly, and clung to me as if she were still eleven years old, and our father newly dead. I remembered how frightened she had been in the days after Papa died. She had not been able to sleep in her room with her women for months. She had slept in my bed with me, until the weeks before I married Louis.

Though she was slight, Petra was a child no longer. Her own two girls were eight and nine years old, and they would both marry in a few years' time. I would have to look to their marriage portions, and find decent men to stand by them. I would not allow my sister's daughters to go to any clod that Raoul might choose: some man who liked to hawk, or some boy with a good pair of hunting hounds.

"Alienor, he has left me."

"Who, Petra?" Though of course, I knew already.

"Raoul. He has married another."

I laughed, bitterness filling my voice with gall. "After all the trouble I went to getting him out of his first marriage? I think not. The pope will not be a fool in his case twice. I paid good money for that divorce. You and he are married, no matter how many doxies he takes to his bed."

"She is pregnant."

I had nothing to say to that. I took Petra in my arms, and held her close while she wept. Though Raoul was much older than she, I saw that she loved him still.

"Shall I have him killed?"

It was a course of action that before I never would have considered. But now that I had seen my father's murderer done to death, such things seemed possible. I did not see how I could let the ungrateful bastard live, after he had made my sister weep.

"No, Alienor, please do not hurt him."

She clutched me hard, and I forced a smile. For her sake, it even reached my eyes. I was a better actress than I once had been. Even Petra could not tell when I was lying now.

"I was only joking, sweetheart. Forgive me. It was lightly said."

I kissed her, and she leaned against me, her tears spent.

"Men are unfaithful ever," I said, knowing that the well-worn platitude would be no comfort to her.

"I know." She dried her eyes on the fur trim of my gown, as no one else alive would have dared to do. "I always thought he would be faithful to me."

Those who served me in Petra's household had told me already of her troubles, but I had been so steeped in mine that I had been able to do nothing but send for her. I would care for her and her girls for the rest of their lives.

As for Raoul, I knew he was dying of a coughing sickness that made him hack up blood. From all the doctors in Paris told me, it was a lingering illness, and a difficult death. I had already decided to let him take what doxies he might. I would leave him to that death, and welcome.

"Where are the girls?" I asked.

"In the nursery, with Marie and Alix."

Her weeping had stopped. Before it began again, as I knew it would, there were things I would speak of, things she must know.

"Petra," I said. "I have news. Come and sit by me."

"Are you well, Alienor?"

My sister had never taken up the new pronunciation of my name. She spoke it as she always had. Only with Petra did I remember my softness, the shadow of the girl I had been long ago, before my mother died.

I saw her fear that I would die and leave her. I smiled again, and pressed her hand.

"I am well," I answered. "I am too strong for even God to kill."

We sat together on the chairs Amaria had left for us in the midst of my Persian roses. I took my sister's hand. "Petra, you remember the dark days, the days after Papa died."

My sister blinked in the soft light of that walled garden. "Yes, Alienor. Of course I remember."

"I did not tell you then, but Papa was killed."

"He drank bad water," she said.

"He drank someone's poison."

Her alabaster skin turned gray, and I thought she might be sick. My hand moved to her arm, holding her up.

"Forgive me for telling you, but you are a woman now. You are old enough to know. I found the man who killed him."

"He is dead?" Petra asked. I saw her strength suddenly, in the soft, deep blue of her eyes.

"He is dead now," I answered.

"You killed him." She watched my face. She knew I would not lie to her.

"I did," I said. "He drowned in the Seine. My man had a hand in it."

"Bardonne," she guessed.

"How did you know?" I asked. "Has there been talk?"

"No, Alienor. He always loved you, even from a child. He will never tell."

"No," I said. "He will not."

"Papa would be glad," she said. "He would be proud of you, if he knew."

"Perhaps he does know," I answered.

Petra's grip tightened. "You do not believe that."

"No. I do not."

We sat in silence then, my sister and I, each of us lost in our own thoughts. She was not devastated, as I thought she would be. Her pain over Raoul seemed to recede with this news I gave her. She was glad our father's murderer had been caught and punished. It gave her comfort, as it had not comforted me.

Petra stood, and raised me to my feet. In her eyes, I saw myself, not as the hero of her childhood, but as the woman I was, my flaws and strengths together. Petra pressed her hand to my cheek as if in blessing.

She knew me, as no one else did, as no one else ever would. Tears rose in my eyes, and clogged my throat. Petra drew me close, and pretended that she had not seen them.

"I love you, Alienor."

I stood in my sister's embrace, and clutched her close. This time, it was she who held me.

"Come," she said. "Let us go in. I would see Marie, and Alix. And you must see my girls."

"Before we go," I said, drying my eyes on my scented handkerchief, "I must tell you. Louis and I . . ."

"You will part, as soon as it can be done."

"You knew?"

"I live in the country, Alienor, but even there, we hear the news."

"And the people in Aquitaine, and Poitou," I said. "Are they angry?"

Petra smiled. She had passed through my lands on her way to Paris. She had seen the people there with her own eyes, and listened to their grievances as she passed. She was always my eyes and ears when she traveled through our homeland, and this time was no exception. "They are angry that Louis was not man enough to give you sons. But they love you. They would follow you anywhere, farther even than Jerusalem."

I kissed her, before we went indoors to fetch our children. Had I been alone, I would have sent a woman for them, but Petra wanted to go inside to see the girls in their nursery.

I would have to leave my daughters with Louis when I went home to the Aquitaine. But they would be gone in a few years' time in any case. French princesses were betrothed young, and raised among their husbands' kin. I felt the loss of them already, as I stood in that walled garden, with Petra's hand on mine. Before Marie and Alix were parted, sent to separate husbands in separate lands, I hoped they would be some kind of comfort to each other, as Petra had always been a comfort to me. I would suffer from the loss of them, once I was gone.

One must cut out one's heart, to be free.

Petra spoke as if she had read my mind like an open book of prayer. "Your girls will be all right. Fear nothing, Alienor. Louis loves them. He will guard them well."

"Yes," I answered. "Louis is a good man."

"You are a good woman," she said.

"Ah, Petra. You are the only one who thinks so."

"Then no one else knows you, Alienor."

I did not answer. Petra took my hand, and led me into the darkness of the keep. We would find our daughters and bring them with us, out into the light.

❈

Petra and her girls stayed for the rest of that summer. I would not send them home again, but kept them safe in my household. They would return to Poitiers before me, after my annulment was secure. During those months, the sun shone more than it ever had, as if offering a blessing on my divorce. Louis' people had begun the arduous work of securing it through Rome.

The Parisians were relieved that they would soon see the back of me. For my part, I was relieved to have someone else shoulder the expense. Bribes in the Vatican cost more than anywhere else on earth.

Still, I was queen in France. And every day, I stood with Louis as he heard petitions in the great hall of the Palace of the City.

One morning in late August, Petra stood with me on the dais. She and I were whispering together, planning to take the girls out into the sunshine that afternoon. We would walk down to the river, to watch my man Bardonne catch fish. Now that my time with my daughters was short, I spent as much of my leisure with them as I could.

So I was not looking when Henry of Normandy first walked into my husband's court. Louis sat on his gilded throne, attending to all and sundry with a patience that had always surprised me. No doubt Suger had taught him that.

As for myself, I felt restlessness rising from the ground at my feet, the sap of life mounting through the stones of the palace, through the soft soles of my shoes, and up into my spine. It made me light-headed, and as hungry for life as I had been in Antioch.

"It is the retinue from Normandy, Your Majesty," Brother Matthew, Louis' new confessor, said. "They have come, my lord king, that the eldest son might be confirmed as duke."

"Indeed? Let them come forward."

If Louis had known about the Normans' scheduled interview, he had forgotten all about them until that moment. Petra's lips quirked, and I had to look away, or laugh outright.

Geoffrey of Anjou, my father's old friend, came forward first and made his bow. His red blond hair gleamed in the sunlight of Louis' audience hall. He was a tall man, and seemed used to commanding all who came before him. He did not walk up to the dais, but stopped ten feet from us, and knelt where he stood. I wondered at this, until my eyes fell on his eldest son.

Henry strode past his father to kneel before my husband. He paced like a lion in a cage, his energy barely contained as he moved forward to greet Louis, as if the King of France were his equal. His eyes were a light gray, but it was the fire in them that I saw first, a brand that seemed to run along my skin, heating every inch it touched. He stepped forward and knelt, his eyes locked on me.

"My lord king. I come to claim my lands in Normandy. I offer myself as your faithful vassal."

At eighteen, he seemed too young to have conquered the great duchy of Normandy where his father, Geoffrey of Anjou, had failed. This boy, Henry, had taken Normandy by force, reclaiming his mother's lands for his own, as his father had never been able to do.

But as I looked into his eyes, I saw that Henry had been a man for years.

Henry's bold gray gaze met mine across the distance that separated us. Though he knelt below the dais at my husband's feet, he seemed the kind of man that, in his own mind, never knelt or yielded to anyone.

His hair was cut short for war, but fell against his forehead in a sweep of dark red. He was a handsome man, with wide shoulders, but he was not a hulking colossus, as one might expect a conqueror to be. He had not worn his sword into the royal presence, but the silk of his tunic strained against the heavy muscles of his arms. As soon as I saw him, it seemed to me that he would be more at home in armor on the field of battle with a sword or mace in his hand.

Even as a boy, no doubt this man's strong chin had dissuaded others from ever taking him too lightly. There was a gleam in his eye, a light that took in all he saw with a glint of humor. I could see beyond that light to an intelligent, serious mind, for no man would have made himself Duke of Normandy at the age of eighteen without skill in politics as well as in war. One might take in the merry light in Henry's eyes, and think him a merry man. But I knew at once that Henry valued respect as much as he valued his own strength. One would be a fool to approach him with easy familiarity, thinking him a man for jokes and laughter only. From the way he carried himself, I could see that one day, Henry of Normandy would be a king.

Stephen of Blois still held England and Wales, the lands

that by rights belonged to Henry's mother, Maude. I saw from the resolution in Henry's eyes that he would make short work of Stephen, and of any who stood too long in his way. He was walking the path of power; I had no doubt that when this man took ship for England, he would reconquer that land just as he had conquered Normandy.

As if he could read the thoughts in my head as he might read a book laid out on a table, Henry smiled at me. A bolt of fire flashed between us, a charge so hot, it took my breath. If Louis had an opposite on earth, surely it was the man kneeling before me.

My husband's cool blue gaze took in Henry of Normandy as it had every other petitioner, with no sign of emotion. Louis gestured, and Henry rose to his feet.

"You are welcome here, my lord duke. Tomorrow, we will confirm you in your office. You will take your lands once more from our hands. Until that time, stay here with us; feast and drink in our hall."

"I thank you for your hospitality, my lord king," Henry said, his eyes on me.

"We both thank you," Henry's father said. Geoffrey of Anjou was a powerful presence as he rose from his knees. Geoffrey stepped forward, so that he stood at Henry's elbow, presenting Louis and his court with a united front. He was never strong enough to hold his wife's lands, but now that I looked into his face, I saw why my father had fought for him in Normandy. There was something in Geoffrey that called on men to follow him. My father had recommended this man to me as a protector, as a friend in adversity. I wondered if Papa had been right, if Geoffrey would have come to my aid, had I needed it, as my father had come to his.

Their audience was over. Indeed, all the petitions for the day were done. Louis turned without a word and left by a side door. He would be at prayer for the rest of the afternoon.

I stood and watched my husband go. His shoulders were stooped, as if he were a man of five and forty. His priests led him away, and closed the door behind him. When I turned back, Henry was standing beside me; Geoffrey of Anjou had approached the dais with him.

"Your father was a good man," Geoffrey said. "Had he been my general, perhaps we would have won."

There was no answer to that, so I offered none. "He spoke well of you, my lord," I said. "Even at the end of his life, he named you as a friend."

"That is my honor. He served well in Normandy, and was wounded for his pains."

I was surprised that Geoffrey would speak of it. Though he had never won the lands that had fallen to his son so easily, I saw no evidence of envy in his eyes. Either he schooled his features, as my father had taught me to do, or he felt no resentment at all.

"Yes," I said. "I remember."

Henry stood silent between us. I thought his gaze might turn to Petra, for men loved her sweet smile and her soft blond hair. But he did not. Though he did not stare like a country clod, he had eyes only for me.

"You are renowned for your beauty," Henry said. "I see that those reports are not exaggerated."

I laughed at this clumsy attempt at flattery. My laughter echoed off the stone walls of my husband's hall, and wrapped us in its warmth. I mocked him, and he knew it. I saw that he did not care.

Louis' people eyed us, and murmured to one another. I sighed. Another rumor started. By night's end they would have me in bed either with this boy or with his father, or with both of them together. I was deeply tired of Paris and all its trickery.

I turned to Petra, and nodded to her. She proceeded toward the inner door, knowing that I would follow.

"If you gentlemen will excuse me, I must be about the business of the keep."

"Of course." Geoffrey bowed, but Henry did not. The young Duke of Normandy still stared at me, and I saw laughter in his eyes. He knew I was no housekeeper. Perhaps my reputation had preceded me, as well as word of my beauty.

"Good afternoon, my lady queen. We will see you again at this night's feast," Henry said.

"Indeed," I said. "This is my kingdom. You could not avoid it, if you tried."

"Who would avoid your lovely presence?" Geoffrey asked. His courtly smile was smooth as silk, but it was Henry who caught my eye as I turned to walk away. It was Henry's gaze that followed me, Henry's warmth that I felt on my skin, until the door closed behind me.

❧

The rains came out of nowhere, as they often did in Paris, so that Petra and the girls were forced to stay indoors by the fire. My sister played with them as if she were not a countess in her own right. She romped and chased them as if she were as young as they. I left them to it. Rain or no, that afternoon I was too restless to stay indoors.

I left the girls with Petra and went walking in my rose garden. The rain was still falling, but had slowed to a drizzle. I drew my wool cloak close around me. The fur lining kept me warm as I walked the damp stone paths. The wet seeped into my boots, so that my hose became wet as well, but I did not heed it. I walked in circles, like a caged bear, round and round that garden without looking at the flowers.

I was alone that afternoon with my thoughts, as alone as I ever was, without even Amaria to attend me. She kept watch for me by the door that led back into the castle keep. She knew these moments without my women were precious to me. Before long, the sun would set, and I would need to go inside to dress for dinner in the hall.

I stood looking at my roses without seeing them, their scent mingling with the smell of damp earth, when Henry came to me.

He was silent, like a great cat. He approached me slowly, as if he feared to startle me. Perhaps he thought me timid, though my reputation surely would have told him other-wise. As he stepped toward me, heat rose between us, then built until I could not catch my breath. I had never felt such power between myself and a man before, not with Rancon, not even with Raymond. Henry's dark red hair glinted in the gray light of my husband's keep. His eyes met mine as an equal; like Louis, he was only a little taller than I was. In my garden, with the rain falling all around us, as I began to fathom the depths that lay behind the gray of his eyes, Henry reached down, and took my hand. His fingertips worried at the diamond Louis had given me, and his thumb played over the ruby signet ring of Aquitaine.

"Do you always stand in the rain, lady, or did you simply come here to meet me?"

I laughed at his audacity. That joy-filled sound swirled around us, binding us like a warm cloak, caressing us both. "I wait for no man, my lord duke. And you might greet me with a little more respect. I am your queen."

"You are," he said. "A man could not wish for a queen more beautiful."

I thought for one breathless moment that he might kiss me then and there. When he leaned closer still, I did not pull away. I wondered what folly I had gotten into, what foolhardiness I hoped to serve by allowing this boy to make love to me in the very shadow of my husband's house, where even the walls had ears.

But Henry did not kiss me. His breath was warm on my lips, taunting me, even as he raised my hand. He kissed my signet ring, his soft lips caressing it. He left my wedding band untouched.

"I looked for you everywhere," he said, his voice low.

"I even checked the chapel, but all I found was your husband at prayer."

"Louis prays a great deal," I said. "He is a good man."

"I am a better one."

"You are a boy."

I spoke more to deny myself than him, but my challenge lit his eyes with fire. He wrapped one arm around my waist and drew me close, easily, as if I were a doxy he had purchased at market.

He did not deny my words, for he did not need to. We both knew I was lying. He smiled at my bravado, a knowing smile that did not belong on the face of one so young. He drew me close, one arm wrapped around my waist, the other moving up into my hair. He cupped the back of my neck in one great hand. I felt the calluses on his palm and fingers snag the bronze strands. My people had said, when I asked for a report of him, that he never wore riding gloves, not when hunting or at war. For some reason, evidence of that knowledge undid me. The calluses on his hands excited me, and any resistance I might have mounted slid away as his lips closed over mine.

It was a soft kiss, much softer than I would have thought to receive from a man so strong. It seemed his strength did not have to prove itself. We both knew that he had vanquished me already.

My mouth opened under his, and I felt his triumph as he shifted his body closer to mine, drawing me against the hard length of his chest and thighs. His sword belt dug into my waist; this thrilled me more, as his tongue plundered my mouth. I could taste all his past conquests, and all his conquests to come.

"Dear God," I said. "This is folly."

Henry laughed low, the sound running over my skin like hands. He caressed my hair, while his other hand held me fast against him. He did not let me pull away.

"It is the sanest thing I've ever done."

"You must let me go."

"Must I?"

I was a beautiful woman, and I knew it. But under Henry's gaze, under his hands, I became a different woman altogether, a pliant woman, a woman who did nothing but want. I was always that woman as long as Henry was touching me.

"Wear green tonight," he said. "Green to match your eyes."

"Why would I do that?"

He smiled, his mouth lowering so that it hovered only an inch above my own. His breath was warm, and I sagged against him, my hands on his chest, holding him back from what we both wanted.

"Let us not lie to each other, or to ourselves, Eleanor."

He did not speak my name as Raymond had. But the name I had borne for Louis for so many years sounded different on his lips. It was a new name, just as I was a new woman, simply because he had touched me.

Henry stepped away from me.

My heart pounded from his nearness, raced with my desire for him, but my mind was clear. I was still myself with him, but better. Perhaps it was possible for a man to teach a woman to know herself. Before that day, I would have said such a thing was not possible.

"I will see you in the hall," he said. "Wear green for me."

"I will not."

Henry smiled. The shadows of the keep had begun to creep up from the ground, filling the walled garden with the beginning of night. Those shadows played over his face, but they could do nothing to dim the red gold of his hair, or the knowledge in his smile.

"You will."

He was gone then, and I was left alone to catch my breath. I had never seen such a man, not in all my travels, not in all my years upon the earth. I noticed then that it was still raining. I had forgotten the weather while Henry was with me.

My hood had fallen when he kissed me, and now my hair was as wet as my shoes. My gown was damp where he had touched me, and the fur on my cloak was matted with the rain.

Amaria came to me then, and led me indoors by the hand. She took me to my rooms the long way, by the hidden corridor that led to my bedchamber. My ladies still waited for me in my sitting room. Seeing that I was in no condition to greet them, Amaria called for my bathwater to be brought into my bedroom, and sent my ladies away.

I stood alone, by my bedroom's only window, and looked unseeing into the dark. Night had almost fallen, but the gray of Paris no longer chilled me as it had an hour before. Now that gray made me think of Henry, and of the color of his eyes. I knew I was far gone, for I could still taste him, and the warm velvet of his tongue.

Though this was true, I did not feel mad, as I had felt with Raymond. This was something new, some new game that Henry had started. Now, for the few days he lingered here, it was for me to play it out.

❀

I was late to the feast, as my hair was still damp from the rain. It took time to dry it out before the fire. Instead of braiding it once more, Amaria drew the bronze strands up into a simpler style, and placed the coronet of Aquitaine over it. I wore no veil, which I knew would infuriate the Parisians, but I was damned in their eyes already.

When I came into the hall, Louis did not chide me for my lateness. Instead, he rose from his chair, forcing everyone at the high table to follow suit. The people sitting below the dais rose as well, so that everyone's eyes were on me.

"What a lovely gown, Eleanor. You are a vision, as always."

I blinked, for though he loved me, my husband rarely offered me compliments anymore. "Thank you, Louis."

The king drew my chair out from the table before a footman could step forward and do it for him. I accepted the wine he offered me, as well as the squab. Everyone else sat when Louis did, and as the king began to eat, everyone else ate as well.

Petra caught my eye from where she sat at Louis' left hand. I winked at her, and she almost laughed, choking on a sip of wine. She thought to sleep in my room that night, but after my time with Henry in the garden, I would be too restless. I would send word by Amaria that Petra might sleep in the nursery with the girls. She loved my daughters, almost as much as she loved her own. Often I wished I had her easy way with them. They loved me, but as queen, I was set apart. As young as they were, both Marie and Alix knew it.

The musicians played quietly in the gallery above our heads. I could hear it over the sound of the talk that night, and I found the lute and fife soothing. I sipped my wine, and ate my spiced venison, raising my eyes only then from the trencher Louis and I shared. I should not have done it, for I found Henry down the table, staring at me.

My color rose, as if I were a young girl or an innocent. No one around us seemed to notice, save for Henry's father, Geoffrey, who glowered at me. No doubt he did not want his young pup of a son running after a married woman. Or perhaps he simply feared to start a war with my husband before Henry was even confirmed in his duchy. Whatever the reason, Geoffrey of Anjou was not fooled by my downcast eyes. He shifted on his bench. His eyes did not leave me, nor did his son's.

I looked up at last and met Henry's gaze. He smiled at me, as if we knew a secret. There was something about him that warmed me, even from that distance. I gave up all pretense at modesty, and smiled back at him.

Triumph lit his eyes, as it had in that rainy garden. He raised his glass to me, a gesture that warmed me almost as much as his touch had. I turned from him then, and ate my food without tasting it. Louis offered a bit of seasoned pork, which I took but did not touch.

I drank my wine, and kept my own counsel until the fruit

was brought out and the minstrels came down from their gallery for the dancing.

The tables were taken up on the lower floor, and the rushes strewn with thyme and rosemary. The scent of those herbs rose from the ground below the dais. I breathed in those mingled scents, as well as the smell of woodsmoke, and took in the light of the evening fires. Lamps burned, hanging from chains above the dance floor. All around that stone hall, the light worked to chase away the shadows, but darkness lined the walls. As I watched, lovers paired off, some to the dancing and others to the outer darkness. For the first time in years, since I was a young girl at home safe in my father's court, I wished I might be one of them.

Henry was standing by me then, bowing so low that I thought he might stoop to kneel. He did not address me but kept his eyes on Louis.

"My lord king, may I have the honor of a dance with your queen?"

Louis smiled fondly. It never crossed his mind that this man, this young conqueror, would have any darker motive but to take my hand.

Henry did not speak to me, but led me by the hand into the motion of the dancers. All eyes were on us, though I would soon be free and no longer wear a crown. Though Louis was casting me aside and everyone knew it, that night, I was still queen.

I tossed my head, so that my hair fell over one shoulder in a bronze cascade. It had begun to come unraveled from the simple style Amaria had put it in. As it fell undone beneath my coronet, I found I did not care. The Parisians looked scandalized, but so they did even when I knelt in church.

"You wore green," Henry said finally, his hand over mine.

We began to move in the elaborate pattern of the dance. I did not have to wait a moment or hesitate to discover which way he intended to move, as I had often done with so many other men. Our bodies moved together without thought, as if we had been born to it.

"Did I?" I asked. "My women dress me. I rarely think to look at their choices, for all my gowns are as fine as the rest."

He laughed low, so that no one else could hear him. He drew me close in the dance, and leaned as if to bow to me, his lips coming close to my ear. "Liar."

I laughed then, all pretense at coolness fled. Henry laughed with me, and all in Louis' court turned to look at us, Geoffrey of Anjou included.

Only Louis did not look down from his dais, for Brother Matthew sat with him. Louis' new confessor had taken my place at table. My husband's fair golden head was bent, listening to all his churchman said. The rest of the court saw Henry and me together, but Louis never did.

Then the dance turned me away, my back to the dais, so that I was moving among the courtiers once more. Louis fell away from me like a dream at morning.

I took in the sight of Henry, standing by my side in his clothes of silk. He had worn wool in the garden that afternoon, a tunic and hose made for riding, or for war. He wore silk now as a king might, but casually, as if he knew his own worth.

As the dance ended, I found myself basking in the light

of his eyes. Here, then, was a man to meet my fire. Here at last was a man to match my strength. What a shame that he was so young, and that I was married already.

Henry returned me to the dais, and bent over my hand. He spoke low, as if offering his fealty, but his voice was not subservient. "I will come to you tonight. Look for me."

He left me gasping at his audacity. I would have laughed, but I had no breath. Louis nodded to me, and I sat once more at his side. I did not stir from the dais again that night.

Before long, Henry disappeared, but his father stayed, glowering at me all the while. I had made an enemy there. Geoffrey of Anjou clearly did not want the likes of me near his son.

But I could have told him, had he had the courage to ask, that I had not chosen Henry. Henry had chosen me. Surely even Geoffrey of Anjou knew the difference.

Chapter 27

❧

Palace of the City

Paris
August 1151

ONCE LOCKED SAFE IN MY ROOMS, ALL MY WOMEN DISMISSED but for Amaria, I knew that Henry could not come to me there in my husband's keep. Still, I hoped for him, as a peasant farmer hopes for rain after months of drought. I called myself a fool, but I sat waiting, a goblet of wine in my hand, my eyes and ears turned toward the door.

There came a scratching at the hidden door behind the tapestry beside my bed. Amaria and I had used that passage earlier in the day to slip past my women. As far as I knew, no one but Louis, Amaria, and I knew of its existence.

At the sound of that scratching, Amaria was on her feet in an instant, her blade out. I rose more slowly, running my hand through my hair. My heart began to pound, as it had when I ran across my father's fields as a girl. It was Henry, and I knew it. He must have followed us earlier, without being seen.

I laid my hand on Amaria's arm, and went to open the door. Henry stood in the dark of the hidden corridor, a lamp in one hand, and a scroll in the other. Perhaps he had written me love poetry, and came now to read it to me. The thought, unlikely as it was, made me laugh as I stepped back from the doorway and let him in.

"My lord duke. You are welcome to this place."

"No duke yet, my lady. That is still for your husband to say, come the morrow."

He spoke of the ceremony that would confirm his position, but we both knew, as all the court did, that such a ceremony was a formality only. He had won his mother's lands back by force of arms. Louis would not stand in his way.

Amaria frowned, closing and locking the door behind him, hiding it once more behind the tapestry of Saint Paul at prayer. Though she frowned, her blade was sheathed and hidden in her sleeve already.

"You may leave us," I told her. "I will send for you, if we have need."

Amaria transferred her glower to me, but left through the front door, to take up her post as guard in my audience chamber. My sitting room would be cold that time of night. She wrapped herself in furs before she left me.

I watched Henry where he stood by my mahogany table. Its top was polished to a high sheen, and gleamed in the light of the candles I had set by. Henry put his lamp down, and laid the scroll next to it.

He shrugged off his concealing cloak, and I had to master myself to keep from breathing in too sharply. He was not conventionally beautiful. He had not Louis' grace, soft features, or golden hair. But Henry of Normandy was compelling. Every catlike move he made called to me. There, alone in my rooms, he reminded me of a great lion turned loose among common men. I had never known anyone like him.

"Do you come to ask for my support against Stephen? You may have it, without asking," I said. "I have always despised weak men." I dismissed his rival for the throne of England with one wave of my hand.

"Have you?" he asked. "That must have made your marriage difficult."

"You are impertinent."

"But not wrong."

I held my tongue for a long moment, for fear I might laugh again.

"I have something to show you, if you would do me the honor, my lady."

I came to his side when he beckoned me, breathing in the scent of sandalwood on his skin. I stepped close, knowing that I tempted him, knowing that I tempted myself. Whatever he thought to show me, we both knew why he was really there. I had drawn a furred cloak around me to hide my lawn shift. His eyes were heated, and he smiled as if he knew what my body looked like, fur or no.

He did not touch me, but opened the scroll on the table before us. He took the lamp, and set it on one side of the vellum to hold it down. In that soft light, I noticed for the first time that his lashes were ginger and bronze, almost the same color as my own hair.

"Look at what I have brought you. What do you see?"

I looked away from him, and down at the vellum spread before me. My lips quirked without my commanding them.

"I see a map," I said. "A map of my lands, the lands of France, and England, the kingdom you seek."

"You see far," Henry said. His eyes were serious now. His lust was still there, but held in check, like dogs snapping at their leashes. I saw that he was a man in control of himself always. It would be no different here in my rooms than on a battlefield.

"When you are done with Louis, these will be your lands again, unencumbered." Henry traced the Aquitaine and Poitou, and all my other holdings.

"These lands I hold already." Henry's blunt, callused finger outlined the borders of Brittany, Anjou, and Normandy.

"The Vexin I will reclaim from Louis," he said.

"Will you indeed?" I arched one brow.

He met my eyes, and smiled. "Give me time, my lady. You will see."

He looked back to the map under his hand, and traced the outline of England and Ireland, pressing his palm down on the kingdom his mother had lost, the kingdom Geoffrey of Anjou could not hold for her.

"England will be mine, in three years' time," he said.

"So soon?"

"Sooner if I have my way."

"And you always get your way."

"Yes."

Henry's gray eyes fired with his hunger for me. For a moment, I thought he might drop his hands from the map he showed me, and take me in his arms. I was trying to tempt him to it, but he did not move. I felt the tension in him, as he fought himself. Not even Raymond had shown the control that this man had.

"Lady, attend me. Just one moment more."

I looked down to the map on the table. Henry cradled my lands and his, those he held now and those he sought to hold, between the palms of his two hands.

"These lands we might claim together, lady, once you are free. If you would have me."

"Have you?" I asked. "Is that not why you have come here? What have our lands to do with that?"

Already, I saw what he was getting at; I saw where he would lead me. But I would not speak it aloud. It would be he who offered all to me.

His eyes met mine again, and along with his lust, I saw his power. It was as potent as anything I had ever seen. It made me sway toward him, until I caught myself, one hand on the table between us. My palm rested between his, on the center of the map. He raised one hand, and laid it over mine.

"Do you think I seek to seduce you for my pleasure only?" Henry asked. "You are queen. You are duchess. And you are mine."

I tried to draw my hand from beneath his, but he held me fast. My breath caught, and my heart thundered. I waited until he spoke.

"We will hold these lands, together. Between the two of us, we will build the greatest empire seen since the time of Charlemagne."

My old dream rose to haunt me, the dream that had died on the road to Antioch. I recoiled from Henry, for I wanted what he offered too badly. He saw my need in my eyes. He did not let me go.

"You will marry me," he said. "You will be my queen."

"You wear no crown yet."

"I will. I promise you. And when I wear one, so will you."

"I wear a crown already."

"How many women have said that they wore two crowns in a lifetime?"

"None."

"You will say it, Eleanor. I will make it so. I will set a second crown upon your head, and we will rule these lands together."

"As partners?" I asked.

"And allies," he answered. "When I am in Normandy, you will rule in England as my queen."

"Your regent?"

"Yes."

"In name only, while your lords and ministers rule in my stead?"

"You will rule in fact, not just in name. I have heard your name spoken all my life. Now I have seen you, and I know you are my equal. No other woman in all the world can claim that. Say you will join me, Eleanor. Say you will be mine."

"What you offer is not possible."

"I have built my life on the impossible. And here I am."

"Here you are."

In the end, I did not hesitate. I had never been one to stop myself from taking what I wanted. That moment with Henry was no different.

"If you will be mine," I said, "I will be yours."

Henry smiled, raising my hand to his lips. I thought he would kiss my fingertips to seal our bargain, but at the last, he turned my hand over in his own, and pressed his lips to my palm. The heat of his mouth caught at the fire already burning in my body, until I thought I would lose all reason. Still, he stared at me, his own fire raging in his eyes. His tongue darted out, and licked the center of my palm, so that I lost my breath.

"Done," he said. "So be it."

He did not draw me to the bed, even then. He raised his other hand from the table, and the map of vellum drew up once more into a scroll. The brush of the pigskin was soft in my ears, a gentle sweep of sound. I stood, transfixed, as Henry drew me closer.

"I have had many women," he said. "But you will be the last."

I knew even as he spoke that he was lying. He was more than ten years younger than I was. No man could stay faithful to a woman for a lifetime, save perhaps Louis. But I found that lie was sweet in my ears. I found myself leaning closer, the heat in my belly rising, as Henry's lips played once more against the skin of my palm.

The firelight surrounded us, casting our shadows upon

the walls. We were cut apart from the world beyond those stones, from the life of the French court, from the life I had known. I felt as if my father lived yet, and stood guard over us in the next room. I felt as if I had never known fear or loss or death. As if the world and all its folly, the price I had paid for power, the price I would go on paying, could not touch me.

I stepped forward, and raised my hand to his cheek.

It was a gentle gesture, not like me at all. Henry seemed to know it, as he seemed to know me; he understood me from the first. I stayed close to him, my palm on the rough sandpaper of his cheek. He had shaved before coming to me, but his beard had started to grow out again already.

"Eleanor," he said. "There is someone else in your eyes."

"No," I said. "There is not."

He did not blink or drop his gaze from mine. It was as if I had not spoken.

"You love a man," he said. "Not Louis."

I tried never to think of Raymond. It did no good to think of him, so I did not. My mind and heart had done my bidding since I was a very young girl. Only now, with Henry's gray gaze boring into mine, did I feel again the pain of what I had lost when Raymond died.

Of course, I could not tell him that. I opened my mouth to lie, but Henry spoke before I could utter a word.

"No, don't tell me. It doesn't matter. I would have no lies between us."

"He is dead."

Henry stared into the green of my eyes. He did not

speak, and for a long moment I wondered if the deal was done before it had even begun. I wondered if he would not raise me up, and take me as his wife, even for the kingdom of Charlemagne, even for the lives of all our sons to come.

He raised his hands then, and cradled my face between them. Something beyond lust bound us, something time could not touch. I saw it as we stood alone with no one between us, no kingdoms, no crowns, no children, no losses. That night, there was only Henry and I, alone together in a room.

He was a man with a duchy he had wrested from the dead, a man with a kingdom still to conquer. I was a woman with a broken marriage and a lost dream, with only daughters to show for the last fifteen years of my life. But Henry did not see that when he looked at me. Nor did he see only the Aquitaine, and Poitou, and all the green and fertile lands that lay between them. When Henry looked into my eyes, he saw my soul. Without all else to play for, the fact that he knew me would have been enough.

"Know this, Eleanor. For us, there will be only one another. I will have no rivals between us. There is only room enough in my bed for two."

I did not answer him at once. I did not fob him off with a smile or a lie or a glib truth. I took him in, the gray of his eyes and the ginger-colored lashes that framed them, and beyond that, his soul, staring back at me. "All right," I answered him. "So be it."

Those words were my seal on the bargain that we had already made. Henry drew me to him and I felt his true strength. The warmth of his arms enveloped me, and for the first time since my father died, I felt as if I were protected, shielded from the world. This was an illusion, but I welcomed it.

Henry's lips were soft on mine, tentative, exploring the contours and the curves of my mouth. He tasted of the burgundy we had drunk at dinner, and of the spiced venison we had eaten at the high table. He smelled of sandalwood, and clean linen, sun-dried and crisp. I pressed myself against him, as if his wholesome light might find its way from the contours of his muscles and sinews, into my bones.

He laughed a little, low in his throat, lifting his mouth from mine. He smiled, and I smiled back at him, for he did not mock me, and I knew it. His appreciation and regard for me rang even in the dark softness of his laughter. Warmth flooded my body, until I thought my blood might catch fire. All this he did with just the sound of his voice, his hand on my waist, the other in my hair.

"You have been too long neglected, Eleanor. You will find yourself well loved in my bed."

I raised my head, and caught his lips with mine. I drew him down with me onto the bed, casting aside my fur wrap, so that my body was clear beneath my shift in the firelight. Henry caught his breath, and his hand trembled as he reached for me. His desire was so strong that I thought he might swallow his tongue. My lust was thick in the air already, shimmering like a mist over my skin. I reached for him and pulled him down to me. He laid his body over mine, his mouth covering my own. Our tongues tangled together, and his hands ran over me, first over my shift, then under it. My skin warmed beneath his callused palms, and I pressed myself against him. He would not be rushed, but drew my shift up and over my head in one smooth motion.

He looked down at me, raising himself on one elbow. He ran one hand over my body's curves, watching my breasts rise and fall with my breath beneath his hand. "You are the most beautiful woman I have ever seen."

I ran my hands along his chest and drew his own clothes off, first his tunic and hose, then his shirt. He was young, his arms and hands burnished from his time in the sun. His muscles were well crafted, as if by a sculptor. He did not look like the Greek statues I had seen in Byzantium. He was too much of a man for that. But he was beautiful.

I pressed my lips against his chest, running my tongue over his skin until he gasped. I rose up over him, and mounted him, as I would a horse. Young as he was, he was no blushing maid. He knew what I was about, and lifted me effortlessly, until I had taken him in, and sheathed him with my inner fire.

We both lost ourselves then, our bodies moving together as they had on my husband's dance floor. This time we rode together as if in a race, a race where there would be two winners.

I felt my climax rising within me like a tide, like a wave at dawn. Henry drew me beneath him, and rode me hard as that wave swamped me. I shuddered, my breath lost. I could not even gasp his name.

He joined me then, his body trembling over mine. He shook as I had done, but harder, as if an earthquake had squeezed the breath from his lungs, as if he would never breathe again.

He fell against me, as if someone had cut him down on the battlefield. He clutched me, his hand in the bronze softness of my hair. I could not move, for he held me fast, his heavy body on top of mine, as a stone on top of a tomb. Let me be dead, then. I was glad to die, if only he lay upon me.

I laughed at this thought. Henry laughed with me, his gray eyes gleaming. He did not move to let me rise. I could breathe, if only barely, so I let him stay where he was.

"There will be more of that before there is less," he said. "I will not let you go."

"Not yet," I answered.

"Not ever. No other man will touch you again. I swear that, Eleanor."

"No?" I asked. "Not even my husband? Not even Louis?"

"Do not name that milksop to me," Henry said, resting his head against my breast. "I am your husband now. I, and no other."

"You, and no other," I answered.

He heard the truth in my voice. He raised his head and kissed me.

We lay close for a long while, his warm body over mine. As I came back to myself, as I began once more to feel my limbs, my hands and feet, I stretched, as languid as a cat in the cream. It was then that I felt the dampness on my belly.

He had withdrawn from me at the last.

I felt a fury rise in me that I had seldom if ever felt. All my hatred for Louis and his weakness, all my sorrow over his constant rejection, rose up in me as one great mass. I thought at first that I would choke on it, or that my silent rage would set fire to the very ends of my hair.

I could not shield my reaction from Henry, because I could not control myself.

"You are angry," he said. "What have I done to offend you?"

"Your seed." I could not bring myself to speak past that one word. My tongue had swelled, this time with ire.

Henry raised one brow, and looked down at my body. He wiped away the dampness with linen taken from my bedside. When he leaned down to kiss me, I turned my head away.

"There can be no son yet, Eleanor. I cannot leave him here behind me."

Henry's voice was soft, his breath warm in my ear. Even so, he did not chide or cajole me. He faced me as his equal, even there, my body naked beneath his.

I met his eyes, the fire in my heart beginning to go out. I saw then how weak I was with this man, how much I cared for him already. He had spilled his seed outside my body, and I had taken mortal offense.

I would have to school myself to subtlety. I would have to guard myself and my feelings well. Henry was a part of me already. I saw that this would be my weakness, as well as my strength.

I held his gaze for one long moment. He did not look away.

"You do not want your first son to be King of France?" I asked. My tone was light, as if I made a joke. Henry knew, however, that I did not.

"My firstborn son is safe at home in Normandy," Henry answered.

He did not soften this news with a smile or a caress. He did not toy with me, or treat me as less than I was. The pain of his other child burned in my breast.

My jealousy warred with my newfound love. That was when I knew that this was no simple bargain, no political alliance with lines clearly drawn. This was something new, something never seen upon the earth. This would be a love affair and a bargain both, a marriage and an alliance together. The Church would never sanction it. Their priests would never say that a man and a woman could face each other as Henry and I did that night, as equals, with no trickery, with no lies or deception, with no false vows between us.

It was his honesty I met when I leaned up and pressed my lips to his. It was his truth I tasted, as he ran his tongue over mine. That night, beneath the canopy of my marriage bed, we met as equals, and took joy in each other's strength.

Henry entered me again. This time he led, as the hounds lead the hunter, and I followed. I gasped under him, my pleasure rising quickly to swamp my reason. Henry did not follow me over that edge until I had tasted that pleasure not once, but twice.

His own pleasure crested then, rising in the gray of his eyes to drown him. We lay together afterward, cast up on an empty shore, where there was only he and I, alone together.

"I love you, Eleanor."

I did not answer, but pressed my hand over his beating heart. He lay down with me again, his body over mine, shielding me from the world. He drew the wolf-fur blanket over both of us, and pressed himself to me, breathing gently into my hair.

"Sleep now," he said. "I will wake you, just before dawn."

I did as he bade me. I slept, deep and dreamless, his body laid over mine. And in the morning, before dawn, he woke me with a kiss, just as he had said he would.

Chapter 28

❧

Palace of the City

Paris
August 1151

HENRY LEFT ME SO EARLY THAT AMARIA HAD NOT YET RE-
turned to me. I rose when he did, drawing on my robe of
sable. Henry ran his hand along it, pressing his palm against
my body, smoothing the soft fur along the curve of my hip.

"Louis confirms my duchy this morning, and then I will
be gone."

"I will see you in the chapel," I said.

Henry smiled at me, a wicked gleam in his eyes. "You
cannot avoid it, my queen. You will be seeing me, off and on,
for the rest of your life."

"More on than off, I trust."

He cocked one eyebrow at me, drawing me close in the circle of his embrace. "For certain, lady. But it will be a big empire."

I found I did not want to talk of duchies or of power, or of the political alliance our marriage might bring. I pressed myself against him, opening the fur of my gown so that I could feel the leather of his leggings against my naked thighs. My breath caught in my throat, and Henry kissed me again, his tongue moving leisurely over mine, as if we had all morning for our love play.

Both of us knew, however, that we did not.

Henry groaned, and I knew he wanted me as much as I wanted him. This was a new thing, this sweetness, knowing that my lover craved my body as much as I craved his. And it was a heady feeling, to bring a man of Henry's power under my sway. I was drunk on it, after only one night.

Henry stepped away from me. I left my gown open, that he might see my naked body in the firelight. I knew he would think of me as I was now, later, when we were apart, both of us surrounded by enemies.

"Until the chapel, Eleanor."

He left the way he had come and I fastened the door closed behind him. Amaria emerged from my antechamber then. She must have been listening at the door, as all good servants do.

Amaria's dark blue eyes met mine, and for once she did not frown. Her smile was soft, like a young girl's, a smile I had not seen on her face in many years, if ever.

"He will make you a good husband, lady. He is full of fire."

I did not answer her, or scold her for her impertinence. I drew her close, and took her hand in mine. I held it only for one moment, but she knew more from that touch than my words could tell.

※

Later that morning, I stood under the canopy in Louis' chapel, my husband at my side. Though we were swearing in the Duke of Normandy, the Parisians cared little, and few had shown up for the ceremony. Henry knelt before my husband, as pious as a monk. I would have laughed had I not been in control of myself. As it was, Henry met my eyes as he rose once more to his feet, and gave me a wink.

Geoffrey of Anjou stood behind a column and stared at me with loathing. I would have thought that he would take more pleasure in this day, since he had worked so hard, and spilled so much blood, some of it his own, to make it so. But Geoffrey cared little for the ceremony. He did not look at Henry at all. Instead, he glared at me, his mouth puckered as if he had eaten something foul. I wondered what in the last day had made him hate me, and so openly, especially since my father had been his fast and loyal friend. His son Henry had taken a lover before. Surely Geoffrey did not begrudge his son a little pleasure, taken in the dark reaches of the night.

As I watched Geoffrey from the corner of one eye, I began to see that he was more intelligent than I had given him credit for. He did not begrudge Henry the hours between my sheets. I saw in the bitterness of his gaze that he had the effrontery to hunger for me himself.

I had spent so long surrounded by the hatred of the French court that I had stopped looking for lust in the eyes of my enemies. As I looked into the dark blue of Geoffrey's gaze, I saw lust as well as loathing. The combination gave me pause, and I took one step back. Louis reached for me, and took my hand. He was not sensitive to the eddies and tides that ran throughout his court, but he was still sometimes sensitive to me.

"Eleanor, are you all right?"

I met his eyes and smiled. Louis had been my ally for almost fifteen years. In some ways I would miss him, though I hungered to be free even with his hand on mine.

"I am well, my lord king. I thank you."

Henry heard our exchange and raised one ginger-colored brow. It came to me then, all in one rush, how much he and I had shared the night before, how much we would still share in the months and years to come. I was giddy with the knowledge that I would have a husband strong enough to meet me on equal ground. I took my hand from Louis' and fingered the jet and pearl rosary at my waist. Brother Matthew came to Louis' side and distracted him, as I knew he would.

I walked out of the chapel surrounded by my ladies. We went the long way to my rooms through the inner gardens. The sun had come out finally, though the ornamental trees still dripped with rain.

Amaria stood guard on one side of me, and my Parisian waiting woman Priscilla on the other, when Geoffrey of Anjou stepped out of the shadows of the keep.

I smiled, thinking that surely he was not clumsy enough to display his enmity before my ladies. But I found I overestimated him.

I stopped, since Geoffrey stood in front of me. I wondered for a moment if he would have the effrontery to touch me, if he would take my arm and drag me into the darkness of the palace.

Geoffrey knew that Henry and I had spent the night together, and in his eyes, the knowledge did not raise Henry as it should have, but lowered me. I remembered suddenly all the distant tales I had heard, even in Poitiers, about this man and his anger toward women. He and my father had been friends all their lives, but even as a child, I had heard how this man stooped to striking his wife, the Dowager Empress Maude, as if she were a recalcitrant mule or a dog. My father had always considered a man's business his own, and I had never questioned it, since there was not a man born anywhere on the earth with the courage to raise his hand to me. But now, as I looked at Henry's father, I saw that his weakness in war was linked to his weakness with women. His fury, however, was strong.

I blinked and took him in, as the red Plantagenet rage I had also heard of mounted in his face, making his skin darken to the color of puce.

"I think you are no better than a whore," he said to me.

My ladies heard him, and drew together in horror, twittering like birds in a hedge. Amaria stood frozen, her contempt like shards of ice. I felt the cold of it on my arm as she touched me.

I raised one hand, and my women withdrew. Priscilla led them out, that they might continue work on the altar cloth for the cathedral at St.-Denis. I waited in silence until they were gone, my smile never wavering.

Geoffrey's color rose, until I thought he would turn purple. I wondered if he might fall at my feet in a fit of apoplexy, and if he did, what on earth I would tell Henry.

"Indeed?" I said. "And who gave you leave to think?"

Geoffrey's mouth opened and closed like a fish cast on dry land. I pressed my advantage while I had it, for I did not know how long we might be alone.

"You are a weak man, and a fool," I said. "This is not Anjou, where women can be bullied at your will. I am Queen of France. I am Duchess of Aquitaine. You will keep a civil tongue in your head if ever again you have the good fortune to speak to me."

"Father, please leave us."

Where Henry came from, I did not know, so intent was I on the new enemy before me. Henry approached from behind, his words a bulwark to shelter me. I watched as Geoffrey swallowed his ire out of respect for his son.

Henry could control him, then. That was to the good. I had come too far, and walked my own path too long, to allow a fool like Geoffrey of Anjou to interfere with me.

Henry touched my arm once, then took his place beside me. It was the gentleness of that touch that silenced Geoffrey in the end. I saw the defeat rise in the blue of his eyes, and drown his reason. Henry had made his choice already. Even Geoffrey, overwhelmed by his lust and hatred for me, could see that.

The Count of Anjou bowed once before turning on his heel and stalking away. I watched him go. His bow had not been for me.

"You have made an enemy there," Henry said, his eyes on his father's retreating back.

"He is not my first," I said.

Henry's lips quirked, and I found myself wishing that we were alone once more in my rooms, that I might feel those lips on my skin again.

"Nor your last," he answered.

I laughed, and the warmth of that laughter bound us closer, so that Henry stepped toward me. He raised one hand, and slid one finger along my cheek.

"I hope I die with your laughter in my ears."

His eyes were on my lips, and I knew had we been anywhere else, he would have kissed me.

"Not for years yet."

"No." Henry's gray eyes met mine. "I still have a great deal to do."

"Does it pain you, that your father loathes me?"

"He loathes power in women. There is a difference."

I thought of the Empress Maude, and of how she should have been queen in England. I thought of Geoffrey of Anjou, and of how a weak man might hate a woman of strength. I had been lucky. As weak as Louis was, in all our years together, he had never hated me.

"I do not trust your father," I said.

"You need trust only me. He is loyal to my cause."

I smiled. "And what cause is that?"

Henry laughed. "Myself."

At the door into the keep, there was a flutter of cloth. A boy came out, a boy only a year or so younger than Henry. He stood in the doorway and stared at us. Amaria must have known him, for she did not order him away.

Henry raised one hand, and the boy withdrew. He left quickly once Henry motioned for him to go, but not before I caught his furtive looks, and his dark red hair. He moved with stealth for one so large, like a skulking beast. Shorter than Henry, this boy was as broad, his arms well muscled, his eyes small. He stared at me for one long moment, but when Henry gestured again, he fled.

"My brother. My father's namesake. Geoffrey the Younger."

"He has an ill-omened look about him," I said.

"You have a sharp eye," Henry answered me, his arm around my waist. I leaned against him, that he might feel the softness of my curves, covered as they were in silk and fur. "He is a thorn in my side, but one I can easily draw out."

"He is your father's favorite," I guessed.

Henry's eyes grew cold. "He was. He still would be, I suppose, but for my triumph in Normandy."

I did not answer. Men did not change their favorite children as women changed their gowns. I saw in that moment that his family was one of hidden depths and valleys. Henry was leaving Paris that afternoon, and had little time to explain the intricacies of his family to me. I would ask after such things among my spies. I must know the lay of that land before I married into it.

Henry leaned down and kissed me, his tongue playing

over mine in a delicious dance that pushed politics and family to the back of my mind. He drew away, and I followed him, so that he claimed my lips again.

"Eleanor, I must go."

"I know. I thought you would be gone already."

"I would not leave without a word between us."

"We have no need of words," I answered. "All our words were spoken last night."

Henry moved back from me, and reached into the pouch at his waist. I saw he had been in the garden before me. He had filched one of my roses from the arbor, a Persian rose with red velvet petals, a rose bred to bear no thorns.

The flowers had just opened the day before. No doubt he had come before the ceremony to fetch this rose for me, or perhaps he had sent someone else to pluck it. Now he held it between his callused fingers.

The deep red rose had not been crushed in the pouch that had borne it, but it had been pressed, so that now the petals smelled of spring, and of Antioch, where I had first seen such flowers without thorns to mar them. Now, as I stood there with Henry, that rose smelled like my future.

"I'm no romantic, Eleanor."

He laid the rose in my hand.

"You will get no poetry from me, nor songs of love. But I will love you, every day for the rest of my life. I need no oath before a priest to tell you that."

I pressed myself against him, my lips on his. He was only a little taller than I, so I did not have to strain. His arms came about me, and clutched me, as if I were water in a desert, as if he were adrift on an endless sea, and I was all that kept him from drowning.

I knew that he meant what he said. Henry loved me for what he saw in me, for my fire and my strength, which reflected his own. My lands had drawn us together, but the fire between us would seal the bond. I knew without his having to tell me that he had searched all his life for a woman like me, thinking never to find one, just as I had never thought to find a man like him. Henry hungered for a strong woman in his life and in his bed; he longed for an equal. He found one in me.

I fell against him; I fell into his kiss, and almost lost myself. His passion for me was so strong, I almost forgot where I was and who. But always, I kept my head. It was I who drew back first.

"I must go, Eleanor. I cannot stay."

"I know."

Henry stepped away from me. The flower he had given me had been crushed between us. The smooth stem was still held fast between my two fingers.

"That is not just a rose, Eleanor. It is a reminder to both of us that when we deal with each other, we must keep our blades sheathed."

I could not imagine a time when we would draw daggers against each other. With passion like ours between us, there was very little we could not settle in bed.

"When you are free," he said, "send for me."

Even from the distance of five feet, I thought his desire for me would burn me alive. I stood in the heat of that blaze, and stretched, like a cat that has come in from the cold to sit beside the fire. I must be careful not to have my tail singed.

"And if you are already in England?" I asked.

I kept my voice light, my tone even, as if I did not care if I never saw him again.

He did not give me a glib answer, as most other men would have done. His eyes were calm, though the fire still raged beneath the gray, ready to consume us both. He spoke solemnly, as if taking an oath.

"From England or Normandy, from anywhere on earth, I will come back for you."

Henry did not speak again, but bowed to me, as if swearing me fealty. He left me there, alone with my waiting woman. As he strode away, he did not look back.

I stayed in that garden for another hour, though my women waited for me abovestairs, though no doubt all Louis' courtiers knew where I was and why. I stayed alone, with Amaria guarding the door. I walked the narrow paths of that rose garden, without seeing the flowers, without hearing the birdsong or even feeling the sun upon my face.

In an hour, I had schooled my looks to blandness. Amaria and I climbed the stairs to my room together, and this time, we took the formal staircase. Before we stepped into the keep, I pressed the rose Henry had given me into my alms purse, where no one else would see it.

Chapter 29

❧

Palace of Beaugency

County of Blois
March 1152

MY ANNULMENT WAS GRANTED ON A FINE DAY IN MARCH AT Louis' castle of Beaugency. The prelates gathered with a letter written in Pope Eugenius' hand. They discussed solemnly our marriage and its barrenness. It was considered barren because living girl children did not count as heirs in France.

My daughters had been left behind in Paris. The loss of them stung me, but I knew that I would see them again. Louis would not keep them from me. And in a few years' time, first Marie and then Alix would be married away, betrothed to shore up the throne of France, sent to seal alliances and bargains made by their father and his ministers.

Long ago, I had chosen and sealed my own fate. And now I was making for myself another.

The meeting of the bishops was quick and, for the Church, strangely lacking in ceremony. Louis and I sat side by side, as if we were strangers, while the churchmen ruled our marriage null and void.

My own seal was called for, as was Louis', and then it was done. The bishops filed out to a great luncheon that Louis' people had prepared. It was odd to eat at midday, but it was even odder to disband the marriage of the King of France. All those men felt the need of a libation, and their paunches showed that they never took their wine without good meat and bread. I would leave them to it. I was going home.

Louis and I stood alone on the dais in that sunlit room. The light of noon slanted in from the windows above our heads. It shone down on Louis' fair golden head, showing traces of gray. He had borne no silver in his hair before he learned of his father's murder. Now Louis would be an old man for the rest of his life.

I thought at first that he would leave me without a word, but always, he was Louis. He had never changed in all the years I had known him. I saw now that he never would.

"I love you, Eleanor."

Louis' voice was quiet, but I knew that his churchmen and my women heard him. They all turned away, as if he had confessed to something vile. As it was, I could not answer him, nor could I touch him. For now we were allies only. I was his vassal, he my liege lord. I would have pressed my hand to his cheek, to offer him comfort, but it was no longer my right.

"May God bless you, Louis. Now, and in all the days to come."

When I spoke, it was not an empty wish. I hoped Louis would be blessed and cared for, just as I was grateful that the caregiver would no longer be me.

Louis left me there in the hall of Beaugency. I watched him go, his churchmen following, as they went into the chapel to take the mass. My Parisian women curtsied to me, and in a flutter of silks, they followed the man who had been my husband. I had paid them earlier that morning with sacks of gold, so they had nothing left to stay for.

Amaria came to my side, and pressed my hand. She would walk with me into my new life. Like me, she was eager to leave the Parisians behind. I did not smile at her, but turned to go, for I knew that Louis' spies were watching.

I kept my step slow and measured as I made my way from that hall. I did not increase my pace, though every nerve in my body called on me to run, to leap upon my horse and ride off into the distance, in case those churchmen might change their minds, and call me back.

Of course, they did not. No one followed me, save the eyes of Louis' spies, as I made my way out into the sunlight of the castle bailey.

My horse waited for me. She was a sleek Arabian mare, all white save for her hooves and for the streak of gold along her brow. I had purchased her in Byzantium. She had come with us all the way back to my husband's lands, and now she would travel with me to mine. For the Aquitaine and Poitou were mine now, not my father's, nor my husband's. I was duchess. And if Henry had his way, once more, I would be queen.

My Arabian mare tossed her head, and I offered her my hand, that she might breathe in my scent. She took a dried apple from my palm, and nuzzled me. Though I had not ridden her often, she knew who her mistress was.

"My lady duchess, she is beautiful. What do you call her?" Geoffrey of Rancon was at my side, holding the bridle of my horse. I had sent for him, and he had come, just as I knew he would.

"Her name is Guinevere," I said.

"A lovely name," he said. "The name of a queen. I only hope that she comes to a better end."

I laughed, and my mirth filled the walls of that bailey. "Of course, she will, my lord baron. She is in my service."

"You will always have my service, my lady duchess, for as long as I draw breath."

Geoffrey lifted me onto my horse. She had been saddled for long riding; I would not ride pillion that day. She danced a little under me, but then she felt my hand on her reins, and she remembered herself. Or more likely, she remembered me, and what was my due. Guinevere stood still, and waited for my command.

Henry had sent me greeting from the Norman port of Barfleur only the month before. He gathered his army, and built his ships, that he might claim England and make it ours. I knew that Henry would meet me in Poitiers, as soon as I sent word to him. We would be married there, with only my people looking on. We must keep our alliance a secret, even now, but I knew that no one would stop us. He and I were not to be gainsaid, not by any man living, nor by the dead. We would make our own way, Henry and I together.

Geoffrey led the vanguard, and my men, come up from Poitiers for this purpose, fell in beside and behind me. Geoffrey took up my standard and held it high. I saw my father's golden lion, flying in the air above my head. The red and gold of Aquitaine shone along its border, catching the light of the sun and holding it fast.

As I turned my horse out of the keep at Beaugency, and took to the open road, my freedom rose up from the ground to greet me with the first spring flowers. My freedom fell with the sunlight on my hair and shoulders, gilding my red veil and gown, which I wore to match my father's standard.

That standard was mine now, more than it had ever been. For the first time in fifteen years, the fleur-de-lys of France did not share its place. There was only my father's lion, now mine, caught in the wind above me. It soared there, as my heart did. I almost felt my father with me that day, his hand on my shoulder.

It was not the kingdom my father had foreseen when I was a child, but the empire Henry and I would build together would stretch farther than the lands of Charlemagne. I would revive my father's dream in another guise, and make it my own. Henry would give me sons to rule after us, and we would reign over our new kingdom as partners for the rest of our lives.

The promise of our future filled me with the greatest bliss I had ever known. I felt as if I, too, might take flight beside the standard that rose above my head. Instead, I touched my foot to Guinevere's side, and she leaped forward into the beauty of the day. I would ride hard, with no one to stop me. For, at long last, I was free.

Afterword

ELEANOR MARRIED HENRY OF NORMANDY IN THE SUMMER of 1152. Henry and Eleanor lived happily together for many years, ruling side by side, he in Normandy and England, and she in Aquitaine and Poitou. Henry won the throne of England from Stephen of Blois in 1154, and Eleanor was crowned queen there, and served as regent whenever Henry was away on the Continent.

Eleanor and Henry had nine children, seven of whom lived to adulthood. William, their first son, named for Eleanor's father, died of a fever before he reached the age of three. Henry the Younger, Richard, Geoffrey, and John were given titles and lands in their own right, while Eleanor and Henry's daughters each married abroad at a young age in service of the crown.

Eleanor's daughters with Louis, Marie and Alix, both married to support the throne of France. Marie became the Countess of Champagne, and though she spent little time in her mother's company, Eleanor's eldest daughter grew into a woman who embodied all the graces of the Court of Love. All her life, Marie of France supported the arts; a patroness of troubadours, Eleanor's eldest daughter was also famous for writing music and poetry of her own.

Eleanor and Henry's marriage began to falter on a personal level in 1166, when Henry met and fancied a new mistress, Rosamund de Clifford. Eleanor and Henry still saw each other often on feast and holy days, but after the birth of their last child, John, in December of 1166, Eleanor returned to Aquitaine, and took up her place as duchess there.

Once Eleanor's eldest sons were old enough, in 1173 she aligned with Henry the Younger, Richard the Lionhearted, and Geoffrey of Brittany, along with the Count of Flanders and her ex-husband, Louis VII of France, in an effort to take over Henry's holdings in Brittany, Normandy, and Anjou. This bid for power failed as Henry defeated his rebellious sons and their allies. Henry forgave his sons, but once he had captured Eleanor, he locked her away for the rest of his reign. Upon Henry's death in July 1189, Richard's first act as king was to set his mother free.

Eleanor ruled through her son Richard, serving as regent when he rode to the Levant on the Third Crusade. Upon Richard's death, Eleanor saw to it that her last remaining son, John, succeeded as king in England, before withdrawing into retirement at the Abbey of Fontevrault in 1199.

Eleanor died April 1, 1204, at the Abbey of Fontevrault. She was buried beside her husband, Henry II, and her favorite son, Richard. Her effigy, and Henry's, can still be seen in that abbey today.

Photo by Belinda Keller Photography

CHRISTY ENGLISH is the author of two historical novels, *To Be Queen: A Novel of the Early Life of Eleanor of Aquitaine* and *The Queen's Pawn*. Christy received her undergraduate degree in history from Duke University.

TO BE QUEEN

**A NOVEL OF THE EARLY LIFE OF
ELEANOR OF AQUITAINE**

CHRISTY ENGLISH

QUESTIONS
FOR DISCUSSION

1. As the novel opens, Eleanor's mother and brother are dead, and she is her father's heir. Would Eleanor have ever become duchess without her father's support?

2. Eleanor's younger sister, Petra, is never considered for a political role by Eleanor's father. Do you think this has a negative effect on Petra's relationship with Eleanor? How do Eleanor and Petra interact in the novel? Do you think that they loved each other, even as children?

3. As a child, Eleanor wants to learn to hunt with a falcon and a hawk. Her father has also promised her that she can ride a warhorse once she is old enough. Why do you think Eleanor wants to establish dominance over these hunting animals, especially hawks and warhorses, two types of animals that are usually reserved for men?

4. *To Be Queen* is dedicated to Eleanor's father, William X, Duke of Aquitaine and Count of Poitou. If she were alive today, what might Eleanor think of this dedication?

5. Eleanor never liked the Parisians, and they never liked her. Why? Do you think her attitude toward her husband's people changes over the course of the novel?

6. For years, Eleanor and Louis are without a child. Who gets blamed for the lack of children? Who was at fault? How does this attitude toward conceiving children differ from our modern point of view? Why?

7. Eleanor and Louis go on Crusade to fight against the Turks in the Levant. Did Eleanor want to take this journey? What was your favorite part of her time in the city of Constantinople? What was Eleanor's favorite thing about that city?

8. When Eleanor reached Rome, she expected the pope to grant her an annulment from Louis. Why did she expect this? Were you surprised when she did not get what she wanted? What was your reaction to the pope blessing her marriage to Louis, a marriage she desperately wanted to get out of?

9. Eleanor was clearly unhappy in her marriage to Louis. What were her reasons for being so dissatisfied with Louis? Do you think she ever truly loved him?

10. When Henry of Normandy walks into the court of Paris, he stares at Eleanor and does not look away. Do you think he planned his seduction of her? Why did she allow herself to be seduced by him?

11. Whom do you think Eleanor will be happier with, Louis or Henry? Why? Is happiness a consideration for Eleanor? If not, what does she base her decisions on? Do you agree with her choices?

12. Eleanor was one of the most remarkable women of her time. She was one of the few women ever to wear two crowns in a lifetime, and one of the few women to rule a duchy in her own right. What attributes of her character allowed her to achieve so much?